4FUN PUBLISHING
ULTIMATE SUPER MEGA BUNDLE (30M/M BOOK BOX SET)

30 SHADES *of* GAY

BEST GAY STORIES OF 2015

WARNING

This book contains sexually explicit scenes and adult language. It may be considered offensive to some readers. This book is for sale to adults ONLY.

Please store your files wisely where they cannot be accessed by underage readers.

* * * * * * * * * * * * * * * * * * *

WANT FREE COPIES OF 4FUN BOOKS?
Just visit the blog and download free copies of 4Fun books:
http://4fun-gay.awesomeauthors.org/

About the Publisher

4Fun Publishing, a member of **BLVNP Incorporated**, 340 S. Lemon #6200, Walnut CA 91789, info@blvnp.com / legal@blvnp.com
NOTE: Due to the highly emotional reaction of some people to works of erotic fiction, any email sent to the above address that contains foul language or religious references is automatically deleted by our anti-spam software and will not be seen. All other communications are welcome.

DISCLAIMER

Please don't be stupid and kill yourself. This book is a work of FICTION. Do not try any new sexual practice that you find in this book. It is fiction and not to be confused with reality. Neither the author nor the publisher or its associates assume any responsibility for any loss, injury, death or legal consequences resulting from acting on the contents in this book. Every character in this book is over 18 years of age. The author's opinions are not to be construed as the opinions of the publisher. The material in this book is for entertainment purposes ONLY. Enjoy.

30 Shades of Gay

Best Gay Stories of 2015

By: 4Fun Publishing

© 4Fun Publishing 2015
ISBN: 978-1-68030-378-0

Table of Contents

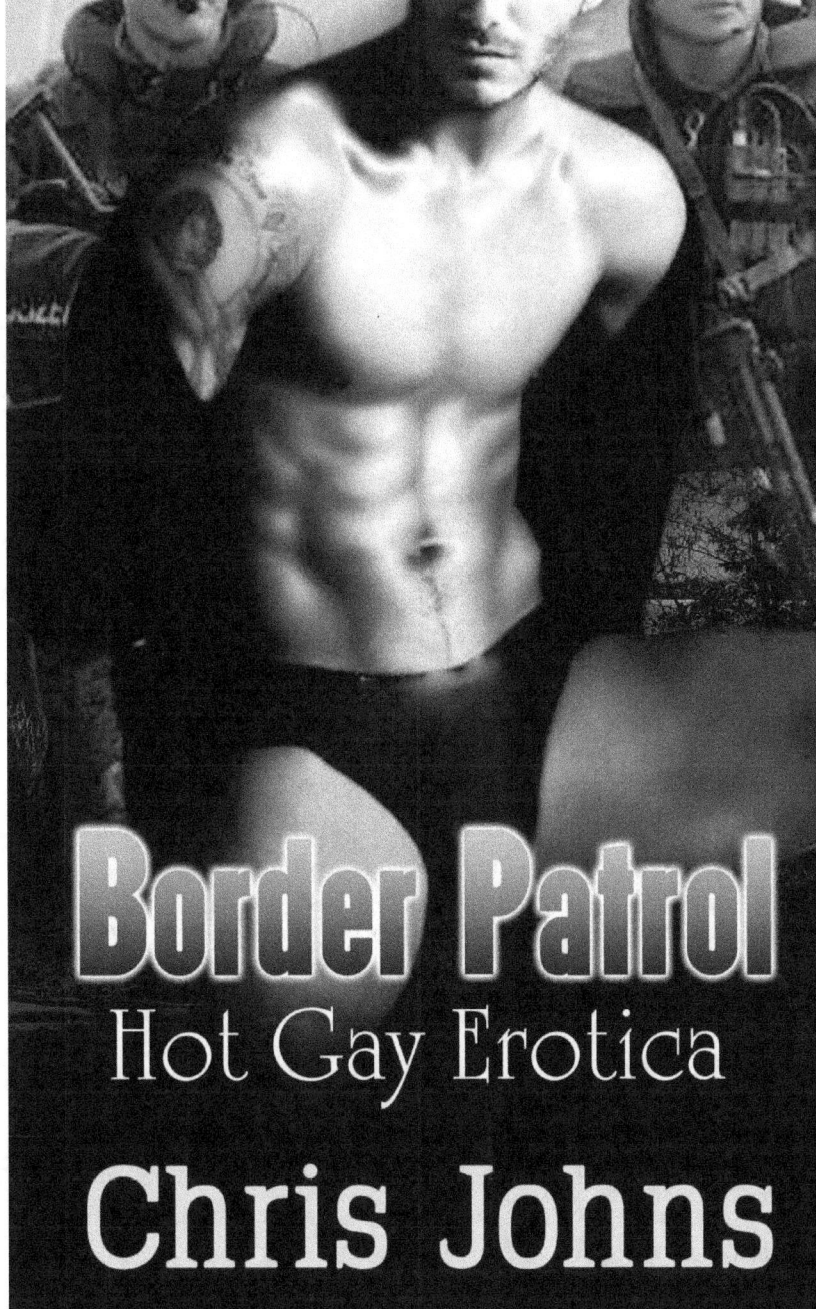

Border Patrol
Hot Gay Erotica

Chris Johns

Border Patrol

By: Chris Johns

Part 1

Patrolling this sector of the border was fine during the spring and summer months. Even in the autumn it was still pleasant, but now, in the winter, it was miserable. The choice appeared to be snow or rain, and always cold.

The patrols were on foot because the forest was too dense for vehicles and of course they were too noisy. The actual border had a fence and a road alongside it, but the commander thought roving foot patrols about a kilometre inside the border would catch more illegals because they would be less careful, now that they were across into Germany. Unfortunately he was proved correct. The patrols along the border road were always finding holes in the fence, but seldom caught anyone. But Heinrich and Jorge had captured hundreds in the year they had been doing it. On one wall in the small compound where they took the captured illegals they had rows of little men, indicating the number they had been able to return to Poland. They had started it as a joke.

"Just like our Luftwaffe Pilots marked their kills on the sides of their aircraft during the war," Jorge had said when they started it.

There was another separate tally in a notebook Jorge kept in his locker. That was the number they had not declared, always the young pretty ones or the just plain sexy. The two young guards were gay and would on occasions, when they captured a particularly attractive guy, offer him his freedom in return for sexual favors. It was fun and in the winter lightened up otherwise dull down time. They were never refused. The young ones particularly would have sold their soul to be allowed into the West so there was never any forced sexual contact; the detainees were offered a simple choice. After they had been stripped and scoped out thoroughly the offer would be made.

"If you look as sexy when your penis is erect as you do now with it flaccid we will let you go, but not until after we have checked how good you can blow us and take our cocks up your arse."

Some were quite enthusiastic others were very resentful but most just accepted it as the price for their freedom.

Petrov was one of the resentful ones, but he had such a superb slim body that Jorge wanted to keep him for days.

"He will get used to it, and then he will enjoy my cock up his arse. If he becomes very good I might keep him in my apartment in Hamburg as a permanent sex toy for use during my time off."

Heinrich had laughed. He and Jorge had been friends since joining the army at eighteen, and had stayed together during their military service, joining the border patrol unit when they had served their enlisted time. The pay was good, the time off was brilliant so despite the rotten hours when they were on duty and the miserable weather in the winter they had stayed. Jorge was the joker and Heinrich loved him like a brother.

The capture of Petrov had been standard. The snow made it so easy to follow the illegals. They stopped covering their tracks about 100 metres inside the border. With their snowshoes on, Heinrich and Jorge could move much faster than the prey over the loose snow so even if they were seen early it didn't matter, the chase just lasted a little longer.

A pistol held to his temple while Jorge cuffed him and fixed a lead to the cuffs soon had him resigned to his fate and he followed without any more trouble. Once inside the accommodation he was released from his restraints and told to strip. No trouble, there seldom was, once caught they knew there was no point in fighting it. They would of course serve time in a prison at home, but then they would try again.

Jorge had a good digital camera, the same as the official one. When Petrov was naked, he took only ones for his private collection. The encrypted files on his computer were a gallery of gorgeous naked Polish boys, many of them with erections. They showed gorgeous cocks and cute butts that Jorge knew he was going to slide his cock into.

When Petrov was naked, Heinrich carried out a body search, making it as humiliating as possible to subdue any thoughts of objection at a later stage.

"Spread your legs and bend over the desk, I am going to check that you are not secreting drugs on your person."

As he was talking, Heinrich was plastering one hand with a lubricant while Jorge had his revolver out ready to use. The humiliation was easy, a slow increase in the number of fingers being used to finger fuck him.

"This one has a really cute butt Jorge, your cock will think it has gone to heaven if you slide in here."

Jorge laughed and got the camera ready when he realized Petrov was not going to fight.

Using his own camera he took full length front and back. What he was faced with was a tall early 20's Polish man. He was slim built with fine muscle definition, slim waist and a gorgeous arse, Jorge could hardly contain himself, he so wanted to cup those two perfect little cheeks in his hands and then spread them so that he could see his little rosebud. Short, black hair, almost black eyes and long, but well-proportioned face made for a very sexy picture.

"You are a very sexy looking man Petrov, if you get an erection and we still like what we see, you will be invited to suck our cocks. Then we will see how good it feels to slide them into your arse. When we have enjoyed your body fully, we will let you go provided you never mention that you were captured if you are ever caught by the authorities."

The boy was obviously thinking about this, was it worth being buggered to get into Germany, and if he allowed it, would they keep their word? The risks he had already taken to get this far made him shudder, and he really didn't want to go to a prison in his motherland, they were quite grim.

Acquiesce and put it behind him when it was finished. He took his hands away from his groin and started to play with himself. When he was erect he dropped his hands to his sides and looked at his captors.

"Oh my God, Heinrich, I don't know about him sucking me, I know I am going down on him as soon as we have showered."

Petrov was surprised and pleased that whatever they were going to do to him, and make him do to them it was going to be with clean bodies, he was badly in need of this shower, he had been running and hiding for days as he approached the border. It would be heaven to be clean again.

Heinrich remained clothed and ready for action as he watched Jorge thoroughly pamper Petrov in the showers.

"This will warm you up Petrov I can see you are still cold from your exposure. My name is Jorge and I am going to take my time to make love to you. I think you are a very sexy man."

Petrov was confused, he was expecting to be raped and humiliated, not pampered and made love to.

"How old are you?"

Petrov told him. "I am 21, Jorge." He said the name hesitantly which made Jorge laugh.

"I am 21 as well, we should be friends."

Petrov relaxed, and as he did so he took in more of this young German who was now being so nice to him. Jorge was bigger than Petrov in build, he also had a big penis which Petrov could see clearly now, and it was bigger than his. The thought of being fucked by it was not the most thrilling, but perhaps it wouldn't hurt too much if Jorge was gentle with him.

"Have you ever played with boys sexually Petrov?"

The Pole shook his head.

"Well, I am going to have lots of fun teaching you how to pleasure me and I will do that by pleasuring you."

Jorge was thoroughly enjoying this. Petrov looked quite fierce but he was proving to be a little darling. He was gently spoken and appeared to have accepted his lot. His German was very good as well. Jorge thought he would probably meld in quite well with the German people. He was of course black haired so not a true Aryan, but lots of Germans were as well with all the interbreeding that had gone on since the war.

Jorge thoroughly soaped Petrov's body before gently fondling his cock and balls. It felt so good. The cock was very hard but the ball sac still had enough play in it to please Jorge. The Pole was clearly excited by all this attention and made no objection when Jorge told him to turn round. The butt was exquisite and Jorge couldn't resist moving in close so that his cock was lodged in the crack between the perfect little cheeks.

"You feel so good, and look so exciting. I know I am going to take you to Paradise."

The feel of another man's cock sliding up and down between his cheeks should have upset him, but Petrov realized he was enjoying it. Jorge continued to play with him and stroke him until he thought he would orgasm if it went on.

"I am almost ready to cum Jorge, you excite me so much."

Jorge was so pleased. He turned Petrov back round, made sure that both of them were free of soap and then dropped to his knees and took Petrov's cock into his mouth. Just a few inches so that he could swab the glans with his tongue. Too much for Petrov after all the stimulation, he came almost immediately and was horrified that Jorge had no time to pull off. The horror turned to surprise when he realized that Jorge was sucking him gently, taking all his cum as he went soft.

"Mmm, that tasted so good, I think I am going to want to do that again before we release you."

He stood up then, took Petrov in his arms and kissed him softly on the lips. This was amazing, Petrov didn't know what to do or say. He loved everything this German guard was doing to him.

Heinrich was watching all of this and was as amazed as Petrov at his friend's actions. They had been together for years, and in this job for over a year and he had never seen Jorge show such affection for a detainee. Usually it was a suck and fuck before throwing them out, but here he was pampering this one in the shower and going down on him, and then kissing him. What on earth was going on?

When Jorge took Petrov through to the sleeping quarters instead of just fucking him over the desk, Heinrich knew it was time to step in.

"Jorge, this boy is just a fuck, he isn't your new boyfriend."

Jorge blushed a deep red as he looked at his friend.

"I'm sorry Heinrich. I have feelings for this man that I have never had for any of the other detainees. I want to make love to him, not just rape him. I know I have to let you have a go as well, but please, be gentle with him when it is your turn."

Heinrich shook his head, but he watched as his friend kissed and cuddled this sexy young Pole.

When Jorge positioned so that they were 69ing he spoke to Petrov.

"Do the same to me as I am doing to you, but neither of us must cum yet."

Heinrich was monstrously erect watching all this foreplay. After a while, he stripped and disappeared to take his own shower. He was going to get in on this action it just looked so erotic. When he came back, still naked, he very quickly came back to a full erection. Jorge now had the prisoner on all fours and he was rimming him. Using both hands to spread Petrov's cheeks wide, he had his tongue buried as deep as he could get it. When he came up for air, he looked at his friend, smiled and said, "This boy is exquisite Hein, I have never had so much pleasure making love." Heinrich laughed.

"I don't think I have ever seen you so happy Jorge, perhaps I should make love to you instead of the Pole when you are finished."

Both young men were laughing and Jorge rolled Petrov over onto his back again, cuddling him before he spoke to him.

"Would you like to watch my friend fuck me after I have made love to you?" Petrov looked surprised, and then amused.

"Yes, I think I would, perhaps he could do it without you fucking me first." That was enough for all three to have a fit of the giggles before Jorge became serious again.

"Please Petrov, I want to make love to you. I think you are so sexy." Petrov was surprised and looked at his captor with a quizzical expression.

"But you don't need to ask, you know I will let you so that I can be free in your country."

"Yes, I know, but I won't penetrate you if you don't want me to. We can both have wonderful orgasms just using our mouths and hands." Heinrich sat down with a bump and a look of shock on his face.

"You aren't serious Jorge."

"Yes, I'm serious. I think this man is special. I want to make love to him for a long time, but only if he is enjoying it."

"In that case I am definitely going to fuck you. I'm horny and this is the first chance of a fuck this week."

Jorge was an anal virgin, he and Heinrich had never indulged in mutual sex even though they were old friends and both gay. He thought about it and realized he was prepared to give up his own virginity to protect this man lying alongside him.

"Alright, you can fuck me after I have finished making love to Petrov."

Jorge returned to the 69 position and brought Petrov to a wonderful orgasm almost the same time as the reverse happened. Jorge was amazed that this boy swallowed all his cum, but was pleased as well. He swivelled back round, and while they calmed down planted loads of little kisses all over Petrov's face, particularly the lips.

"All right Hein, where do you want me? You'll have to open me up first or you will damage me because I'm a virgin."

Petrov was amazed that this German was going to give up his anal virginity for him.

"I want you over the desk, like we normally have the illegals."

Petrov watched, mouth agape as Heinrich squatted behind his friend and started pushing fingers into him. It was incredibly erotic and he got a monstrously hard erection on. Heinrich noticed it and pointed it out to Jorge.

"Perhaps I should let him fuck you after I have taken your virginity my friend."

Jorge looked at Petrov's straining cock and wondered.

'Let me get Heinrich satisfied first and then I will think about it,' was what Jorge thought and what he said to Heinrich was.

"I'll see after I find out whether I like it."

Heinrich lubed himself and Jorge's arse before gently sliding over his sphincter. Naturally it hurt to start with and Petrov noted the pain in Jorge's eyes. When it went Jorge told Heinrich he could continue. It looked so erotic Petrov was almost peeing pre-cum which didn't go unnoticed.

"Mmm, I should have been doing this for the last three years Jorge, you feel incredible to fuck."

"I think I should have let you. I know how good it feels to fuck, but I had no idea it would feel so good having a cock sliding in and out of me. Perhaps in future when we fuck the illegals I will let them fuck me afterwards."

"When I finish Petrov I think you had better be ready to take my place, this slut is obviously enjoying having a cock in his arse."

"You're right, but Petrov, I want you to make love to me on my bed not here."

This was getting so raunchy that Heinrich sped up and fucked Jorge hard to orgasm. Both young men squealing with the pleasure as Jorge came at the same time.

Petrov determined he was going to be very gentle with this odd man who was being kind to him, but was obviously a homosexual.

When they were on the bed with Jorge on his back, Petrov did the same as they had been doing mutually earlier, but added to it was gentle finger fucking of Jorge's anus. When he was sure Jorge was excited enough, he put some lube on his cock and entered him in the missionary position. Very quickly, he realized it looked incredibly erotic having this young German lying under him with that huge cock lying along his tummy and the very nicely shaped butt accepting his penis with quite obvious pleasure. The feelings running through his body defied belief. He had made love to girls at home, but none had been this exciting. His cock was being caressed by Jorge's arse as he slid in and out, taking him off to outer space with the incredibly erotic sensations.

He didn't last long, and despite only having cum a few minutes earlier Jorge didn't either. Their orgasms were very intense and Heinrich who had watched in awe slipped quietly out of the bedroom realising there really was something special occurring between the other two.

Jorge and Petrov, as they calmed down stroked each other's torsos and kissed each other tenderly on the lips, not taking their eyes off one another.

"I would like you to do that to me sometime Jorge. I want to give you the pleasure you have just given me."

"I want to as well Petrov, for a long time, forever."

Petrov was surprised.

"But you can't, I must leave here mustn't I?"

Jorge had been thinking and made this suggestion.

"Heinrich and I only have two more days before we are due time off. If you stay with us here I will drop Heinrich off as usual and then we can drive to my home in Hamburg where you can stay with me. I have a little money so we can buy you clothes and try to find you a job. Illegal immigrants are employed all the time, sometimes on very low wages, but you wouldn't have to pay for accommodation so you would be ok." Petrov was amazed that this young German would do this for him.

"Why would you do that Jorge?" Jorge blushed and replied very quietly without looking at Petrov.

"Because I think I am falling in love with you. You thrill me like no other lover ever has done."

Surprise wouldn't come close to describing the emotions Petrov was feeling at that declaration.

"I am so flattered Jorge, but I'm not even sure I'm gay. You have been a wonderful considerate lover, but I have never touched another boy sexually. I will let you fuck me because what you have given me was very special, but I may never want it again."

Jorge smiled shyly.

"I don't mind. I can live in hope that when we have made love a few times, even if you only let me fuck you once, that you may like it enough to stay with me."

"I would like that. I won't feel under pressure and you are very nice." When Jorge told Heinrich he almost exploded.

"Are you serious? If he is caught, and found to be living with you, you'll lose your job and go to prison. Your life will be ruined."

"I know, but I'm going to do it, we'll be careful and we'll have a story that won't implicate you, so it is only ourselves that we need to worry about."

"You're mad, are you in love with him or something?"

Jorge dropped his head again.

"Yes, I think I am. He thrills me so much he takes my breath away." When Jorge admitted his love, Heinrich's attitude softened.

"Be careful then my friend, I would hate to lose you. You are like my brother Jorge and I love you as well."

Petrov was both happy and amazed that these two loved each other but not sexually, well, apart from this one time that he had witnessed.

That night Petrov was so pleased, Jorge just cuddled him all night. The next morning, instead of being locked up while the other two patrolled, he was told he could spend the day in their quarters and they would see him just before dark. They caught two more illegals that day and radioed for the wagon to come and pick them up. Petrov was hidden when the collection van arrived and then showered and ate supper. After supper Jorge asked Petrov if he could make love to him tonight.

"If you don't like it, and don't want us to be lovers I will still take you to Hamburg and help you while I am time off."

Petrov realized he could have the best of both worlds and all he had to do was let Jorge fuck him once.

"Alright, we can try it."

Love making took on the same pattern Petrov had witnessed before, except that it was his arse that was being opened up this time. Jorge was very gentle, making sure he was very relaxed before adding each new finger. When he had reached four, he fucked him gently with them, continuing to use his tongue and other hand to keep pleasuring him. Petrov thought he was going to heaven. Jorge kept hitting his prostate always gently, and always stroking it before pulling out again. When he introduced his penis he only slid the glans in before remaining still and just stroking Petrov's cock and balls. It was so erotic and sensual that Petrov's eyes were as wide as saucers with surprise. Jorge's cock felt incredible as it slid in a little bit more on each in stroke as he fucked gently. By the time he had all of Jorge's enormously long man rammer inside him he couldn't believe the feelings, and after a few long strokes he thought he was going to leave this planet. It felt wonderful, more sensuous than anything he had ever experienced before.

"Oh, Jorge, what are you doing to me? That feels wonderful."

Jorge was so happy, he fell forward and kissed Petrov so passionately it had both of them gasping for breath.

"I am glad, I love you so much already, I will always want to please you." This was incredible, Petrov wanted this to go on forever, but, eventually the feelings for both of them were too much and they started to orgasm, very close together, and so intensely that they started screaming.

Heinrich was so worried at the volume of the screams that he burst in on them, just as Jorge fell forward onto Petrov's chest and both of them burst into tears. It was incredible; Heinrich had never seen anything like it. The other two were crying and kissing, uttering stupid words of love. He turned and left them, shaking his head in wonder.

Part 2

Time off came round and the plan Jorge had suggested worked. When they dropped Heinrich he admonished them to be careful and told Jorge he would see him in two weeks' time. Jorge and Petrov drove on to Hamburg.

Jorge's apartment was very comfortable. It was only one bedroom but a spacious reception area, open plan lounge dining area and kitchen. The bathroom was off the bedroom and that was where both young men went first, to get rid of the travel dirt.

Jorge loved this part of their relationship. Washing each other always resulted in them cumming in the shower, it was so erotic pampering each other, always spending much longer on the groin area than anywhere else.

Petrov still marvelled at the length and hardness of Jorge's penis every time he got an erection and he would have a little snigger when he realized how much he enjoyed the feel of it sliding into his anus. Just a week ago he thought he was a good heterosexual boy, now he loved the feel of a huge cock in his arse, but he also loved to feel his cock sliding in and out of Jorge. The agreement was that they could both fuck and be fucked as the mood took them. They both loved it so after only a few days their lovemaking was stupendous.

The next thing for Jorge was to get Petrov some more clothes and it was wonderful shopping with his new love. They couldn't afford to be extravagant but they didn't need to.

It was during one of these shopping expeditions that they were spotted by a young officer of the border patrol that knew Jorge. He got close enough to hear them talking and picked up on Petrov's accent. In itself not notable but being a border patrolman the officer was suspicious. He followed them to Jorge's apartment, before going to a local cafe to think about what he should do, and to check with his headquarters on Jorge's record.

The officer, Kurt, found out that Jorge and his partner Heinrich were old friends and were both gay. Their record of captures was impressive so they were obviously dedicated patrol men. What should he do if this other young man was an illegal immigrant?

Kurt rather fancied Jorge but because of his position he had never been able to make contact in a social environment. He knew that Jorge and he were the same age and that Jorge and his friend Heinrich had served together in the army before joining the border service.

Finishing his coffee, Kurt decided he would call on Jorge under the guise of finding out if he was happy with his routine as a border guard.

He knocked on the door of Jorge's apartment which was opened by Jorge dressed in just a pair of athletic shorts. He was obviously freeballing and looked as though he was partly aroused. Kurt wondered if he had caught him just about to have sex.

"Good afternoon Lindeman. I am Lieutenant Kurt Muller from HQ, may I come in?" Jorge was obviously flustered. He looked nervously back into the apartment, patently looking to see if Petrov was hidden.

"Ah, yes Sir." Petrov was hidden in the bedroom so that was no problem.

"I have some questions to ask you about the border patrol, but first I would very much like to look round your apartment."

Without being replied to Kurt headed straight for the bedroom and was rewarded immediately he opened the door of it by the sight of Petrov also clothed only in shorts, sat nervously on the edge of the bed.

"Ah, Jorge, and who is this young man?" Jorge jumped in quickly.

"He is just a friend, visiting me, Sir. We were just getting changed to go out."

Kurt walked up to Petrov, stuck his hand out and said,

"Hello, my name is Kurt, I work in the same service as Jorge."

Poor Petrov fell for the easy manner. He jumped up, put his hand out and replied.

"Hello, my name is Petrov, I am pleased to meet you."

"And where do you come from?" Jorge jumped in quickly hoping to salvage what he guessed was a disastrous slip.

"My friend comes from close to the Swiss border, Sir."

Kurt laughed.

"Ah yes, with his good Polish name and his accent I can tell. Perhaps he would like to show me his papers."

Neither needed to reply, the look of anguish on both faces told Kurt all he wanted to know.

"Let's all go and sit down shall we?"

Jorge and Petrov sat next to each other, and the looks that passed between them made it obvious they thought it was all over for them.

"Jorge, I have looked at your record. You and Heinrich are easily the most dedicated and successful pair of guards on the border so I don't want to make trouble for you. Let me tell you what I think is going on here. Petrov is an illegal that you picked up on the border, but for some reason didn't hand over to the collection vehicle. Looking at the pair of you I am guessing that you are attracted to each other to the point, Jorge, where you were willing to risk prison to help Petrov. Correct me if I am wrong so far."

Jorge looked up miserably, at his officer.

"No Sir, you are correct. It has never happened before, but when we picked up Petrov, I was very attracted to him. I want to help him settle here long term but I don't know how to go about it."

"Well what you have done is patently not the right way. I am, and have been for a long time, attracted to you as well Jorge, but being an officer I didn't feel it was appropriate to make any advances. Now however I would like to make love with both of you, and if you agree I will help you legalise Petrov's position."

Jorge was suspicious, this seemed too easy, but he was prepared to grasp at any straw to keep Petrov with him.

"Willingly, Sir, happily, if I can keep Petrov as my lover."

Petrov was not happy having a third person in their relationship, and how many more might there be later he wondered, but like Jorge, he realized they had no choice.

"Good. In that case why don't you both call me Kurt and show me where I can get undressed and showered. I presume you both did that as soon as you came in from shopping."

He was grinning and it became infectious. Jorge and Petrov looked at Kurt together and decided he might be an interesting body to play with as a side line, both grinned and Jorge got cheeky.

"Petrov and I would be delighted to undress you and shower you Kurt. We both love clean bodies to play with."

That comment set the scene and Kurt could not believe how erotic they made undressing and showering him. Both Jorge and Petrov kept their shorts on and the resulting erections covered by their thin shorts were extremely erotic for Kurt.

Showered and dried, and now all three naked and hard, Kurt spoke.

"When the Gestapo interrogated prisoners during the war they often stripped and humiliated their captors hoping to make them talk. Of course they did unspeakable things to them often injuring and mutilating them. I would love to use the same technique with you two as a role play game. I won't, of course, hurt you or mark you in any way, but I have fantasised about being able to do what I like with young sexy men. I will only ask that we do this once, and then I will help Petrov get papers to remain here. I might however ask you to make love to me occasionally Jorge, you have the most incredible penis."

Jorge thought this could be fun. He was surprised that Kurt was flexible as well, being happy to take and give cock. He wanted Petrov to himself, but he wasn't going to turn down the chance to fuck this sexy officer.

Kurt was very slim and shaved all his body hair, emphasizing the more than adequate length of his cock. Jorge would enjoy taking that inside either orifice.

"Now my Polish friend, you will tell me how your escape network to the West works."

Petrov looked absolutely stunned. He had no idea that the Germans knew there actually was an organised network that had found a way to bypass the patrols on the Polish side of the border making the only hazard to overcome the first kilometre inside Germany. Kurt picked up on it.

"Oh my God, there really is an escape network. We had no idea. I'm sorry Jorge, I will have to take Petrov in for interrogation, this is much too big for me to let pass."

Jorge was gutted.

"Please Kurt, there must be an alternative. If Petrov tells you all he knows, couldn't you fabricate where you obtained the knowledge."

Kurt had to think about this. He would almost certainly get a promotion if he could stop, or at least slow down the number of defections across the border.

Petrov was thinking very fast. If he divulged all that he knew it would jeopardise the escape plans of many more Poles. If he didn't, he would be interrogated by the Germans first, and then returned to Poland where the interrogation would be as brutal as the Nazi regime had used during the war. He didn't believe he would be able to hold out against sustained brutality, so, reluctantly he decided he would try to strike a bargain with Kurt to be able to remain here.

"If you will tell me everything you know Petrov I will tell my superiors that I am unable to reveal my source because it would be too dangerous for his well-being. That part is certainly not a lie. Your authorities are as eager as mine to stop this illegal traffic."

Petrov reluctantly told Kurt everything before they resumed their play time, now a little more subdued than originally planned. It wasn't much fun so Kurt stopped it.

"I'm sorry, I didn't want to ruin our fun but this is so important. Let's forget it for today. I will call on you again when we are all more relaxed."

It was several days before Kurt called again. When he did he was wearing the triple pips of a captain and was obviously in very high spirits.

"I owe you so much Petrov, look, I am now a captain, that should not have happened for several more years. Your reward is to be the interrogator and use me as you will for the remainder of the day."

Now, all three young men were in high spirits at the thought of unbridled sex for the next few hours. Showers were taken but when they were all clean and dry Petrov and Jorge put shorts back on to make believe they were the interrogators and Kurt was the prisoner.

The next hour was interesting from Petrov's perspective. They spit roasted Kurt, and then, to cement his position, Petrov choreographed Kurt fucking Jorge, he knew Jorge wouldn't mind, and Kurt had already stated he wanted to make love to Jorge.

Three well satisfied young men sat around Jorge's lounge afterwards and Kurt explained how he was going to get Petrov papers to make his stay legal.

"I will work on it with Petrov while you are away next time Jorge. I think I can also find him a job."

Jorge and Petrov were delighted, but a few minutes later Kurt spoilt it a little for Jorge.

"Jorge, I don't believe that you could have done this without the knowledge, and probably collusion of your partner Heinrich, so, I am coming on an inspection tour of the guard posts and will work it so that I overnight at yours. I will then enjoy using Heinrich's body the same as we have done this afternoon."

Jorge was quite upset to begin with, and then he thought how much fun it could be if Kurt fucked Heinrich. He would love to watch that, and he didn't mind if Kurt and Heinrich fucked him so he told Kurt his idea and had them all laughing. Petrov tried to sound hurt that Jorge was going to have more sex when he was away, but it didn't sound convincing.

That night, Jorge told Petrov his thinking. "When we have satisfied Kurt and he leaves us alone, I don't want to make love to anyone else but you. I know we will be apart for half our time, but now that I have a lover I will try to get a posting to headquarters so that I am home almost every night. I really do love you Petrov and hope we will be together for a long time."

Love making that night was tender and sensuous, incredibly satisfying for both young men.

Things did work out for Jorge. Heinrich wasn't too upset being fucked by Kurt and was even less upset when Kurt and he spit roasted Jorge several times.

"Now my friend, we must find you a boyfriend. Of course, Kurt will take payment from you to help regularise his living and it will cost you several deep fucks from his man rammer." Jorge laughed and Kurt did as well, casting lustful glances at Heinrich.

Two good things came out of Kurt's involvement with Jorge and Petrov. Petrov was given permission to remain in Germany and Jorge received a posting to headquarters to help develop plans to make all of the patrols as successful as his and Heinrich's had been.

Heinrich received a new partner who was also gay and was admonished by Kurt to make love to the new partner rather than pretty

Polish boys. The advice was taken and Jorge was delighted to find Heinrich on his doorstep one day with his new boyfriend.

Jorge and Petrov went on for years as lovers until the iron curtain disappeared and Poland was free of Russian control.

"I love you Jorge, but now I must go home to look after the family that I deserted to come to the West."

It was a tearful goodbye and Jorge couldn't hide his hurt at Petrov's desertion. Kurt realized and over time he and Jorge became lovers, remaining together for more years, both serving in the border control department where illegal immigrants were now more likely to be from Turkey than the old Soviet bloc.

End of the 1st Story

Chris Johns

My Street Urchin

The Filipino Adventure

Gay Romance Erotica

My Street Urchin
(The Filipino Adventure)
By: Chris Johns

Chapter 1

I was getting used to Manila now. I had been here four times before and I could usually stay for a week or ten days. There were so many boys available for sex that the cost was peanuts, particularly as the peso wasn't a hard currency, so black market rates for American Dollars were ridiculous. It meant I could have a boy all night for about $10 and short time for pocket change. I would sometimes have three or four boys a day just for a quick shag or a blowjob. I know that wasn't very moral of me and years later, when I developed a conscience I did feel guilty about the way I had exploited the poverty. I'm talking about the late 70's, of course.

Live sex shows were spectacular, real hardcore sex only a few feet from me. If the boys in these shows were tasty, I would take one out for the night and repeat his performance in my hotel suite. Other nights I would go to the clubs where a higher class of boy would be available, but still not cost me much. I had discovered that if I brought packs of designer underwear with me I could get one of these boys for the night with a single pair of designer briefs, well, not even designer ones. I could buy Haynes in packs for just a few dollars, but they were like gold dust to these guys.

I was obviously getting choosy because one night I didn't see anything I fancied in the club. I had gone for the dancing, but wouldn't have passed up the chance of a night companion. It wasn't far to my hotel so I decided to walk even though it was after 1. I was only about a hundred yards from my hotel when I saw the boy come out of the shadows as I passed an alley way. Not very big and not at all threatening as he slid up alongside me and keeping pace with me, spoke.

"I'll let you fuck me, Mister, if I can stay with you all night."

Not an unusual request. These boys slept under market stalls or in alley ways, usually wrapped in an old blanket, if they were lucky. They were invariably dirty with clothes that hadn't seen a washing machine in months. I would usually give them a few Pesos and send them on their way, but this boy spoke like an American rather than a Filipino, so I waited until we came up to the next street light and stopped. I turned to face him and he looked up at me with a quizzical expression on his face.

"What?"

"I wanted to have a look at you. You aren't Filipino, are you?"

"Half of me is, the other half is an American Sailor."

That wasn't unusual, street girls never took precautions and neither did the sailors.

He was quite small and only looked like a kid.

"I can't take you to bed, you are too young."

He stood as tall as he could, so, about 5 feet 6 inches, pulled his shoulders back and said, "I'm eighteen."

I thought, 'yes, eighteen months', but said, 'prove it'. He took out his national ID card and yes he was eighteen, so I immediately thought, fake, but, he was quite cute, and he was desperate, I could tell, which probably meant I could do anything I liked to him and he would let me.

"If the night porter will let you in, I'll let you stay for a little while at least."

Jesus, (J pronounced like an H), was the night porter and was used to me. I always checked in to a suite as me +1 so that when I had a boy stay overnight I could take him to breakfast with me before sending him on his way. I tipped him quite well at the end of each stay and he gave me no problems.

"What's your name, Boy?"

"I'm David Betchek."

"I'm Chris, come on then let's see how you fare with the porter."

ID card was genuine according to Jesus so we ended up in my sitting room. In the bright lights I had a better look at him. His clothes were better than the average street boy, but they were filthy, and he wasn't much better. I had been in a smoky club so I was going to throw all my clothes in the washing machine, tumble dry them and iron them the next morning even though I had plenty. I didn't want smoky clothes contaminating the remainder of my stuff.

"Take all your clothes off, David, we'll throw them in the machine with mine. I guess that means you are staying the night."

He was naked before me, stood with a broad grin on his face. I told him to empty his pockets onto the coffee table and then I shoved everything into the machine, except his underwear, which was beyond redemption as far as I was concerned. I threw them in the waste bin and told him I'd give him a new pair in the morning. I was certainly building brownie points with this boy. I came back and looked at his few possessions. A tatty old wallet that looked empty, a few coins and his ID card.

Next was the shower. His hair was a revelation; it had looked a mousy grey/brown, but that was dirt. The true colour was rich dark brown, medium length. His eyes were dark brown and not very expressive, but that changed as he became comfortable with me and they came alight. The remainder of him was perfect for me. He was quite small, no real muscle definition, just a nice shaped body with virtually no hair. For a Filipino boy he was well endowed, but I put that down to his American father, uncut, but quite a small foreskin. His head was fully uncovered when he was still only chubbed up, a very cute butt made it for me.

I thought that making love to him wouldn't be difficult.

I on the other hand was early twenties, similar build to David but about six inches taller. I was considered an attractive man with my curly mid brown hair and matching eyes. I was circumcised with a good length cock and decent sized ball sac. I know I needed to start working out or I was going to lose what little definition I had.

I gave him a thorough shower because he was so dirty, the result of course was a very hard boy cock. When we were both rinsed off I couldn't resist going down on him for a quick suck. It was great, but I wasn't going to let him cum in case we could make sweet music together.

"When you are dry, David, wrap a towel round you and join me in the sitting room."

He looked a little apprehensive as he sat opposite me.

"Tell me a little about yourself."

"Not much to tell really. Mum told me my dad was a sailor she met in Subic Bay. After she had me she had to keep going to bed with other men to keep us both. I must have had a couple of hundred dads at least as I grew up. Mum died before I could finish school, but I spent a lot of time with American kids so I never spoke like a local boy. I became a street kid after that. I try to find work and do make a little money, but never enough to have a room so when I really want a bed to sleep in I proposition a guy as he comes back to his hotel and get a good night's sleep for a fuck, or sometimes just a blowjob."

I thought what a shitty life he must have led.

"Do you like being fucked and giving blowjobs?"

"Sometimes, if the punter is nice to me, but mostly they just want to get their rocks off and then they fall asleep. I could plunder their wallets easily, but I never have."

"Well, I would like to give you a blowjob and then fuck you, but I promise I will be gentle and considerate with you."

He nodded, looked at my groin again even though he knew what he was going to get.

"That's ok, Chris, you can do anything you like to me as long as I can sleep here."

I wasn't particularly kinky most of the time so I intended to do what I said. He was a delight, putty in my hands. We did go 69ing for a while before both of us had very intense orgasms. I still wanted to play so as soon as I was recovered I made him turn over and come up on his knees, with his legs well spread.

"Drop your head onto your arms, David, and make yourself comfortable."

I started playing with his ass with my hands before moving in close and licking his cheeks while I played with his cock and balls to get him an erection again. I guess he was over six inches long so I could have lots of fun when he was hard. While I played with his butt I licked his balls and sucked his cock before going in with my tongue to rim him. He told me later he had never been rimmed before. I knew he enjoyed it because he had another mighty orgasm. I felt it coming so I quickly ducked my head down to catch it in my mouth, quite a load. I then concentrated on his love tunnel with my tongue and fingers until I was reaching overload myself, then I lubed us both and entered him. Despite my size, he was so relaxed I went straight in and fucked him with long slow strokes. We were both cooing as we reached another climax, only one lot of messy cum on my bed, which we cleaned up after we had calmed down.

"That was really good, David, I hope you are up for that again in the morning."

He was glowing. "Oh yes Chris, that's the best sex I've ever had. I've never been rimmed before, that was amazing."

He was gushing and I pulled him into me, kissed him goodnight and he turned to spoon into me. I loved it.

The next morning, he made the coffee while I ironed his clothes. He showered and I gave him his new underwear. He loved them. We went down to the restaurant for breakfast and he ate enough for two men. I wondered what I was going to do with him. I didn't want to just send him back to where he had been last night, but what else could I do? I had another couple of days before I had to go back to work. I was a geologist for an oil exploration company in the Middle East. Not very experienced so I worked under a senior guy, but I got loads of holiday, about four months a year taken every couple of months depending on workload. I bit the bullet and decided to keep him with me.

"Would you like to go back to the suite and do to me what I did to you last night?"

His reaction was so over the top I was creased up with laughter, but the result was we were back in bed a few minutes later. The boy was incredible. He made love to me like never before in my life. When he fucked me I was so spaced out I had several orgasms. His cock was pure joy to have roaming around inside me. I was wasted when he eventually pulled out and we lay panting.

"Wow, I think you had better stay with me to do that again."

He looked at me, not sure whether I was speaking the truth. He didn't say anything though so I didn't. I had planned to go on a trip that day to do some wild water rafting. I decided to still, but I asked David if he would like to come with me.

That day isn't important, except to say that just watching the fun David was having was worth it. He was like a little kid. I didn't speak Tagalog, but watching him interact with the Filipino lads in the canoes I knew he was having a ball. We had both stripped down to our underwear for the rides because I hadn't thought about us getting wet. The boys put our clothes in plastic bags so that when we reached the bottom we could towel off and go back to Manila dry, but commando. Both of us were wearing briefs and showed healthy bulges in our pouches. Both of us got touched up a few times as well, but we weren't worried. I was quite flattered really, and when we got erections the boat boys made us laugh with their suggestions.

Back at the hotel we showered and I gave David another pair of briefs from my pack. He was so pleased and was a complete joy to watch. I got loads of very intense kisses and a bucket of thank yous'.

It was too early for dinner even though we had only snacked at lunch time and it was also too early for sex. Well not really, but I didn't just want a quickie with this boy. We went out to a swish bar in the Hilton and it was there that I realised his clothes weren't good enough. We had a quick one and left. I dragged him into a menswear shop and bought him a complete set of clothes. He really looked good so we went back to the Hilton and sat in the lounge chatting and drinking until it was time for dinner. I took him to a good restaurant and watched with joy in my heart as he tasted different dishes. Our waiter was middle aged and I think he guessed at our relationship as he bought us a selection of the starters in nibble size portions. David had a huge T Bone steak for his Entree and I was amazed that he still found room for a large portion of apple pie. We went back to the hotel then, too full to do anything but sit and watch TV for a couple of hours. We did it in just our briefs because neither of us wanted to crease up our street clothes.

We went to bed quite early. I asked David to make love to me, and I would do it to him before we slept. The boy used his previous experience, plus I think a big dollop of affection for the day I had given him. His cock was so much fun to pleasure and then when he used it to ream out my insides I was definitely in cock heaven.

The next day was my last full day and I wanted to do something for him until I could come back. I asked him what we could do to protect his new clothes and give him a base to start building his possessions.

"I have an American friend. He is in the navy but based here so he is only away at sea a little. I know there is a locker room that you can rent lockers in. He keeps a load of personal stuff in his because he is gay and he doesn't want the navy to know. I could probably get one there, but I don't have any money."

We found out details, took a taxi to the location and I bought three months for him. We put the key on a chain round his neck so that he wouldn't lose it. Before we locked it up I slid $200 in without him seeing it. I was going to give him some more when I left.

"I want to see you again when I come back, David, is that ok?"

He looked at me, a little disbelieving.

"I mean it, I've really enjoyed being with you and I can be back here in a couple of months all being well."

"I'd like that as well, Chris, I'll keep my new clothes nice so that we can go out together, and I'll try to get more work so that I can pay my way."

We said no more on the subject and just tried to enjoy the day, knowing that at lunch time the next day I would be off to the airport and back to work. We took in a movie and giggled through most of it because we made out in the back seat like a couple of kids. We wandered through Harrison Plaza after that and watched some of the boys trying to pick up tourists and other expat guys.

"Did you ever do this, David?"

He blushed, nodded his head and replied, "Yes, when I had nice clothes, but as they got worse to look at I didn't fit in."

He was right of course. I had picked up boys here, but they were always smartly dressed and charged premium rates for their services. I didn't ask him if he was going to do it again. I didn't feel it was my place, I didn't own this boy.

The next morning he gave me contact details for his American friend so that I could tell him when I was coming back. I wouldn't let him come to the airport with me so we said goodbye as I climbed into my taxi. I kissed him on both cheeks and slipped a bundle of Pesos into his hand. He was crying as we pulled away and I knew I was going to be doing some investigation to see if I could get him a job in Abu Dhabi with me.

Chapter 2

There wasn't a lot of work offshore when I got back so my company settled me into an apartment in town.

"I think we are likely to have a couple of years work for you in the desert, Chris, so get settled here and forget about offshore for now. Lots of seismic work. Pretty boring, but at least you'll be able to use all your theory training to analyse test sheets."

I wasn't worried. Abu Dhabi was only an hour or so from Dubai along the coastal highway and I had a good car. I could spend time up there if I got bored here. In the event I got friendly with one of the helicopter pilots and started spending time at the company club near the airport. It was quite a cool place. Nice bar, big swimming pool, cinema and a night club at which they held dances and shows. Richie told me they had just received approval to have a full time steward and they were going to bring one in from the Philippines. My brain went into overdrive then and I started delving into the agent and the qualifications they would be looking for.

The details suited me fine. They would select a boy for suitability and then train him in Manila before bringing him into the Emirates. I had to come clean with Ritchie then so that he would keep me informed, and I made friends with the employment agent. Ritchie was funny.

"Bugger, my Gaydar needs servicing. I never pegged you as gay, Chris. Like to come to bed with me tonight?"

My Gaydar was shit as well. I had socialised with Ritchie occasionally since we met when he flew me out to an island for a check on some survey equipment. We had gone in a Jet Ranger, just the two of us. I had to check some wave equipment so it was swimming trunks for me and a small dinghy with an outboard to work from. Ritchie stripped to his underpants and came with me.

"I'll handle the dinghy, Chris, and you just tell me what you want."

I did note he was very buff, but never had a thought he might be gay. He told me he thought the same about me.

The agent made it clear that if I wanted to select the boy who would do the steward's job he had no problem with it, of course it was going to cost me, but the cost wasn't too bad so we shook on it and I told him what I was going to do and when.

I telephoned David's friend and told him when I would be back in Manila.

"Tell David to meet me at the same hotel as last time. I should check in midafternoon on the date I have given you."

He promised to tell David and I was humming, waiting for the time to pass. We would need to get him a passport and introduce him to the training team in Manila. They would organise his visa and travel when he was ready to travel and the helicopter company would pick up the tab.

I arrived as planned, no David. I telephoned his friend, sorry he was away at sea. Had dinner, still no David. I knew there was a gay club near the hotel that did really raunchy sex cabarets.

I decided to go to try to cheer myself up. The lights had already dimmed when I arrived and I was shown to a table with a waiter holding a penlight. The show started with a boy lounging on a sofa. I did a double take. He was wearing an identical pair of briefs to the ones I had given David. He was a big boy all round. Great body and he filled the pouch of the briefs so that they were nearly bursting. He was lit by a spot light and another one was roaming over the stage until it picked up a little boy crawling on all fours towards the big one.

I nearly wet my pants, it was David. He had a load of whip marks on his back and across his naked buttocks. He looked awful and I wanted to cry. He stopped at the feet of the big guy who looked at him and then just said, 'suck'. David peeled the briefs off and then sucked the guy, changing positions to give all the audience a look. The guy was huge and after a few minutes, he pushed David back and cock slapped him quite hard. God knows where they found a local with a cock that big, it was certainly the biggest I had ever seen. Then he pulled David back in to suck some more.

Next, using a foot, he hooked a can of Crisco out from under the sofa and ordered David to lube his ass and be ready to take a real man. One hand playing with the monster's balls, his mouth engaged sucking the monster cock, the audience could see David scoop the Crisco up and use it to fuck himself with increasing numbers of fingers until the monster hauled him up by his hair and pushed him over the sofa. With no finesse, the cock entered David in one movement. David screamed but the guy power fucked him, pulled out as he came all over David's back and then picked up a whip. He beat David with it as he crawled off stage screaming at him that he was a useless slave and would pay for it.

The lights came up and an announcer said that the slave would be brought back for some extreme double fucking sex and a more painful beating strung up.

I couldn't believe David had dropped this low in just two months considering I had left him with a reasonable amount of money.

David and the other guy came out front after that, David in just a g-string so that you could see his much abused back, particularly his ass. When he saw me he ran back behind the stage. I got hold of the big guy still wearing David's briefs and slipped him a note to bring David out to me even if he had to drag him. He thought that would look good so he did and made David kneel before me. I took his hair from the giant and thanked him. When there was just David I forced his head up so that he could look at me.

"Why?"

He started to cry.

"I wanted to have lots of money when you came back so that I could buy you things."

"And have you got lots of money?"

He shook his head. "They make me do this for nothing now. I'm not allowed outside. I really am a slave."

I looked around and could see the bully watching and the manager hovering quite close.

"Do you still have your locker?" He nodded. I could then see the key round his neck.

"What personal stuff do you have here?"

"Just my old clothes and my ID."

"Can you get your ID?"

He nodded.

"Go and get it, you are leaving with me."

"They'll kill you before they release me. Please go, I'm not worth it."

"I love you David, and you are coming with me, all the way to Abu Dhabi."

Shock didn't even come close to describing the look on his face.

"As long as we can get you a passport you are coming to Abu Dhabi to work."

He cried then, "They won't let me, they'll kill both of us."

I looked around and thought he was right so I told him.

"Well you've made your bed, now you can lie on it."

I said it quite loud, stood up and shoved him out of the way. I went up to the manager and asked for my bill.

"Useless little shit, I tried to improve his lot when I was here last time. Doesn't have the sense to improve himself. I'll be back for the next show, I want to see him whipped good for his stupidity."

The manager was pleased, particularly when I gave him a sizeable tip.

I went straight to the local police station, got hold of the duty inspector, told him the story and asked him what we could do to get David out whole. I guessed what was coming so when he quoted a figure I halved it, we ended with a figure I could live with.

"You get all of it when we are clear of the club, with David and his ID card, nothing before."

The inspector grinned at me. "Very wise when you don't know who you are dealing with. Why don't you go back to the club, we'll join you at the appropriate time."

I got the best table in the house for the next show. Two big guys dragged David on this time and strung him up by his wrists. He looked terrible and I wanted to cry.

The two monsters took turns fucking him before the guy from last time came on with a whip. He had just started administering blistering strokes when the lights went up and the place was full of police.

David was taken backstage and dressed before being led out by a policeman. The other three performers were led out in cuffs and the manager was admonished to clean up his club. I realised then it was all a game. The inspector tried to prise extra money out of me to release David but I put up a good argument and I had David in my suite soon after.

I was crying as I washed him gently in a warm shower. His poor abused body looked awful. I put him to bed and left to see Jesus. I told him what I needed and he delivered it to my room a little while later. I spent ages then making sure all of the whip lines that had drawn blood were cleaned thoroughly. I dressed them all and then covered him with a sheet before settling down in my armchair to watch over him. He became very feverish and I spent half the night trying to cool him with cold compresses. His fever broke before dawn and he settled into a calm sleep. I had breakfast sent up for me, and David eventually woke about mid-day. He looked a lot better than when I had brought him here twelve hours previously. His eyes were deep sunk, and he had obviously lost a lot of weight. The second he saw me he broke down, curled up in the foetal position and sobbed. I cuddled him and told him I loved him and was going to look after him. Nothing worked and I ended up sending for a doctor who sedated him.

I had a full month's leave this time and I needed it. David returned to me very slowly. He felt so ashamed at what I had seen, and at his own degradation at the hands of the manager and his goons. He told me he was systematically fucked every day after he started doing shows there.

While he was convalescing I started the process of getting him his passport. Thank heavens for a corrupt society was my thought because although it cost me a lot of money I had his passport before I had to return to work.

We never made love that month. I thought he was much too fragile. The week before I had to leave, we went to clear his locker and I was amazed, the $200 US I had left for him was still there with the new clothes.

"I wanted to be able to buy you a present when you came back."

We never mentioned it again, but he did buy me a present when we were safely together in Abu Dhabi.

I introduced him to the training school where he would undergo his training as a club steward. They told him that as soon as he was ready he would be processed into the United Arab Emirates.

I was almost ready to go on my next leave when he arrived. Ritchie arranged for both of us to meet him and settle him in. He had his own room and private bathroom within the club. Ritchie was the manager as well as being a line pilot so we had no problems.

"Most evenings he will finish at 11, he doesn't have to sleep here. On nights that we have entertainment he'll finish too late to leave the compound. He doesn't need to be here for work until 11 in the morning because the club doesn't open until 12. He won't have to do any catering, just bar service, and he will have to keep the club clean. I handle all stock ordering and money control. I'll sign you in as a permanent guest so you can buy drinks and come and go as you please."

"I don't know why you are doing this for us, Ritchie, but know I will owe you for the rest of my life."

He looked between the two of us, grinned and said, "Mmm, I might come calling to collect sometime. You are, after all, two very sexy guys, and I'm not exactly swamped with gay lovers here in this Islamic state."

I realised then that he was right, we would have to be careful.

"What's your routine for the next 48 hours, Chris?"

"I'm free. I am not going anywhere for my leave so I can work or not as I please for the next month."

"Alright, I would like David for two hours after lunch tomorrow and probably the same the next day before he starts full time."

David looked at me and grinned. I took him home with me then.

We got to the bedroom ok, but then I just stripped him naked and inspected him minutely. His skin was clear of all the nasty whip marks and bruising. His body had filled out and returned to normal. I stroked his cock, watching his eyes as I did. He came to a beautiful erection and tears filled his eyes.

"It's ready for you, Chris, whatever you want to do with it."

I didn't reply to that comment, but I told him to turn round, spread his legs wide and bend over. He did without hesitation. I spread his cheeks wide and examined his rosebud. It patently wasn't a virgin anus, but it was very neat, looked perfect and there was no obvious scarring.

"Were you given an anal examination by a doctor before you came here?"

"Yes, Chris, he was very thorough."

"And you are perfect internally?"

"Yes, Chris, he told me he could see where I had been sodomised, but that it was all healed and there was no scarring."

I turned him round again, took him in my arms and kissed him.

"I love you, I love you so much, I just wanted to make certain you were healed physically. I don't know what your ordeal has done to your mind, David, so I am not going to instigate anything sexual with you. Whatever you want from me you can have, but you make all the first moves so that there is no chance I will traumatise you with any of my actions."

The tears were running down his cheeks now and I gently thumbed them away before leaning in to kiss his eyes.

"I want you to take me to bed, make love to me and bury your little Chris as deep in my ass as it will go," and then he laughed through his tears.

"I love you too, so much. I never expected someone to take care of me again."

I don't know how long it took me to enter him. I know we both came several times. I never dreamt in a million years that I would fall so head over heels in love with a street boy I picked up in Manila.

David settled in happily. Ritchie and I were in the bar most nights but he gained in confidence so quickly we never needed to help him out. If it got very busy Ritchie used to help, he told me he loved being a barman.

I stayed with David in his quarters occasionally, but his bed was a bit narrow for comfort. Our love life settled down, it was always intense because we grew together, but I loved him so much, and I guess it was reciprocated.

Ritchie tried to get into a sexual liaison with David, which upset him and he told me.

I knew that we owed Ritchie big time and I told David.

"I'm not suggesting that you go to bed with him, but you can be very nice to him considering what we owe him."

David thought about it. "I don't mind having sex with him, Chris, he is very sexy, and he has a fabulous ass, but I wouldn't ever do it without you."

I thought about it and wondered if it would make David more comfortable if that bit of tension was removed from his life. I approached Ritchie.

"Ritchie, David tells me you have been hitting on him and he is very uncomfortable with it."

Looking very contrite, Ritchie replied.

"I'm sorry, Chris, but I'm as horny as hell and he is so sexy, plus I know he is gay."

"We both owe you big time and don't feel that sex with you would hurt us. David thinks you have a very sexy ass, and I do too. The problem for David is that he would feel very uncomfortable having any kind of sexual liaison with you unless I was there as well. So, this is the score. You can come over to my apartment one evening and control what we do together for a couple of hours, no holds barred, except that in David's case you may not use cp on him at all. In my case don't get over enthusiastic. I do have to be able to sit down to work."

Ritchie giggled and I joined him.

"After the first time if you want sex with us again you can join us by appointment but we all take turns at choreographing the session. Be warned, both of us want to feel your love chute caressing our cocks."

"Ooh, lovely, I can't wait."

"Are you a bottom then, Ritchie?" I asked in a surprised tone.

"Sometimes, really I'm very flexible, I'm not exactly kinky but I do enjoy being in the middle for a spit roast, or on either end, and I think a little cp can be very erotic."

My turn for a good laugh.

"It sounds like you and I were cut from the same cloth. David fucks like no one I've ever met, and he has a gorgeous cock to do it with. I've never been a happier bottom than I am with him."

"This all sounds great, Chris. I have wanted to fuck your cute butt since I saw you in swim trunks that day."

"Ditto, so when are you coming round?"

He thought about it. "What's your programme the day after tomorrow?"

"Nothing, I'm still officially on leave."

"Good, can I come over tomorrow night? I'll bring David with me and can I stay the night?"

"Yes to both, I'll tell David. I suggest you give him a blowjob and vice versa to start things rolling, he'll be more relaxed then."

"Sounds good to me," was Ritchie's reply and he toddled off, a happy bunny.

The next night I had a relaxing evening knowing that David would have had a sleep in the afternoon so that despite working he would still be up for a sex session. We had discussed it and he quite shyly said he thought that would be fun.

When they arrived David said he would like a shower first so off he went and Ritchie and I stripped so that we would all be naked together. I couldn't resist touching Ritchie when he was naked and very quickly brought him to an erect state. Of course, he did the same to me and we were caught as David came back to the bedroom.

"We're all ready for you, Lover, but Ritchie is master of ceremonies tonight."

We all laughed at that comment and Ritchie looked at David's flaccid cock.

"I think the first thing to do is make that pretty piece of man meat erect. Why don't you get comfortable on the bed David and let Chris and me pamper you for a little while."

Perfect. David was relaxed because I immediately leant over him and started kissing him as Ritchie started playing with his cock and balls. He was erect very quickly so I moved aside to let him watch but started stroking his torso and playing with his nipples. We very quickly had him spacing out with all the caressing and touching, licking and sucking. He loved it and patently so did Ritchie. It was delightful to watch my lover begin to lose it and the little squeals of pleasure as he orgasmed had me smiling broadly. Ritchie gulped down his sperm and I leant in again to kiss him.

Ritchie sat up then and looked at David and I snuggled together.

"I was going to get David to return the favour, but I think he should give you a blowjob, Chris, while I open him up and plant my baby in his love chute. After that, you two can do anything you like to me."

David was grinning at that comment and spoke up very quickly.

"Ooh, lovely. I want to play with your butt for a long time and let your insides caress my baby maker."

Ritchie and I both looked at David in surprise. Where on earth had he got hold of that expression? David guessed what I was thinking by the look on my face.

"You forget, Chris, I spend every night listening to the American and British pilots and engineers talking in the club."

Then he laughed and we did as well.

Ritchie's attack on David's butt showed his experience and his kink. His tongue was working overtime trying, successfully to tongue fuck my baby. David was doing his usual wonderful exciting of my nether regions, amplified by the messages going to my brain from my eyes. The more enthusiastic Ritchie was, the more David became. I disgraced myself, cumming very quickly. I was ready to go again quite quickly though because Ritchie entered my baby and that site was incredible. He only fucked him for a few minutes before having him turn over into the missionary position and with me holding his legs well back and wide he entered him again and David took me in his mouth. I was erect again in no time. This was turning into the most fantastic spit roast I had ever seen. David was loving it, and that was the most important thing in the world to me. When Ritchie orgasmed he took the two of us with him, it was fantastic. Ritchie dropped back onto his haunches and just looked at the two of us.

"If I'm going to be piggy in the middle next time I think we should finish with you in the middle, Chris, and me reaming out your butt."

I grinned, that was how I would have played it as well, but I would miss out on fucking Ritchie and I definitely wanted to do that now that I had seen his butt, which was incredible. It was beautifully muscled, and when he was lying on his tummy, legs spread and his gluts tensed I almost came on the spot. Spit roasting him was terrific. David surprised him with his ability. I knew of course because we swapped top and bottom frequently. I deliberately pulled his legs down close to the bed just to get the most incredible view. David's tool pistoning in and out of Ritchie's butt soon had him squealing with pleasure. That worked for me, too quickly unfortunately because I came very quickly despite having orgasmed before. It was great to watch the finale though with Ritchie continuing to squeal as David pounded his butt. The orgasms were pretty impressive when they came and it took the two of them quite a long time to calm down. We cleaned up then before deciding whether to go for the third one.

"I would love to do this again guys and start the ball rolling by spit roasting Chris. If you say we can I'll happily go to bed now provided David and I can 69 in the morning."

That's what we did. I didn't mention that I hadn't had a fuck because my two blowjobs had been terrific. We were three in a bed with David in the middle spooned into me as he usually did, so Ritchie just spooned into David. We all agreed the next morning that the sleep had been very satisfying.

The next morning I had a no touch orgasm watching Ritchie and David blow each other. It was so erotic because both of them were enjoying some arse play as well. I knew I was going to have Ritchie's butt next time after he had fucked me.

We arranged another threesome for the following week and I told Ritchie that I would control this one and that I was going to fuck him while I had David punish him for hitting on him when I wasn't there.

"I don't think you should get away with trying to take my baby to bed so next time you can have your spit roast, but afterwards I'm going to ream out your love tunnel but have David spank you at the same time."

Ritchie grinned. "Oh well, I suppose it was only a matter of time before you saw my masochistic side."

That surprised both David and me, but it also got me planning exactly what we were going to do to our friendly pilot.

The spit roast was lovely on the next little orgy. David was feeding me his lovely penis, making it very erotic for him and me both. He fucked my face while I played with his balls and his rosebud. I only fed him the one finger, but I could strike his prostate, and did. When I tapped it he deep throated me and I could massage his cock with my throat until he pulled out again and I just swabbed his glans with my tongue. While all this was going on, Ritchie opened me up very quickly and slow fucked me. He kept stopping, and just remained embedded fully in me while he played with my cock and balls. I knew why, he was making it last as long as he could. Definitely no complaint from me, he was good, very good. It almost made me relent on what I was going to do to him, but not quite. When he saw David emptying his balls into my mouth he sped up and I felt his orgasm just as I started mine, almost perfect synchronisation. We cleaned up then and I told Ritchie to prepare for punishment.

We started the final session with Ritchie on his tummy in the lounge. He spread his legs as wide as the sofa would allow and bent them at the knees before tensing up his gluts. He grinned at me as I took a photo.

"I'm going to keep this one for posterity because I doubt I will ever see a sexier arse. Of course it is going to be a different colour by the time we finish tonight."

David slid up onto the sofa at Ritchie's legs end and started playing with the cheeks. I jumped in very quickly, kneeling at the side and told David to spread the cheeks so that I could start playing with the rosebud. We both played for ages. I started reaming Ritchie out with my fingers until I had all five digits from one hand sliding in and out without too much trouble.

"Right, Slut, into my bedroom on your knees on the bed, legs well spread, head and shoulders on the bed."

He was perfectly positioned by the time David and I joined him.

"Right, David. Lube Ritchie and yourself and fuck him. Kneel well back because as you fuck him I'm going to spank him."

Christ, that looked erotic. I straddled Ritchie, pushing his back further down on the bed, which emphasised his butt even more. David entered him and fucked slowly with long strokes. I spanked each cheek in turn, making him feel them, but not too hard. I kept up the spanking while David fucked him and realised Ritchie was hugely turned on by it. I kept it up until David orgasmed by which time Richie had done it three times.

"Turn him over, David. I'm going to fuck him in the missionary position and you are going to take over the spanking."

What transpired had me multiple orgasming. With his legs pulled well back and wide, held in place by David holding them underneath his arms, Ritchie's arse was held high for me to fuck him and his lower butt and upper legs were available to David. I fucked fast and hard, and David was spanking the lower butt and upper legs quite hard. It must have hurt because Ritchie was squealing like a scalded cat. But, he was orgasming almost from the go. By the time I pulled out he was firing blanks and his butt and upper legs were quite red. I thought David might have gone over the top but Ritchie's comment when he could talk scotched that idea.

"Oh, God, that was the most incredible fucks I've ever had. Can we do it again?"

David and I just dissolved with laughter as I spluttered out. "You masochistic fuck slut."

He grinned at me and replied, "You'd better believe it."

We had quite a few threesomes over the next couple of years. Ritchie was promoted to an operations contract manager but continued to manage the club. I was promoted as well and took over as senior geologist ensuring several more years here.

David came to England with me for several of my holidays and met my family. No trauma, I explained to Mum and Dad how I had met David, leaving out the gory bits. They loved him so I knew when the time came I would be able to bring him home with me. We went through the civil ceremony as soon as we could because I would want him to have British citizenship when I came home to roost.

Things worked out how we planned. I was thirty when my contract was terminated. The oil company gave me a very generous bonus and David resigned from the club and came home with me. Ritchie was sorry to see us go but his sendoff was an incredible night of sex with us.

It took us a few months to sort David's immigration status during which time we lived with mum and dad. All settled and I started job hunting. The North Sea was the place for my experience and I was soon employed at Aberdeen. We bought a lovely home outside of the city. David learnt to drive and got a job in a hotel as a barman. He was so good and such a hard worker that the manager had promoted him within a few weeks and he became head barman. I spent quite a lot of time offshore but that was just an excuse for incredible loving sex every time I came ashore.

We never went back to the Philippines, but once settled in Aberdeen we did start using our holidays to travel and we went back to the Far East several times to Thailand and Cambodia. We were quite naughty in both countries, taking pretty boys to bed. Ritchie had made us realise how much fun threesomes were, and they spiced up our sex life.

We did hook up with Ritchie again a couple of times when he also ended up in Aberdeen, but when he found a proper boyfriend we stopped the sex but enjoyed social contact. He still had that amazing butt, well into his forties and both David and I would joke about taking him to bed to give it a good workout.

I never expected that taking a little street urchin to bed in Manila would end up giving me the love of my life, but that was how it worked out. Before we retired, David became the manager of the hotel and I the Chief Pilot of my company.

After we met, Ritchie was the only other lover we had, discounting the Thai and Cambodian boys who were always just one night stands.

End of the 2nd Story

Chris Johns

FOREIGN SEDUCTION

GAY EROTICA

Foreign Seduction

By: Chris Johns

<u>Part 1</u>

"You are going to Marignane, Teo, for the Puma Conversion." Teo nearly flew over the desk to kiss his operations director. His dream come true, he had been flying the Allouette III since getting his licence and desperately wanted to move up to the large twin engine choppers. He knew that meant no more Nigeria, he would either go to Iran or Indonesia. He prayed it would be Indonesia, the boys were beautiful and the regime much less oppressive.

Luck smiled on this young man. He passed the conversion course with flying colours, did his command flight with the chief pilot of Aero Spatielle and was off to Indonesia as a Captain.

Djakarta was a tip but he only stayed there long enough for the corruption to allow him an Indonesian Air Transport Pilot's Licence and a work permit in less than seven days.

"You will have a young Indonesian first officer Teo, younger than you even."

The manager laughed as he said it because Teo was only 22, the next youngest Puma Captain was more than 10 years older than him.

"Don't trust him to do much more than fly the machine, you do all the navigation and planning and definitely all the fuel uplifts. I want you to take a machine to Salawati Base. They are expanding the operation by bringing in another rig. I hope your sling work is good."

(The operation was called Heli-Rigging – small drilling rigs that could be dismantled into loads small enough to be slung under a helicopter and moved around land areas not suitable for roads, i.e. Mangrove swamps. All support for these rigs was flown in including the port-a-cabins that the crews slept in.)

Teo had done sling work with the Allouette so no problem, the loads would be bigger that was all.

"Stop at Sorong heli-base to pick up spares and Jefman Field to pick up anything that is there for the base camp. The chief pilot expects you on site in three days. I suggest you plan today, leave early in the morning and overnight at Balikpapan, you can make Salawati the next day."

Teo was over the moo. His first flight in the country would be across most of it.

A car took Teo out to Pondakcabe the next morning to the company airfield where his machine was out and loaded ready to go. He checked all the fuel tanks were full before he started his externals. Half way round and a very flustered two striper came running up.

"I'm sorry I'm late Captain, my driver was late picking me up."

He got that all out before he realised this Captain looked about the same age as him.

"What are you doing?" were his next words.

"I'm pre-flighting our aircraft ready to leave for Irian Jaya, I assume you are Tom Prajitno?"

"Yes, but you can't be the Captain, you aren't old enough."

Teo laughed and put out his hand.

"Thank you Tom, but I can assure you I am Teo Rykal and the Captain of this puma. Let's get finished up or we are going to be late."

Tom was not particularly happy, this didn't look right. Nearly all the Captains on the Pumas were about forty, this man was only half that age.

Settled into the flight deck with all doors closed Teo looked at his unhappy co-pilot, smiled and said, "I like to do challenge and reply on checklists Tom, so if you read it out we'll get going."

Tom took out the checklist and started reading it watching Teo carry out the check and acknowledged it. He liked this system, it made sense and nothing was forgotten.

"If you do radios Tom I'll fly the first leg to Surabaya and you can do the other two to Bandjarmasin and Balikpapan."

By the time they had taxied in to dispersal for fuel at Surabaya, Tom knew that Teo was indeed a Puma Captain, his flying was perfection. It gave him huge incentive to fly well the next two legs and by the time they shut down at Balikpapan he felt he had not disgraced himself.

They had a long day the next day, 9 ½ hours flying but they landed at Salawati before dark, having completed two refuels with three long legs.

Don Carpenter was the chief pilot, a very pleasant ex R.A.F. Wing Commander. He personally greeted Teo and Tom when they had shut the Helicopter down.

"Just bring your bags boys, the engineers will deal with the aircraft. Leave them all your paper work Teo, you can sign the 700 (the aircraft log book), in the morning."

They were shown to a pleasant port-a-cabin with a twin bedded room and private bathroom.

"You'll almost certainly be flying together so you bunk together. Drop your bags and come for a drink with me before dinner, slum it tonight and then you can shower before bed. No hurry for the morning, breakfast goes on until 0930 so be late and see me in the office at 1000."

Teo liked this man. He was tired and a good night's sleep was sensible if he was going to be familiarising himself with a completely new operation.

After dinner Teo and Tom retired to their quarters and started to strip for a shower, both realised at the same time that the only place to get naked was in the bedroom. The bathroom was too small for anything except their ablutions.

"I guess we can't really be coy about our bodies Tom, not enough space. We're both boys with similar equipment so shall we get this out of the way straight away. I'll show you mine if you show me yours."

Both young men laughed hysterically at that and peeled off their underpants together, stood up and scoped each other out.

Teo looked his co-pilot in the eye after running his eyes over everything in sight.

"Very nice Tom, I won't have a problem looking at that every day."

Tom blushed, was his Captain coming on to him?

"Me neither," he said in reply.

Teo watched Tom head for the shower after agreeing to go second and felt a stirring in his loins. Tom Prajitno was one very hot cookie with an incredibly cute butt. Teo had never been to bed with a

Southeast Asian boy even though there were plenty of Indonesians in Holland, but he had always wanted to, he thought they were as sexy as they come. If there was anything less than perfection in what he perceived as the average Indonesian it was that most of them appeared to have quite small penises and Teo was a bit of a size queen. He liked to top but he liked to have a lovely big cock to play with while he was fucking its owner. If Tom only had four or five inches, Teo thought, he could live with that, just as long as he could slide his monster between those two sweet cheeks sometime. Huh, some chance of that, was his next thought.

Tom came back from the shower now with his towel wrapped round him so Teo went for his and cleaned his teeth. Tom was in bed when he got back so Teo didn't know whether he slept naked or not. He slipped into bed himself with nothing on and he knew Tom was watching.

"I'll set my alarm for 0900 Tom, that will give us an hour for shower and breakfast before we have to see the Chief Pilot. Goodnight."

Tom returned the goodnight and turned the light out.

Well, he had now had two days with this new very young Dutch Captain, he admired his professionalism as a pilot and liked his easy going nature. The best part was the age gap of only two years, it would be great to have Teo as a friend not just as his Captain. It would be even nicer if Teo came on to him the way he thought he had earlier.

Tom had played around as a boy and realised he liked boys much more than girls but in his profession he had to be careful. If Teo did come on to him he thought it would be wonderful to suck on his cock and see how big it was. He had heard that European men generally sported about six or seven inches and that was very exciting. He was an anal virgin but thought he might like to be a bottom for Teo. He would also like to fuck him, but he didn't think there would be much chance of that.

The next week was manic. The new boys flew almost maximum hours every day to make sure they were up to speed for the next rig move. The other pilots loved it, sat around all day doing very little while Teo and Tom flew their butts off.

"Teo this has probably looked very unfair loading you and Tom with all the work this week but when we do the next rig move you have to be very slick picking up and dropping loads. You will be flying at max gross weight most of the time with minimum fuel for your sorties, Tom will need to be sharp working out fuel loads when the Load Master calls your load weight as you are in bound. Or probably your best bet is to let him fly the inbound leg and you work out fuel loads. Heavy loads you fly, less stressful loads let Tom fly. Let him fly any legs that you only have internal cargo or passengers."

Don was very keen that the new young Indonesian First Officers get plenty of stick time.

The beginning of the second week Don told Teo and Tom to spend the day watching the Load Masters and their crews working on the ground.

"I'll issue you with coveralls and goggles, Teo."

Teo loved to watch the loading crews at the beginning of a working day, they were gorgeous. One in particular who he played Badminton with some evenings was instant erection material, but after a couple of hours work they were smothered in dirt from the helicopter down wash as they came in for loads.

Just about every helicopter hangar in the world appeared to have a badminton court marked out on the floor and Indonesians were great Badminton players. Rudy Sartono had been world champion for years and was something of a national hero. Teo's little hottie was also a Rudy and a more than adequate player as well. Teo was the best of the European players and would invariably end up playing a singles match against Rudy as a climax to an evening's sport, he never won but he and Rudy became friends. The Loadies used to play in their underwear which meant the ugliest boxers Teo had ever seen. He determined that when he came back off his next leave he would bring a pack of good boxers for Rudy and pass the present off as a gift for him being such a brilliant player, and then hope to see him in them one day.

The load masters lived in the main camp because they were all Westerners. The loadies lived in a small complex close to the hanger. Teo had seen it inside one night when he had walked back talking with Rudy. He was appalled, it was incredibly basic with double bunks in little cubicles, thin mattresses, no fans, no air conditioning and yet the boys were always happy and smiling.

Teo brought the subject up with the senior load master one night.

"What you have to realise Teo is that most of these boys come from pretty primitive backgrounds. Their accommodation here is a step up for them in the same way that it would be for you if we put you into The George V in Paris."

Teo was amazed.

Meanwhile, in their cabin Teo had made a couple more comments to Tom that could be construed as a come on if Tom picked up on it. A few weeks together and Tom felt he should try to progress this relationship with his Captain. The opportunity came after their second rig move was complete. The crew bar was almost empty one night when Tom and Teo were off flying for the following day allowing them to sit later enjoying some cold beers. A little alcohol loosens most people's tongues and Tom was no exception.

"You don't talk about girlfriends, Teo. Don't you have one back home?"

"No Tom, not into girls very much. How about you?"

"Me neither, women are so difficult to understand, men are much more comfortable company."

"Yeah, but it's more difficult to get your mate to scrub your back than it is your girlfriend."

Teo thought this might give Tom an opening if he was interested, and it worked.

"I can't think why, have you ever asked?"

Bingo, this was his first real opening and Teo wasn't going to miss it.

"I haven't, but when we get back to the cabin I'm going to have another shower and ask my mate to wash my back."

Teo was smiling as he said it so that he could say it was only a joke if Tom backed off.

"Mmm, I think your mate will say yes, and he's an excellent back washer, he has very sensitive hands."

This was getting interesting so Teo thought he would take it a step further.

"Well in that case I might not stop at asking my mate to do my back, I can ask him to do my front as well. I like the idea of sensitive hands washing all of my body."

"Your mate would find that interesting as well, particularly if it was reciprocated..."

Both young men grinned at each other and in very quick time finished their beers.

Tom wasn't kidding. When he started to wash Teo, even before he had touched anything remotely erotic, Teo was sporting a monster erection.

"I'm at your waist Teo, would you like me to go lower?"

"Oh crikey, yes please, you were right about having sensitive hands."

Teo spread his legs as wide as the shower would permit when Tom started washing his arse cheeks, so Tom slid his hand down Teo's crack and washed there, all the way through to the back of his balls. He gasped as Tom's fingers played around his rosebud. Inside thighs came next and down to his feet and then Tom suggested he turn round.

Teo was blushing as he turned because his erection was so hard it was hugging his belly.

"Sorry Tom, but your sensitive hands are responsible."

Tom was grinning like a Cheshire cat at what he could see. Teo had a perfect penis about eight inches long. It looked fabulous, dead straight, quite thick and with a foreskin that had drawn back clear of the glans with Teo's erection. The head was pink and a lovely bell shape with a pronounced ridge at the base of the glans. Tom thought he would die if that was to move in and out of his anus it looked so erotic.

"Well, it does make it easier to wash."

Of course the whole front got washed but that took only a couple of minutes, washing cock and balls took long enough for Tom to make the cock spit a large quantity of sperm. Teo loved the sensitivity of a soapy hand playing with his balls at the same time as another hand was gently wanking his man meat.

"Oh God that was good Tom, I don't know if I'll be that good for you."

Tom grinned again.

"I don't mind, I know it will be so exciting just having you touch me there."

Teo leant forward and just touched his lips to Tom's.

"I hope so because I want to give you so much pleasure and later maybe make proper love to you. I think you have a very exciting body and I like you so much as a person."

Tom was over the moon. He thought he could fall in love with his Captain without any problem but he realised man on man love with this European was only going to bring eventual heartache.

Living for the moment was good. Teo had magic hands as well but Tom nearly fell over when Teo rinsed him off completely then dropped to his knees and started licking his cock. It was heaven for both young men. Tom was a lovely light coffee colour and his circumcised cock was the same colour as the remainder of his body. It was probably a little over five inches long, slim and with a nicely proportioned ball sac hanging below. Teo had plenty of practice at sucking cock and very quickly had a mouthful of Tom's sperm. He kept sucking on it gently as it went soft to make sure he didn't waste any before relinquishing it and standing up. Tom was speechless, just looking in amazement at Teo until he moved in and gave him a very passionate kiss on the lips.

"You taste as sweet as you look Tom. That was fantastic."

Tom nearly fainted. "Thank you Teo, promise me you will do that again."

"Oh yes, promise, every day if you like."

They dried off and went back to the bedroom.

"I doubt we will be able to sleep together Tom, the bunks really aren't wide enough but would you come to my bed for a cuddle before we sleep?"

Tom loved it. Teo stroked him all the time he was talking.

"Tom, you have a truly perfect bottom. Would you let me make love to you properly sometime and bury my cock in it?"

"Oh yes please Teo, you are very big though. Are you sure you can without killing me?"

"Sure, I will open you up very carefully before I try to put it inside you."

"In that case, yes please, we have all day tomorrow to enjoy each other's bodies. Can I make love to you as well? I would like to feel my penis inside you. I have never done either before."

Teo giggled, "We could end up spending the whole day in bed at this rate."

"Ooh lovely," and both young men dissolved in boyish giggles.

Teo ran his hand through Tom's sleek black wavy hair and kissed him again.

"I think we should go to sleep now, it looks like we are going to have a busy day tomorrow."

Both laughed again and Tom snuggled in close to Teo speaking softly into his chest.

"Just let me enjoy the feel of your body for a few more minutes."

The next thing Teo knew was waking up still cuddling Tom, both of them sporting their morning hard ons. Teo looked at the clock, 0700, he hoped no one had come in during the night and seen them because he realised they had not locked the door.

'Mustn't make that mistake again, we could be in trouble if we aren't careful.' Was Teo's thought as Tom snuffled a little, rubbed his nose and pushed his woodie into Teo even harder than before.

Teo stroked his new lover and thought how lucky he was. The only other boy that he really lusted after was Rudy and the chances there had to be close to nil. Also Rudy was very assertive so Teo thought it was very unlikely he would be submissive at all.

They returned to the port-a-cabin after breakfast and locked the door before stripping very quickly and falling onto Teo's bed again for lots of kissing and cuddling.

Tom was too excited to want Teo to take a long time making love to him so he told him.

"Teo, just open me up and fuck me this time, will you. I want to feel your penis inside me so much, you can make love to me next time."

"Mmm, but only if you promise to do the same to me. After that we can make slow love for the remainder of the day."

Teo was almost cumming as they went 69ing. He started to rim Tom first, he loved licking all round his rosebud. It was such a pretty little thing and the surrounding butt cheeks were gorgeous. He soon moved on to fingering him, gradually opening him up until he had four fingers fully inserted and rotating. Watching his first finger slide into Tom's anus made Teo gasp. It looked so erotic and felt so incredibly sensual. The whole picture was a delight. Tom's twin butt cheeks, so tight and so small, a pretty pink anal entry, the perineum was hard and prominent, and as Teo found out very sensitive. He tickled the back of

Tom's balls where he found another region of excitement then came the cock, as hard as rock, but still with that lovely silky feeling. All this time Tom was playing with Teo's cock and balls, taking Teo's cock in his mouth was a new and exciting experience and thinking about it entering his anus nearly had him cumming as well. Teo turned round, slipped Tom's legs over his shoulder and lubed up his anus, as he was doing the same to his own cock he told Tom.

"I know I am not going to last very long this time lover, you are just so exciting to touch. But I promise when I make love to you I will remain inside you for a long time."

"I don't mind Teo. I just want to feel that monster inside me."

A little pain as Teo's head slid over Tom's sphincter, but that soon went he was so relaxed. Teo took it very slowly in an attempt to last, but looking at the incredible sight before him was too much and he very quickly shot a serious load of sperm deep into Tom.

Falling onto the bed alongside Tom, Teo whispered, "Your turn now lover and then we'll explore paradise together."

Tom loved it, this was his first time and sliding into Teo was amazing. The feeling as his penis was encased in soft tissue was almost beyond description. Like Teo, he couldn't last very long and Teo didn't help by working his butt muscles.

"Oh God Teo, I'm cumming, I'm cumming."

Teo was smiling broadly at the expression of ecstasy on Tom's face.

Two very satisfied young men were lying grinning at each other when there was a knock at the door. Teo kept his cool and just called out, "What is it?"

"Very sorry to disturb you Sir, but the Chief Pilot would like to see you in the office."

Quick shower and both pilots went to see why they were being summoned on their day off.

Don was very apologetic.

"Teo, Tom, I'm sorry to disturb your day off but there has been some serious military activity in Sorong overnight. We don't know what is going on so we are bringing tomorrow's Bintuni flight forward to today. Will you two fly it and take your day off when you get back. You will have to overnight and come back tomorrow."

Teo grinned. He would have liked to spend the day making love to Tom, but Bintuni was the French survey camp and the food was always superb so they went, no problem.

Bintuni was fun, but very cut off and with their radio unserviceable there was no contact with base. Teo and Tom were not worried. They loaded their passengers after breakfast the next morning, having refuelled and checked the helicopter. Flight time would put them on the deck at Salawati in time for lunch and Teo let Tom do all the flying so that on final approach he handled the radio while a happy co-pilot flew the finals to landing. Teo was surprised that no one talked to him from base and as they turned for finals he could see quite a lot of military activity around the whole camp.

"That looks a bit sinister Tom, all those soldiers on an oil base camp."

Tom agreed but there was no choice in where they landed.

As soon as they were on the deck the chopper was surrounded by soldiers all pointing guns at the people as they deplaned. Tom and Teo were the last off and were approached by a young officer.

"You will come with me."

Tom tried talking to him in Indonesian but was told to be quiet.

"I don't like this, Teo."

That comment cost him a rifle butt in his kidneys. Teo was furious at this unwarranted brutality and helped his co-pilot and lover the remainder of the walk to see a Colonel who looked nasty.

Mr. Nasty addressed Tom.

"Can you fly that machine?"

Tom was intimidated by this very forceful approach.

"Yes, Sir."

"So we don't need this white man?"

"Well, yes Sir, we do. The Puma is set up for two pilot operation."

"Why?"

"I have no idea Sir, but the co-pilot is needed for all emergency operations involving the hydraulics and for other systems management in the event of an emergency requiring one pilot to be on the controls uninterrupted."

"In that case I will keep this creature alive to assist you when we want to fly. He is to be treated like any other animal in this camp though, and animals don't wear clothes. Tell him to strip everything except his boots."

Tom looked at Teo and relayed the Colonel's order.

"I'm not stripping naked Tom, what the hell is going on here and who is this guy?"

The Colonel replied in perfect English.

"This guy currently controls whether you live or join your colleagues in the mass grave being dug as we speak so I suggest you follow every order given to you by an Indonesian national whatever that order is. Now strip."

Teo did in quick time but felt very foolish stood with all the soldiers looking at him.

"You will be accommodated now in the quarters that the load staff used. You will feed with the ones that remain there and you will make yourself available to any of them that want you for any purpose, the same with people in the main compound here."

Teo looked at Tom, shrugged and started walking back down the hill to the loadies long hut. Force of habit, he went via the Puma he had just flown to talk to the Indonesian engineer he could see inspecting it.

"She is fine, Syarif. There were no faults on the flight back. I will sign the 700 as I go to my quarters. What has happened to the Chief Engineer and the other English Engineers and Load Masters?"

Syarif looked devastated.

"They were all shot, Captain. All expatriates have been killed except you. The loadies are digging a mass grave for them now. I don't know who these people are but they are monsters. The Indonesian Oilmen have been told they must run the operation and the Indonesian engineers have been told they must service the Pumas."

Teo wanted to reassure him that everything would be ok but he didn't know how.

"Just do as they ask Syarif, you know I will help anyway I can."

"I know Captain but I don't think you will be able to do much, the Colonel is obviously going to treat you badly looking at the way you are now."

Teo almost laughed, he had almost forgotten he was naked. He did manage a smile as he left to fill in the aircraft log.

Once in the loadies quarters he didn't know what to do with himself. No one wanted to talk to him, they just looked but kept their distance. Boys that he had joked with while they played badminton now looked away from him. Nothing to do so Teo lay on a bunk that appeared unoccupied and fell asleep. His next conscious action was to grunt as he was kicked awake.

"Get up you, that isn't your bed."

Teo looked up and it was Rudy, his eyes immediately registered disbelief.

"Why did you do that Rudy, I thought we were friends?"

"Well you are wrong. I used to cringe at your condescending way of talking to me."

Teo was angry at that.

"That is bullshit and you know it. I have always treated you with respect and as an equal."

"Huh, well you certainly will now if you want to keep the hide on your body. Now follow me, I will show you where you can sleep."

Rudy took him to the end of the hut, to the darkest corner and showed him a ratty old mattress of palm leaves that had obviously fallen into disuse.

"You will sleep here. You will be brought your meal at meal times but you will not eat with us. Now you will come with me for your first lesson in obedience."

Teo followed his one-time friend out to the hangar and across to the corner where they kept the keep fit gear and the water skiing equipment. They all used it during their free time, not just the expat pilots and engineers. Nearly all the loadies were there watching and Tom was stood off to one side with tears in his eyes. As Teo looked at him he mouthed the words, "I'm sorry, Teo."

"Get on the weight bench on your back."

Teo looked at Rudy who almost screamed his next command, "Now you scum."

As soon as he complied two more loadies strapped his torso to the bench and then pulled his legs up and secured them to the weight bar as wide as they could spread them. Rudy picked up one of the ski boat paddles and with no preamble gave Teo ten good hard strokes across his buttocks. He could feel that Rudy was not really putting his weight behind them. It was almost as though he was just going through the motions.

"I think I will give you another ten after I have finished with you."

Rudy was flexing his muscles, so to speak, showing off his new found power over an ex-pat.

Tom jumped in then.

"I am sure the Colonel will be delighted if he is so bruised that he is unable to fly, Rudy."

Realising he had to be at least a little bit careful he grinned.

"Of course you are right Captain, but to make him realise I want respect and obedience he can give me a blowjob."

Tom was flabbergasted, "What, here?"

Rudy grinned as he started to strip off his shorts, "Yes, why not, he is only an animal as far as the Colonel is concerned. I heard him say so."

"That's disgusting Rudy, he was your friend and this is how you repay his friendship."

Rudy shrugged and moved round to Teo's head.

"Look at what you are going to suck on and play with slut, make sure it is the best blowjob you can give."

As Rudy's soft penis slid over his lips, Teo thought how much he had wanted to do this, with affection though, not under duress and with an audience. It got worse, he noticed the engineers coming to have a look at what was going on. How would he be able to face them to talk professional talk with them after this?

He was sucking on Rudy's cock until it was erect and then he was told to play with it and with his balls. While he was doing that he could feel fingers worrying his anus and other hands stretching him.

"Mmm, he has a nice little pink man pussy. I think we should take turns fucking him as well as letting him suck us after Rudy has finished."

About a dozen of them fucked Teo until Tom got really stroppy.

"We have to fly in the morning. If you keep this up he is going to be unfit and I have the names of everyone who has abused him, which I will give to the Colonel when he can't have a chopper."

That cleared the hangar, except for the engineers and Tom.

The senior engineer said to Tom,

"We spend more time down here than anyone, we can keep Teo with us all day working on the aircraft. He will be able to sleep comfortably if he wants to in one of the aircraft cabins. But what about after work, that's when the others are going to abuse him?"

"I don't know, I'm going to have to talk to the colonel. You should be ok tonight Teo so come and have a shower in our old quarters."

Tom pampered Teo in the shower but didn't make any sexual advances. He thought Teo had enough of that for one day. They did some serious kissing and Tom promised to try to get better conditions for him.

At dinner in the main mess that night and Tom, full of trepidation, approached the colonel.

"I'm sorry to trouble you Sir, can I have a word with you about my captain?"

"He's not your captain, you are his, what is it?"

"Knowing how much you dislike white men and seeing Teo naked, the loaders and handlers abused him to the point where he would not have been able to fly tomorrow if I had let them carry on. Please let him live up here in this camp Sir, even if you keep him naked. Otherwise we are going to have three Pumas serviceable and no flight crew even for one."

The Colonel had already planned extensive use of a chopper so reluctantly he had to make concessions for Teo.

"Very well captain, if you are prepared to have him in your cabin he can sleep up here from tomorrow onwards. He can eat with us as well but he will remain naked and you will be the captain on the flights."

"Thank you, Sir."

Tom almost ran down the hill to tell Teo. Rudy heard and was furious, he was hoping to make love to this sexy European everyday. The scene tonight had been to impress his fellows, he wanted Teo as a lover and he had fucked it up. When Tom had returned to the main camp Rudy called Teo to his cubicle.

"I'm sorry Teo, I wanted to impress my fellows with my power but what I really want is for you to be my lover. "

Teo was not feeling particularly charitable towards this guy even if he was as cute as all get out.

"I would have liked that Rudy. I have always thought you were very sexy and having seen you naked and hard today I know we could have brought each other much joy. Tonight though I am so sore internally that I think it might be unwise for you to fuck me again. I can however reverse roles or just give you a blowjob that isn't forced on me."

"Will you Teo? You can do anything you like to me tonight as my punishment for degrading you earlier."

"That will be nice. I have showered in my old cabin so if you are showered as well I would like to make love to you."

Rudy beamed, he began to realise that this white man really was something special. He knew he would not have forgiven Teo if their roles had been reversed.

Teo made slow and considerate love to Rudy, marvelling at the beauty of the boy, his hard muscles but soft skin, his butt was a work of art that Teo fucked for ages without cumming. His own soreness and pain made it easy to last and by the time both young men had their final orgasms the air was wild with the smell of sex.

"Oh God Rudy, you are incredible. What a lover you could be in different circumstances."

Rudy actually cried into Teo's chest.

"I'm sorry Teo, I'm so sorry. I liked you the first time you came to play badminton with us. You were always so nice to us, I was stupid earlier."

Teo kissed him softly and whispered, "Never mind, I'm sure it will work out in the end."

They cuddled up together for the remainder of the night. The next morning there was very little work going on around the camp. Most of the Indonesian staff had not been senior enough to run it and were wandering around aimlessly. The Colonel picked up on it and realised he had made a mistake killing all the Americans and Europeans. Needing to vent his anger and give himself time to recover the situation he sent for Teo. With most of the senior staff in the recreation area he addressed them.

"I want department heads in my office now. The remainder of you can keep this thing here for your entertainment. You can do anything you like to him as long as he is left fit to fly if I need him."

With that he walked out telling Tom to join them as well.

Teo was left standing in the middle of the floor with all the middle echelon from each department looking at him. They all tended to be quite young university graduates from good families and had all been very friendly with this young Puma Captain.

Frans Suharto was a Chinese Indonesian and he and Teo had become good friends because they were both Jazz fans.

"I daren't clothe you Teo because I am sure the Colonel wouldn't hesitate to terminate me, but please, come and sit here with me until we see what is happening."

"No."

Both men looked over to where the one word had come from. It was the senior store man who was an obstructive oaf. Teo had run up against him when trying to get the ski boat repaired. He was as bad as the Colonel, hated white faces.

"I am going to fuck him after I have beaten him."

Nobody said anything. Frans shrugged his shoulders and whispered to Teo, "Sorry."

The store man walked to the centre of the room.

"Stand here slut, legs spread and hands behind your head."

Teo naturally complied. Whatever else, he wanted to live, and disobeying an Indonesian wouldn't help that situation.

The man walked round him grinning like an idiot, spanking his bottom and striking his penis until he had Teo crying with the pain level in his cock.

"Bend over slut and pull your arse cheeks apart. Let everyone see where my cock is going."

Again Teo did as he was told, blushing with the shame and humiliation. The man pulled his rock hard cock from his trousers and made Teo suck on it. He fucked Teo's face violently for a few minutes holding him in place by his hair before moving behind him, holding his hips firmly and ramming his cock in all the way. Teo screamed. On top of last night's damage, this new assault was horrendously painful. He collapsed with the pain overload and Frans stepped in.

"That is definitely enough. I doubt Teo will be fit to fly now so I am going to inform the Colonel."

The store man was quite frightened and when Frans came back with the Colonel who, seeing the state of Teo, pulled out his pistol and with no preamble shot the store man, told Frans to do what he could for the white man and returned to his conference.

Two good things came out of that for Teo, another solid friendship and virtually no more abuse. It was soon round the camp what the Colonel had done and everyone realised that Teo was important in this new regime.

There were a few staff who took him to bed though, he was after all a very sexy well put together young man. His greatest pleasure though was his nights with Tom. They made love frequently with great tenderness. Rudy got his share as well, always apologising to Teo for taking advantage of his position.

Teo laughed the first time he did it and took the boy in his arms, kissed him quite passionately on the lips and standing back to scope out the whole of Rudy's front said, "Anyone as sexy and gorgeous as you can take advantage of me every day. You are a very beautiful boy Rudy and I am honoured to serve you."

Rudy cried the first time Teo said it and hugged this man he was patently falling in love with. Unfortunately it was reciprocated and Teo realised he had got a problem. He loved Tom as well. Both of these Indonesians were spectacularly sexy and nicer than Mum's Apple Pie, as the American's would have said.

Tom was a bright lad and picked up on Teo's problem. Cuddling in bed one night he spoke to Teo about it.

"It is very unlikely that we could have more than a few years together Teo however much we love each other, so if you love more than one of us it isn't going to matter in the long term. I know you like Rudy very much so don't feel guilty about making love with him as well."

Teo was surprised.

"Thank you Tom, I do love you but Rudy is so cute and sexy."

"Mmm, I know, remember I watched him rape you and force a blowjob on you. Done with love I can see how that would be enjoyable."

Both young men laughed and Teo feeling cheeky said, "Perhaps we should have a threesome then."

Tom wouldn't look at Teo as he whispered his reply.

"I think I would like that."

Scene set then after a little further discussion.

Frans unwittingly facilitated the action by dispatching a helicopter to a remote camp to see if anything could be brought out now that it was not being used. Rudy was now the senior load master so he was designated to go. When they got there to look at it they found that the port-a-cabin that had been used by the camp boss had a double bed in it. They opened all the windows to air the place while they checked out everything and by the time they had finished it smelt quite ok. They found a full tank of fresh water and had a Mandy shower scoping each other out until they were giggling like school girls.

"I think we should have a round robin of spit roasting," Teo said, while they were drying. "Who wants to be first in the middle?"

Tom and Rudy looked at each other with slightly embarrassed expressions and Teo realised he was the common factor having made love to both but they had not made love to each other.

"I'll go first. You can both do anything you like to me and then I will suck one of you while the other one fucks me. Let's just go for it, we'll worry about making love some other time."

They all grinned and ran for the bed.

Teo loved it. He ended up sucking Tom while Rudy reamed out his butt. It was fantastic having a cock in each end. When they came Teo said, "That was incredible. Can I stay here and you two just keep changing ends?"

More laughter and Tom looked at Rudy and said, "I'm pulling rank Rudy, I am going in the middle this time."

Rudy didn't mind, he knew he was going to get his turn.

Teo said, "You can remain that end Rudy. Tom has the sweetest love tunnel. I think you ought to feel it caressing your cock and then Tom can feel yours. I am quite happy to get two blowjobs."

Another shower when they were finished and three well satisfied young men checked everything was done before manning up and flying back to base camp. Rudy sat in the jump seat between the two pilots couldn't resist leaning across and fondling Teo. There were lots of giggles, three very hard cocks and red faces when they landed because the engineer meeting the aircraft was ogling the bulges and Teo's prominent erection.

He laughed when he had finished looking and said, "Mmm, can I come on your next trip, it looks like it may be an exciting event."

Four laughing young men now. Teo helped the engineer put the chopper to bed and Rudy and Tom went to report to Frans.

The Colonel's regime may have been oppressive and at times frightening but certainly in the helicopter world there was plenty of fun and games.

All good and bad things eventually come to an end. Three months after the takeover Teo and Tom were flying a sortie with some soldiers in the back when they received a call over the radio from a strange station.

The base was on the next island and was the relief force coming to restore the rule of the president. It was arranged that they would land at the new station and the soldiers in the back would be captured and replaced by the new soldiers up to the maximum Teo felt could safely be carried and they would return.

Clothes were found for Teo before he disembarked and the relief force Colonel briefed him. They were given a very quick demonstration on the use of pistol and machine gun, offered one of each and some spare magazines, fired a few shots and were returned to their chopper.

They had the use of a short runway and Teo overloaded the aircraft by some extra troops taking 24 in all knowing that he would probably make a fairly heavy landing when they got back but not dangerously so. There were now 26 armed men, 24 of them being commandos so with luck the element of surprise would be sufficient to see success. If Teo kept the chopper running they could escape again quickly; if things went wrong, at least denying the colonel the use of helicopters.

In the event it was a massacre. Most of the enemy troops were in a barrack hut and were slaughtered in the first five minutes, for the rest it was a mopping up exercise. The enemy colonel was captured, Teo and Tom flew him back to Djakarta for his trial. When they returned to Salawati base Teo was the new Acting Chief Pilot while new more senior pilots could be recruited to replace the slaughtered ones.

The appointment became permanent at the behest of the oil company because they perceived that Teo had been a bit of a hero and had helped protect company property, plus the fact that all the senior Indonesian staff were singing his praises.

Rudy remained Senior Loadmaster, moving to the main camp and Tom very quickly got his command making him an even younger captain than Teo.

The three of them enjoyed lots of very hot sex for the next few years until Teo was returned to the main base in Holland as operations manager and Rudy joined him to supervise all logistics for Indonesia.

Tom was left behind as Chief Pilot at Salawati base and he took a new lover, Frans, who had tried to protect Teo.

The four would meet up occasionally either in Europe or Indonesia and for Frans the most exciting event there was a foursome, realising his dream of making love to Teo that he had since first seeing him naked.

These happy young men didn't change as they moved into middle age and remained friends. Teo with his Indonesian lover Rudy, and Tom with his Indo/Chinese lover Frans. For Teo the odd dalliance with Tom was always special and their respective lovers realised it without rancour facilitating at least one private loving session between these two flyers on every occasion that they met.

End of the 3rd Story

Gideon Elliot

Heart's Desire

Gay Romance Erotica

Heart's Desire

By: Gideon Elliot

<u>Part I</u>

The sun was bright. The day was cold. The clear blue sky, deep like the white of a child's eye, was frozen. It did not seem like winter was coming to an end.

Chris stared out at the river wondering if he had made the right decision. He wondered if his best friend Archie had not made the better decision, choosing to skip college and take a job writing software for Moonglow. He would start with a salary of fifty thousand a year minimum. There was no telling, he said, where he would go from there. Fifty thousand a year and he would be only nineteen!

Chris had been offered a similar position. They had told him the same thing. The sky was the limit, Wally, the recruiter who spoke to him at the job fair in the high school gym before Christmas had told him. Despite the harsh economic environment, things were vibrating at Moonglow. They had an optimism that was way out in front of the general sense of gloom and defeat that marked and marred the Zeitgeist.

"Obama's going to digitalize all the medical records in the United States for a start," Wally said, "and we've got the software to do it better."

But Chris was uncomfortable and unable to commit himself. He told Archie he was not sure what he wanted.

"Come on, dude," Archie said. "Did you ever think you could make that much money doing something you'd do just for fun anyhow?"

"I know," Chris said, strangely lacking enthusiasm.

"And we'd be together, just like we are now."

"Yeah," Chris said. "I know. But, I don't know. I can't help it; I don't know."

He was dissatisfied with his response and its passive insistence. But that was all he could say. If there was anything else to say, it was in hiding in some dark recess inside him. He was unaware of it; except for a vague presentment of he did not know what.

"Well, I know," Archie said. "You're like...a masochist. You can't just enjoy something good when it happens."

"Maybe," Chris said. "I gotta think about it."

"What's to think?" Archie said. "You think too much and it will vanish. They want an answer by Saturday. I said yes already. What's holding you back?"

Chris shrugged without saying anything.

Saturday, he stood looking out at the river watching his breath as it condensed in the air. Maybe he was making a mistake. So be it. It was his to make.

***

"You blew that one," Archie said on Monday at school. He was angry. He was hurt. He took it personally.

"We could have been together," he said, resentfully, but you killed that possibility.

***

Chris's mother had been just as enthusiastic about Moonglow as Archie. She was similarly incensed at what she called his lack of enthusiasm. "You want to be a letter carrier like your father for thirty-five years and then collapse one day and spend the last two years of your life dying?"

"That's not what I'm saying," Chris muttered half audibly.

"As far as I can hear, you're not saying anything. What is the matter with you? Are you losing your ambition this early in the game? Huh?" She tossed back her head and her long neck stretched and a hank of her long blond hair flew over her shoulder. She was still a young woman. Her husband's death had freed her from subservience to a man who was a dozen years her senior. She felt the life inside her, and she was eager to let it out.

"No," Chris muttered.

"Are you on drugs?"

"I'm not on drugs. I don't know what my ambition is." Even as he said it, Chris knew that it was not true. It hit him, as hard as he tried to duck. He'd given up on what he really wanted to do. He daydreamed of acting. It was an amorphous desire. He was ashamed of it. He did not trust himself. He lived a lot in fantasies. Being an actor was just another fantasy.

***

He had not told anyone, not his mother, not Archie, no one about the college application he had mailed. It had been Mr. Gorman's, his guidance counselor's idea.

"You don't seem happy about programming, although your grades are stellar."

"It's ok," Chris said.

"Only ok?"

"Yeah."

"What would be better than ok?"

"I don't know," Chris said.

"I don't believe that," Mr. Gorman said.

"I want to be an actor, but..."

"But?"

"But that's a fantasy."

"It is right now. But it could become a reality if you set yourself to it."

***

After that meeting, at Mr. Gorman's suggestion, and with a no-interest loan from the guidance counselor, to be paid back whenever he could, of 125 dollars, Chris submitted an application to a university famous for its theater department.

Mr. Gorman agreed to let him use his office for the return address, too. Chris had explained the tense situation at home with his mother, at first only as an excuse for cynicism and apathy. Then he found himself desperately pouring out his confusion to the counselor. He could not understand her fury, she who had pursued her life so sideways, especially since his father's death, suddenly, now, had wanted to see him regimented. It was killing him, flattening out his spirit. He could not take it. Gorman knew the only way he could reach the boy was by creating an alternative.

Chris' mother took it like bad news when he told her that he had been accepted with a full scholarship at a prestigious Ivy League university. "A scholarship is not a salary, she said."

Her response did not come as a surprise to him.

"Please don't sabotage it," he said.

"I'm not sabotaging anything. I just want to know what in the world going to a fancy school is going to do for you in the way of learning something that's going to allow you to make money." She was looking intently into the bathroom mirror, applying makeup. Chris was standing in the doorway looking at her. But she was not looking at him. As she spoke, she spoke into the mirror.

"Money is not everything," Chris said.

"Spoken like a person who has never had to pay rent or electric bills or grocery bills or telephone bills or hospital bills his whole life!" she retorted.

***

Chris prevailed. But from the beginning of May, when he got the acceptance letter until mid-August when he left home, it felt more like a defeat than a victory. His mother was distant and broadcast an air of betrayal or indifference in every word and every gesture.

Archie, once bound so inextricably to him, once his choice was clear, avoided him all summer. He didn't even answer his portable or respond to an SMS. Chris did not press it. He was getting himself ready for a new life.

***

It was the second week of August. In three days Chris would leave for New York. It had been decided that he would take the bus. All he was taking were two suitcases and a laptop.

It was the last day he would spend by the lake. As had been the unusual case the whole summer, he was by himself again. Archie had managed to avoid him even at the lake. Today was an exception. They saw each other at the same instant, Chris from the edge of the water, Archie as he scrambled down a rocky slope. It was too late to turn back. Besides, he was driven by momentum and gravity, two pretty compelling forces.

So he hurtled down the hill. But something tightened in him as the bare souls of his feet slapped against the flat rock which jutted out over the lake. He took a spot as far from Chris as possible, at the edge of the rock, at a right angle to Chris, not really very far, given the size of the ledge.

Chris felt the snub although there was no reason for it to surprise him. He dove into the lake from his perch. He pawed the hard skin of the water with the cups of his palms as he churned across its surface. Then he burrowed underwater. As he shot through the cold, containing all his breath, an impossible elation took hold of him.

"What the fuck is going on?" he said breathing freely and deeply, climbing back onto the ledge. "Why are you cutting me?"

"Don't play dumb. It does not become you," Archie said.

"What are you talking about?"

"If you really don't know, then there's nothing I can say that will make you."

It was more than Chris could bear. He burst out laughing.

"What are you laughing about?" Archie said, indignation struggling to suppress an eruption of sympathetic giggles. He was overcome by the sight of his once-friend's lovely, fluid body slick with wet.

"I don't know," Chris said, biting his tongue although he was itching to say: because you sound like somebody's fucking wife. Instead, he said, "This whole thing is ridiculous. We were best friends. Now you avoid me."

"I didn't turn down the job at Moonglow," Archie said.

"Because you do something does not mean I have to do the same thing," Chris said, letting go. "That's not what friendship is. It's more the mark of a jealous and possessive love."

Archie felt bruised by this. A wound opened inside him. He was humiliated. Humiliation did not sit well on his strong young frame. Chris felt him cringe inwardly, and then he understood.

Chris was perched on a rock facing Archie and the water. "I have a joint," he said, stretching and dragging his knapsack over to him. "Wanna make believe it's a peace pipe?" He lit it, dragged on it, and extended it to Archie. Archie wavered an instant but then took it and inhaled.

Archie stumbled over his breath as he exhaled, gasped, caught some air in his throat, and began to cough. His fits of coughing became involuntary, tears filled his eyes, and he broke into sobs. Chris moved nearer to him to comfort him. Archie was embarrassed. Chris took the joint from his fingers, snubbed it out, and put his face near Archie's.

"Are you alright?" he said even as he realized he was obviously not.

Archie hardly answered and only gasped.

"I know you're not," Chris said, gently.

Without saying anything Archie threw his arms round Chris and buried his face in Chris' neck. All Chris could do was stroke the back of his friend's neck. Then it was his skull he was stroking. But it was more like caressing. Then taking Archie's cheeks in the palms of his hands, he lifted his head and looked at him.

"I want to kiss you," Archie said.

"I want to kiss you, too," Chris said. "But I am leaving in three days. You know that. I still am."

"I know," Archie said. "I know. That's the way it is. I'll get over it. The world is full of people."

But the words were secondary, for even as he said them, his lips and Chris's were touching. It was clumsy. It did not go further.

"I'm sorry," Archie said.

"There's nothing to be sorry for," Chris said.

"I have to go," Archie said, although he had not swum. "I guess it's Goodbye," he said.

"Goodbye, Archie," Chris said, sealing the lid on the coffin.

***

Freshman year was a revelation for Chris. He came; he saw; he changed.

He came to the campus a boy torn by confusion. What happened with Archie had severely shaken him, not just the last encounter, but the whole course of their friendship. He had been a nerd. He hung around with Archie, another nerd. They were both nerds. They took long walks in the deserted industrial parts of the town many nights. They spoke endlessly, hypothesizing distant galaxies and fantasizing impossible creatures.

But Chris began to change the beginning of the last year in high school, when they were seniors. Archie's dishabille began to trouble him. He began to scan himself in the mirror for imperfections. He began a war in himself against any kind of flab, physical, mental, emotional. He undertook to read the complete plays of Shakespeare and to listen to all of Wagner's operas. He began swimming every day. That drew him to use the gym.

Archie had noticed that Chris was less available than he had been. And he was dressing differently, attentive to what he wore. His body was different, too. Archie did not like it. But he said nothing. When they were together, Chris acted as he always had, but it was different. Archie would not have put it this way, but Chris had acquired elegance.

Chris was changing from within. It was natural to him. It was his own growth. Consequently, he was less aware of how much he had changed than those who knew him were. He felt more like himself than ever. He liked it.

Chris saw -- better to say -- he felt, from the moment he set foot on the campus, from the first day at the university, that he had entered a world of desire and possibility. He was dazed by the feeling of the air, as he breathed it into his lungs. *That* had never felt so gladsome before in its passage. Nor had he ever felt more like himself and less like his shadow. This was something new. It was exhilarating. He felt empty, ready to be filled. It happened. He was. The change was organic.

He joined the theater department, began to act in short plays, took singing and even ballet classes as well as gymnastics. His voice deepened, became a rather mellow baritone. He was six feet tall, a hundred fifty pounds, lean, muscled, and ruggedly handsome.

Larry was handsome, too, even beautiful, and to protect himself he had assumed the role of a hyper-masculine, athletic, uncaring, unapproachable young man. His tuition was fully funded by a track and swimming scholarship, and he excelled at both. He had put himself down as a business major. He excused himself from any girl's desire for a sexual attachment with the excuse that he was in training.

One frustrated date asked him when he told her that, "For what, celibacy?"

He laughed good naturedly. "Feels like it," he said.

"You don't have to," she said.

"Yes, I do," he said.

His real interest was theatrical set and costume design. He kept it to himself until Chris told him after swim practice that he was a theater major.

"No shit!" Larry said, lighting up with surprise.

They became friends quickly, despite Larry's being two years older than Chris and scheduled to graduate two years before him.

As a senior, Larry took an apartment off campus, and no one raised any objection when Chris chose to live there, too. They did not begin their friendship as lovers.

They sat many nights over a few beers or some vodka sours and spoke about their early lives. Chris told of his father's death and the chill that had come over everything those two years that his father was dying while his mother carried on doing what became only her duty with no other concern than to express her virtue under duress and distress. But once he was dead, it was different. She became different, vulgar and hungry. She had no trouble meeting men or bringing them home, intruding into his life with something he could not handle.

Larry's father was a carpenter who had the reputation in the small town he came from of having slept with many of the women in his neighborhood. The fights between his parents were sporadic and made the air tense with violence, but they always ended in bed. He often heard their wild growling. He longed for something finer. In high school he had been rather morose and withdrawn despite his popularity.

"I realized I had this power that I did not want of getting people to need me to like them," he said.

"What a burden!" Chris taunted him.

"I know," Larry said. "But it is. I don't want demands put on me."

"You'd rather be seduced." The words had jumped out of Chris' mouth.

"Maybe," Larry said, laughing thoughtfully.

"Shall I seduce you?"

"Maybe you already have," Larry said.

"How did I manage it?"

"I think it was when you said you were a theater major. Somehow it made me think that I could be. I mean, you did not look...I don't know how to finish that sentence. You just made me feel like it was possible."

Everybody said you had to take his course in Homer.

Chris was in awe of him.

"At that moment, with that confrontation," he said, "all our attempts at interpretation prove to be insubstantial. Interpretation is revealed to be the bloodless thing it is. The only valid response to the poem, the only response that can make the experience of the poem the experience of poetry is your experience of the encounter as the overwhelming visceral illumination that it is."

A lock of his dusky golden hair fell over his forehead. Without thinking or missing a beat and with the hand that did not have a copy of "The Iliad" open in it, he brushed it back, only to have to do it again after it defiantly tumbled back down. He was adorable, and though he was not vain, he knew he was. He knew how to use it too, to draw attention and keep it.

"Apollo does not signify anything allegorical or metaphorical. This is 12th century Greece, B.C.," he continued. "He's one of the Gods. Gods were not allegorical or metaphorical. They were actual, relentless and terrifying, terrifying in a thrilling way, in the way that indomitable power is. When Diomedes hurls himself against Apollo in the ecstatic fury of his battle fever, hot from his victory over Aeneas, Apollo thunders out a warning to him.

"If you want to do interpretations, make up meanings, I can't stop you," he admonished the class, "but I can caution you. All this scene is, what is at the root of this story's power," he explained, "is the encounter of a magnificent and furiously raging mortal striving with and then deferring to an ineffable and aroused God. There is an explosion of power so intense that it recoils back on itself. It becomes an implosion. That encounter is nothing but itself, and it is existentially terrifying. It brings together the forces of anger and eroticism. They combine in a kinetic confrontation between a man and a God."

He could not have held his audience better had he been a star of the theater. His class was charged with drama and charisma. Students sat on the window sills and radiators. They crouched on the floor in the corners of the classroom, notebooks thrown open, but hardly anyone took notes. Everyone was listening.

***

Everyone on the faculty called him Eddie. He called himself Eric. It was his middle name. It was his mother's name with the 'a' trimmed off in recognition of his masculinity. She had been a concert violinist who had been more devoted to her career than to him. She did not know who his father was. There had been several men around the time, and none of them was eager for a child. Mostly he was raised by his grandmother, a pretentious woman with a large apartment on the Upper West Side of Manhattan and a thick German accent. She beat him with a paddle if his report card was less than perfect.

He was not married. He was courtly and flirtatious with women. At the semi-annual holiday parties he danced with nearly the entire female complement of the faculty and the administration with courtliness and gallantry. But he was always out of reach, impervious to any grasp. He was open, affable, unavailable, and irresistible. He was tenured and had published several books and numerous journal articles.

***

Chris sat in the first row in his class, basking in his sense of awe. He had copied his staccato style of speaking, his well-fitting ribbed cotton turtle necks worn under an autumnally-brown tweed jacket, and his leather coat.

"You are falling for him. Definitely," Larry said. "You're under his influence for sure. This is going to hurt."

Chris looked at him uncomprehendingly.

"Not you," Larry said. "Me. Already I can feel you drifting."

"I don't know what to say," Chris said.

"There's nothing to say," Larry said.

They had been sleeping together. And they had stopped. Their passion had flared. Then it ebbed. Chris had taken the spare bedroom with the divan for himself.

It was the leather coat that did the work and took Chris where he never thought he could go.

"I like your coat," Eric said, walking beside him down the granite steps outside Bluehouse Library into the early and perhaps deceptive springtime. Perhaps deceptive because snow was known to come yet again, even after such sweetness, before winter could be confidently forgotten. This year it would not. But they could not know that, yet.

Chris blushed, giggled, and shrugged.

"It looks good on you," Eric said. "But the two of us walking together like this, we might be mistaken for a pair of upper-mid-level Nazi bureaucrats. My rooms are over there." He was pointing to the upper floors of an old Victorian mansion across the street and down the block. "Can I interest you in a pot of tea?"

"I'd love to," Chris sputtered, unable to camouflage his excitement.

"Why do you dress like me?" Eric said, carelessly, as he hung Chris' coat in the closet beside his. Chris blushed again.

"Please don't be embarrassed," Eric said. "I am flattered."

"I admire you and I want to model myself on you," Chris gulped, figuring that honesty was the best defense. But he was to be outdone by a master at the game.

"Have you thought about what it would be like to have me inside you?" Eric said.

The question would have seemed weird, shockingly odd, even incomprehensible, had not Chris so often imagined slowly stripping seductively and watching Eric watch him doing it, had he not felt his rectal muscles clenching and loosening as he imagined Eric inside him. He took a breath. He took the leap. "I'd like that. I want you inside me," he said. "Yes, I have."

Eric smiled. He brought the young man to him and pressed him close. He kissed him. "You got to me too," he said.

"I only daydreamed about it," Chris said.

Eric unbuckled Chris's belt. "Take your shirt off," he said. He watched as Chris pulled the shirt over his head. Then he removed his own, enjoying the way Chris gazed at him.

"It will feel like I'm making love to myself," he said, teasing, following the contours of Chris's naked chest with spidery finger-tips and touching his lips to Chris's and then backing away.

"You like to work out," Eric said, taking hold of Chris's firm nipples.

"It turns me on," Chris said with a shiver.

"Do you work out?" he said, looking at Eric's smooth and well-wrought torso.

"It turns me on," Eric said.

Daylight was gone. They lay together in Eric's bed, slowly dancing their way to ecstasy.

"Tell me how you feel," Eric said, looking at Chris looking up at him.

"I feel like I'm worshipping you," Chris said.

Slowly they interwove themselves.

* * *

"You don't have a television?" Chris said, in the morning, returning to the kitchen with his empty coffee mug, looking for a refill.

"No, I don't have a television," Eric said, smiling, looking at Chris' well-wrought figure, nearly naked except for his black bikini underwear. With his cup extended as Eric tilted the pot and poured some coffee out into it, he seemed to Eric posed to be an old Greek or Roman marble of a beautiful young man. "Michelangelo would have appreciated you," he said.

Standing aside, had he been able to, Eric would have seen that he too constituted a figure in that ensemble, as he stood arm outstretched, chest gleaming, pouring the coffee into Chris' cup.

"But you do have a laptop," Chris continued.

"I could not live without it," Eric said.

"I'd like to hear you say that about me," Chris said.

"With or without changing the pronoun?" Eric said.

"That's for you to determine," Chris said.

They were silent. The agreement had been made.

"Let's shower, and then you ought to get going," Eric said.

"What happens now?" Chris said as he looked at himself in the mirror and brushed his hair.

"What do you mean?" Eric said.

"Are we?" Chris said but shifted from words to gestures, shuttling his right hand back and forth through the charged and empty air.

"Are we what?" Eric grinned.

"I don't know," Chris said, hesitating. "Do you want to see me again?"

"I'm going to see you in exactly one hour and fifty-three minutes from now and talk to you about Diomedes' third encounter with a God, when he would have slain Ares, if Gods could be slain," Eric said and took a swallow of coffee. Chris frowned.

"You are teasing me. I mean this way, like this?"

"Like this?" Eric said, drew Chris to him in a full body embrace, and kissed him with his tongue.

"Yes," Chris said, "like that."

"Get dressed," Eric said. "I'll see you in class. Come to my office after your last class, which is over...when?"

"At three."

"I'll be there."

"Yes, Sir," Chris said, and went out into the morning light-hearted and confident.

Breaking with Larry was not easy. As far as Chris was concerned, it was not necessary.

"I don't think I'm ready for an exclusive relationship with anybody," he said. I don't understand how my friendship with Eric affects how we are with each other at all."

"Don't be coy," Larry said. "Friendship."

"You want me to choose between the two of you?" Chris challenged.

"That's what life is about."

Chris shook his head in exasperation. He could not be held back, and it kept happening. It was suffocating him; it had been the same way with Archie.

"Not for me," Chris said.

"Of course not," Larry said. "You don't decide anything. You just shift for yourself however you want, as if no one else were involved. You follow your fancy."

"What else do you want me to follow?" Chris said, laughing with indignation, "Yours?"

"Yes," he said, "take me into consideration."

"You mean follow your desires instead of mine. No thank you."

"What are you going to do this summer?" Eric said, his hand on Chris's shoulder as they passed under the marble arch and sauntered through the alley formed by the facing lines of newly blossoming apple trees.

"I was thinking of going west to pick grapes," Chris said.

He had decided not to think about things that were impossible, and maybe, he said to himself when he tried to piece things out, it would be a good thing to go into some open spaces and get away from everything for a while, so that the new shapes could take and solidify.

"That's not a very good idea," Eric said.

"No," Chris responded surprised.

"No," Eric repeated. "A better idea is to spend the summer with me in Greece."

"Are you serious?"

"I'm doing a seminar in Athens the last two-weeks in June. Then I'm free for the rest of the summer. Our trip would be paid by the university. I always stipulate a traveling companion. I don't like to be alone."

"Poor baby," Chris said with an appealing, teasing pout.

"Then you'll come with me," Eric said in triumph.

"At your beck and call, master," Chris said with a graceful swooping bow, your devoted warrior and acolyte.

***

The Aegean Sea breaks its waves on a sable-colored sandy shore. Marvelous rocky caves and arches tower above it on the beach. Great rock walls, too, are submerged within the depths of the water. Only their crowns and peaks break the surface forming alleys and mazes of blue water for swimmers to negotiate like the narrow streets of antique villages.

As worthy of the gaze as these rocks and caves or the resonant horizon filled with an immense emptiness of blue that brings the gaze to it and fastens it there -- were the two masculine figures standing in the wet sand by the edge of the water gazing at the declining sun that was turning the blue sky purple. Their lithely muscled, supple, sun-brazed bodies glittered with perfection. Their scant black bathing suits showed that perfection. They turned, embraced. Their bodies touched and hardened and they drew their breaths together in a long surrendering kiss as their desire flared.

Swimming, they broke their strokes against the strong Aegean, the hard-breasted, blue-chested, sun-crested Aegean, embracing its throbbing water. They returned happily winded to the beach. Clasped in each other's embrace, body pulsed against body as their breathing, dancing, settled to a steady joy.

"I'm sorry we have to go back to Athens tomorrow," Chris said, as they climbed up the steps built into the cliff above the beach. The sun had set and the evening's darkness was quickly deepening. "Even though I like Athens," Chris added as they unlocked their bicycles.

"You like picking up dope at dusk on Odos Sofokleus."

"It was good grass," Chris grinned. He was aroused already, ready to ignite at the slightest thing. Feeling how powerfully Eric had taken possession of him drew a wave of desire to flood him. Neither of them had ever felt it like that before. Now it had become the way it was with them always. They lived for each other.

"You could stay here forever."

"I could."

Tired from the sea and the sun, they lay stretched out in their bed only covered by a sheet. They turned and embraced. They kissed as if they were dreaming. They kicked off the sheet and held each other breaking the boundary between bodies. Chris looked up at Eric dazed. They fell asleep still joined.

They woke and began to dance inside their glow, rushing together into a bright gold pneumatic landscape. They faced each other like ancient warriors. Their torsos were like bronze breast plates. Their touch was like the hurling of lances. They subsided into each other's arms. They slept again. They woke again. The moon was full. It shone thru the window. The window opened on to a terrace. The terrace gave out onto the vast and black Aegean. It was nearly two in the morning.

The night sky beckoned. They kissed and smiled. They put on white trousers and loose-fitting white shirts which they left unbuttoned. They went slowly, facing traffic. There was an occasional passing car that illuminated them and the trees along the roadside, and then it was gone. For an instant the dark was darker, and then they could see each other's faces.

Eric had his arm round Chris's waist. Chris walked snuggled against Eric, his cheek pressed to Eric's. They stopped. They kissed. They looked at the moon. They embraced. They flamed at the touch of their muscular flesh.

They arrived in Athens in the heat of the day. They took a cab to their hotel. The room was spacious and clean. It was air conditioned. The bed was large, fresh, heaped with a huge comforter. They slept under the happy weight of the quilt, enlaced in each other's arms. They woke. It was evening. They walked in the falling light to a café at the foot of the Acropolis.

End of the 4th Story

Gideon Elliot

UNSTABLE
Emotion

GAY ROMANCE EROTICA

Unstable Emotion
By: Gideon Elliot

Chapter 1

I was becoming like one of those perverse, introspected, isolated characters in Dostoevsky novels, wandering around, not in the gray and gloomy winter of St. Petersburg, but in Amsterdam, and spending my afternoons and late nights not in filthy taverns but in hip hash and coffee houses.

I had a cheap attic room overlooking a canal, in an old house owned by a middle-aged numismatist with an international reputation, Heinrich Mengelbaum, whose grandfather had managed to outwit the Nazis and survive.

Unlike Raskolnikov, I harbored neither desire nor plans to kill my landlord, and often sat listening, attentively, to his stories of loss and survival, and told him of my own life and, sometimes, late at night, over some aqua vita and hashish, of the times my soul, soaring, came to the surface of my body, of those moments I prize more than anything, the ones I lived for and too often lived without.

Mengelbaum was a widower. All he had left of his wife, whose framed picture showed her to be a beautiful Hungarian girl - hardly a woman - was Johannes, the son she had borne and died doing so.

Of such sweet mettle was Mengelbaum made that the boy was his beloved and there was no admixture of resentment in the man's love. Moreover, Johannes inherited his father's loving disposition and his mother's beauty.

"You wouldn't believe what it was like to be young, then," Mengelbaum said, glancing back and forth between me and Johannes, who sat at the table with us, his ubiquitous sketch pad in front of him, making quick studies of his father and me.

Mengelbaum was referring to the period right after the war. "Our hearts were open with joy and contracted with grief. Here was life, again. And there was death, forever, always lingering at the doorway of the future; the horror of the past could not stop infiltrating the far reaches of the present. Life teased like a neurotic girlfriend who couldn't make up her mind if she wanted to go to bed with you or never see you again."

***

I smoked my hash straight in an old Chinese pipe, without tobacco. And I drank a strong, sweet, cinnamon-laced Greek coffee, several cups a day. The first was at five-thirty in the morning. I rose each morning at that time, did a half hour of exercises with free weights, showered, squeezed a glass of orange juice, took a bunch of vitamins, and had a second cup of coffee very hot and very sweet. The aroma of cinnamon stayed with me throughout the morning as I wrote.

I wrote every day without interruption until one-thirty. Then I hit the streets and had lunch in a hash and coffee house. Even then I wrote, sitting over a bowl of vegetable soup with fresh bread and Gouda cheese, a little stoned. Sometimes Joachim was around and I'd go home with him.

Usually, I slept in the early evening, and went back out later into the night, roamed the streets and cruised the hash and coffee houses. I generally got to bed by three.

It had been six years since I'd left the United States, and I hadn't gone back yet and did not wish to.

Actually, I had become frightened of the country, the way you might be frightened of someone who is not really who he seems. There is something, too about lying itself that is very frightening, the immense denial it proclaims of your right to exist. The United States had become a country whose government had been usurped by liars, who would not even stop at committing murder in their battle to make falsehood appear to be truth. And too many of its citizens seemed to be going out of their minds.

I was happy to see Joachim standing at the counter at the Way Back. He saw me and smiled as he handed me a pipe by way of greeting.

I accepted the pipe and took a big hit, feeling my head go loose immediately, my flat gut tighten, and my cock get hard in anticipation.

Before I could exhale, his lips were on mine and he was sucking the smoke out of my lungs and taking it into his, pinching my nipples hard to get every last breath out of me.

"It's nice to see you," I said.

He breathed out.

"I was afraid you'd be upset."

"You set the rules. I follow."

Joachim looked at me, half in admiration, half skeptically.

"It's true," I said. "I've been totally reconfigured since I met you."

"How so?"

"Nothing bothers me. Everything turns me on. I'm high all the time. I mean I'm running on the energy you arouse in me."

He was groping me as I spoke, and staring into my eyes with a cool detachment which completely enthralled me.

"Being with you is a trip to heaven," I said. Even as I said it I was succumbing to the complex authority of his presence.

"I'll be back in two weeks," I said. "It won't be long."

The night was warm and we were strolling together by a canal, holding hands and pressing our shoulders together.

"For me it will be long," Joachim grinned and drew me to him in a kiss.

"Are you scared?" he asked afterwards, looking hard into my eyes, making sure of the truth of my answer.

"Scared?"

"You said," he answered, "America scared you and you did not wish to go there."

"I'll be back," I said.

How could he know how my heart raced, excited, despite my fear! I had hit the big time.

America had become an ache in my heart -- an empire built on war, illusion, and mendacity.

New York was unlike the city I had once known. The angles had changed. Streets which had been there were gone, and ones which never were suddenly had glassy skyscrapers standing on them.

Farrell drew on an unlighted pipe as we walked along the new promenade along the Hudson.

"You must be in heaven," he said, referring to the book award.

"I don't even know how to think about it."

"Well, I read the book, and you're amazing."

I blushed, and tried to hide it by blurting out anything that would come to me.

"You used to be able to stand right on the edge," I said, leaning against the tubular fence extending from the cement. No barrier to the river.

"Come here a lot?"

"All the time."

Farrell looked at me, understanding.

"The trucks were over there," he said.

"Hemingway," I said.

"Served him right," Farrell said.

And now we knew that we knew each other.

"When do you fly back to Amsterdam?" he asked.

"Saturday morning. It's to Paris."

"Will you have dinner with me tomorrow night? After the reading? Just us? Not business, just friendship."

"Sure," I said.

"But you don't have to wait till then to come up to my place."

"I won't," I said, extending my hand, which he took and brought to his lips.

***

"You make my cunt open up," I said, teasingly, as he blew kisses on my neck, "but I'm not sure I want you to fuck me."

"May I kiss you?"

"Yes," I said, and his lips were pressing me into him before I could take in a breath.

"You're starting to make me want you," I said.

Finally, he did not, but I left him in friendly spirits. I took him to a happy orgasm and caressed him with admiration. He was the sort of man I admired, but not the kind I surrender to.

I winked when I kissed him in the morning and said "Ciao." He grinned.

***

My book was in all the bookstore windows. It was prominently displayed in the Astor Place store.

There I was, an infinitely reproducible cultural commodity: me, a book, with a dust jacket, stacked up pyramidally, offering to reconfigure reality with strings of words, in sentences that came from beyond where we are and go both nowhere and where we want to be. It took my breath away to think of all the human channels I would flow through.

I had to keep hold of myself or I would explode with vanity.

The reading went well. First I spoke, and watched the crowd and saw how many young people, male and female, were there admiring me. I let myself enjoy it the way you let yourself fall sleep in the arms of a caressing sun under an infinite azure sky on the shore of the Aegean.

Once I begin to read something I've written, I usually feel good about it. It astonishes me. I'm ready for the embarrassment, but instead I feel the thrill of discovery.

"I've been writing," I said with a faux-sheepishness that is really the opposite of self-effacing, when the clapping stopped, "what maybe can be called poetry. I wrote this on my flight over here, when I got to thinking about the painfulness that America has become for me:

> The president speaks
> Rodents jump out of his mouth
>
> Rats jump off his tongue
> Poisonous snakes slither off his lips
>
> The reptiles fall to the ground
> They curl around his feet
>
> The rats land on their paws
> Softly striking the carpet
>
> In the frenzy of freedom

They rush through the doorways

They swell on the street and spread
The plague they carry is loose

The lice of the president's lies
The lice on the rats from his mouth

Cling to us all

Carried beyond the seas then breed
A great plague in the desert"

Afterwards, I stood around with a plastic flute of champagne in my hands answering friendly questions, gently flirting, and being charming until Farrell hustled me out and took me to his room and slowly licked my nipples.

***

I landed in Paris. Joachim met me at CDG. We stayed for a week, in a little hotel on a crooked, winding street not far from the river.

The moon hung like an amber halo beside the giraffe's neck of the Eiffel Tower.

We got into a cab and rode along the Seine watching the amber-gold, illuminated buildings of Paris reflecting in the water.

In our hotel, the steps turned round an invisible center, a column of unencumbered air. We reached our room. Joachim unlocked the door and pushed me in and kicked the door shut with his heel and took me to him. He stuffed himself with my kisses until I was gasping with desire for him and felt the wonderful hardness preening inside his jeans. I brought it out and kneeled before him and slowly took him in my mouth. With my true heart's reverence, I began an act of worshipful surrender and felt the pulse of his responding. He pulled me up to him and wet his fingers in my mouth and then lubricated me. Gazing at me, he entered me as only he can. I knew him and he was mine and I was his and this is what I was whispering when the breaths half-formed in my throat did become actual words.

We took a train back to Amsterdam on a Tuesday evening.

We sat watching the French countryside dissolve into the night.

"Look," Joachim said, but he was not pointing at the dusky landscape running by us like frames of film over revolving sprockets. He was showing me a small, red velvet box, the kind rings come in.

"I opened it."

"Yes," I said and kissed him.

Inside there were two small silver rings, for the nipples.

Back in Amsterdam, we fell dead into my narrow bed asleep in each other's arms.

***

"It was a very handsome stamp on the envelope," Mengelbaum said as he held the door open for us and we walked into his airy living room with plank board floors. Thank you."

"It's good to see you again," I said.

Joachim stretched out his hand and shook his when I introduced them.

Mengelbaum poured out four shots of vodka (Johannes was sitting in his pajama bottoms and a sleeveless undershirt, his nineteen-year-old's radiant physique glowing), and we clinked our glasses and sipped the vodka.

"I need a bigger place," I said. "Joachim and I are going to live together. I'm going to have to find something. I hate to leave you."

Mengelbaum smiled.

"Why are you smiling?" I said.

"Because one floor below the roof where you are now, I just happen to have three large rooms with a kitchen and a separate w c, airy and facing the canal."

Chapter 2

Joachim was gone when I opened my eyes. His place in the bed, beside me, was empty; the sheets and his pillows were no longer warm with his body's nighttime warmth.

"Joachim," I called, like a frightened child calling for his mother.

The apartment was empty but for me, however.

Outside, the sky above the canal was clouded, dappled with gray and intensely luminous patches of white, like silk rumpled in bunches, with darts of pale green lining the peripheries.

On the old pine table in the kitchen, a glass of squeezed orange juice waited for me, and the things for my coffee were laid out. The smell of fresh coffee still in the bag was heavy.

I looked out the window, beyond the canal. In the distance, I saw Joachim out on his morning run, all in black, in his scanty black track shorts, high black sox with the yellow band around his muscled calf, his coltish thighs with ropes of muscle gleaming, and his tight sleeveless black shirt over his Roman torso. He even wore black leather running shoes.

I sat at my desk in my black briefs and a burgundy robe because there was a poem that was bothering me to be written. It had been a repeated occurrence recently. I would hardly begin to think about Joachim and it turned into a poem.

Together, we will sleep one sleep,
Joining both our heads in one dream.

A light and densely-hued shadow
Will flicker a hypnotic rhythm
Joining us in one pulse.

Twined together in each other's sleep
How will we know we are not really only one?
How will we be able
To tell anymore
The difference between kissing and breathing?

I finished my coffee, and finally got into the shower, adjusting the water when a swift gust of air parted the shower curtain.

"Mind if I join you?" a naked Joachim, drenched with grimy sweat, asked as he stepped in under the shower with me and pulled me to him with a playful brutality which thrilled me.

I kissed him as furiously as he was kissing me and got hold of his tongue before he got mine, and I pulled him to me as if his tongue were the rope of a lasso I had slung around him.

I held him in my power until he rallied and pulled me by the nipple tips until I was dancing, knees dipping, in front of him with my head tilted back and my mouth open breathlessly to receive his kisses.

I pulled away and reached for the soap.

"You are one grimy man," I said, beginning to soap the back of his neck and working my hands down the front of his chest, soaping the smooth, pale skin and the well-wrought muscles which made him so wonderful to look at.

He pressed his mouth to mine and worked me as if he'd devour me. He brought me all the closer and contained me more entirely in his power, pushing two strong, soapy fingers deep up into me, wiping me out, stripping my soul, turning my brain around with his eyes.

I clung to him and writhed under him and turned to him with an intensity of tropism, like the open flower following the sun.

He was above me. We were stretched out on the terrycloth mat on the bathroom floor. He rocked and writhed inside me and took me with the power of lightning. He made pain sing with pleasure and pleasure extend into the borderland of pain.

I gasped as his tongue touched the depths of my throat, and his living, throbbing, hard and propulsive masculinity took me beyond endurance. I cried repeatedly his name in frantic surrender.

"Have you heard from your publisher?" Joachim said.

"Yes,' I said.

He was silent, waiting for me.

They will tape the interview here with me at VPRO.

Joachim held the envelope up to the light before opening it. He looked at the address. It was a bold handwriting. He opened it. The letterhead announced an independent affiliate of a major American studio. Above a signature in the same bold hand was a short note.

"I saw your film," it said. "I want to see you. Meet me Tuesday, at three o'clock, at the American Bar."

The American Bar in Amsterdam is a clean, well-lighted place. I would never go there. Neither would Joachim. But that's where the producer said he wanted to meet him.

It did not turn out to be what Joachim had expected. He was naive. I would have been, too. It was our time for recognition. This was just one more instance.

Joachim must have been surprised, no, more than that, he must have been thrown entirely off balance by the outright, undisguised antagonism which met him.

I can only imagine it. And I do repeatedly, always somehow magically intervening the moment before to prevent it.

What happened there does not really happen in daily reality.

There is death all around us, all around. There are single mad murders that make the headlines and wars, and wars within wars with their inexhaustible, unquenchable wildfires of killing. All those who are provoking and promoting them try to keep them from being reported at all. And the headlines about them are made in the numerous and competing propaganda offices of all the combatants.

Nevertheless, that Joachim was the next moment shot point blank in the chest made no sense. It was an impossibly incongruent event. His body slumped down in the booth. He was dead. The bullet came from behind.

Joachim's interlocutor was unhurt. Of course! He was part of the whole plot, the decoy to get Joachim where they wanted him, those enemies of liberty and liberation, and those triple agents who provoked and inflamed the world's conflicts and supplied every side with venom.

The gunman, with a scarf covering his face just about up to his eyes, fled out the door before anyone knew what had happened.

***

"*Geliebter*," Johannes said tenderly, looking straight into my eyes, the landlord's shining son whom Joachim and I had taken as our friend.

I held him tighter and sobbed more grievously.

Outside there was a thunderstorm, I began to laugh. I was laughing and crying at the same time.

It had exploded, and all the tears of the world washed over my heart and beat their way through me, finally emptying themselves out whether or not I would. I was vomiting tears. And it had not yet ended.

Johannes held me and said nothing. He only held me. And I sobbed, as grief and the relief of grief released twisted inside me. It was the kind of twisting you have to do when you're undoing knots, and it's much more a painful process than tying the knots originally was.

These were love-knots I would never have untied, but now they had been torn, cut, and the more brutally they had been pulled at, the tighter they had become until I could no longer breathe.

Now as Johannes held me and stroked me, my breath began to flow smoothly, slowly, somewhere else; somewhere in the distance, the thread of life was keeping alive some other body, not me.

my eyes are burning; my head is bent
with the weight of unspent tears

the future is a bullet to the gut
shot from the gun of the world

the men who have never been tired
the executioners of sleep
now threaten us
those are guns that were their eyes

hope is a ghost
a lost memory
the song of youth
only an old man can sing

End of the 5th Story

Gay BDSM Erotica

Erotic Aggression

GIDEON ELLIOT

Erotic Aggression
By: Gideon Elliot

Chapter 1

It is a truism in this age, whose insights into human motivation have been shaped by the psychoanalytical hermeneutics that were introduced by the great Viennese physician, that great virtues are often the contrivances by means of which equally great vices present themselves as socially acceptable, without risking condemnation, and that, frequently, can bring upon their practitioner general approbation and enviable accolades.

Such it was with Martin Bower who from the earliest age found inordinate pleasure in the dismembering of small creatures while they still enjoyed, as it were, to have the breath of life throbbing in their diminutive corpuses. Plucking wings from flies and butterflies, and their thready legs from spiders, as his teeth clenched intent with the discharge of a rage that animated him, affected him with such personal excitement that it was never in the performance of these malicious surgeries but that the configurations of his countenance did not reveal the most intense and furious sympathetic sensibility with the creatures that were the objects of his mutilation.

Rather than being openly performed, these experiments in the assertion of power over nature were enacted secretly. The outward show the boy made as he grew into a handsome adolescent forecast nothing but grace, charm, and a deferential respect for others. This impression caused to be conferred upon him praise and admiration by all who could share in the responsibility for the quality of his growth and by all who were fortunate enough to observe in the young man the happy results of their efforts toward his education. At the age of thirteen he announced that he intended to be a surgeon when he grew up.

At University, his classmates admired him and his teachers esteemed him. He was recognized for intellectual brilliance and for emotional availability. His capacity to be compassionate, especially as he listened to stories whose narrators were rightfully angry, and his gratifying response to their tales with an uprush of anger, made him the first ear to turn to.

His first foray into cruelty lasted just under two years and he was done with it by the end of his junior year. Nor did it hamper the reputation for receptivity, availability, and affability, for genuine friendliness that made him shine -- in classes and in general on the campus. His devotion to cruelty was enacted in the odd recess each life can find, and it brought him into a parallel universe where he became someone else who was pretending to be him most of the time.

When he began at the University, Bower's father had given him an open-top two-seater car of a creamy pale Dresden green. The dashboard was of oak wood. The seats were of leather died a deep oxblood. In this car, from time to time, he left the campus and lonely along unlovely highways, he watched the road disappear beneath the car's wheels as he raced towards fulfillment of boundless desire.

He had discovered the club entirely by accident when he had gone to a remote village in search of the tranquility that a hamlet near a forest and a gently meandering stream can afford a young man of sensitivity and sensibility who is besieged by the excitements of an urban situation and a busy social routine intermixed, in his case, with an on-going course of rigorous studies, for his desire and determination to be a surgeon never wavered.

Hidden behind an imposing and antique stone wall that stretched along one side of a gently sloping dirt road across from the forest where he had wandered having left his car in a shaded and out-of the-way grove, was a castle – at least a castle was what it most resembled – upon which he had stumbled some weeks ago because, as the day was hot, he had stripped off his clothes and, leaving them on the bank, plunged into the river and begun swimming with a strong and easy stroke until he had reached a turn in the river. It opened onto a prospect that gave him a surprising view of that marvelous stone structure, hidden, for the most part, by the wall he had seen from the road.

It would have been an event of no consequence had Bower seen the grave pile and having seen it turned round to return to the bank upon which he had left his clothes, and near which his convertible was parked.

But circumstances greatly shaped by chance, a force whose origins are far from being transparent to the understanding, made it otherwise.

On the bank, quite close to the river, there composed into undeniable focus for the powerful swimmer a scene of even more commanding aspect than the edifice itself. It was of someone being beaten, whipped actually. The moment of his apprehension was also the moment of his response. Charging with a powerful stroke, he reached the shore and sprang out onto it from the river, oblivious to his own nakedness. He ran up to the scene of –it was not altercation, but attack, and cried, "Put down that whip. He is bleeding."

"And so will you be. Back off," cried at him the marvelous specimen of brawn brandishing the whip, his erection straining. But instead of backing off, Martin threw himself forward and, grabbing his opponent by one shoulder, yanked the whip out of his hand.

"What are you doing?" said the boy who lay in the tall grass bleeding, overwhelmed by the swollen masculinity that the naked man inhabited, and in awe.

Having interrupted something he thought he had been drawn to do as a courier of virtue, he soon became enmeshed in it to the full measure of his vice. Interrupted in their mystery, the participants were enraged and began together to pound the intruder in an embrace of blows, but with protean magnificence he slipped through their fingers and took his position before them with whip in hand, a naked circus master, as he cracked the whip on the earth before them and sent up clumps of dirt. Astonished, they held back and marveled. The whip was an extension of the arm that swung it, and danced in the same way that the muscles in the arms did.

"Who are you?" the one who no longer brandished the whip demanded as if still the master.

"I'd rather you answer that question regarding yourselves," Martin answered.

"You may not be happy if we do. You must come with us if you would know. But you've been warned."

The young man who had been beaten was hardly less naked than Martin, who let them guide him despite some wariness, keeping hold of the whip, as they walked, in front of him, to the castle. He wore only a black leather G-string; the straps of a leather harness crisscrossing his slim torso.

Inside Bower had to suppress a laugh.

"It surprises you," a young man, some five or seven years Martin's elder, inquired walking into the anteroom where Martin waited with the whipper – whom he had stripped of his whip – and the eager victim.

"No," Martin said looking directly at him with a warm smile, "that is what makes me laugh -- the pleasure of finally seeing openly what had hovered at the edges of my awareness."

Chapter 2

When he returned to the University the following afternoon, Bower told no one. He told no one of the cell in which he had spent the night, nor of the half a dozen others similarly incarcerated, not as prisoner but as torturer. It was not guilt that kept him from speaking. He did not feel guilty. He experienced the kind of exaltation being in love is reputed to induce. He was walking on air, and like a lover, understood implicitly that speech to anyone about the rituals of love could only dishonor them, especially when the rituals were such as he understood would bring shock and censure were they known. It would be called debauchery, at best, even by his open-minded acquaintances had they known the erotic ceremonies of Cruelty and Suffering that had become his spiritual nurture.

* * *

The Student Union was a masterpiece of deception. From outside it seemed to be a drunken and cockeyed, nevertheless perfectly balanced, edifice of mirroring glass. Inside, that glass was translucent and made anyone inside feel as if there were no boundary between the world outside and this protected space. The building's skin from within was a window forked by tough, curving, intersecting, tensile, supporting aluminum rods.

It was late in the afternoon. Martin's eyes were tired. He rubbed them as Elsa spoke. When vision came back to him, he turned and looked at the boy passing in the middle distance before them. Elsa felt his attention go. A blank space opened before her. It became impossible to make sense of anything. She forgot what she was saying.

Martin turned back to her. She appeared to blush. It was really anger, but she stifled it and rifled his hair.

To say that she had designs on Martin would be speaking accurately. Her parents would disapprove of him. But that was a big part of the attraction. She was rebellious and she was experimental in her rebellion. Her mother's disposition was starchy. She could tolerate no deviations from the way she thought the world ought to be. But Hanna

Blume had gotten under the girl's skin better than Elsa knew, and anyone who gave thought to the matter could see her acts of rebellion as nothing less than the clearest declarations of loyalty. She had entered a fight she wished to lose

"You're not here at all, are you?" she said bringing his head nearer her with the palm of her hand on his cheek.

He responded warmly when she kissed him and felt a frightening possibility of surrender.

"Let's go to my room," she said.

He consented. The day, because it was spring, had extended itself and as they walked in the late evening only the slightest suggestion of night was beginning to plant itself into the texture of the falling day. Across the campus they trod hand in hand with the liveliness of the young when they are imbued with the excitement of budding eroticism and the anticipation of its steep increase before they let burst together the great storm of joy.

He spread himself out above her and became a steely cloud and gently enveloped her in his mist as she dissolved in the moist warmth of their mutual rain. Afterwards he wished for a cigarette because he had engraved in his mind images in black and white from early French New Wave Cinema movies.

"You've changed over the last few weeks," she said looking up at him as he leaned on his right elbow, his entire body twisted somewhat to that side but not so much that he would become unplugged from her, and drew her to him.

"Oh, yeah," he said. "How?"

"In a good way," she said with empathic sincerity. "It's like you'd grown, like you've settled into yourself." She kissed him and he responded. The last sparks of their earlier explosion flared and spent themselves until after the shimmer of fading all feeling was gone but the utter joy of relaxation.

* * *

The top was up and Martin was protected from the downpour as he sped through the unusually dark evening over the dirt road beside what he had called the castle but later learned had been a monastery. He had settled into himself.

* * *

"You really intend to become a surgeon," Elsa said.

"Yes," he said.

"And when will you have time for me?" She was flirtatious and petulant and something else was lurking. He had to get away. It did not go on long. Martin told her one evening after classes that he was going to stop seeing her because her demands on him were too consuming and kept him from giving himself to his preparations to be a surgeon.

"You take the time we have," he said to her "and squander it, you ruin it, resenting the time we don't have rather than making the time we do have count for something."

She mocked his sentence but it did not matter. He left her. His heart was heavy -- for her. For himself, he was glad. His heart was light. He was free again of bondage to the conventions he had already managed several times to get free of. The curse of life was to be in other people's clutches.

Chapter 3

The wind was refreshing. His head needed to breathe. It was too long he had been holding on. Now he raced down the interstate until he came to the grass-edged dirt roads and took the one on the left through a forest until the meadow by the river where the monastery stood. The sky was drenched with stars. Inside, he sat at one of the long bars and drank a vodka martini. A jazz trio backed a singer going through parts of the Cole Porter Songbook. There were few members at the bar and most of the chambers on the second floor were not being used. But all of that was of no account. Richard walked in and for Martin a cloud lifted. He was tall and although thin, it was a muscular, compact thinness. His sandy blond hair caressed his skull and his head was balanced precisely upon the lean pillar of a strong neck. They kissed in greeting.

"I wanted to see you all week," Martin said, embracing him.

"I could not get you out of my mind."

"I'm hard for you all of the time."

"I want you now," Richard said and pressed his mouth to Martin's.

"Come," Martin said, pulling away. They swallowed the last of their drinks and took the rose marble steps to a chamber on the second floor where the balcony looks down at the fountain in the atrium. The room had been prepared for them.

"Come inside me, please," Richard said. "I am such a vulnerable slut when I am with you. You don't know how much I need you."

This unguarded confession of desire pierced Martin's own reserve and acted upon his nerves with an electricity that is unrepresentable by language although it is searing in the flesh. It was intolerable to feel. It was a clawing, craving demand on his flesh. He did not want to accede to it.

"Fuck off, faggott," he said.

Richard looked at him with dumbfounded amazement. "But you," he began, but before he could finish, Martin had slapped his mouth shut with a sharp crack on the cheek.

"You still want me inside you?" Martin said.

"Oh, yes," Richard affirmed nodding his head.

Bower pulled open his shirt and stood torso bare, broadcasting his impenetrable masculinity. He raised his chin and slowly turned his back on Richard, who had fallen to his knees. Bower walked out of the room onto the marble terrace outside. He leaned up against the marble parapet and looked down at the powerful spray shooting upwards in the fountain at the center of the atrium.

Richard could not cope with it. He felt a sudden emptying out of his belly. Inexpressible grief and despair overwhelmed him. "Martin," he cried. Bower walked back into the room and locked the door behind him. "It's not a game," he said. "It's a matter of power. I have it. You don't. That says something about you."

Richard did not like hearing what Martin was saying. He knew it was true and it made him numb. He wanted the power of words, tender that becalmed the spirit with abundance of affection.

"You'll sleep on the floor," Martin said, looking down at Richard and opening the door to admit the boy whom he had summoned when he stood at the parapet.

Take me into bed with you, please," Richard begged.

Martin ignored him. He was excited and like iron: he gazed at the boy: the more he frustrated Richard, the stronger he felt. He swelled with the pride of being unyielding. He held the boy and drilled him with kisses, oblivious to him as he possessed him. He let him go.

Richard stood immobile by the doorway, his gaze fixed on them; his heart, pricked by an icy knife, wept as it beat.

Martin left the boy and approached him.

Richard fell to his knees. Martin pushed him to the ground. When his lips were near Martin's feet, he stretched to kiss them, but Martin kicked him away. Richard curled up on the floor, lay still, unable to sleep, unable to move.

"Are you alright?" Martin asked Richard, the next morning, once he had sent his night's companion scooting out the door. He extended a hand to help him stand.

"A little bit sore," he said, bent.

"This will straighten you out," Martin said, taking hold of Richard's nipples and pinching them hard. It did.

Richard could hardly contain the gratitude he felt when Martin kissed him. Martin sensed it, but it did not infuriate him. It warmed him.

He felt tenderness toward the gentle soul he dominated. He was set up as a protector by the natural scheme of things. It could be a burden, but it could also be a joy. He kissed Richard warmly and left him for another time.

Chapter 4

The winter sun was strong and already suggested spring's approach. Elsa kept Martin in her sights despite his defection.

"Where do you go?" Elsa asked, as she walked up beside Martin, acting as if they were still a couple.

"Go?" Martin said.

"Yeah, when you go away for a weekend or a night."

"Into another world."

"What the hell does that mean?"

"Just what it says."

Elsa frowned at this evasion. "I want you to stay in this one," she said.

"I told you it was no go. I'm going to go into whatever world I want to."

"You want me to be a boy," she said knowingly, as if having unmasked him.

"I want you to get off my back."

"You don't know what you want. You don't know if you want a girl or a boy, and it's for sure you don't know how to make me feel like a woman."

"If that's true, what do you want from me?" he said, guiding them off the cobblestone path onto the grass and then standing beside an old, tall, spreading chestnut tree. He took her in his arms as if he were her father or her brother. "Look, I don't want to take anything away from you," he said, as if talking to a child, looking straight at her, "but I can't surrender myself to you either. Demanding that, you will only frustrate yourself even more."

She heard his words but let them slip past her. She felt his body outlining hers as he held her comfortingly. She sighed and looked up at him and he understood she wanted his mouth on hers and her breath flowing at his rhythm. He was moved by her need and desired it at that moment, too, but he knew that if he recognized and satisfied that need he would not subdue it but stimulate it. And then it would corner him, trap him. He held back and then he withdrew.

"What?" she said.

"I am only cruel to be kind," he said.

"You're full of shit," she said.

"It's getting dark," he said. "I'll take you to the edge of the park and then we can go our own ways."

"I don't need your help to walk across the campus," she said coldly, "even in the twilight."

"I know you don't," he smiled. "I'm going this way, then. Take care of yourself."

He left her in knots. She could not figure out if he was deliberately trying to or if he was just so incredibly stupid. But he was not stupid. She knew that. Her pain was that much deeper. It lasted for several months. The langor lasted with little abatement throughout the summer and the only thing that defeated hopelessness was the inexorability of routine.

He disappeared, or as good as had. Every now and then she spotted him at a distance and knew not to go near. She cursed herself for spotting him, dreading the grief it would bring to her day.

She learned in the fall that he had transferred. Some kind of fast track program that put him in medical school a year quicker. Whatever. He was gone. And she was glad. So was he. He was living with Richard, not quite as lovers, but with Richard in submission to him. It was very convenient. He began medical studies and was cared for, fed, soothed, stroked and adored by someone.

"It's not that you love me. I can tell you don't," Richard said, placing a mug of coffee on the counter in front of Martin. "You just like how it feels to have someone completely at your disposal, to take care of every need."

"Absolutely."

"I'm a convenience."

"You are a necessity," Martin said, lifting Richard's chin with his index finger and delicately biting his lips, as if tasting him. "Actually, a little bit of a luxury."

* * *

The hailstorm had come on unexpectedly; moments before there had been sunny skies. But ice pebbles came with a frightening force banging relentlessly on the windows. Martin stood, still without his shirt and barefoot although he had pulled his jeans back on.

"You don't need a new car," Richard said smiling, "for example. You over indulge yourself. You are just out of school. You've just gotten a job in the best hospital in New York."

"You don't know what I need," Martin said slowly, emphasizing each word with a slight squeeze of Richard's pointed nipples.

"Ok, what do you need it for?" Richard said, hardly able to think.

"I want it. Isn't that enough?"

"Is it?"

"You tell me."

"No, it is not."

Martin tilted his head to the left and jutted his jaw forward. "To each his own," he said.

"Aren't you ever satisfied?" Richard said.

"I'm always satisfied," he said. "You're the one who's continually frustrated."

"That's because you keep leading me on and then withdrawing."

"Poor Uncle Wiggly," Martin said, taking Richard's cock between his fingers pinching it and letting it go after a few searing frets and slides, drawing him near to the edge but pulling him back until he was dizzy.

"Take me there," Richard begged. Martin let go his cock and before he registered, cuffed Richard's wrists together behind his back. Richard froze immobilized, statuesque, surrendering to sensation as Martin ran his hands over his body and dug his fingers into his flesh and made him feel like he was sculpting him.

He stood back, gazed at him, took his jeans from off a nearby chair and got into them, pulled a polo shirt over his chest that showed it all the more, tongued Richard's lips and left him.

Elsa had not had an easy time. She had been burned by the anger her failed relationship with Martin aroused in her. She seethed when she remembered. The only thing, she imagined, that could satisfy her, would be if he could be made to recognize what he had done and if he could be made to repent it. She bit her teeth. She had no way of getting that. That's what the fall was, the beginning of consciousness. Memory becomes a torment and resentment becomes the dominating passion. He had unfastened himself from her. The best thing she could do, she knew it, was to get purged of it all – get it out of her mind and out of her system. That took will and concentration. For their triumph over regret and resentment, she knew, there had to be an object. She needed a discipline, something to concentrate on. It was the Law, with its precision, particularity, and especially with its dependence on ordered argument, that captivated her.

Upon graduating, she was lucky enough to land a job at the Morrison Agency, a firm specializing in public relations and celebrity damage control. She was sharp, incisive, and, when need be, ruthless. She rose from intern to associate in a matter of two years and after another three years to an executive position; she left Morrison to open her own office. She did not solicit any of the clients she had at Morrison to switch, but a number of her clients, hearing of her new venture, followed her, and her agency thrived.

She was often bored when not working. She began a relationship with Tom, a good-looking guy a few years younger than she was whom she had hired as her assistant. But the more she attached herself to him romantically, the less she became able to maintain her superior status with regard to him. Her sense of need humiliated her. She was stuck, and it was only after she discovered, before anything serious occurred, that he had begun doctoring invoices so that he could skim part of the fees off for himself that she dismissed him from her employ and her bed.

It was a transforming experience for her. "I've been a fool," she said, sitting in Bernie's Helicopter, the rooftop bar on Spring Street under a canopy of summer stars.

Marcia contradicted her, as friends will. But Elsa held her ground.

"A fool."

* * *

"This looks interesting," Richard said as he handed Martin an invitation that had come in the mail inviting him to attend an interdisciplinary conference and moderate a panel on the varieties of dominant/submissive relationships. He accepted and they flew to Seattle.

* * *

"You don't mean what you say," a streaky blond woman with dark eyebrows, slim cheeks, and high cheekbones said to him.

The crowd around him had thinned out. Martin was collecting his papers and arranging them on the lectern, looking down, but as she spoke he glanced up at her.

"How can you tell?" Martin said with a smile and a glance at Richard.

The woman would not be put off with a question for an answer. She looked at him intently and he could see what he thought to be a degree of animosity. She was defying him to look at her. That drew his gaze despite himself to her. Each time their gazes met, however, he would not engage but withdrew his. His papers conveniently needed his attention and he turned to arranging them and slipping them into his leather shoulder bag.

"You think you're better than anyone else," she said casually, as if their conversation were genial.

"Excuse me," he said, astonished.

"I could destroy you if I wanted to," the woman said.

Now Martin looked at her, unwavering.

"Yes?" he said. And there was no doubt about either the power he commanded or his confidence in its depth.

She blinked and walked away.

"What was that about?" Richard said.

"I don't know, but a lot of that sort of thing is happening lately."

"It gets you on edge," Richard said.

"No," Martin said, thoughtful, "I seem to get people on edge."

End of the 6th Story

Gideon Elliot

A *Second* CHANCE

Gay Romance Erotica

A Second Chance
By: Gideon Elliot

<u>Chapter 1</u>

The stars fired the heavens with magnesium jets of desire. They burned in his eyes as he walked by the river. Never had he suffered such grievous despair as now he was feeling. He was flaming with desire and aching with the fear of feeling it.

The trucks were rolling under the West Side Highway and the moon looked like it would fall out of the sky, but it continued there nevertheless and it turned into a pallid stream of light, a band stretching across the black surface of the Hudson.

There was nothing to do but to go home and to go to sleep, hoping that the band of light might transform itself, in sleep, through sleep, into the multi-foliate shape of a dream -- such a dream as makes sleep more appealing than waking. But a dream can bear pain as well as pleasure, recapitulate torments undergone as well as realize wishes.

He woke confused. He had been a slave in a red Moroccan palace and wore only a cloth of gold skirted round his hips. He stood high like an Egyptian with his nipples stiff and commanding.

First thing he had to do was to try to remember what he had done last night.

Everything had been going smoothly in the days, the weeks, and the months before. He thought he had it beat this time. Miriam had been tender. She was no longer talking about leaving him and taking the children with her as she had that night two years ago when she'd called him a rotten bastard and cursed him for continuing his gay cruising even after the birth of the twins.

He had felt guilty enough to listen to her shouting without trying to defend himself. He did not want to go to Dr. Nostrand, but he did. For the sake of his marriage, he did. He pressed his lips together and vowed to give it his best shot. He'd been trying to beat this thing since he was twelve!

Nostrand took him by the upper arm and guided him into his office.

"Please," he said, pointing to a leather chair.

"I feel pain."

"You feel pain."

"I want something I'm not allowed to want. I feel something I must not feel."

"So it feels like pain when you have to stop yourself from feeling what you feel?"

"It feels like pain, yes."

"Then the solution is simple. You must feel what you want to feel and feel also that you are afraid to feel it. Yah. Expose all the feelings. Right now they are powerful because they are in hiding, waiting in ambush, using the darkness you are providing. They can jump out at you at any moment and overpower you because you can't see them."

"Yeah."

"So if you give them darkness, they can only get stronger and bide their time. No. You must acknowledge those feelings, bring them into the open. In the light you can see them. And then you can discard them."

So Andrew felt what he knew he felt. But now he felt it like it was something that existed, yes, but was not necessarily his. He could just pass it by.

Andrew thought it had worked. Miriam did, too. She had let down her guard. So had he.

So it was strange that suddenly -- (suddenly?) -- he was overwhelmed, as if he'd been hypnotized and given a post-hypnotic suggestion, by desire he did not want to have.

It was a hot August night. Miriam had flown with the children to her parents in Sussex for a fortnight, and he was busy at the office every day.

He got home Friday after seven, having spent a very long day doing research and writing briefs in the Spenser trial, which was on the docket before Judge Hermandiez for the second week of September.

"You're wasting your time, darling," O'Brien said, leaning against the window and watching the sunset illuminate the glass panels of a skyscraper neighboring the one which housed their offices.

"Huh?" Andrew said

"You're wasting your time. You'll never win this one."

"Whose side are you on?" Andrew said with indignation.

"Everyone knows Hermandiez is a ball buster."

"Maybe," Andrew said. "But, then again, maybe I got tough balls."

"Oh, butch!" O'Brien cried. "But, really, honey, you're a pussy."

Exhausted, hungry, unable to shake off O'Brien's smarmy insinuation, when he got home -- or was it just the heat? His mind was grinding on nothing, like the wheels of a car spinning in sand. Eating or resting, both were impossible.

He showered, shaved, toweled himself dry. He was pleased, turned on at how good he looked in the mirror. What a fool he'd been in his twenties when he was still caught up in a superficial gay boy sensibility and thought that thirty-seven was old.

He hadn't gone to The Web since, since he had tried to turn...to re-establish things with Miriam. But tonight, even as he drifted over there without being deliberate about it, once he was inside, he realized that a part of him had known all day long that that was where he was going to wind up.

* * *

He went home with a guy named Max Harrison who lived in a high-rise off Ninth Avenue on Twenty-third Street.

Harrison was a few years younger than Andrew, slightly taller than him, and well built, nicely muscled. His body was firm and hard.

"I'll give you a massage," Harrison said, sensing the tension that prevented Andrew from responding to him. "Lie down."

Andy stripped down to his black boxer briefs, smiled, and then took them off. He lay face down on a narrow bed in a long, narrow room painted maroon, lit only by candles.

Harrison warmed scented oil, lily of the valley, rubbing his palms together. He began with Andy's lower back, spreading out, slowly, gentle circles, warming his back with kneading fingers, playing the cords of his neck as if he were fingering a recorder. And like a recorder,

Andrew began to sing in long high moans the tune being played upon him, the song of desire and surrender.

But before desire could peak or surrender drive him into wild submission, he spilled himself in a slow and senseless ooze.

"I can't stay," he said jumping up suddenly.

"It's okay," Harrison said, hoping to calm him. "Would you like some coffee before you go."

With shaking fingers he could hardly button his shirt or tie his shoes. He fled from the place into the street in panic.

* * *

It would have been the end of it, and everything would have been fine, except for one thing which made the situation incomplete and therefore unfinished and therefore a dangerously, damagingly lingering one. He could not stop thinking about Harrison. Or, at least, his body could not stop. And whenever his body thought about Harrison he became furiously sexually aroused.

When he went up to Harrison at The Web the next night when he was standing at the bar, Harrison snubbed him. It made sense. What else could he do? Andrew had walked out on him last night, left him high and dry. He was not a shrink or an eleemosynary institution for confused faggots. And he did not need serial blue balls. So he turned his back. It made sense.

But Andrew said, "I'm really sorry about last night, and I want to try it again."

"What the hell do you think I am?" Harrison turned from the torso and said.

"I know," Andy said. "I freaked out."

"What's it to me?" Harrison said. "I don't force people to be with me, but once they do choose to be, I expect they want to, that they know what they are doing."

"I'm really sorry," Andy said, "but I can't get you out of my mind."

"What do you want from me?" Harrison said, amusement and disdain expressing themselves in his voice and on his face. "Do you even know?"

"I'm not sure I do," Andy said, "but I know I can't get you out of my mind."

"Tell you what," Max said. "I'll give you a second try, but there have to be some stipulations."

"Stipulations?" Andrew said.

"Stipulations," Max repeated. "You know what that means?"

"I ought to," Andy said. "I'm a lawyer."

"So much the better," Max said. "Stipulations."

"Complete obedience, complete passivity, unconditional surrender."

He sounded like the very devil extending his most alluring possibilities.

And Andrew said he'd sign the contract. He meant it metaphorically, but the words felt eerie.

"Go home, now," Max said.

"What?" Andrew said not expecting that.

"Go home, now," Max repeated.

"But I thought..."

"There's no need for you to think," Max said, gently, consolingly, as if speaking to a confused child.

* * *

"But nothing happened," Andrew said hoping that would be enough. It was almost true, too.

It was not enough.

Miriam crushed her cigarette out in the seashell ashtray on her desk and exhaled a cloud of pungent smoke at the same time.

"What happened happened inside you," she said. "Whatever actually transpired is not important. What's important is..."

"My god," Andrew shouted. "You want to control every electrical impulse that tingles through me."

"I thought we had come to the point where you were able to acknowledge responsibility for your own behavior."

He took a deep breath and he felt the isolation in his heart that he had been damned with from birth. And every time it had been succoured, it was only temporary. But isolation was solid ground. Everybody else was a phantom you had to watch out for.

He moped around the house when he was not at work.

But at work, he felt himself in another world, free in the solitary of his active mind, formulating doctrines and making sense of human action through the mediating grill of the law, which, it seemed to him, was the only thing able to make experience sensible.

"I don't know what to do with you," she said.

He shuddered inside and held the ears of his soul to keep his tranquility undisturbed, but listened with the ears of his mind to try and figure out how he could improve and prove himself more satisfactory to her.

But sometimes he got tired of that and saw himself made up and costumed, serving in a candlelit chamber a beautiful boy who adored him, to whom he had surrendered his very soul.

* * *

He had in a stupid moment, given one of his e-mail addresses to Harrison.

"I will expect you this Friday at 9:30 at the bar at The Web."

That's all it said.

Andrew was inclined to ignore it but was drawn to linger over the message and read it again and again.

* * *

Miriam was irritable Friday morning as she was packing her small bag for a week in New Orleans where she was going for The National Book Association's annual convention. There were three titles, important books by important figures, a political memoir, a historical romance, and a critique of the policies of the present American government that she had particular interest in. She had shepherded them through printing and wanted to supervise how they were marketed, too.

She ought to have been excited. But she was uneasy. She reviewed the possible causes: anxiety about flying, fear that her books would not be well received, the same misgivings she always had as a mother leaving the children for any length of time. Sure, all those were possibilities. But, no, it was Andrew. Something was unsettled. She could not put her finger on it. But there was something disquieting in the air between them.

"Oh, well," she sighed and cleared her mind.

She was cheerful at parting when she got into the taxi for the airport, regretting that she had been irritable.

"Don't be too lonely without me. Don't let the kids run you ragged. Don't wear yourself out at work."

"Any do's?"

"Do think of me when..." She blushed. "You know when."

"And don't you exhaust yourself either," Andrew said. "The books are wonderful, and I know you'll be able to place them."

He left her and picked the kids up from school and took them to the health food restaurant for dinner and read the next chapter of Silas Marner to them before bed.

Once they were asleep, he mixed vodka and grapefruit juice over ice and sipped slowly as he looked over his e-mails.

As if in a trance, he changed his clothes to an old, torn pair of jeans and motorcycle boots.

He stood in front of the mirror trying to decide whether to put on a white sleeveless athletic shirt or a black one. He played idly with his nipples which seemed to stretch with undefined desire and stiffen.

He chose a square-topped white tight-fitting top.

"Margie," he said, speaking into his cell-phone. "It's Andrew. Is it ok if I go out for awhile and you keep an eye and ear open for the kids?"

Margie was a downstairs neighbor. She had a key to the apartment and often looked after the kids when Andrew or Miriam wanted to go out.

"Sure," she said. "Mind if I go through your DVD collection."

"Not at all, Marge."

"Or if I fall asleep on your couch?"

"Of course not. Thanks so much! There's some cold Raki in the fridge, too."

* * *

It was chilly enough that he could wear his leather jacket but still not so chilly that you couldn't leave it unzipped.

He was a little self-conscious about his nipples, but he also liked it, the way they pressed against the tight fabric. He breathed deeply and stretched his pecs upward.

The smell of beer hit him as he pushed his way into The Web and over to the bar.

"Hello," Andrew said to Max.

"I want a vodka martini," was all Harrison said, but it was clear he expected Andrew to bring it to him.

"Yes sir." Andrew had intended it to sound cheeky. But it didn't. It didn't sound anything out of the ordinary.

Andrew came back with the martini for Max and had gotten one for himself, too.

Harrison laughed and waved a finger.

"No, no," he said. "That is not done. You don't get anything for yourself without getting my permission first."

Andrew pulled a disbelieving face and Harrison said in a low voice, smiling, as if he were speaking of love, speaking slowly, "If you're going to be my bitch, you're going to follow my rules. Put your drink down next to mine. You drink if and when I say you do."

By the time he left the bar, Andrew, with Harrison's permission had drunk enough martinis to make him stagger giddily.

"You really ought to not drink so much if you can't hold it," Max laughed pressing him tightly to himself, steadying him as they walked.

"But you said I could," Andrew teased back, looking into his eyes and stumbling because he could not see what he was doing.

"And do you do everything I say?" Harrison asked with an amused grin.

"I do," Andrew said. "I absolutely do."

"How do you account for that?" Harrison taunted him.

"Because...just because."

Chapter 2

It really did not need to be New Orleans. Inside, it hardly was. There were identical hotel rooms painted Dresden green. There were long corridors gussied up to look like a street lined with bistros. There were Grand Ballrooms, one painted a butter color; the other, avocado. There were silvered hot plates at long buffets. But outside, it was New Orleans. She left the hotel and walked around the quarter glad that it had been preserved.

"Well, I'll be."

It was Richard Spurge from Harper's new religious division.

"You still mad at me?" he said falling in step beside her.

"I wasn't mad at you," she said. "I was just bothered that you were doing that. I remember you from college, Richard. Bertrand Russell: Why I Am Not A Christian. Thick paperback. Remember? It goes against everything you once...I mean..."

She stopped, blushed, stumbled verbally but picked herself up.

"You're, I don't know. You could do better. You... Books are for opening people's minds, not closing them. So I got angry because you know that, or you once did. And now, you're acting like you don't know it anymore."

"You know, you're beautiful," he said.

"When I get angry?"

"No, when you get thoughtful and analytic."

She looked at him suspiciously.

"No, I mean it. I know what you're saying. But you don't understand. Sometimes you have to go where they put you, or you don't get to go anywhere and you won't even have a home to stay in if all you want to do is just stay home."

She shook her head. Darkness and concern showed themselves in the furrows she made in her brow.

"Do you want an anti-depressant?"

"What?"

"Do you want an anti-depressant?" she repeated. "It's quite mild. I couldn't go on sometimes without. Might do you good."

"With you concord is an event within discord," she said carrying a bag of groceries into the house up the flagstone path.

Andrew preceded her by a few steps carrying the heavier bag and fumbling for his keys.

"I want a relationship," she said, "where, when discord happens -- I know it has to -- discord is an event inside concord, surrounded by it."

"What are you saying?" he said, pushing open the back door into the kitchen,

"I'm not going to go on like this." she said, standing by the table upon which she had just set down her bag.

"What do you want to happen?" He hesitated to ask. He was ashamed of the passivity he felt himself locked into.

"I want you to leave."

He looked impassively into the void.

"What about the kids?" It was not insistent. It was a murmur.

"When have you ever cared about them?" she said reproachfully. She still stood by the table, not moving. He wished she would so he could move. It was as if he could not move unless she released him.

"And now you're using them to make yourself look pitiable," she continued.

She spat the last words. There was nothing you could say. But everything was off. She was right. What could he argue? Discord was at the center of their marriage.

"Oh, don't look like that," she said. "I won't buy it. I know you're just waiting to go. But you're too guilty to say what you want. People like you are dangerous."

* * *

"You're somewhere," Max said, rubbing Andrew's shoulders.

"Yeah, I sure am."

"Tell me. What's going on? Where are you?"

"I'm on Thirty-Second Street."

"I don't understand."

"I'm living in a hotel on Thirty-Second Street."

"Not at home?"

"I have no home."

Silence.

"Miriam kicked me out."

"What will you do?"

"I don't know. The only thing that keeps me going is work."

"Thanks," Harrison said, teasingly.

"This – you and me – it doesn't feel real, Max. I'm sorry. I don't know. It's like kids playing follow the leader."

"You mean that?"

"Half and half. I mean it feels good but..."

"But now there's nothing keeping you from making it real."

"You mean?"

"What do you mean?"

"Are you talking about us living together?"

"Do you want to?"

"Me moving in here?"

"There's a spare room, although I think we should share the bedroom."

"But I'm supposed to feel bad."

"And you don't?"

"May I be honest?"

Max nodded assent.

"The thought of living with you excites me very much, of being that close to you. It's a feeling I've only experienced fleetingly. I never thought it was really meant for me."

"That means you don't have to go home. You can sleep here tonight."

"I'm free."

"You're home."

* * *

Richard Spurge took Miriam to a small restaurant on Mercer Street where they ate octopus and stuffed red peppers.

"I can't believe it," she said, fingering the stem of her glass of a 1988 Pommard.

"Can't believe what?" Richard said.

"That you do the kind of work you do."

"Oh, no," Spurge laughed, hoping to insure he could keep the subject floating rather than have it crash down all around them and blow up like a bomb.

"Don't worry," she said. "I could get used to going out like this."

He took her hand from across the table and put her fingers to his lips.

"I hope so," he said.

On Spring Street, she asked him to put her in a cab. When he protested, whimpering while pursing his lower lip and frowning, she said it was not that she would not sleep with him but that she would not sleep with him tonight.

* * *

"The future has already happened and we are moving towards it," Andrew said, passing the joint back to Max.

"We make the future and guide it towards us," Max contradicted him and then took a toke and held his breath.

"Oh, I don't know," Andrew said. "Does it matter?" He turned and looked at Harrison. The sky was dark and heavy. It was sure to snow.

"Have you heard from Miriam?"

"She does not answer my calls, and I'd just as soon not talk to her anymore."

"The children?"

"It's an expense I can bear."

"I mean not seeing them."

"They're ok. Richard's a nice man. He'll take good care of them, and with the monthly stipend I send plus the investments I've made for them, they'll each be able to go to college, and more."

"So now you are twenty-one again."

"Eighteen."

* * *

The Web was full of college students. Billie Holliday was on the juke box singing "It Was Just One of Those Things."

Derek was nervous. He was not comfortable standing in a bar hoping people would look at him and afraid, at the same time, that they would.

"You have not been doing this for long," Max said to him, touching his palm to the boy's cheek.

"No, sir," Derek said with a mid-western accent.

"Don't be nervous. You're very hot," Max said, pressing his palm against the young man's chest.

Derek blushed and dropped his eyes.

"Don't disappear," Max said, his palm dancing over the area of the boy's genitals.

"Say thank you," he said, as he cupped them in his palm.

"Thank you," Derek said, suppressing a giggle.

"Do you like him?" Max asked.

"He's very pretty," Andrew said. "I want to kiss him."

"I want to kiss him, too," Max said.

And he brought the boy to him and gave him a kiss full of his power. It made Derek shudder with desire. He wanted to be opened.

When Max let him go, Andrew did not wait but took his mouth with a delicate reach of his fingers and brought it to his and kissed him dreamily and long and languorously until the boy was helplessly dizzy with desire.

"Come," they said, leading him out of the bar.

"Who are you?" Harrison asked Derek once they were on the street and heading to his penthouse on Twenty-third Street.

"I was born in Kentucky. My father is a colonel in the army. My mother was a nurse but became a full-time housewife. We moved around, but we spent the last two years in Arizona. I'm studying theater at Columbia. Does that say enough?"

"Enough for now." Harrison smiled with a wink. "Theater!"

"My father doesn't like it. He wants me to go into the military."

Andrew took his other hand and kissed it gently, the upper side and then the open palm.

"But you know what you want," Max said.

The kid smiled grateful at the acknowledgement.

In bed, they stroked him and gazed at the opalescence of his flesh, and lost themselves in the voluptuous innocence of his fresh, spring-young body.

Andrew put his mouth to the boy's and felt swept towards him by the current of his breath. The ocean of his blood beat on the shore of his desire and with his kisses he swam inside Derek.

Derek held on to him and writhed, lost in the amplitude of his own sensations.

As he writhed like that, Harrison slid one hand beneath his jeans and slowly worked one finger into his granite ass. With the other hand he went under his t shirt and felt the warmth radiate from his chest. He took hold of one nipple between his thumb and first finger and slowly, gently began to knead it. His finger dug deeper into Derek; he increased the force with which he rubbed his nipples.

The boy saw the cloudless blue sky of Arizona rolling forever in translucent azure billows.

End of the 7th Story

Gay Romance Erotica

SENSUAL SURRENDER

GIDEON ELLIOT

Sensual Surrender
By: Gideon Elliot

It is hard to explain this. Shit! It is simply hard to talk about it. It can look crazy. Maybe it is.

We had without my noticing become very serious about what had once been a diversion. Julian pretended to be my master and I pretended to surrender to him. I was submissive and his slave. It really was very hot, sexually more arousing than anything I had ever experienced before. But it was a game. Really. That's how it started.

He would pretend to hypnotize me and I would pretend to fall under his spell and into a trance. And there were times when we really could get into it. Then we started raising the ante.

* * *

One night we went to hear the B minor Mass at Carnegie Hall with some friends. Afterwards we sat around in an all-night place, and with no prompting from us, the conversation turned to a current political scandal. A respected political figure, respected, at least, until the scandal broke, was photographed at an airport going to Guadeloupe with a male hustler. His defense was that it was not him. But there was the picture, and no one had any doubt that it was him, and that was before his male escort began to give rather detailed interviews all over the place.

From there we got onto the subject of hidden sexual identity, of sexual power and sexual surrender.

"It's not enough to be in love?" Doris said.

"It's not a matter of love," Tony said.

"No, it's about power," Kendra said.

"Exactly," Julian said.

But I was yawning. I was not able to suppress the yawns. I tried at first and then gave up trying to. It was late. I'd worked all day and, just my luck, I'd have to go into the office Saturday morning. So being the gentleman he is, Julian made excuses for us, as our friends remained behind, sitting in a corner booth longing for cigarettes and drinking one brandy more than they would have had they been allowed to smoke.

* * *

The street running along the park, Central Park West, was quiet and tree covered. They walked for a while saying nothing, breathing deeply, holding hands.

* * *

"You know I wonder if this stuff we're doing" – I knew he would know what I was referring to – "is not working a little bit."

"What do you mean?" Julian said.

"Well," I said, "I kind of feel your presence enveloping me all the time and I feel like I want your approval. I kind of feel," I stumbled with embarrassment, but pressed myself to finish the sentence, "like I want to submit to you all the time, to be in a hierarchical relationship with you. It goes against my belief in equality."

"No kidding," Julian said. "How does it feel?"

"It drives me crazy with desire – and shame."

"It gets me excited just to hear you speak that way," he said.

"Really?"

"Really."

Julian hesitated before he spoke. "Being your master turns me on."

And that was it. I didn't even have to ask. He knew what I wanted, and so did he.

* * *

When this conversation transpired, we had not been living together long, perhaps three months. We had not originally moved in together. I answered his ad for a roommate and he had no problem with me and I moved in. Then we discovered each other.

Of course looks were involved. We are both healthy young guys who are into keeping their good looks looking good and care about fitness, style, and clothing. We did not go to a gym but we began working out together at home, old fashioned calisthenics enhanced with twenty pound weights. And it did not seem to bother either of us to see the other one in a state of semi-dress or complete undress on the way to the shower, etc., or so I thought until one morning that issue changed the dynamic of our relationship.

Julian smiled at me in the kitchen and said "Good morning" – it was around the third week I'd been his roommate – as we met there for awakening through coffee, each emerging from his room. Julian was a beautiful eyeful in a snowy white tank top that highlighted his attention commanding nipples and a pair of silky black briefs that showed him off beautifully. I usually wore nothing. The house was well heated.

"I'm not sure I approve of that," he said. He was not smiling.

"Of what?" I said.

"Of you walking around like that. It's too free. Cover up a little, cover the genital region. Just a little bikini type thing, something. You ought to show some modesty."

I was not sure I was really hearing what I was hearing. "It bothers you that I don't have clothes on?" I said, trying to orient myself.

"It is not a matter of what bothers me," he said.

"What is it then?" I asked, puzzled.

"That's just what it is about," he said without raising his voice but fixing my attention. "You ought to know without my telling you. You ought to be able to sense it. But I've noticed that you don't have a sensitivity for other people. You are always focused front and center on yourself."

I did not think so, but what good would it do to object and have him overrule me? He was unshakably sure that his comprehension of me surpassed my own. Arguing was not going to get us anywhere. The more I asked, as I tried to understand him, the more annoyed and angry he got at me. I tried, therefore, not to rebut or deny whatever he said. I tried to conciliate and be as agreeable as I could. But it did not work, either.

The only thing I could do then was withdraw. That is what I did. I went to the bathroom, washed my hands and face, and took a pair of low rise black briefs from the closet there, and got into them.

I had left my coffee in the kitchen. Julian was leaning against the table and looking out the window. He turned to look at me when I came back. Did he momentarily smile? I think so.

Did it affect me surprisingly? Yes, it did. It made me...can you understand how I use the word?...it made me flash. Does that convey anything? A quivering shot of color effervesced inside me. I saw it and I felt a tremor loosening way deep down. I hardly knew what was going on.

He was still stern, but the animosity was gone, I could tell -- along with his way of making you feel not that you are not there but that your being there is of no consequence to him. I didn't care. It still felt good just to be around him.

"You look good," he said, his way of acknowledging the storm had passed. "It's very sexy."

"Thanks," I said, having no right, or reason, really, to be ungracious if he was not being officious. And the truth is my heart was fluttering, excited by his attention.

"Touch your right nipple with your right index finger," he said.

"What!" I shrieked.

"Shut up and touch your nipple," he said, letting his grin explode.

I did as he said, although I could not help laughing.

He stood up and walked over to me and took me around the waist and pulled me to him so that the outlines of our hard cocks were rubbing.

"Is this alright with you?" he said looking directly at me.

"Yes," I said, beginning to giggle again and dropping my eyes.

"Stop giggling," he said.

That's how we started, and from there...

He made me look back up and kissed me very gently and sweetly, easing me into his power. He stroked my chest almost without touching it, making the nipples dart out to him like screaming teenage girls reaching for a hot performer. I arched my back and was lost when his lips fell on mine and claimed me. His breath was a new air and I breathed it as if it were pure oxygen. He held me in his kiss and we both became more violent. We clawed at each other and felt the cold hard strength of our muscles pressing against each other, as if each of us was determined to push his way into the other.

Then he fingered me and held me there. I knew what I wanted. He knew I did. It was what he wanted me to want and played his finger inside me in such ways as to make sure I continued to want it more and more. He smiled at me and he stopped. He kissed my nose.

"I've got to go to work," he said, his voice low and smooth. "More later."

I was dazed and insatiably hungry for him, and just when I thought I was going to explode in an uncontrollable series of combustions, he was gone and I crashed back into myself and went around all day not knowing what had hit me.

As our time together grew, however, I think we've gotten to know each other and to build up our trust in each other pretty well. Each time I thought about the extent to which he exercised power over me, I became very excited. I realized that I liked the way his power felt and that I wanted to show him, to have him see it, to affect him with my admiration and esteem.

I had to tell him, and I was embarrassed and frightened, embarrassed at getting off on being submissive, and frightened that he would take it as unappealing self-contempt and withdraw from me and become inaccessible. But that did not matter as much as my self-imposed absolute obligation not to hide anything from Julian. And it did not happen.

That Friday night after the concert, when we left Doris and Kendra and Brian and Tony at the bar and walked home along Central Park West, I found the nerve.

There was a big moon, the air was fresh and clear, and I found myself unable to keep what concerned Julian from him.

After I told him about my fantasy of being his slave for real, on our walk home along Central Park West that night, I felt a weight lift off me. I felt better than that: he did not turn from me but admitted that the idea excited him.

It was then, too, that I said that I wanted him to put me in a trance. He was a psychologist.

"I don't do that," he said.

"Well even if you didn't, you could," I said.

"What do you mean even if I didn't?"

"When you consult on advertising campaigns, aren't you helping your clients consider what best is going to put the greatest number of people into a trance? That's what advertising is."

"Maybe you're right," Julian said. "But that's not the issue."

"What is the issue?" I said, unsure whether I was confused or he was being difficult.

"Whether I want to," he said. "How much I want to pay the kind of attention I'd have to."

"Do you want me to beg?" I said. "I will."

He mussed my hair and smiled. "No, you don't have to beg. But it does turn me on, to think of you like that."

That's when my lessons in subordination began.

Lessons in subordination?

Exactly. It is not easy becoming a submissive person even if submission turns you on. And now it became no longer difficult for me to admit just how much it did turn me on, does turn me on. But being turned on by the idea, by the fantasy of being submissive and actually being submissive are two different things.

* * *

He twisted my nipples and gazed into my eyes. He slapped my hands away when I reached to touch his nipples. I moaned and swooned like a fool. I longed to suck his nipples. The more frustrated my desire, the stronger it became until I was vanquished by confusion, unable to distinguish between him and myself. I wanted him inside me and I began to beg. I knelt at his feet. I felt my knees could not support me. I touched the arch of his foot with my forehead. I looked up at him in supplication and took both of his palms in my hands and kissed them.

"Stand up," he said.

Trembling, I did.

"Sleep in the bedroom you used to use from now on and be available whenever I summon you."

"Yes, sir," I said.

I knew I would honor his decisions and follow his instructions, willingly, despite the tinge of grief that colored my being put at a distance. I had lost him. Strange, just when he had agreed to embody my fiercest and most repressed desire.

I did not know if he was angry at me and kicking me out of his bed and ending our relationship or by his banishment of me, beginning a new kind of relationship and serving my wishes. But it was not my place to figure anything out.

The rituals we devised, rituals of domination, of deference, and of submission were really ways we found of decorating a life that was pretty usual. I say we because, despite my subordination, I initiated aspects of our relationship by the way I presented myself.

* * *

Julian was not in private practice or part of a hospital. He actually was, as I have said, a consultant who had established a thriving clientele, among which he counted several of the largest and most well know firms, not only advertising firms but the personnel departments of many corporations.

He had a small office in the Empire State Building. From there he traveled around the city and sometimes beyond, to the Midwest and the West Coast when business required it.

His field was called Consumer Motivation and he worked on advertising campaigns for consumer products, corporations, and, especially, once money was set flowing by the U.S. Supreme Court in the Citizens United decision, for political candidates and political issues. In other words, he went to the office every day, like most other men in his socio-economic class.

I had just gotten tenure and I was teaching Shakespeare and Milton at NYU.

I often felt humiliated by the intensity of my need for him and immeasurably injured when he dismissed me without any recognition that there was a very special bond joining us together, when he paid little or no attention to me and showed little or no affection towards me. The worst was that it really seemed like he was not even trying to make a point by ignoring me, freezing me out in order to show the extent of his anger at me or displeasure with me, but that, simply, he had truly become oblivious to my existence and got on fine without me.

I hurt and attempted to remain stable and cheerful and lock my anxiety and desire away. It became routine for me to fall into painful despondency from time to time, to look at him and feel rebuffed.

"But it is not love," he responded after I told him how I felt.

"What is it then?"

"Pride," Julian said.

"Pride?"

"And it has to be broken, quickly and once and for all. Afterwards, you will feel much better, like after a triple by-pass." He smiled and remained unapproachable.

The doorbell rang. A young man holding one beautiful long-stem red rose asked me when I opened the door if Julian lived here. Before I could answer, Julian appeared, stripped of his shirt.

"Marcel," he said. "Come in and welcome." He took the flower from him and embraced him, kissed him, but only with so much display as to suggest there would be a later when they were alone that…

"I will not be five minutes, and I'll be ready. Come with me while I finish dressing." They did not even snub me. I was just not there for them.

They left; I was alone, and there was nothing I could do. Whether I sobbed or moaned or wished in my inner heart to be caressed, or condemned the moon, it did not matter. I hardly existed. I existed hardly. In words, only in words! Empty words!

Despite myself I waited. I waited for him to come home. It was impossible for me to be easy until he was home and we were together alone, even if he was angry.

"You broke something," he said when he got home a little after three, angry that I had waited up for him.

He pulled off his tie and tossed his jacket on the couch.

"I loved you," he said. "But you couldn't feel what that means. Now I use you. And that turns you on."

"You don't love me?" I said.

"Not anymore. How can love and domination occupy the same space?"

"Julian," I said as I moved forward in supplication, risking taking him in my arms when he pushed me away even before I could touch him.

I lunged at him to cling. He pushed me away again with disdain and walked out of the room, into his bedroom, and turned the key in the lock.

I do not know how long it was before I began to cry. At first it was fake, self-pity, a show, but after some churning the anguish caught and turned to grief and I began sobbing for real. It was then that the door opened and Julian walked into the room and got into bed beside me and held me to him and embraced me as I cried in his arms.

He kissed my tears and his fingers played slowly spider wanderings on my neck. My sobs turned to deep breaths when he put his lips to mine. He made his way down my back with the same spider dance of his fingers until he brushed me where he enters me and I shivered with excitement.

* * *

The December night, the last night of the year, began before the afternoon was over and Jordan stepped out of the shower and surveyed his clean-shaven naked body in the full-length mirror, examining himself for imperfections and pleased to find favor in his own eyes and eager to present himself to Julian, a Christmas gift as it were ready to remain always ready beneath his tree. Julian, however, was not there to receive his present. For most of December and until the end of February he was out on the West Coast working on a series of projects.

Jordan dried himself with the thick towel, rubbing his chest more than it needed to be dry but hardly enough to diminish the longing, the longing that swelled like an erotic miasma clinging to and encircling his nipples like a halo.

To these nipples he then applied a solid coating of bronze eye shadow and saw them stiffen when he raised his arms in the ritual of styling his hair.

Snow was still falling and the streets and roads were covered with snow and most of the cars had vanished from the roads, their pride and mobility curtailed by a simple operation of nature.

Jordan stood by the curb wearing a pair of thigh high boots and wrapped in a thick fur coat, worn over very little, a black thong, a pearl necklace, bronze-tinted nipples. He was protected by an umbrella held over him by the doorman who also held the door of the cab that he had summoned open for him.

"Happy New Year," he said, intoxicated with the gay merriment of the last night of the year and by the annual gift of $500.00 that Jordan had given him in the lobby.

"Happy New Year to you, too, Mr. Jenkins," Jordan said, and the cab took its way cautiously through the park to Madison Avenue.

The radio was on, but rather extraordinarily, the driver was listening to the eighth string quartet by Shostakovich, and Jordan was unable not to comment on it. But the driver took offense, perceiving condescension where Jordan would have denied there was any.

Guilty for the unintended misstep and a little humiliated that what he thought would establish a friendly connection, a camaraderie of appreciation became the grounds for animosity, he gave the driver a five dollar tip, but it did not ease his discomfort. If anything, Jordan thought as he made his way under the steel and glass deco awning, it emphasized the distance between the two of them.

The doorman poised on a stool at his small lectern desk inside, pointed to the elevator on the left side of the wainscoted hallway. Four E he said without being asked. Jordan took the few marble steps to the ornate, waiting elevator. He kept his coat closed. He was alone in the elevator and was shivering…

End of the 8th Story

Hank Brooks

Forgiven

The Ghost of Jed Harding

Gay Romance Erotica

Forgiven

The Ghost of Jed Harding

By: Hank Brooks

Jed Harding and Isaiah Hauser were classmates at the United States Military Academy in West Point, NY. They met on their first day there in August, 1857, when they were assigned side by side cots in the Plebe barracks. The cots were assigned alphabetically. They became instant friends even though they had little in common except that they were both entering The Academy, and seeking careers in the military.

Jed grew up on a plantation in Georgia. His family owned over two hundred slaves who worked tirelessly in the cotton fields, and in the mansion he called his little home. He had two younger sisters, and his father was a widower. His mother had died in a small pox plague about ten years earlier. He was a handsome lad of British descent. He stood six feet tall; his hair was a dark blond and slightly wavy; his eyes were blue; and his body reflected the truth that he had worked side by side with the slaves in the fields when it was necessary to do so. Even though he treated his slaves well, they were still disposable chattel in his mindset.

Isaiah was born to a farming family also. He was of German descent, and a true Yankee from Connecticut, where his family grew tobacco. He wasn't poor, but he was far from rich. Still, compared to many of his friends, he was a person of means. He looked nothing like Jed except for the brawn. He was 6'2" tall; his hair was black and straight and fell to his neck; his eyes were brown and seductive. Seductive eyes did him no good at all. He came to The Academy an eighteen year old virgin.

As they made up their cots, they introduced each other and when they shook hands, they knew that they would be friends. Jed couldn't wait for them to shower together. He was anxious to check out his new friend, and he was not disappointed. Isaiah was about five fat inches of flaccid beauty. His foreskin was skimpy and Jed liked that. Jed himself was about a quarter of an inch shorter, but just as fluffy, and he grew to about seven inches. He had too much foreskin and only about half of it retreated when he was hard. Isaiah's ass was round and bubbly, and Jed hungered to put his cock as far up that ass as he could. For the first time that he could remember, he pictured Isaiah's cock entering his own ass and even his mouth. He was smitten with desire. He started to grow hard in the shower and forced himself to turn away and think of terrible things.

The Plebes had no break from their arduous routines until Thanksgiving. Jed lived too far away to go home for so short a furlough. He would not be returning to Georgia until Christmas break. Isaiah begged him to come home with him. Of course, he accepted immediately.

It was a short coach ride to Poughkeepsie, New York, then a ferry ride across the Hudson River, and another coach ride to Greenwich, Connecticut. Isaiah's father, Hans, would be picking them up at the coach station in Greenwich, and transporting them to his farm some twenty miles away. They would be leaving The Academy early Wednesday morning and arriving home late Wednesday afternoon.

Hans embraced his son warmly, and Jed was jealous. His father never showed him any affection. When the coach approached the Hausers' home, Jed was surprised at how small it looked next to his magnificent plantation home, but when he entered, he was struck by the cozy, inviting feeling he felt. The house had only four bedrooms. Isaiah's parents occupied the largest room, and his two younger brothers had the two smallest bedrooms. Isaiah's bedroom was smaller than his parents' and larger than each of his brothers.

"We'll be rooming together," he told Jed. "Come, I'll show you my room and we can freshen up before dinner." The room contained a single size bed that was no bigger than the cots they slept on at The Academy. Jed was overjoyed, even when Isaiah said, "If we're too uncomfortable, I can sleep on the floor."

"No way," Jed thought.

While they were changing from their uniforms into civilian attire, farm attire at that, Zachariah and Benjamin burst in on them. They had just come in from doing their chores. Zach was sixteen and Ben was fifteen. They wrestled Isaiah to the floor and played with him lovingly. Again Jed grew jealous. He could never play with two younger sisters like this. When everyone settled down, and introductions were made, they went downstairs to meet Isaiah's mother, Greta.

Jed was expecting to meet a short plump hausfrau. Imagine his shock to meet a tall, attractive, blue eyed blonde. She did not look much older than Isaiah. She and Isaiah hugged until Jed thought they would break each other's bones. Much to his surprise, she gave Jed a big hug also, and a kiss on the cheek.

"Isaiah has written so much about you," she said. "I am so delighted to meet you. Now all you men can get out of my kitchen and dinner will be ready in a few minutes."

When they were in the living room, Jed asked how many acres the family owned.

"Eighty," Hans answered proudly.

"That's wonderful," Jed replied. "We have about fifteen hundred. How many slaves does it take to run the place?"

Hans and his sons turned white.

"Good heavens man. We run the place ourselves. At harvest time, I hire farm hands from amongst our neighbors. Some men even join us from the city to make extra money." Jed found this unfathomable, but wisely he said nothing.

Greta made a stick to your ribs, Yankee winter dinner: New England clam chowder, pot roast, home-made bread, apple pie and hot tea. The weather had dropped a good twenty degrees in the past hour and the family appreciated what she had cooked. The house had chilled considerably and Hans and his sons added wood to the several fireplaces, and they stoked the fires. It was Jed's first time away from Georgia. He knew it would be much colder than at home, but still he was surprised. He also realized that winter had not really set in yet, and he wasn't looking forward to what lay ahead. The efforts of the family had considerably warmed the lower level of the house, but Hans said, "Be sure you all have extra blankets tonight." He looked at Jed. "The only fireplace upstairs is in the master bedroom," he explained. Jed was delighted.

After dinner, Jed and Isaiah were questioned by the family, who wanted to know what life was like at The Academy. Jed kept sending Isaiah telepathic messages. He was afraid they would talk all night. Finally Isaiah got the message. "Jed and I have been up since before dawn," he said. "Would you all please excuse us? I, for one, need to get some sleep."

The cadets put on coats and went outside to use the outhouse. "I hate chamber pots," Isaiah proclaimed. "I only use them as a last resort. I have a couple in *our* room." Jed barely heard him. All he could think about was that in just a few short minutes they would be lying in bed together.

When they entered Isaiah's room they found a basin filled with warm soapy water and some dry towels.

"Your mom's a wonder," Jed said. "She thinks of everything." Jed surprised Isaiah when he stripped off his long johns and washed his balls and cock as well as the rest of him. Then he put his underwear back on. Isaiah was embarrassed into doing the same.

The bed was small and they were indeed forced to lie close to each other. Jed loved it, but Isaiah was uncomfortable. The silence in the room was very dramatic, especially since the two friends usually talked non-stop.

Finally Isaiah said, "I'm glad we got the extra blankets. It's nice and warm under here."

"It's too warm for me," Jed lied. "I'm taking off my long johns." He jumped out of bed, stripped naked, and climbed back into the warm bed. The lack of space permitted him to push up against Isaiah's body. Now Isaiah may have been a virgin, but he knew the feel of a hard cock pushing up against his thigh.

He froze, not knowing what he should do. Then he thought better of making a thing of it. Young men of eighteen got hard all the time. It didn't mean a thing. Why he had a boner himself right now.

"Why don't you strip also?" Jed asked. "Our body heat will keep us warmer than any blankets."

Isaiah didn't have to be told twice. In seconds, both boys were naked, and now instinct took over. They were facing each other and Jed's lust made him throw caution to the wind. He pushed hard against his best friend and began to rub his boner against Isaiah's hard cock. As he did so, they both began to purr.

Suddenly Jed ducked under the blankets, and Isaiah felt the strangest, most wonderful sensation. His cock was warm and wet. It took a few seconds to realize that Jed had taken his cock into his mouth, and was running his tongue up and down the underside of the hardest ever, biggest boner, Isaiah had ever had. He was unfamiliar with an orgasm. When it started to build in his body, he was scared, but it felt so good, he would not have stopped it if he could. He figured if Jed was trying to kill him, he'd have to explain his dead body in the morning.

Jed could sense that Isaiah was near and he sucked harder. Isaiah came gushing in Jed's mouth. He started to scream and forced himself to stifle it. The walls in the house were paper thin.

Isaiah was afraid to move. He had no idea what had happened to him, but he did know that he wanted more, and he wanted to give Jed the same pleasure. In a few minutes they were lying side by side again. Their bodies were pushed together and Jed put his lips on Isaiah's lips. It was Isaiah's first kiss, and he didn't know what to make of it, but he liked what he felt. Soon Jed's tongue was forcing open his lips, and their tongues were tickling each other. Isaiah was breathless. He was even more shocked when Jed whispered, "I love you, Isaiah. Please fuck me."

Isaiah was overwhelmed by Jed's admission of love, but he had no idea how a man fucks another man.

"I'll do whatever you want, but you'll have to show me how," he told Jed.

"Please," Jed pleaded "love me too."

"I want you to let me suck your cock too," Isaiah said. "Then you can teach me how to fuck."

That night, after recovering from the joy of fellatio, they fucked each other twice, using only spit as a lubricant. In the early morning hours, they lay huddled together. As he fell asleep, Isaiah whispered, "I love you too, Jed."

Jed almost didn't want to go home for Christmas and for the two week summer break, but he had to. He would have preferred to have stayed behind with Isaiah and to make love with him. It got easier when they were upper classmen. They had many weekends off. They would go into the nearest town. One of them would book a single room at some hotel, and they would make love all weekend.

They were due to graduate on May 15, 1861. One month before graduation, Fort Sumter was fired on, and the long expected War Between the States began.

"I have to go home," Jed announced.

"What about us? This isn't fair," Isaiah sobbed. "I love you. This conflict has nothing to do with us."

"Have you learned nothing from these past four years? We have to put country and duty above all personal considerations. I just received a wire from my father instructing me to go to Clarksville, Tennessee. My commission in the Confederate army is assured. Apparently we are amassing our troops there as a focal point for an invasion of the north."

Jed grabbed Isaiah and kissed him passionately. 'Stay safe, my love. We'll meet after the war no matter who wins." He ran off leaving Isaiah sobbing.

Two weeks later while a good hunk of the confederate army was amassing in Clarksville, they were beset upon in the middle of the night by almost five thousand Union soldiers. The surprise attack decimated The Rebel stronghold. Among the dead was a young officer named Jed Harding.

The ghost of Jed Harding was convinced that Isaiah Hauser had betrayed him. He could not get any rest, and he devoted his eternity to taking revenge on Isaiah's descendants.

2013

Carlton Hauser made an important family decision. He took a semester off from Yale to do so. Shortly after he inherited his four time great grandfather's house in Greenwich, CT, he decided to raze it to the ground and sell the property. The house had been the site of where all his ancestors, and he himself, had been born, and where they all lived as children. But the house was almost one hundred and fifty years old. There had been too much renovation and band aid repairs to save the old place. It needed to be totally torn down and rebuilt. Now it was a question of whether he should throw good money after bad, or not.

There was another consideration in making the decision. Every one of his ancestors had died in this house. The deaths occurred under mysterious circumstances, shortly after their wives gave birth to their first son. It was deemed to be a terrible family curse, but every succeeding Hauser said that it was pure nonsense and lived, or rather died, to rue their words. Carlton knew that he could live here safely, but decided not to tempt the fates. He knew that he would never have a son.

On the evening before the bulldozers were due to arrive, Carlton went through the house one more time to assure himself that nothing of value, sentimental or monetary, was left behind. He thought he spotted something on a shelf high up in the armoire in the master bedroom. Sometime over the years, the armoire had been affixed to the wall, and so it had become part of the house, and would be destroyed along with it.

He reached up and was surprised to find a dusty old journal on the top shelf. He wondered how it could have been missed by his father, and all the grandfathers before him, but he could not come to any clarifying conclusions. He himself would never live as a married adult in this house, so he could not imagine how it could have been missed by so many fastidious housekeepers.

He dusted the book off with his handkerchief, and concluded his search of the house. When he was satisfied that nothing was left, he went back to the small apartment he had rented in Greenwich. The book was tucked under his arm. When he got home, he dusted the book further with a clean rag, and laid it carefully on his bedside table. Then he showered to wash away all the grime he had acquired in the decaying house.

He was too tired to read the book that night, and he decided to tackle it in the morning. He fell asleep more quickly than he had ever fallen asleep before. In his sleep he had a vivid dream. It was so real that when he awoke, he remembered every detail and every word.

A handsome young soldier in a confederate uniform got into bed with him, and kissed him full on the lips. He could feel the kiss, warm and wet, and he got an erection. The officer spoke to him. You look just like your forefather, Isaiah. It hurts me to see harm come to you. You are the end of his line. The curse will end with you. The apparition kissed him again and he had an orgasm.

The orgasm woke him up. He had to get out of bed and change the bed sheet. He was very disturbed by the dream, and the fact that at the age of twenty-one he had a wet dream. This time he could not fall asleep so quickly. He tossed and turned most of the night. He finally fell asleep about four in the morning and slept until eight.

When he awoke, he clearly saw the young officer sitting on the edge of his bed and smiling at him. He blinked his eyes and the ghost was gone. He was sure that he was imagining it all, and at some level he was disappointed. The young man was so handsome. If he was real, Carlton would have made a move on him.

After breakfast, Carlton made himself comfortable on the sofa and opened the journal. The script was old fashioned, and each letter was executed with a flourish. He found it difficult to read, but he didn't give up. Somehow as he stared at the script, it got clearer and clearer to him. He read the first entry.

April 15, 1861: Yesterday the War Between the States began at last. I fear that I am the first casualty. I lost my beloved Jed, not to gunfire, but to separation. He has been summoned to Clarksville, somewhere in Tennessee, to receive his commission in the Confederate Army. I am certain that should we both survive this conflict, we will find each other after the war. We love each other too much to be separated forever. I have no idea how I am to survive without him. How can I engage in combat knowing that Jed might be at the other end of my rifle. I may die of a broken heart before any rebel bullet can pierce it.

Carlton could not believe that his ancestor Isaiah Hauser had written these words. Fuck! He thought. He was gay. Why didn't he wait for Jed? Why did he marry? He read on, hoping that the journal would answer these questions.

April 22, 1861: Graduation was moved up three weeks because of the war. I received my commission today, and all of us new officers were assembled in the dining room at The Academy. We were addressed by a general, who was more than a little drunk. He told us that a spy in rebel territory had informed the proper authorities that the rebels were massing in Clarksville for an invasion of Union territory. I grew sick. I wanted to vomit. I knew that Jed was among them.

He went on to tell us that we would be among the officers leading the surprise attack on the rebels before they could attack us. I wanted to die, but I had to hide my emotions, lest my fellow officers attribute my feelings to cowardice. I cheered as loudly as they did when the general concluded his speech.

When we were dismissed, we went back to clear out our barracks. The best part of our clothing would be shipped home. We kept only our combat gear, some of which we were newly issued.

May 15, 1861: Today should have been my graduation day. Instead it was the worst day of my life. At the crack of dawn, we fell upon hundreds of rebels in a camp in Clarksville. Most of them were still asleep and never knew what hit them as our bayonets pierced their hearts. I did not kill a single rebel. Instead I searched every face looking for my beloved in a useless quest to keep him safe. By nightfall the few of them remaining alive surrendered, and we returned to our camp with the prisoners. Jed was not among them, and I feared the worst. Optimistically I prayed that he had not been in the camp at all.

May 28, 1861: Our high ranking officers have intercepted a list of rebel dead at Clarksville. As I feared, Jed was among them. I want to die, but I must go on. I am too full of grief to write anything further today.

December 14, 1863: I hate this war. It took away my life, my Jed. I haven't seen my family in two years. My brothers are in the war. Every day I pray for their safety. I hate living in a tent in an open field. I fear I will get sick and die, if a rebel doesn't get me first. I would welcome death. Perhaps there is a heaven and I will be reunited with my love. I have no need to live another day in this hell.

June 11, 1866: The war has been over for some months now. I was wounded in the leg in the final hours of the war, and I will limp badly for the rest of my days. I have been discharged from the army with a small pension. My father has arranged a bride for me. I will meet her tomorrow and we are to be wed in a fortnight. I fear that I might not be able to perform my husbandly duties, but I will give it the same effort I gave to the army, when my heart was never in it. Is there a man on this earth more tortured than I am?

June 13, 1866: Molly is a beautiful young girl. I must admit I like her very much, and I think she likes me.

June 1, 1867: In just a day or two I shall be a father. For the first time since Jed was torn from my arms, I feel that I may have something to live for.

June 5, 1867: Today, unto me, a son was born. I named him Jed.

Here the journal ended, but Carlton knew why. Isaiah was thrown from his horse and killed a few days later. It was considered a freak accident. Isaiah was a cavalry officer, and a wonderful horseman. So how could this have happened? In his head, Carlton heard a voice say *THE CURSE!*

For some reason, Carlton could relate to his distant ancestor who was as gay as he. He lay prone on the sofa, closed his eyes, and began to cry for Isaiah's loss. He prayed that someday he could have a love as deep as Jed's had been.

He imagined that he heard someone else crying. He listened and he was certain he did. He opened his eyes, and there was the young rebel kneeling on the floor next to the sofa. He was as solid as any living person Carlton knew.

The two sobbing men reached out and touched each other.

"You're real," Carlton said. "Are you Jed?"

Jed nodded. "He was innocent all along," he sobbed. "How could I ever have believed differently. Forgive me, Isaiah, and ask all your progeny to forgive me as well." He laid his head on Carlton's chest and Carlton began to stroke his hair.

"I can only manifest for an hour or so," Jed said. "Please make love to me, Carlton. You look just like your four time great grandfather, Isaiah. That is, except for one thing. You are circumcised."

Carlton laughed. "Yes, yes, Jed let's make love. Come with me into the bedroom." When Jed stood up he was as naked as the day he was born. Carlton quickly shed his boxers, and they fell naked together on Carlton's bed.

"What did you and Isaiah like to do the most?" Carlton asked.

"We would get each other as hard as possible with our tongues and then we would fuck each other."

"That sounds perfect." Carlton twisted around into a sixty nine position. He went right to work, and ghost or no ghost, he felt Jed's hot warm tongue bathing his throbbing cock. Even more incredible, he could taste Jed as clearly as any other guy he had ever been with. He even had a little struggle pushing back Jed's foreskin.

Later he unloaded easily into Jed's man hole. When Jed fucked him, he was aware when Jed had his orgasm, but he felt no body fluid entering his gut. He did feel Jed getting softer and falling out of him. They lay perfectly still for awhile, basking in the afterglow.

"I have to go now," Jed announced. "I've stayed too long seeking revenge, and it was all for nothing. I've got to go find Isaiah and all his descendants and ask them to forgive me. Oh Carlton, I can see a great white light beckoning to me. I really have to go now."

Jed got out of bed. He was draped in a beautiful white robe and his essence glowed with a bright white aura. Carlton stared after him in total awe, as Jed slowly faded away.

"I hope you find Isaiah," he yelled at the disappearing ghost. "I hope you find all of them, and when you do, please tell each one that I love him."

End of the 9th Story

HANK BROOKS

Love, Sex, Religion

DIVINE GUILT

Gay Romance

Divine Guilt

By: Hank Brooks

I lay on my stomach, almost not breathing. I was waiting patiently, expectantly, for Mark's cock to enter my virgin ass. Moments ago his greasy finger had scouted the territory he would soon invade. Then a second finger, and finally a third, entered me. They were well oiled, and I hardly felt discomfort as he reamed and stretched my asshole, making sure that I would be ready to receive him. When he removed his fingers, I felt empty inside.

I shivered involuntarily when I felt his cockhead find my minimal opening. I was frightened and totally aroused at the same time. Mark had placed a pillow below me, raising my buttocks to greet him. He was straddling me doggie style and I was faint from wanting him so much.

"Are you ready?" I thought I heard him whisper. But now, years later, I'm not sure that he had said anything at all.

I think I whispered back, "Yes, I'm ready. Fuck me. Please fuck me. Fuck me now."

Maybe an inch of his cock entered me and then stopped short at the sphincter which blocked his way. I was glad that Mark, fully erect, was no more than six inches of uncut glory. I couldn't imagine anything bigger than that taking my virginity. He wasn't too thick either, but not at all thin. I had passed turds larger than his prick, and I lost some of my fear when I first saw him in his present state. He was so hot and horny. I could hear his cock screaming to enter me and find release. I wanted so much to please him.

"Stop me if it hurts too much," he said. I could barely hear him.

"It doesn't hurt at all," I answered him and he thrust suddenly past my opposing muscle. I nearly screamed out from the awful pain, but I bit my tongue. I had read enough, and heard enough, to know that the pain would soon give way to pleasure. I knew that when he was fully inside of me and started to stroke, his cock would massage my prostate and I might even cum before he did. In addition to all that cerebral knowledge, I loved Mark with all my soul. There was nothing he could do to me sexually, that could possibly hurt me.

He kept on entering me until I could feel his pubic hair on my hairless butt. Then he stopped and lay perfectly still. He let his upper body fall slowly on top of me until we were lying parallel to each other. I could feel an occasional twitch of his cock inside of me, but still he did not move. The pain was gone, and the knowledge that the man I loved was inside of me added to the pleasure I felt. I thought that life could not get any better than this.

"Are you all right?" he asked with genuine concern. I prayed inwardly that his concern meant that he loved me too, and that he feared hurting me. All the while his tongue was tickling me inside my ear.

"I'm great and I love it," I answered. "When are you going to stop talking and fuck me?"

Mark laughed as he began to stroke his cock in my love nal. He came out just far enough to keep from falling out, and when he reentered, he went all the way in. I felt a strange tingle growing inside of me and I realized that my body was aching to cum. I assumed that my prostate was being stroked by Mark's prick.

In the beginning, Mark deliberately stroked slowly and stopped often, but after a short while his stroking became more regular and I could feel his pace quickening. His breath was becoming shorter and shorter, and I knew that he would cum any second. I was so consumed with the fact that I was about to pleasure him, that I almost didn't realize that I was about to cum myself. As I shot my load into the pillow, I constricted my asshole involuntarily. With each spurt of my orgasm, my ass closed tightly around Mark's cock. He could no longer delay his climax. My constrictions put him over the top. I waited expectantly to feel his fluids fill my gut, but I didn't. It took me a minute to realize that Mark had put on a condom. It was the right thing to do, so why did I feel so cheated?

Mark lay on top of me catching his breath. Neither of us wanted to move. We would have stayed that way all night, but Mark's cock grew smaller and he finally fell out of my asshole.

***

Just a few days earlier I was lying in my college dormitory bed, a nineteen year old virgin. I had just finished jacking off, and my cum was coating my pubic hair. I was sobbing bitterly into my pillow. My masturbation fantasies had not taken me to the realm of Venus, but rather to Vic, the hunk who was captain of my college football team. Vic and I were in the same Phys Ed class, and I got to see his muscled body three times a week in the showers after class. I had to think of maggots crawling up and down my body to keep from getting hard.

During the past few months, I had finally let myself consider the fact that I might be homosexual. The very thought of it sent shivers up and down my spine. I was raised devoutly Catholic, and I was convinced that I would go to hell if I acted on my masturbation fantasies. On the other hand, I was convinced that I would go crazy if I didn't, *and soon.*

Whenever I had homosexual fantasies, I felt an absolute need to do penance. I would run to church and offer as many prayers as I could remember, and promise God that I would purge these thoughts from my brain. A lot of good that did! I wanted to confess my sins, but I could not mouth the words, especially to a priest.

That night I made a decision. Instead of another useless church visit, I decided to call a telephone number I had put in my wallet at freshman orientation. At the orientation we were all ushered into a huge gymnasium where at least one hundred tables had been set up. The tables were full of literature and one or two people sat at each table. Every fraternity, sorority and club at the university was represented. I had little interest in any of them, but I strolled up and down the aisles dutifully. At last one table caught my eye. The table contained several publications and a plaque which read: *GAY AND LESBIAN COALITION.* A very unattractive woman and an equally unattractive man were seated behind the table. I wanted desperately to stop and speak to them, but I didn't dare. After much prodding by myself to me, I practically ran by the table, picked up some literature and was off before the two gays could speak to me. I was out of the gym before they could recognize me or call after me.

I didn't dare read the pamphlets in my dorm room for fear that my roommate would see them. It was an empty fear because he was never there. He slept at his girlfriend's off campus apartment almost every night. I enjoyed my privacy, but I committed the deadly sin of envy, and I confessed that sin often to my pastor. It was a ready substitute for my sin of homosexuality. In the end, I decided to wait until I knew for sure that my roommate would not be in for the night and I could read the pamphlets fearlessly. Several weeks passed before I got up the courage to read them even though he was never around.

The pamphlets were not too revealing. One advertised support groups for gays. Several were requests for donations for various AID's charities, and one was a newsletter from the local Gay and Lesbian Community Center. I read with interest the announcements of the various gay groups which met at the GLCC. As much as I would have wanted to attend a weekly meeting of gay college men on Wednesday evenings, I knew I never would. On the last page, tucked away in a corner, there was a little blurb encouraging gay men and women to call the Center Hot Line if there was something bothering them which they needed to get off their chests, or they needed to get help with.

One evening I decided not to use the church as my crutch. After guiltily jacking off while fantasizing homoerotic situations, I determined to call the number I had harbored in my wallet since orientation. I stared at the phone for long minutes before getting up the courage to call. Finally, with great trepidation, I punched in the Hot Line number. I shook with unreasoning fear as I heard the phone ringing at the other end. It rang four times and I was about to hang up in relief when I heard a friendly voice say, "GLCC Hot Line, Mark speaking. How can I help you?"

I was frozen and couldn't answer until Mark asked, "Is anyone there? I promise I don't judge, and whatever you tell me is as privileged as the confessional." That very "Catholic" reference reassured me and I said, "Hello Mark. My name is Jason."

"It's nice to speak to you, Jason. Now, how can I help you?"

"I'm not sure you can," I sounded doubtful.

"Well if I can't help you, maybe I can refer you to someone who can," Mark answered optimistically. "Just tell me the reason for your call."

There was something in Mark's voice that allayed some of my fears. Still I hesitated and when I did speak, I stammered a lot and I wasn't sure I was making sense.

"I think I might be gay," I stammered out. I waited for Mark to respond but the line was silent. It was my turn to ask, "Are you there?"

Finally Mark asked, "Is being gay a problem, or does being gay create problems? There's a fine difference you know. Most people who call are troubled about being gay, and it's a big problem for them. Others don't mind being gay, but sometimes it causes problems for them, like at work or school for instance."

"I'm afraid of being gay. I'm afraid I'll go to hell. I'm still a virgin, but every time I fantasize about homosexual sex, I feel obliged to run to church and ask God to forgive me. I know how much he hates homosexuality, if not homosexuals themselves." I started to blubber. I was angry at myself for giving in to my tears, but I just couldn't help it.

"God doesn't hate anyone," Mark said adamantly. "He loves all his creations, flaws and all. What makes you think that being a homosexual or just thinking about it will get you into hell?"

"The Bible," I answered with authority.

Immediately I heard Mark laugh snidely. "Listen Jason," he said, "the Bible was written by men, not God. If you tell me that God spoke through those men and they merely recorded the 'Words of God' I will tell you that they were mortal men, and their mortal prejudices came out in interpreting 'God's words.' Anyway nothing is more badly interpreted than biblical passages and their meanings. Jews can spend years arguing over the meaning of a single sentence in the scriptures, and Christians are a very close second. That alone proves that 'God's words' were often misinterpreted, and certainly badly translated from the original writings."

"I've heard those arguments before," I said. "I'm not convinced. I live in mortal fear that I will spend eternity in hell."

"You're a tough one," Mark said." Usually when I reassure a caller that he won't go to hell, they are convinced, at least for the moment. But I can't seem to convince you. Look, Jason, I'm here at the Hot Line every Friday night from six to ten. Why don't you meet me at the end of my shift next Friday? We'll have a cup of coffee and talk."

"What makes you such an expert?" I asked in a very mean spirited way.

"Well Jason, I accepted my homosexuality very early in life, and I have never had a problem with it, nor has it ever caused me a problem. Well, once it did. A girl fell in love with me in the eighth grade. I never encouraged her, but when I told her I was gay, she slapped my face."

I started to laugh.

Mark continued, "So you see, I'm an expert. In addition, I was raised Catholic so I know where you are coming from."

"You were raised Catholic?" I asked. "Does that mean you aren't a Catholic anymore?"

"I attend a gay church now. It's Christian and that's all I care about. I'm comfortable there. I had a Jewish boy friend once, and we went to a service at the gay synagogue. I felt at home there too. Do you know why Jason?" Mark asked rhetorically. "Because they told me there that God loved me, and I was assured that He didn't give a hoot about my sexual orientation."

"OK," I said. "I really do need to talk about my fears. They are driving me crazy. I'll come down to the Center next Friday about a quarter to ten."

"Give me your telephone number," Mark said. I immediately grew suspicious. I had a vision of being kidnapped by some cult.

"Why?"

"Just in case I can't make it next Friday, I can call you. Unforeseen things happen you know."

I reluctantly gave Mark my number and we hung up. The rest of the evening, before I fell asleep, I kept wondering if I would have the courage to go to the Center and meet Mark. I was just dozing off when the phone rang. I was pretty surly when I answered.

"This better be good if you are calling so late."

"Sorry Jason. It's Mark. I hope I didn't wake you." Something happened then that I had never experienced before. My heart skipped a beat.

"No," I stammered. "I'm still up."

"Rather than wait until next Friday, how would you like to go to church with me on Sunday?"

"Roman Catholic?" I stupidly asked.

"No," Mark replied. "It's the gay church. The service is a good mixture of a Catholic Mass and a Protestant service. I think some of your fears might be allayed, when you see that you can be religious, have faith, and still be gay. Unfortunately you were programmed to believe that homosexuality was a sin, and if that wasn't a sin, then homosexual acts were. I want you to see that it's all hogwash."

To be honest, I had no wish to attend any church other than my own, but I had made a decision to seek help in exorcising my demons through means outside the church, so I reluctantly agreed to meet Mark. To be even more honest, I was anxious to meet the wise man with the kind voice on the other end of the phone line, and I didn't want to wait a whole week. Mark gave me explicit directions to the church, and said to meet him at 9:45 AM on the church steps.

"How will I know you?" I asked.

"You can't miss me," he said. "I'll be standing on the steps looking for you. My hair is fire red; my eyes are blue; and if that's not enough for you, my face is covered with freckles. I'm twenty now, and my doctor says that the freckles will start disappearing soon. In fact they should have been gone by now. Also I attend the University, so you may have seen me on campus."

After we hung up, I began to picture Mark from the description he gave me. Of course I exaggerated his beauty, and found myself whacking off, dreaming that he was down on me and sucking away with joy and abandonment. When it was over, I sobbed loudly and asked God a hundred times to forgive my sins. I vowed not to meet Mark on Sunday and to attend *my* church instead.

Sunday morning dawned cloudless. The temperature had dipped below freezing during the night. The freezing weather actually warmed me. Suddenly I thought of Thanksgiving only two weeks away. I would be home in a comfortable, familiar environment. I would be surrounded by people who truly loved me because they didn't know my secret. *Would they love me if they knew?*

I looked over at my roommate's bed. It was empty as usual and a good thing. My seven inch, circumcised cock was hard as nails and protruding through my boxer shorts. I had to pee badly. I grabbed a heavy bathrobe, put on my slippers, and ran to the bathroom. While I was peeing I made a mental plan to ignore the early, unseasonal cold, take a shower and go to church.

CHURCH! Suddenly I had butterflies in my stomach. Did I have the guts to meet Mark this morning? While pondering this monumental question, I became aware that although I was all peed out, my cock was as hard as ever, maybe harder. The mere thought of meeting Mark, surrounded by gay men, kept it that way. I began to have a conversation with myself. I was doing that a lot lately.

Wuss! I admonished me, *you want to find out if you are gay or not* (like I didn't know) *and if you are gay, you've got to exorcise your demons. You've got to learn to live with being gay the rest of your life. If you don't, you might as well kill yourself.* I shuddered at the thought of suicide. Mortal sins were a lot on my mind lately.

So I took my shower and dressed for church (overdressed as it turned out.) My heavy winter jacket was still in my suitcase. I retrieved the case from the top of the closet and removed the jacket, proof positive that the crisp autumn weather might be gone for another year, and winter was upon us. Even though I had convinced myself that I wouldn't go to a gay church and meet Mark, I had studied the city's bus routes, and I knew exactly how to get there. I was pleased that I didn't have to make any transfers. The bus that I often took to the downtown business and shopping area of the city continued on, and in less than half a mile it was in a very gay section of town. The church was located there.

I got off the bus and walked two blocks east. I turned right and there it was. I was pleasantly surprised and shocked. It was a real church, damn near a cathedral in its ornateness. I spotted Mark immediately on the top steps. He was wearing jeans and sneakers. I didn't know what was underneath his jacket, but I could see that it was not a dress shirt. I was wearing my dark Sunday suit, business shirt and tie, and dress shoes. I felt a little foolish, but convinced myself that it was better to be a little overdressed than inappropriate. I figured that I could always remove my tie.

I approached Mark cautiously, held out my hand, and in a frightened voice asked, "Are you Mark?" Mark looked at me and broke out into a huge grin.

"You must be Jason," he said. "You're just as I pictured you, prim, proper and very wholesome. But that's not to say that you aren't drop dead gorgeous." His first sentence may or may not have been a compliment, but his second sentence made me blush.

"You're very good looking also," I stammered out.

Mark completely ignored my outstretched hand. Instead he threw his arms around me and gave me a warm and welcoming bear hug. I loved it and tried to cover my shock.

"Let's get inside where it's warm," he said. "I didn't want to miss you and I have been waiting out in the cold for nearly a half hour. I was afraid you wouldn't come, but I'm glad you did. I'm hoping you'll be glad also." We found two seats in the dead center of the sanctuary. The church must have had at least two hundred congregants already seated and plenty more men and women were still coming in. It boggled my mind to think that all these people were gay. I even recognized some guys and a couple of girls from school, but I averted my eyes from them.

When I was sixteen I had a buddy who was Episcopalian. One Sunday he came to my church and on another occasion I went to his. The two masses were not too dissimilar. "We're Catholic Lite," my friend told me jokingly. The service here at the gay church was very much like the Episcopal service. It wasn't until the homily that I realized why Mark wanted me to be here.

The sermon concerned itself with Jesus's belief in diversity. All people of every faith and persuasion were welcomed into his Father's Kingdom. Up until then, his own people would not have allowed unclean Gentile's into their Temples, but Jesus believed that all of mankind was inclusive. At no time in his short ministry did Jesus say that homosexuals or bisexuals or lesbians or transgendered people would be excluded. *That's true,* I thought, and I did indeed feel a tad better. This man of the cloth, standing at his pulpit, was actually telling me that clean or unclean, I was loved and would be welcomed into Heaven.

During the sermon, Mark had taken my hand and now he was squeezing it a little harder than gently. I wasn't even aware of it until the sermon was winding down. I looked at him and he looked at me and we smiled at each other. My body was aglow with the warmth and the love of all the congregants. I even took communion together with Mark, and failed to feel that I was sinning because it wasn't being offered by a catholic priest.

I smiled inwardly when I realized that I was lusting after Mark, and had no guilty feelings at all. Even the minister, during his sermon, made a reference to his 'partner.' This place was an incredible pool of love, but I saddened when I realized that I could never tell my family about me or this church.

At the end of the service we left the church and shook the minister's hand. Then Mark led me to the social hall which was in a separate building. The church provided a good supply of diverse beverages and sweets. While we each had a cup of coffee, several of Mark's friends invited us to join them for lunch.

"Not today," Mark declined. "Jason and I have business to attend to. We'll take a rain check."

"Where are we going?" I asked.

"To my apartment. I'll make us lunch" Mark said. "I intend to begin the long process of exorcising your demons. How do you feel about everything so far?"

I answered honestly. "I feel scared. I feel like a traitor to my faith. I still feel like I'm on the express train to hell, and I want to run into a catholic church to pray."

"Boy," Mark said. "Lesson one can't come a moment too soon."

"How will I get home?" I asked, coming back to reality.

"Not a problem. I'll drive you back to your dorm."

When we got to Mark's apartment, I was surprised. Given Mark's age and the fact that he was a student at my university, I expected to see an extension of a sloppy dorm room. I was so wrong. His apartment was small but neat. It was sparsely furnished, but it contained everything a young man could possibly need for his comfort. I was very impressed and told him so. The apartment had a small kitchen with a tiny table and two chairs. There was a bedroom, living room and bathroom.

Mark hung his jacket in the front hall closet, and he hung mine there also. He showed me around and when he reached the bedroom, I saw that the double bed was neatly made. Mark removed his sneakers and put on a pair of slippers.

"Give me your jacket, tie and shoes," he said. I obeyed orders, and Mark miraculously produced another pair of slippers which he offered me.

"We might as well be comfortable," Mark said. He led me to the kitchen and bade me sit on one of the chairs while he made us cheese omelets, which he served with Kaiser Rolls and coffee. While we ate, Mark began to speak. He sounded very much like my philosophy professor. He was very clinical, and I was disappointed. I expected he might be a bit sexually provocative. Correction! I hoped he would be sexually provocative.

"So you're a virgin." He made it a statement rather than a question. "I find that rather sweet." He patted my hand. "Let's get started."

He took our dirty dishes and flatware to the sink, rinsed them and put them in the dishwasher. He was a neatnik!! He motioned for me to follow him and we sat down comfortably on his sofa.

"Do you believe in God?" Mark asked me staring directly into my eyes. His question stunned me. All I could do is nod my head.

"Tell me what you believe God to be?"

I had to think awhile before I answered, "Spirit."

"Good spirit? Bad spirit? In between spirit?" Mark asked. I thought he was mocking me, but I wouldn't be fazed by him.

"Why good, of course."

"Define good," he demanded.

"Perfect, infallible," I responded immediately.

"Then if God is infallible, do you think that his creations are less than perfect?"

"Yes, we are all sinners."

"Then if we are all sinners, who gets into heaven? Maybe I should ask, does anyone get into heaven?"

"Of course," I said haughtily. "Those who repent and atone for their sins."

"But don't we sin again immediately after we repent? After all we are fallible and constant sinners."

Mark seemed to have a rebuttal for everything. I was beginning to become very uncomfortable. In fact, I was beginning to feel foolish, but I wasn't ready to expel my fears just because I felt that way.

"Where is all this leading to?" I asked.

"Nowhere!" Mark answered. "I just wanted to show you that even if you and I were to make love this very second, it would be no less a sin than the other hundred you seem to feel you commit on a constant basis every day. But you should know that no sin would be committed in my eyes. Is it more of a sin to make love, than to send young men to die in senseless, fruitless wars?"

"Are we?" I asked

"Are we what?"

"Going to make love this very second?"

"I'd like that," Mark said. "I feel a big need to save your immortal soul. I know we just met, but I have feelings for you. Surely God would not punish me for loving another human being, one of his creations no less. Have you stopped believing that God is love?"

Before I knew what he was doing, Mark leaned into me and started to kiss me. The biggest wonder of all is that I responded immediately. Our lips parted and our tongues began to duel. If this was the road to hell, the highway was awfully beautiful.

Instead of surrendering to the joy and the passion of the flesh, I was suddenly overcome with guilt and I pushed Mark away from me.

"What's wrong?" he asked.

"I can't," I sobbed. "It's contrary to God's will."

Mark did not let go of me. He was holding me tight and I allowed it. How can I deny how good it felt to be held by him? I loved him but I cringed at the very thought of such a damning scenario.

"You're wrong," Mark said very quietly. "It is God's will. Just look at how quickly we fell in love. I see it as having been arranged by our guardian angels. I feel God blessing us. Don't you?"

Mark continued to hold me. He caressed the back of my head and ran his hand down my back, finally caressing my buttocks. All the while he was whispering softly in my ear. "You have nothing to fear. I love you. I want to make love to you for the rest of my life. Please don't run away from me. I love you. I love you. I love you."

After a long period of soul searching, I said, "I love you too Mark, but I am still in fear for my immortal soul." I wept silently on Mark's shoulder. I could not push him away. Instead I pulled him closer to me and began to kiss his cheeks. I realized then that his cheeks were wet. All the while he had been whispering in my ear, he too had been quietly crying. My heart melted. Suddenly I made a decision, and I spoke too loudly in Mark's ear.

"Yes, Mark, I do love you. I don't know if I'll go to hell or not, but while I am here, I want to spend the rest of my life with you." I put my lips on his and we began to kiss passionately.

"I won't do anything you don't want to do or that will gross you out," Mark said. "Let's take it nice and slow. I'll do all the love making. You just lie back and enjoy it. When you want to, you can do whatever you want to me. I'll be patient and wait for as long as it takes."

Mark led me to the bedroom where he began to undress me. The minute he unbuttoned the first button on my shirt, I got an erection. My first thought was to hide it, but it finally dawned on me that an erection was exactly what Mark would want me to have. When my upper body was naked, Mark began to undo my belt. That was the point at which I got my courage up. I asked him to stop for a moment, and I lifted his tee shirt over his head. Now we were both naked from the waist up.

I expected Mark to return to my belt, but he surprised me by pinching my nipples instead. My whole body vibrated. I had no idea that a man's nipples were so erogenous. I played with his nipples also, wanting to give him the same pleasure. Then Mark bent down and started to suckle and take little nips on one of my nipples, and then the other.

"I'm going to faint," I informed him. "I need to lie down." Without further ado, we stripped the rest of our bodies by ourselves and got into Mark's neatly made bed. We were on top of the bed cover as we came together in a passionate kiss. Mark rubbed his cock against mine. I made no move to stop him. I had dreamed of this moment forever, and I didn't give a damn at that moment if I went to hell or not. I vowed to make love to Mark as long as my strength, and his, held out. I decided to worry about hell later on.

Mark began moving down my body. He kissed my neck, lapped at my nipples and my belly button, and finally reached my pubic hair. For some reason I feared that he would stop at that point, but he skirted around the hair and started to lick my balls and my inner thighs. I was no longer in a conscious state. I was euphoric and concluded that this must be what a "religious experience" felt like. Coming back to my senses, I wanted to reciprocate, and while I was at it, I could make another fantasy a reality. I twisted my body around and took Mark's cock into my mouth, just as he took mine. I paid attention to the way he moved his tongue and his lips, and I tried hard to emulate him. I played with his balls as I sucked him, just as he did to me.

I felt his balls constricting and I knew he was close. I panicked at the thought of his spunk rushing into my mouth, but I did not stop. I was determined to go to hell in style. Apparently Mark was more adept at delaying orgasm than I was, and I felt myself coming. I couldn't let him know because my mouth was full of his cock, but I was relatively sure he could tell. When I came, I did have to stop sucking him as I cried out in utter abandonment. Mark did what I expected and according to my fantasy. He swallowed every drop of my cum.

We lay back exhausted. After a short while, Mark leaned over and kissed me. The smell of semen was on his lips and for what it is worth, that aroused me, and I remained perfectly erect. "Let me satisfy you now," I said.

"Can I fuck you?" he asked me. The fires of hell appeared before me, but I answered. "Please fuck me. I have fantasized what it would be like for years."

"Turn on your stomach," he told me.

I lay on my stomach, almost not breathing. I was waiting patiently, expectantly, for Mark's cock to enter my virgin ass. Moments ago his greasy finger had scouted the territory he would soon invade. Then a second finger, and finally a third, entered me. They were well oiled, and I hardly felt discomfort as he reamed and stretched my asshole, making sure that I would be ready to receive him. When he removed his fingers, I felt empty inside.

I shivered involuntarily when I felt his cockhead find my minimal opening. I was frightened and totally aroused at the same time. Mark had placed a pillow below me, raising my buttocks to greet him. He was straddling me doggie style and I was faint from wanting him so much.

"Are you ready?" I thought I heard him whisper. But now, years later, I'm not sure that he had said anything at all.

I think I whispered back, "Yes, I'm ready. Fuck me. Please fuck me. Fuck me now."

Maybe an inch of his cock entered me and then stopped short at the sphincter which blocked his way. I was glad that Mark, fully erect, was no more than six inches of uncut glory. I couldn't imagine anything bigger than that taking my virginity. He wasn't too thick either, but not at all thin. I had passed turds larger than his prick, and I lost some of my fear when I first saw him in his present state. He was so hot and horny. I could hear his cock screaming to enter me and find release. I wanted so much to please him.

"Stop me if it hurts too much," he said. I could barely hear him.

"It doesn't hurt at all," I answered him and he thrust suddenly past my opposing muscle. I nearly screamed out from the awful pain, but I bit my tongue. I had read enough and heard enough to know that the pain would soon give way to pleasure. I knew that when he was fully inside of me and started to stroke, his cock would massage my prostate and I might even cum before he did. In addition to all that cerebral knowledge, I loved Mark with all my soul. There was nothing he could do to me sexually, that could possibly hurt me.

He kept on entering me until I could feel his pubic hair on my hairless butt. Then he stopped and lay perfectly still. He let his upper body fall slowly on top of me until we were lying parallel to each other. I could feel an occasional twitch of his cock inside of me, but still he did not move. The pain was gone and the knowledge that the man I loved was inside of me added to the pleasure I felt. I thought that life could not get any better than this.

"Are you all right?" he asked with genuine concern. I prayed inwardly that his concern meant that he loved me too, and that he feared hurting me. All the while his tongue was tickling me inside my ear.

"I'm great and I love it," I answered. "When are you going to stop talking and fuck me?"

Mark laughed as he began to stroke his cock in my love canal. He came out just far enough to keep from falling out, and when he reentered, he went all the way in. I felt a strange tingle growing inside of me and I realized that my body was aching to cum. I assumed that my prostate was being stroked by Mark's prick.

In the beginning, Mark deliberately stroked slowly and stopped often, but after a short while his stroking became more regular and I could feel his pace quickening. His breath was becoming shorter and shorter, and I knew that he would cum any second. I was so consumed with the fact that I was about to pleasure him, that I almost didn't realize that I was about to cum myself. As I shot my load into the pillow, I constricted my asshole involuntarily. With each spurt of my orgasm, my ass closed tightly around Mark's cock. He could no longer delay his climax. My constrictions put him over the top. I waited expectantly to feel his fluids fill my gut, but I didn't. It took me a minute to realize that Mark had put on a condom. It was the right thing to do, so why did I feel so cheated?

Mark lay on top of me catching his breath. Neither of us wanted to move. We would have stayed that way all night, but Mark's cock grew smaller and he finally fell out of my asshole.

I am now fifty years old, and Mark is fifty-one. We have not spent a night apart since that wonderful day we first coupled. Mark makes me happy. He makes me want to live every day in his presence. I no longer believe I am doomed to hell. Rather, I believe that God or some guardian angel brought us together. Our union is truly blessed.

I kept my secret from my parents until I graduated college. When I came out to them they refused to talk to me, and told me never to contact them again. I was distraught, but Mark's parents took me under their wings and welcomed me into the family.

Two years after my parents disowned me, I heard from them. They asked if I would please come home for Christmas, and to bring Mark so that they could meet him. Mark's parents agreed that it was more important for us to go to my home for Christmas than to spend the holiday with them.

We attended Christmas Mass with my parents. They acted like nothing had ever happened. They made Mark feel that he was part of the family. At one point during our holiday dinner I looked quizzically at my father. I said nothing at all, but he read my mind. Smiling at me he said, "I didn't want to lose you, son."

The best part of the reconciliation was that I truly stopped believing that my love for Mark was a sin. More importantly, I came to hope that night that my parents didn't see me as a sinner either.

End of the 10th Story

As You Are

HANK BROOKS

As You Are
By: Hank Brooks

How long is it appropriate to mourn for someone you loved deeply, and is lost to you forever? Is a week enough? A month? A year? Five years? Never? Forever?

If someone cut off your right arm, when would you stop missing it? In a week? A month? A year? Five years? Never? Forever?

Perhaps it would be better to word these questions differently. Maybe I should ask how long SHOULD one mourn for a lost love? I am getting sick and tired of my parents, and my friends, telling me that it is time that I got over his death. "You're still young and good looking," they tell me. "Get on with your life. Don't bury yourself with Frankie. After all, it's been five years now."

Francis Ryan Harrison! My love, my life, dead at twenty nine. Mowed down at the pinnacle of his life by a drunken teen ager, who showed no remorse at his trial; who left the scene of his crime and left Frank to die. Had he remained at the scene, a simple phone call might have saved Frank's life. Two years for involuntary manslaughter, sentence reduced to probation for a first offense. Still no gratitude shown. Still no remorse evident. Life is not fair. He has been gone nearly five years now. It isn't fair, not to him, not to me.

I loved him so much. I miss him so much. Frank, with whom I shared life's most intimate moments, most intimate pleasures, I still love him. Often I think of killing myself so I can be reunited with him. But I won't do it. What if there is no God, and what if I never get to be with Frank again? Worse yet, what if there is a God, and he sends me to hell for murdering myself, and I never see Frank again for all eternity? The thought is unbearable, and so I stay my hand.

Each day, I rise and go to work. I perform my duties robotically. I no longer love my work or have any interest in it. I just want the day to be over so I can go home and get into bed, our bed, Frank's and mine. I pretend he is lying beside me. I can smell his essence, especially the musky smell of his cock and balls. I long to kiss his mouth, tickle his ears with my tongue, suck his balls and run my tongue up and down the shaft of his uncut cock.

Each day it gets harder to imagine myself doing those things. The memories are dimming, but my mourning and the misery of living life without Frank is constantly with me. No dimming or diminishing there.

Since Frank was murdered (I will always consider it to be a cold blooded murder, no matter what the law says) I have had no sexual desires to be with anybody else. I have no libido to speak of. Occasionally I jerk myself off, but even that is a rare event. I might as well become a monk. Now in my mid-thirties, I even have a wet dream now and then. What next? Acne?

I hardly eat real food any more. You would think that I would lose weight and waste away. Not so. I eat junk food, and all the wrong fast foods, so I have put on a lot of pounds since Frank's murder. Too bad that he isn't around to enjoy my "love handles." I stopped working out at the gym, and what muscles I had are quickly turning to fat and flab, but I don't give a damn. My parents have a good cry every time they see me or talk to me. My friends have given up on me. None of them want to be anywhere around me anymore. I don't blame them. I am virtually becoming a hermit, and that life style is my choice. I don't mind at all.

I still watch television on occasion, but I have no idea what I am watching. Sports? Old movies? Talk shows? Reality shows? Don't ask me. I am clueless. I am the first to admit that I have become a useless human being. I'm sorry about that, but I simply can't function anymore without Frank. I haven't bought a new piece of clothing in five years, and that's what brought me to The Gap.

I wrote those words in my journal a few weeks ago and now I am beginning to come back to life. Allow me to continue writing in my journal. It helps me to clear my head.

I awoke on the fifth anniversary of Frank's murder. It was a beautiful, late spring morning, and for some reason I felt that I could not bear to spend yet another lonely day in the apartment I had shared with my love, especially on the anniversary of his death. I made myself a cup of coffee and nothing more. This was intended to be my breakfast until I could grab a hamburger with fries and maybe an apple pie at McDonalds.

I put on a sport shirt, but quickly changed to a polo shirt. I could not button up the sport shirt without creating unsightly gaps that showed off my burgeoning tummy. Then when I put on my favorite jeans, I couldn't close the waist without sucking in a few inches. My love handles were bulging over my belt. I looked in the mirror and realized that they were no longer love handles.

I was displaying layers of fat, and I was well on my way to becoming an obese individual. My impending obesity did not happen overnight, and I had to ask myself why I had not noticed it before today. I could only wonder what my ill-fitting clothes made me look like at work. For the first time in five years I gave a rational thought to me, myself, and I. I vowed to go back to the gym and lose these excess and unwanted pounds. Would you believe that I actually felt guilty that I had these thoughts, the thoughts of an alive person? My Frankie was dead and I wasn't supposed to have a thought in my head concerning my appearance. To me, at that moment, I had committed a mortal sin.

I sucked in my gut, got in my car and headed for the mall. When I got there, my first thought was to go to the food court and have something sweet for breakfast, brunch now, maybe a sweet roll and more coffee. I realized what my thought process was, and I was angry at myself. I did something else instead, something that made me proud, and then guilty again. I spotted a group of "mall walkers" taking their morning exercise, and I decided to join them.

I walked around the mall with them for nearly an hour, but I didn't speak to any of them. When they dispersed, they nodded at each other as a sort of goodbye and they did not exclude me. I got the oddest feeling. Wouldn't you? It was my first social interaction with other human beings in five years. (My work environment was not social.) I felt guilty again at first, but then I suddenly felt good about it, and I smiled back.

Later, when I browsed around at The Gap, I selected two new pairs of jeans and three new sport shirts. Up to now I had always bought medium sport shirts. I selected three large ones. I knew that they would fit, but I wasn't sure about the jeans so I headed for the dressing rooms. There were several of them available, and as I walked toward one, I was passed by a very young man who entered right into the room I was headed to. He was beautiful. I'd put his age at 19 or 20. He was about 6'

1" tall. His straight black hair was shoulder length. I couldn't see the color of his eyes. He was wearing a tank top that was really too tight on him. His muscles bulged beyond belief. His jeans were tighter than mine, on purpose, I'm sure. The dressing room had a saloon type door. I could see him from his shoulders up and from his shins down. I was transfixed by his beauty and I just stood there staring at the dressing room. I had no sexual thoughts about the young man at that time. I just stared and admired what I saw.

All he took in with him were jeans, so I was confused when he stripped off his shirt. His muscles bulged even more. Then he dropped his jeans and stepped out of them. His legs were so muscular, I wondered if he was a dancer. I expected that he would immediately try on a pair of jeans, but instead he preened for a bit in front of the mirror. He was admiring his cock no doubt, or at least that's what I thought. I was still frozen and made no effort to try on my own selections. I just continued to stare at the guy; what I could see of him, that is. I was shocked at myself. I was turned on by another human being for the first time in five years. This guy had finally fired up my long dormant libido. I thought about celebrating, and of course, that conjured up thoughts of food, so I quickly erased the idea.

The hottie bent down for a moment to put on one of the pairs of jeans he had taken in with him. At that moment I was diverted and my eyes happened to glance over to the clerk at the register. He was gawking too. He must have seen me staring as well, and that embarrassed me, so I finally went into one of the dressing rooms.

While I tried on my selections, my mind began to race. I was trying to figure out ways to meet this guy. I was sure he would be gone by the time I tried on the jeans. How wrong I was. He was still preening when I was finished. I could have paid for my purchase and left, but I continued to browse.

Hottie came out of the room and went to the clerk who had been staring at him. The clerk completed the sale without once displaying any of his emotions. I was standing right behind hottie at the register and I whispered in his ear, "Meet me at the food court. I'll buy you lunch."

Without missing a beat, he replied, "Not this time fatso."

That brought me back to reality quickly enough. I was devastated. I knew I had gained weight these past five years, but I didn't realize how much. The hottie ran off and I put my clothes on the counter. As the clerk ran up the sale, he smiled at me and said, "Hot hunk of man isn't he? That was quite a show he put on for us." I smiled back and left the store. I just wanted to get home to my hermitic life, and to my solo man cave, after having been caught making a fool of myself.

In spite of how much I couldn't wait to bury myself at home again, I made two stops on the way. The first stop was at the gym where Frank and I used to work out. I renewed my membership. I looked all round and did not see one person who worked there five years ago, or who worked out there five years ago either. Then I stopped at a super market. I bought some healthy foods and vowed to start exercising and dieting immediately. I didn't even care if I had to get rid of the new clothes I had bought today. I figured that some AIDS charity would be glad to have it.

When I got home there was a message from my mother. I rarely returned my parents' calls any more, but this was a new day somehow, and I listened to the message.

"I know I'm wasting my breath," she started, "but I'll give it another try. Cissy, Dan and the kids are coming for dinner Friday night. Your dad and I would love for you to come also. Please call me back. I love you."

"I love you too, Ma," I said to the answering machine, and I called back.

My sister, Celia, her husband, Dan, and my two nephews had tried to include me in their lives since Frank was murdered. Until that awful day, she, Dan, Frank and I were as close as family could be, but I had shut them out like I did everybody else. They tried to reach out to me and I rejected their efforts, driving us further apart.

My mother answered after one ring. When I told her I was coming, she shrieked into the phone.

"Have some pity on my ear drums," I laughed.

"Davey," she said, "I love you so much. I miss you so much." Then for fear of offending me she added, "I miss Frankie too, you know."

"I know Ma," I said. "I'll see you Friday evening. What time?"

"Come at five so we can talk a little." She had second thoughts.

"Come whenever. This is your house too." I kissed her mentally on her forehead.

Over the next few weeks, I began to work out regularly and dieted intelligently with the help of a coworker, who is married to a nutritionist. At the end of three weeks, I had lost twelve pounds. My face lost its bloat and I actually began to see a glimmer of my old self. Every day I prayed that I would run into the hottie again. This time he would find me desirable and then I would reject him and have my sweet revenge. It became an obsession. All of a sudden I began to whack off again amidst fantasies that I was making mad, passionate love to the hottie. Better yet he was returning my love making.

As I lost weight, I began to realize how old and tired my wardrobe was, and I started to replace a good deal of it. I bought whatever I could at The Gap, but I had an ulterior motive. I was hoping to run into the hottie again. During that process, I began to chat regularly with the clerk who also had eyes for my hottie. He was not good looking and his body was very average (who was I to complain?) but he was my age and we had a lot in common.

Imagine my shock when Teddy asked me if I would like to have dinner with him one night. I was tempted, but I viewed it as being unfaithful to Frankie or at least, unfaithful to his memory. I had to say no, but we had become good enough friends that I felt that I owed him an explanation. I didn't want him to think that I was spurning him.

"Ted," I said simply. "I'd like to do that, but I'm in mourning for my late partner, and I'm just not ready yet."

"Please," Ted said, "don't think of it as a date. Let's just be two friends having dinner together. I won't push you for anything or demand anything from you. I promise. Besides, I've been told that I have a great shoulder to cry on."

Ted's argument was compelling. I still wasn't sure, so I said to him, "Please give me your home phone number and I'll call you soon."

"Only if you give me yours," he replied. His eyes suddenly turned from mine and I looked to see what he was staring at. There was my hottie (hotter than ever) browsing among the tank tops.

Insensitively, I left Ted and strolled over to my hottie and began browsing as well. I made sure to accidently bump into him and I mumbled an apology.

"It's Ok," he said and he smiled at me. It seemed that I didn't disgust him this time.

"Do you shop here often?" I asked.

"Oh, yeah. It's my favorite store."

Just then, a beautiful young woman approached him and said, "C'mon Frankie, we'll be late for dinner."

It was all I could do to keep my composure. His name was Frankie and worse, he must be straight, judging by the beautiful girl calling him to dinner. I could never handle all of that. Seduction was out of the question.

I must have slumped where I stood, because I heard Ted ask me if I was all right. I didn't answer until I felt him shaking my shoulder. "Yes," I said. "Let's have dinner together soon. Would tonight be too soon? It's not a good time for me to be alone."

"Tonight would be fine," he answered simply.

"Are you sure about this? I may not be very good company."

"It'll be fine. We'll go some place quiet, where we can both talk."

At dinner, Ted took my hand. I let him. "Frank and I met at a house party in the home of a mutual friend," I began my narrative. "He had just arrived from Chicago to begin his first job in the New York office of a large law firm. My friend knew Frank from his days at the University of Chicago Law School. I must admit that it was not love at first sight. Frank was so good looking, I falsely assumed that he would be very vain, and I sort of shied away from him. It was he who eventually came over to me. I was talking to our host and he politely waited for a break in the conversation.

"He smiled at me and said, 'Joey here tells me that you and he work together.' It was an inane opening and I realized that he was trying to start a conversation with me. I think Joey realized the same thing and he suddenly disappeared. He told me later that it was a deliberate attempt at match making. Obviously it worked."

"Are you going to tell me that it was love at first sight and you slept together that very first night?" Ted interrupted me.

"Not by a long shot. Frank intimidated me. Nobody that good looking ever showed an interest in me. We chatted cordially for awhile until I was able to break away from him. A few days later he called me at work. He asked me to have dinner with him. I was stunned, but I accepted. FYI we slept together for the first time after our third date." I put my head down and started to cry softly. "I'm sorry," I said.

"No need to apologize," Ted said. I looked at him and saw that tears had welled up in his eyes also. I foolishly believed he was crying for Frank. He already knew how Frank was murdered. "I lost my love also," he said simply.

I suddenly realized how selfish I had been. I had only thought about myself. I was full of self-pity. I had divorced myself from the world at large. I had let myself grow portly due to gluttony. Damned if I wasn't a sinner. But here was a fellow human being who was suffering too. He was still holding my hand. I placed my free hand on top of his, and asked him how he had lost his love.

"Jimmy was killed by a land mine in Iraq," Ted stated simply. It was obvious that he would say no more. We sat in silence for a long time. Our hands were still clasped. Finally Ted said, "It's been a wonderful evening. I've enjoyed it. We should do it again soon."

I didn't know what to say so I just nodded. When we left the restaurant we went our separate ways. Ted promised to call me soon for another non dinner date. I was content that Ted was satisfied to be just friends. After that we had dinner together at least one day a week on the weekend. We went to a few shows together, and one day we actually went roller skating. We were both so inept that we could not stop laughing at each other. I actually laughed with another person. After I got over my shock, the guilt returned. I know now that I had what they call survivor's guilt. It's a terrible thing, really.

I still could not bring myself to go out with friends who had been mutual friends with Frank and me. I stupidly avoided seeing these old buddies. As my metamorphosis continued, all that would change.

The next big awakening came after Ted and I had been "seeing each other" for about seven months. I was now thinner and more solid than I had been before Frank's murder. I went to The Gap for some much needed new clothing and there was my hottie at the tank tops again. Ted was with him seemingly trying to assist a customer. He and hottie were obviously flirting with each other.

I grew insanely jealous, but not jealous of the hottie. I was jealous of Ted flirting with someone who wasn't me. Is that insane? I was convinced that I could never love anybody ever again. I couldn't believe how I was feeling. I never entered the store, and I ran a country mile.

I didn't see or call Ted for nearly a week. Finally he called me to find out if I was OK and wondering where I had been.

"What's it to you?" I grew belligerent again, like I had been during the beginning of my mourning period. "I'm sure you took that hot little number home and got plenty of action." I practically spat at the poor guy.

"What the fuck are you talking about?" Ted spat back at me. I told him how I had seen him and hottie flirting with each other and he started to laugh.

"You're a bigger jerk than I thought. I flirt with all my customers who I think are gay. It adds considerably to my commission check. In case you haven't figured it out yet, I care about you. I care a lot about you. I enjoy being your friend and doing things together, but I want more from you. I've been really patient, hoping you would come back to life. I loved Jimmy just as much as you loved Frank, but I have to continue my life. He would have wanted me to. Don't you think Frankie wants you to be happy? Do you think he wants you moping around and shutting out everyone who loves you? I love you, you blind fuck."

I was stunned, and Ted left me incapable of a response. The silence was forever until finally Ted hung up the phone. After I hung up at my end, I fell onto my bed and cried for hours. I begged Frankie over and over to forgive me for my unfaithfulness. I swore I would never love another. All the while I was telling Frank these things, I knew that Ted's tirade was harsh, but true. I began to think that I was falling in love with him. It would explain my jealousy. That realization made me beg Frank to forgive me with even more fervor.

I don't know how long I lay on my bed. I know that I was curled up in a fetal position and I was crying nonstop. The crying was what I needed. When Frank was murdered I was bitter and unforgiving. I felt that I was as much a victim of a cruel and unfair life as he was, but I don't remember ever crying. Now that I was, it was wonderfully cathartic. I also remember lying there feeling cold and hungry. I was finally diverted from my self-pitying reveries by a knock on my front door. I was such a hermit I couldn't imagine who it could be.

The knocking only grew louder. When I still didn't answer the door, the knocking grew louder still. "You might as well answer the door," a voice said. "If you don't I'll call the police and your landlord to make sure you're alive." That did it. The last thing I needed was a scene which would be witnessed by all my neighbors. I got out of bed and opened the door.

Ted stood at the door and I barely recognized him. He looked worse than I did. His eyes were red and swollen and his hair was uncombed. He definitely looked like he had been crying too. He didn't wait for an invitation. He walked in and closed the door behind him.

"Forgive me," he pleaded. "I'm so sorry. I had no right to say those things to you. Who am I to tell you to stop mourning Frank? I'm not even over my loss yet. I just put on a better show than you. Please, please, I beg you to forgive me. I'll never butt into your life again." He turned and started toward the door.

I grabbed his arm and turned him to me. My head was full of a million mixed emotions, but only one thing came to my mind. I wanted desperately to kiss this man. He was the best friend I had in the world. He was the only friend I had who could imagine my agony. I held him to me and placed my lips on his. He responded by clutching me tighter.

His lips, warming mine, triggered all my emotional memories. Instinctively I parted my lips as he parted his, and I felt his tongue tickling mine. I was instantly aroused and pushed my growing cock against his body. Without any conscious thought my arms ran up and down Ted's back. I caressed his butt, and I remember thinking that it wasn't as round and firm as Frank's. I really couldn't care less. I was aroused and I was falling in love and I wanted desperately to express these feelings with Ted.

I led him to my bed which was wet with my tears. Ted was fully dressed, but I was wearing only my boxer shorts. I took them off and lay down on the bed. I held out my arms welcoming him into my bed and into my arms. Ted undressed quickly. Seconds later we were wrapped up together. Our bodies were pushed together and seemed to be desperately trying to meld into one. I felt his cock rubbing against mine. Everything was happening so fast I didn't even remember seeing him after he undressed. I wondered if he was cut or not, and how big he was. I really didn't care, but Frank had been uncut and I sort of hoped it would be true for Ted also. I wasn't about to ask him. He had rolled me on my back and his tongue was descending down my body.

When he started to suck my cock, I sobbed and mumbled out loud, "Ted, I am so sorry." He stopped sucking me, and jumped back to lie beside me.

"Am I moving too fast?" he asked.

"No, No. I'm sorry we waited this long. Please don't stop. It's been an eternity." Ted smiled at me and kissed me again before he went down on me. I came in his mouth faster than I wanted to. He scooted up to lie beside me again and he began to kiss me. We shared my cum.

"Just give me a moment to recover," I told him.

"You don't have to, if you don't want to," Ted said. "I'll understand."

"Oh, I want to," I assured him. Moments later I discovered that Ted was cut. I wasn't disappointed. I sucked him with all the passion I could muster up. The moment I felt his balls shrinking I stopped. I kept him on the edge. He hated me for it, and he loved me for it. I reached in the drawer of my bedside table and found some old condoms. I wondered if they were still good. They seemed to be. I unrolled one on Ted's pleading cock. I also extracted a tube of lube from the drawer. It was so old it was more liquid than gel but it did the trick. I lubed Ted's cock and my ass and I sat down on him. Frankie had an oversized cock and I guess I hadn't shrunk much, because Ted slipped right into me with relative ease.

I can't describe to you, how wonderful it felt to have a good size cock up my ass again. I fairly swooned. I rode him up and down. Ted was moaning and thrusting like a mad man. When he came, I could feel his cum coating my ass. The rubber hadn't held after all. I couldn't care less. It felt real good to have cum coating my ass again. Celibacy sucks.

When I felt Ted's cum spurting into me, I was suddenly filled with guilt again. I forced my rational self to take over and I knew that Frank would want me to be happy. I began to believe that maybe Frank and Jimmy were orchestrating this whole thing. It made me feel better.

We languished in bed for a while and then we showered together. After the shower we cuddled in bed, and as we were falling asleep I asked Ted in a baby voice, "Will you be my feller?"

Ted laughed. "You bet I will," he whispered in my ear.

"In that case," I said, "you are stuck going to dinner with me at my parents' home Friday night and meeting my whole family. We have dinner together every Friday."

"No problem," Ted laughed. "We face my family on Sunday."

"My family will love you," I said.

"And my family will adopt you," Ted concluded as we drifted off.

I write this narrative one year to the day after Ted and I entered into our committed relationship. I have grown to love him more every day, and he claims it's the same way with him. We never forget Jimmy and Frank. If your heart is big enough, you can love more than one person in this lifetime. To answer the question I asked at the beginning, I will never stop mourning Frank's loss, but I have found love, peace and serenity with Ted.

End of the 11th Story

HANK BROOKS

BLOOD WORK

Rewarding His Good Heart

Gay Romance Erotica

Blood Work

Rewarding His Good Heart

By: Hank Brooks

The handsome, thirty-one year old doctor was a pulmonologist, who plied his trade in Los Angeles, CA. His father liked to brag jokingly that he raised a smart kid, because he was a lung doctor in a city where nobody could breathe. Cal would snap back, "I'm also a hung doctor." That gave them both a good laugh.

The nurses at the hospital fairly swooned when he entered one of their wards. He was an even six feet tall. He had soft wavy hair, which was the golden-brown color of a crust of bread. His eyes were a deep brown. His nose was straight, and his square chin had a small cleft in it. When he smiled, he developed a small dimple on the right side of his full, rosy lips. He was single, and he spent many leisure hours working out in a gym near his apartment. The results were obvious. His muscles bulged underneath his lab coat. The aforementioned nurses, of the female persuasion, were swooning in vain. Dr. Calvin Baxter was a dedicated homosexual.

"Dedicated" may not have been a good choice of adjective. Cal was gayer in theory than in practice. He was, to be more accurate, a dedicated workaholic. His profession, and his hours in the gym, left little time for making friends and having sex. He did have one fuck buddy, whom he called upon once or twice a month. Alfie was a nice enough guy, but he had little in common with Cal. When they coupled, they satisfied their lustful needs, barely spoke, did not have a meal together, and went their separate ways. They never socialized. Alfie was happy anyway, because Cal's cock was nine inches when aroused, and pretty hefty as well. It was the biggest penis Alfie ever had the pleasure to service and satisfy. In between meetings, Cal would whack off in the shower, if he felt the necessity, but that was only once a week at most.

Dr. Cal had one more distinguishing attribute. He had an uncommon, but not totally rare, blood type. He was B Positive. He was associated with Cedars-Sinai Hospital, and most of the doctors or staff there preferred to use B Positive blood transfusions for B Positive patients, rather than using O Positive, the universal donor blood. As a result, he was often called upon to donate blood to a needy patient. He rarely knew who got his blood and he never made inquiry.

There was one nurse on the pulmonary ward with whom Cal was particularly friendly. He had lost his own mother when he was sixteen, and Madeleine Allen reminded him a lot of her. They would have been the same age, but the resemblance ended there. Physically they were totally different. Cal's mother had been short, blond and slightly plump. Maddie was tall, at least 5'7". She was thin and had dark blond hair. What made the two women so alike were their kind and sensitive natures, and the fact that they both loved Cal in a very maternal way.

Cal was making rounds one Thursday on a beautiful spring morning. Maddie was accompanying him, when suddenly she completely broke down in the middle of rounds. She was sobbing so badly that he stopped his rounds and took her aside. Lovingly, he wrapped her in his strong arms and asked her what was wrong.

"I'm sorry to be acting this way," she said. "I know how unprofessional it is. I was going to wait until after rounds to talk to you."

"Well, talk to me now," Cal said. "It seems like the appropriate time."

"It's my son Cody," she started to say, and then she could speak no more.

Cal had never met Cody, but Maddie spoke of him often. His father had died when he was in middle school, and Maddie had raised him by herself. He was very bright, and had graduated from UCLA summa cum laude a year earlier. When he applied to medical school, although Cal had never met him, he gave Maddie a glowing letter of reference for him.

Cal grew concerned. "What about him?" he asked.

"Cody needs a kidney transplant. Both of his kidneys are diseased."

"Good heavens," Cal said. "He's only twenty-three."

"He's suffered most of his life," Maddie sobbed. "I'm giving him a kidney, and Dr. Feldon and his associate have agreed to do the operations right here at Cedars."

"When will it be?" Cal was really concerned.

"That's the problem," Maddie said. "There's so much red tape, it could take another couple of months. Cody had to take a year off from med school, because he's on dialysis. He's home with me now."

"How can I help?" Cal asked sincerely.

"Cody and I are both B Positive," Maddie said, "and I know that you are also. I was hoping you could donate a pint of blood at legal intervals, so we might have several pints by the time of the operations. I'm donating my own blood for myself as well."

"Of course I will, Maddie. I'll go right to the blood bank after my shift, and designate the blood for Cody."

Maddie nearly crushed Cal with her hug. She kissed him on the cheek and said, "Let's get back to work."

Every Friday evening after work, Cal went home, showered, and changed into casual clothing. Then he picked up his father at his apartment, and the two bachelors went out to dinner. The day after he learned about Cody, he took time to call his father to tell him that he wanted to pick him up a half hour earlier than usual.

When George Baxter was seated and belted in Cal's car, he asked, "How come so early this week?"

"I have to make a house call," Cal said without further explanation, and he proceeded to set his GPS.

He pulled into Maddie Allen's driveway, and asked his father to join him because it would take a little time. George looked a little baffled and Cal added, "I want you to meet my favorite nurse."

"He must be quite a hunk," George jibed facetiously. Cal ignored his father, who was constantly making fun of his gayness. Cal knew that he was only pulling his leg.

Maddie answered the door. She let them in and Cal introduced her to his father, who smiled broadly at her.

"I was really surprised when you said that you wanted to drop in this evening, Dr. Baxter," Maddie remarked.

"Please call me Cal outside of the hospital. I wanted to meet Cody."

"Yes, Cal, he's dying to meet you too. He's not on the dialysis machine right now, and he said he wanted to meet you in the living room. He dressed for company, I'm afraid."

"He shouldn't have bothered."

"I'll call him," Maddie said.

Cody came out of his bedroom, and introductions were made. Cal thought that he was gazing at an angel. Cody was about the same height as he was. He had brown hair, blue eyes, a strong chin and a very thin, frail body. Cal thought that if the operation was a success, and Cody had the strength to build up his body, he would be a stunner. Cal was surprised at himself for being so attracted to this sick young man.

"Let's go into the kitchen," Maddie said to George, "and leave these two alone for a bit."

As soon as they were alone, Cal asked Cody "When do you go back on the dialysis machine?"

"In about four hours. Why?"

"Well, you are looking pretty fit."

"I feel pretty fit," Cody interrupted.

"I'd be honored then if you and your mother would have dinner with us tonight."

"Gee, doctor, that would be wonderful."

George and Maddie, Cal and Cody, might just as well have been seated at separate tables. Maddie was getting all of George's attention, and he was being charmed by her warm and inviting personality. Cal and Cody were busy talking about medical school, and Cody's aspirations for the future.

"I'd like to be a nephrologist one day," Cody announced.

"Of course," Cal said. "It's funny, but most every specialist I know chose his specialty because someone in his family, or he himself, had a history of the disease. When I was a kid I suffered constantly from bronchitis. I had to be hospitalized a couple of times, and now I'm a lung specialist."

Cody laughed. "Does that mean that all orthopedic surgeons were devilishly wild kids, who were constantly breaking their bones?"

That got them both laughing. Cal took Cody's hand and held it in his own. Cal wasn't even aware of what he had done, but Cody's excited heart skipped a beat. After a few seconds of complete silence, Cal realized how intimate he was being with a straight man, and he ascribed Cody's silence to being shocked at his audacity. He quickly withdrew his hand, and he said with relief, "The food's coming."

Cal wanted desperately to be with Cody, so he made it a habit, over the next few Fridays, of taking Maddie and Cody to dinner with him and his father. George was delighted. In fact, he asked Maddie out for a Saturday night date. She declined because she didn't want to leave Cody alone, but she asked George to please come over for dinner, and to spend the evening with them.

All during George's visit, Cody kept asking him to tell him everything about Cal, and George let slip that Cal was gay. A lump grew in Cody's throat. The poor boy was a virgin. Because of his illness, he had little strength left for school, much less for sexual activity, but he knew for a certainty that he was gay. He felt no pressure to come out…yet. He began to ponder how he could let Cal know that he was gay, and that he had strong feelings for him. In the end, he decided that he would say nothing until after his transplant, and make certain that he was going to recover.

While waiting for the operation to be scheduled, Cal cajoled the pretty nurses in the blood bank to look the other way. He lied, and answered 'no' to the questions about homosexual activity. He knew he was healthy, and decided that a little white lie was in everyone's best interest. If he was breaking the law, he reckoned he should go all the way, and he gave more blood than was allowed. By the time the operation was finally scheduled, there were eight pints stored for Cody, and five for Maddie's use.

He took the morning of the operations off, and he and his father paced the waiting room. The two operations took a long time, and George told Cal that he needed to leave for a while, but he would be back soon.

Cal was not much for religion, so George didn't want to tell him that he was going to the hospital chapel. The chapel was deserted when he got there. He sat down in the last row, bowed his head and began to pray silently. After a few minutes, somebody sat down beside him. It was Cal.

He also bowed his head and prayed along with his father. Neither said a word to the other. After a short time, they returned to the waiting room to wait for results.

Once reseated, Cal put his arm around his father's shoulder. "You really like Maddie, don't you, Dad?"

"I think I love her, Son. I haven't felt like this since I first laid eyes on your mother." He winked at Cal, and added. "You're feeling something more than a friendly interest in Cody also, aren't you?"

"I wish I didn't. I'm sure he's straight."

"I guess," George mumbled.

Just then Dr. Feldon came into the waiting room. He smiled at Cal and shook his hand. "Everything went smoothly. It was text book surgery, and they are both doing fine," he said.

George mumbled, "Thank God," and Cal just grinned.

"They're both awake and in recovery right now, but I'm sure you can see both of them by this evening."

"Thanks Dave," Cal said, grabbing Dr. Feldon's hand and pumping it hard. Father and son allowed themselves to breathe, and went out for a late lunch.

George and Cal were constant visitors to the Allens in the hospital, and then at home when they were discharged. Going into the operation, Maddie had a strong and healthy body. Her recovery was much faster than Cody's. She was back to work in five weeks. Her co-workers greeted her with several bunches of flowers. She particularly cherished the dozen red roses from George Baxter.

Cal got into the habit of stopping off at the Allens' house on his way home from work. At first Maddie and Cody had a private nurse, but after two weeks, they discharged her. It was about the same time as Cal stopped calling Alfie. Alfie was also discharged, so to speak. By the time Maddie went back to work, Cody was managing very well on his own. He was gaining weight, and his ashen complexion was beginning to get some color.

On the first Saturday evening after Maddie returned to work, George made a dinner date with her. He arrived at the same time as Cal in separate cars. Cal was carrying a bag of Chinese food.

"This is dinner for Cody and me," he announced. Cody's face lit up, and he actually blushed, giving him a healthy and beautiful look. As soon as their parents left on their date, Cody started to set the table for dinner, and of course Cal helped.

They sat down at right angles to each other and their knees touched. Neither one tried to remedy the situation, and they purposely kept bumping into each other. As Cody reached for a soup spoon to start attacking his won-ton soup, he accidently dropped it on the floor between him and Cal. Both men bent down to retrieve it at the same time and bumped heads.

"Ouch," they said in unison.

"I'm so sorry," Cal said. He fell to his knees and wrapped Cody in his arms.

"I'm fine," Cody said. "Really! Hey, man, I've got your blood in me. That practically makes me a superman."

Cal laughed. "Do you mind if I hold you anyway. It makes me feel good, and I've wanted to hold you like this since I first laid eyes on you. If I've made you totally uncomfortable, I'm sorry. I'll never do it again, but please remain my friend."

"Cal," Cody said, "you're dad told me that you are gay. I am also." He looked into Cal's face and their lips came closer and closer. Soon they were locked in a passionate dueling match. Weapons: Tongues.

Cal broke it up. "Let's eat first," he said. "You need to regain your strength. We'll talk about this later."

After dinner, they sat together on the sofa and began to "make out," as the old expression goes. "Not tonight," Cal said seriously. "I'm going to call Dr. Feldon and ask him how soon it would be safe for you to have sex."

When Cal called Dr. Feldon the next day, he was told that Cody could have sex any time, as long as it wasn't too wild. Even so, Cal remained very constrained with Cody. They began to suck each other's cocks. Cal allowed himself to orgasm, but he wouldn't bring Cody to a climax. Cody objected, but deep down inside, he was also a little worried about how his body would react.

During the next couple of months Cody regained his strength. He put on weight, exercised in rehab, and his ashen complexion became ruddy and healthy. His new kidney showed no signs of rejection. The proof that all was going well, was how pleased Dr. Feldon was. Cody even arranged to return to medical school to begin his second year.

Cody and Cal made real love to each other just before Cody returned to school. They had begun to fondle and caress before this, but Cal had refrained from allowing Cody to orgasm. Now four months after surgery, they went all out. Cal brought Cody to his bachelor pad for the first time. They both undressed slowly and just stared at each other, without touching, for a long time. They admired what they saw. They were both cut and had firm, fat erections. Cody was about seven inches long. Finally Cal took Cody's hand and led him into the shower. They cleansed each other's bodies for what seemed like forever.

Cal took hold of Cody's cock and began to caress and stroke it gently. When it was slick and scummy with soap, Cal directed Cody to fuck him. Cody slipped in rather easily. Cal was leaning against a wall, and his ass was jutting out invitingly. Cody wrapped himself around Cal's body and began to pump slowly as he stroked Cal's cock. It didn't take the love starved young medical student long to cum. He wailed loudly and clutched Cal harder.

"Stay in as long as possible," Cal instructed. "I want you in me forever. I love you so much."

"I love you too," Cody sobbed in Cal's ear.

Of course, Cody couldn't stay in too much longer, as he was growing limp. When he fell out of Cal, they reversed position. Cody was a virgin and it was more difficult for Cal to enter him. Undaunted, Cody urged him on, and finally he was all the way in, and neither man was moving.

Cal could feel Cody's body relaxing so he began to pump. Unfortunately he came after just a few strokes, unable to constrain his emotions.

"That was fantastic," Cody announced, and Cal made a silent resolution to attempt to delay his orgasms as long as possible.

After the shower, they dried off and got into bed. Their intention was to fondle and cuddle for awhile, and then Cal would take Cody home. But they fell asleep and Cody spent the night in Cal's bed.

One week after Cody completed his second year of medical school, he walked his mother down the aisle. Cal acted as his father's best man. Standing beside their parents as the minister united them in holy matrimony, Cal and Cody beamed at each other. They couldn't be happier.

At the small reception after the ceremony, Cal whispered in Cody's ear, "We're brothers now. How would you like to engage in a little incest later?"

"Now that's what I call a plan," Cody answered, "I can't wait for later." He kissed Cal in front of God and all the wedding guests.

End of the 12th Story

Gay Romance Erotica

BODY SWEAT

Hank Brooks

Body Sweat
By: Hank Brooks

My name is Godfrey. Don't laugh. I'm a Brit. People call me Godfrey. Nobody wants to shorten it to God.

I have a friend named Ralph. Everybody calls him Ralphie. His companion of thirty years died of cancer two years ago. Ralphie lives next door to me on the third floor of a high rise in Ft. Lauderdale, Florida. He is sixty-two years old, two years older than I am. He stands an even six feet tall and he's too skinny, so he looks like a bean pole. Even though he could use a little more meat on him, I personally think he's a very attractive man

He's not all skin and bones. The remains of past glories are evident. Some residual muscle and sinew give his body some texture. He is almost hairless, but he has a thick bush of pubic hair. His cock is cut, and it hangs about four inches flaccid. He still gets hard to six inches. Gravity and time have wreaked havoc with his ball sac, which hangs a good two inches below the tip of his cock. His hair is still mostly a golden brown, but there is enough gray to hint at his age. His chin is square and manly. His eyes are what attract me the most. They are a beautiful emerald green. Sometimes, they seem dull to me and sometimes they shine as if they were made of enamel.

We are good buddies and have many mutual friends. Our social lives are not lacking, and if anything, we are too busy. A quiet night at home is a welcome rarity. We are not lovers, but when tricks are slim, we sometimes have sex together just to relieve the tension in both of us. We always enjoy both our social and intimate times together, and I have often wondered why our relationship has never blossomed beyond being good pals.

Our apartment building is located in a section of Ft. Lauderdale called Wilton Manors. I say it is a section of the big city, but actually Wilton Manors is separately incorporated, and has its own municipal freeloading politicians, just like any other city.

Right across the street from us is a gay bar and restaurant, one of many in the area. This one, I'll call it, Day's End, (they take enough of my money; I don't need to give them any free publicity by using their real name) caters to an older crowd. If someone under forty is there, you can bet he's looking for a daddy. Ralphie and I have no delusions about that, should one of the "youngsters" approach us.

The restaurant has outdoor tables which are rarely used. In the winter it is too cool and windy, and in the summer it is steaming hot, humid and even windier. More often than not, Ralphie will be the only one availing himself of outdoor dining, or should I say outdoor sipping? Ralphie will buy a drink, retreat to an outdoor table, and keep that drink alive for hours. That brings me to the reason, dear readers, that I have decided to tell you this tale.

My good friend Ralphie has a fetish. I was going to say *terrible* fetish, but that would be unkind and certainly unfair. A fetish is a fetish, and I am a real believer that a person's fetish is as sacred as any admission in a confessional. Whatever turns you on should be treated with respect and tolerance.

It is no secret that summertime in South Florida is hot, humid, sticky and downright intolerable, but not to Ralphie. He is obsessed with sweaty, young, and hard as nails, male bodies. On the streets of Wilton Manors you will often sight young gods jogging in just their gym shorts, or gliding along on skate boards, in a state of near nakedness. Their bodies drip with manly sweat. The sweat sparkles in day light, and shines even brighter at night by street light. The aroma of the heady man scent wafts across the air to Ralphie's nostrils. He can sit for hours at his outdoor table, sniffing the magnificent bodies, and enjoying the eye candy these men are offering him.

When one of them jogs by, Ralphie hides his erection under the table, but his palm rests on his package and he strokes gently. He has no hopes that one of these sweaty specimens will come on to him, but he gets off on just watching their bodies dripping and glistening from their exertions. Sometimes when Ralphie's horniness peaks, he will ignore the tent in his shorts, run into the bar, and pull me out. We will go to one of our apartments and fuck our brains out. I have no complaints about a little nookie, and maybe that's why I am so tolerant of Ralphie's fetish.

One exceptionally hot, sticky day, Ralphie sat at his table. He was wearing bare minimum for him; a tank top shirt, no underwear, a pair of shorts and flip flops. Ralphie saw a running figure coming toward him. He was jogging at a pace which was beyond reasonable for this kind of weather, and in this climate. Suddenly the man hunched over. He continued to run doubled up for a few yards further, and finally came to a halt right in front of Ralphie. He sat down right on the concrete sidewalk, trying desperately to catch his breath.

Ralphie immediately went to his assistance. The sweat was coming out of every pore in the man's body. Ralphie smelled the sweat and felt it. His whole body tingled, along with his cock. He helped the man to his feet and sat him at his table. He handed the jogger his drink, which was now nothing but water from the melted ice cubes.

"Drink this," Ralphie ordered. "I'll be right back." In minutes Ralphie returned with a damp cloth and a tall glass of water without ice. He put the wet cloth on the man's head and bade him drink some of the water – slowly.

This gave Ralphie an opportunity to study the man. He was about five feet, nine inches tall and solidly built. He appeared to be in his late forties, as evidenced by a receding hair line. His thinning hair was dark red and left evidence of the redheaded, freckled-faced kid he might once have been. He had blue eyes set a little too close together, but it didn't mar his exceptionally good looks. Ralphie had never really gotten a good look at the guy's package. Things had happened too quickly and now the table covered his manhood.

The man's breathing was very slowly returning to normal. He was no longer gasping for air and his respiration rhythm was nearly steady. Ralphie just stared at him, enjoying the aroma of his sweat, and gawking at how it ran down his chest in tiny rivulets. He waited for the man to speak. At long last, the man put down his glass and extended his hand for Ralphie to shake.

"Thank you," he said simply. Ralphie just nodded at him, trying desperately to drink in as much of the man's scent as he possibly could. "My name is Leonardo," the man said. "Don't ask me why. I'm not Italian. Last name's Chandler, in fact. My friends call me Leo." He hesitated and then added, "My former friends, that is."

Ralphie vowed to investigate that last remark a little further. It sounded so ominous. "I'm Ralphie," he said, shaking Leo's hand. "You haven't been here in Ft Lauderdale very long, have you?" Ralphie asked.

"Just a few days. How did you know?" Leo asked.

"No idiot would run at such a fast pace in this climate. You are obviously oblivious to this fact."

"You're a regular Sherlock Holmes," Leo observed. "You're absolutely correct. I moved down from Portland, Maine just three days ago. I'm staying at a motel, but I'll be able to move into my own apartment early next week. I just signed a lease this morning."

"What brings you here?" Ralphie was nosy. "Business?"

"In a way. I'm a freelance film producer. I have done a lot of work down here because I can film all year in every season. I fell in love with the area and the gay friendly folks in Wilton Manors, so this is where I chose to relocate."

Ralphie's cock tingled. The guy was gay, but way too young for him, fifteen years or more too young. Ralphie had to know more. "But why move from your home if you can come down here as often as you need to?"

Leo started to laugh. He was on to Ralphie's probing. "I guess you won't be happy with less than my autobiography," he said, laughing. He took a long breath and said, "I fell into the trap a lot of young gay men fall into. I thought if I got married, had kids, lived in the mainstream, I could kick the habit or at least bury it." He looked out at the street and yelled at nobody in particular," "Hey young fools, if you're gay, *be* gay. Don't try to be what you aren't." Then he turned his face back to Ralphie's and went on.

"I continued to have sex with men during my marriage. Each time, after an encounter, I would swear never to do it again, but the urges were too strong. The only thing I am grateful for is that we had no children. My wife is a high powered attorney and she didn't want any." Leo stopped his narrative and seemed to be gathering his thoughts. Finally, he continued.

"One day she went to Boston on a case and was supposed to be away for two nights. I brought one of my fuck buddies home. It was rare that we could spend a whole night together, and we wanted to take advantage of the situation. To cut to the chase, the opposing attorney pled for and got a continuance. Sybil came home early and walked in on us while Frank was butt fucking me. I have slept in a hotel ever since that night. She sued for divorce, but it's an easy divorce for me. She makes more money than I do, and she doesn't want anything except for me to get out of her life."

Ralphie said, "I'm so sorry."

"Don't be," Leo sighed. "I'm happy and relieved. I couldn't have loved Sybil very much. I find that I don't miss her at all."

To change the subject, Ralphie asked, "Where are you moving to?"

"To that building right across the street," Leo said. Ralphie's eyes lit up in absolute delight.

"That's where I live," he proclaimed a little too loudly, "on the third floor."

"No shit. That's great," Leo said. Ralphie hoped that he meant it. "I'm on the second," he added.

Suddenly Leo stood up and said to Ralphie, "I can't thank you enough. You probably saved my life. I've put it off, but now that I signed the lease for the apartment, I've got to go buy some furniture."

He was about to leave when he asked, "Maybe you can steer me to the best place to buy. I don't need anything expensive, just sturdy."

"You're in luck," Ralphie said. "I'm an interior designer. I can get you better furniture, and with my discount, you'll end up paying less than for inferior stuff."

"Wow, you'd do that for me? That's fantastic," Leo said grinning from ear to ear. "It smells like I have to go home and shower and shave. What do you say we meet back here in exactly one hour?"

"You're on, buddy," Ralphie said. "I'll see you back here in exactly an hour."

Leo took possession of his apartment on the following Wednesday morning. He and Ralphie spent an hour or so cleaning the place up, even though it was delivered exceptionally clean, newly carpeted, and freshly painted. Leo's affordable designer furniture arrived at 11:30 AM. At 2 PM, a friend of Ralphie's came over and installed window blinds, which were designed to block out sun and some heat. As soon as the blinds were done, Ralphie took Leo to the Broward Mall, where they bought kitchen and bathroom accessories, linens, dishes, cutlery, assorted towels, knick knacks, wall art and just about anything else Leo would need to establish his new home.

Two days later, Ralphie was hanging up the last picture in Leo's designer decorated apartment. Everything else was in place, and the apartment looked like Leo had been living there forever. Leo came up behind Ralphie and put his arms around Ralphie's waist. He had to reach up to nibble Ralphie's ear, but he did, and he kept nipping at Ralphie's ear lobe.

"You've been a godsend," Leo said. "I couldn't have done all this without you."

Ralphie twisted around and stared into Leo's eyes. Leo had not previously realized what piercing green eyes Ralphie had. He was awestruck by the beauty of those eyes. They were facing each other now, and Ralphie's muscle memory came into play. Without any conscious thought, he thrust his erection against Leo's body, only to discover that Leo was in a similar state. They could only smile at each other.

Leo nodded toward the bedroom. "My bed is still a virgin," he declared. "Would you like to help me remedy that awful situation?"

Ralph had never let himself dream that this younger, handsome man would ever want to have sex with him. He was speechless. All he could do was nod his head and move toward the bedroom.

Nobody was in a rush, but still Leo said, "Slowly, love, slowly."

Ralphie's knees buckled. He called me *love*, he thought. I must be dreaming.

They undressed each other very slowly, permitting their hands to wander across each other's bodies. When at last they stood facing each other, they allowed themselves plenty of time to examine the body that they were about to invade. Ralphie stood three inches taller than Leo, but Leo was solid muscle and slightly stocky. They probably weighed the same. Ralphie was cut and six inches in his erect state. Leo was uncut, at least a half inch longer, and slightly wider around. His purple head protruded from his foreskin and Ralphie could not restrain himself. He fell to his knees, cupped Leo's balls in his hand and began to suckle the beautiful knob.

Leo gave Ralphie time to suck him to an extreme state of hardness. Then he pulled away and said, "Ralphie, sweetheart, I want desperately to fuck you." Ralphie looked up at Leo and smiled. He ran to a dresser drawer and removed condoms and KY Jelly. He knew just where they were. He had bought them and given them to Leo as a present. He had placed them in the drawer himself. After he handed the condoms and the lube to Leo, he sprawled out on the new mattress, flat on his back.

Leo squeezed out a glob of the goo onto the fingers of his right hand. He began to insert the lube into Ralphie's ass. He put on a condom and used more lube to coat his cock. Ralphie was shivering in anticipation. Leo positioned his cock at the entrance to Ralphie's urging hole, and began to penetrate. He tried to go slow, but he slipped in effortlessly. He didn't realize what an experienced old warhorse Ralphie was.

By now, Leo wanted desperately to cum, but he didn't move a muscle. He laid his body on Ralphie's and began to kiss him. Their lips parted and their tongues began a duel worthy of Zorro. Leo could resist no longer and he began to pump slowly and sensuously. His pulsating cock found Ralphie's prostate, and Ralphie began to wiggle and moan in sheer ecstasy. In fact, Ralphie came seconds before Leo spilled his jism into the condom.

They lay spent, holding and hugging each other until nature took its course and Leo slipped out of Ralphie's bum hole. Leo rolled over. He was still wearing the condom. "Next time we'll change positions," he said as he got out of bed and headed for the bathroom to clean up.

When Ralphie heard Leo say *next time* his mind went into overdrive. Leo wanted him. He really wanted him. It was not a one-way street, nor a one night stand, as Ralphie had believed.

Ralphie jumped out of bed and followed Leo into the room. "Would you mind if we showered together?" Ralphie asked. Leo didn't answer. He pulled Ralphie by the arm right into the shower stall. There, they took extra delight in washing and soaping each other's cocks, which had again risen and hardened. Leo soaped Ralphie really good and turned his back to him.

"Fuck me," he said, positioning himself. Ralphie had to scrunch down a bit, but he lined himself up and started to enter without a condom. Neither man gave it a thought. He met more resistance than Leo had, but he got in and they started pumping in rhythm. Ralphie reached around Leo and grabbed his cock. He started stroking it, and it wasn't long before he felt Leo's cum coursing through his throbbing rod. When Leo came, his ass constricted, and Ralphie came with a loud, primeval scream. His jism exploded into Leo's guts.

When they were dressed, Leo said, "I'd like to take you to dinner tonight."

"Haven't you paid me enough?" Ralphie asked.

"This isn't payment," Leo explained. "Later maybe, when I go down on you, that will be interest on the payment, but tonight is a date. I'm asking you out on a date."

By now Ralphie believed that he was dreaming or maybe that he had died and gone to heaven. He actually began to cry.

"Why are you crying?" Leo asked.

"Are you sure that you want to date an old fart like me?"

"You're far from old," Leo said. "Anyway I go for older men. The guy Sybil caught fucking me is seventy-one."

"OK then, but I insist we go Dutch."

"If that's what you want, that's fine with me."

"I have one more request."

"What's that?" Leo asked.

"Please don't call me Ralphie. I hate it. Call me Ralph."

From then on, it was all uphill for them, and downhill for me. Ralphie and Leo always ask me to join them for dinner and movies and stuff, and sometimes I do. However, I lost the other side of Ralphie. I lost my fuck buddy, but you need not fret for me. I have plenty of others, but none like him. Nonetheless, I couldn't be happier for him, for both of them, and we are all still good friends. That's what matters.

End of the 13th Story

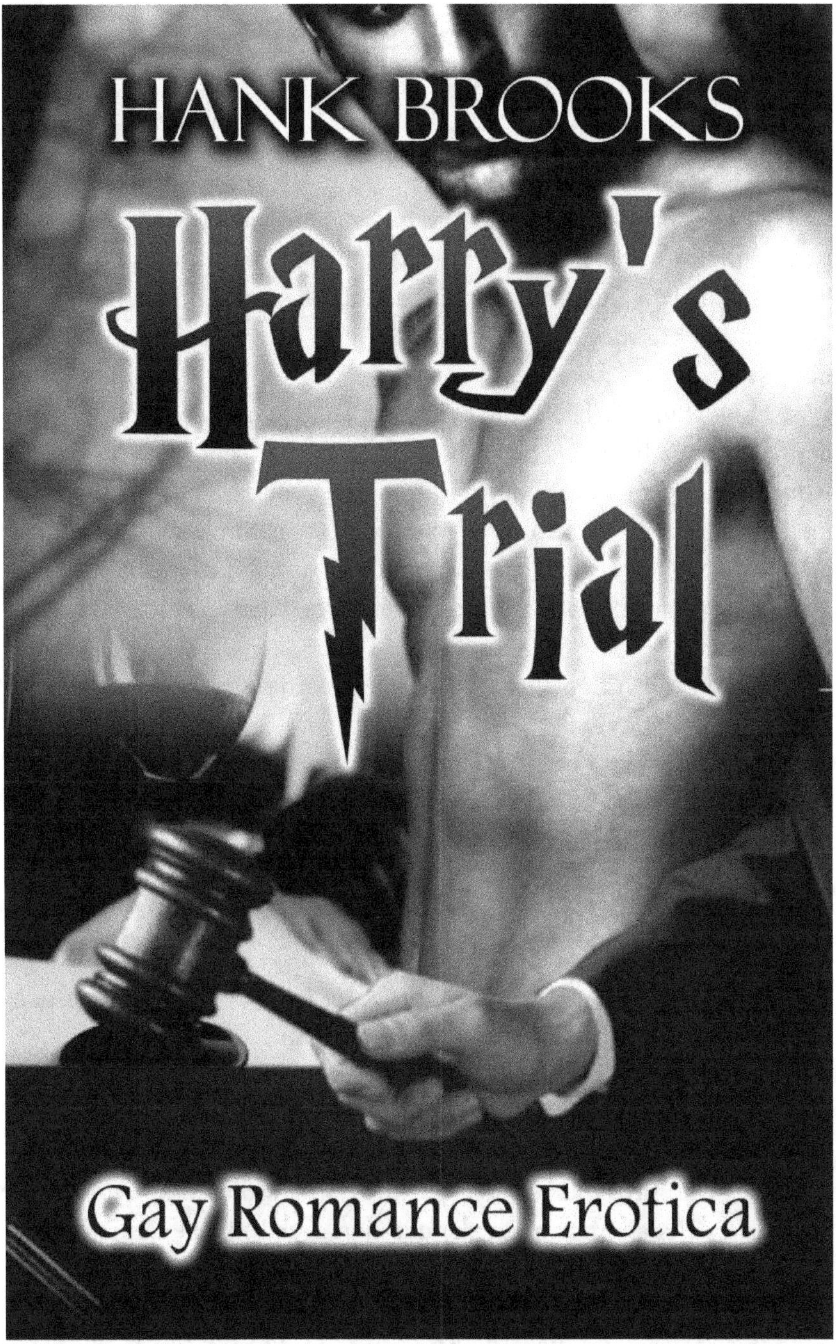
HANK BROOKS
Harry's Trial
Gay Romance Erotica

Harry's Trial

By: Hank Brooks

The thirty-something, very undistinguished looking gentleman, was waiting to be called to the witness stand. Nevertheless, when he heard his name called, he was startled, and he jumped out of his seat. Against his attorney's advice, he had elected to testify in his own defense.

Now that he had actually been called, his life seemed to collapse around him. All his energy was sapped, and he could barely struggle with his body in its effort to walk to the witness stand. It took a monumental effort to step up onto the raised platform, swivel the chair around, and take a seat. No sooner did he sit down, then the bailiff asked him to stand again while he administered the oath. That took another major effort.

He heard the bailiff's voice. "State your name for the records please."

"My name is Harold Hampton."

Finally he was seated and ready for whatever would come. He took a deep breath and glanced furtively at the female judge, who was shuffling through some papers. He couldn't help wonder if a male judge would be more sympathetic.

He heard his attorney's voice. "Did you kill your wife, Mr. Hampton?" He was taken by surprise. He had expected the question, but not so quickly, and not right at the beginning of his testimony. He gasped and tried to regain his composure.

"Yes sir. I killed her while I was trying to defend myself. It was an accident."

"You say you accidently killed her while trying to defend yourself?" His attorney made the question sound like he didn't believe him. Whose side was he on anyway? "That's very interesting, Mr. Hampton. I would like you to tell the court the circumstances which led up to this accidental death. But before you do, I would like to introduce two pictures into evidence." He glanced at the judge. "One picture was taken at Mr. Hampton's wedding, and the other was taken two months before Iris Hampton's death."

The prosecution objected. It was expected that they would object to every motion presented by the defense. The defense had done the same to the prosecution.

"Where are you going with this, Mr. Jancowski?" the judge asked.

"I'd like to show the jury that Mrs. Hampton had put on tons of weight since her wedding, and was perfectly capable of being physically abusive to her husband. He weighed less than half of what she did at the time of her death."

"Overruled," she informed the prosecutor, "Let me see the pictures." Iris was a wisp of a thing in the wedding picture, and a big fat sloppily dressed woman in the second picture. The judge was slim and pretty, and Harold could actually see her wince when she looked at the second picture. She instructed the bailiff to show the pictures to the jury. They had the same reaction the judge had, especially the men. He hoped that weighed in his favor. No pun intended.

The judge nodded her head at Mr. Jancowski.

"OK." He said to Harry. "Tell us the circumstances of your wife's accidental death."

Harry sat back in his chair, and allowed himself to relax for the first time since his trial began. Until now all the witnesses had testified against him, especially Iris's family. They asserted that he completely ignored his ailing wife, and let her shift for herself, even though she was bed ridden. Now he had his moment in court.

His mind quickly reviewed the years from the happy youth he was when he met Iris, to the miserable human being he had become throughout their years of marriage. He began to edit his life, trying to figure out what was appropriate to reveal to the jury in order to gain their sympathy, and what events he should leave out.

***

Harry Hampton was a true cellophane man. He grew to be a skinny, 5'8", brown haired, brown eyed, weak chinned man. He wasn't bad looking, but he didn't have a face that would make anyone look twice either. He went through high school with a C+ grade average, and did not participate in any after school activities. A few girls caught his eye, but when he got up the courage to ask for a date, they turned him down. After awhile, he just stopped asking.

Harry had one really close friend, Jimmy Potter, who was just as non-distinct as Harry was. Like Harry he wasn't bad looking, but he just didn't have any charisma, nor would he demand any attention. He was an inch taller than Harry. His hair was a shade lighter than Harry's, and his eyes were a dark blue. His luck with the ladies was just as bad as Harry's was.

In college, they began to indulge in homosexual activity as often as they could, and they continued it into college, where they were roommates. To be fair, neither of the two boys considered the possibility that they might be gay. They were merely using each other for gratification, but only until the "real thing" came along, that is to say, the right girl.

By the time they were juniors, both boys filled out, grew to their adult heights, and spent some dollars on stylish haircuts and stylish tight fitting jeans. Girls actually began to talk to them.

Jimmy was the first to stop wanting gay sex. He started dating a freshman co-ed when he was a senior. She was kind of cute, but more importantly she put out, and a lot. She wanted even more sex than Jimmy could give her, but he managed to keep up with her by definitely excluding Harry from his love life. It wasn't long before they were talking about marriage.

Harry met Iris in his senior year at a party in the student union. She had just come to the university to do graduate work in nursing. She was just under a year older than Harry. She wasn't pretty, but she was exuberant and perky. Her bubbly personality overwhelmed Harry. He was unprepared for her aggressiveness toward wanting to have sex with him, and he foolishly mistook her for the "real thing."

They were married after Iris got her MS in nursing. Harry was already working in the accounting department of a large manufacturing company. Iris got a job at a nearby teaching hospital as a nursing supervisor and trainer. Between them, they made a very good living, and their life style was free and easy. They had fun together and life was good. In spite of it all, Harry often longed for the sex he had with

Jimmy. He sometimes pretended Iris was Jimmy when they were making love. He wondered if Jimmy had the same feelings, but he would never ask.

The change in Iris took place slowly over the first five years of their marriage. At first Harry didn't even notice it. One morning when they were dressing, Iris was having trouble with a zipper. She asked Harry to zip her up. He struggled, and suddenly the zipper ripped away from her nurse's uniform. Harry realized that Iris was putting on weight. She always had a better appetite than he did, and she always ate more than he did, but he marveled that she never gained weight. That seemed suddenly to be changing. For a moment Harry was elated. Maybe she was pregnant. That thought evaporated quickly. Suddenly Iris began to yell at him. It was uncharacteristic for her to raise her voice or use profanity, but she did.

"Fucking idiot! Fucking oaf! You ripped my favorite uniform. Can't you do anything right?" Harry stood looking at her dumbfounded. Unused to such awful behavior from her, and not knowing what to do, he finished dressing and left the house. He decided that he would have breakfast at a Burger King near his office that morning until Iris simmered down a bit. After Harry left, Iris went into her closet and found a white wrap around dress that wasn't even a uniform. Nonetheless she wore it to work that day.

She never did simmer down. She was gaining weight rapidly, and she knew it. Instead of getting a hold of her unhealthy eating habits, she ate more and more of her fatty junk foods. The unhappier she became, the more she ate. She was never without a bag of junk food in her hand.

She blamed Harry for all her misery. Their sex life slowed to a crawl, and at some point, when Iris's weight exceeded 250 pounds, Harry wouldn't have slept with her if he could. The sweat built up between the folds of her skin and she always smelled foul, no matter if she had just showered. She took up so much of their bed that Harry finally moved into the guest bedroom. He whacked off almost every night dreaming of Jimmy.

Their once tranquil home became a battle zone. From the minute they got home from work, she blamed him for all her miseries. Everything was his fault. Harry became the chief cook and bottle washer. Iris was just too fat to do anything around the house. Eventually she lost her job. Now, in addition to working all day, Harry had to wait on Iris hand and foot, prepare their meals and clean the house. All the while he heard her on the phone complaining to her mother what a useless oaf he was. Harry didn't know what road to turn up next, until fate intervened.

His boss wanted to hire a new assistant for Harry. The business was growing fast, and Harry was growing with it. He was now the manager of the finance department. Estefan Lopez, a drop dead gorgeous Latino, had been working for the city in the audit department. His pay was low and his job was a dead end rut. He was looking for a better opportunity. He was only four years younger than Harry, and Harry's heart almost stopped beating during the interview. In fact, at one point, Harry lost some of his pent up restraint, when at the end of the interview, Estefan said, "Look sir, I'm gay, and if that's an issue, I'll leave right now. I want to be open and above board about it so we won't have any problems down the pike."

Harry only hesitated for an instant. He winked at Estefan and said, "That's no issue at all. The job is yours." He left Estefan wondering about the wink. They shook hands on their new relationship and Estefan said, "Everybody calls me Steve, Mr. Hampton."

"Everybody calls me Harry, Steve."

Harry could not bear going home after work, and he found excuses to work late with Steve. Steve didn't seem to mind at all. They even began having dinner together after work. When Harry got home and Iris ranted for hours about how he didn't give a shit for her, he just kept silent. At some point, Iris usually passed out from booze, and eventually Harry went to bed with her vile words ringing in his ears.

One night at dinner, Harry told Steve about his life with Iris and how miserable he was. Steve put his hand on Harry's in sympathy. An electric shock went through Harry's body. He got bolder. "I was homosexual all through high school and most of college," he blurted out. He stared at Steve and waited for a reaction.

Steve closed his hand tighter on Harry's. "I thought so," he said. "I've always felt you were a gay man crying to come out. I'm really glad about it Harry, because I'm very fond of you." He squeezed tighter. "It would be great if you came home with me tonight."

Harry never thought of Iris once as he and Steve made love. He couldn't believe how good Steve's cum tasted. He had never liked Jimmy's jism much. He stayed as long as he could and reluctantly left at midnight. He went into Iris's room to check on her. She was snoring away, and the stench of wine on her breath was unmistakable.

The next morning she resumed her tirade. She called him an inconsiderate son of a bitch, because she had to make her own dinner, and he certainly knew how hard it was for her to get out of bed. When she demanded to know what time he came home, he said that he came home early, but she was sound asleep. He told her that he cleaned the dishes and went right to bed. As he left for work, her final words were, "You never think about me, just yourself, you selfish bastard. You better get home in time to make me dinner tonight."

Nice, he thought. Her bedside table was fully stocked with junk food, designed to last more than one month for a normal person. Harry thought, it'll be gone by noon.

The next day at work, Harry and Steve acted like nothing had happened between them, but about ten o'clock Harry went to the men's room. Steve followed him in. He locked the door behind him and grabbed Harry's crotch. Harry moaned as the two men kissed passionately. Then they peed and went back to their desks.

After that, Harry spent as much time with Steve as he could. There was no denying how much they loved each other. Steve kept pressuring Harry to leave Iris and move in with him. He kept pointing out that if Harry wasn't around, she would get out of bed and fend for herself. It might be the best thing that could happen for her. Still Harry wasn't convinced, and he continued to take all her abuse. At the same time he could overhear her on the phone telling anyone who would listen, that he never did a thing for her.

The final straw came one night when Harry was sound asleep in the guest bedroom. Iris threw open his door, and all four hundred pounds of her (or more) waddled in. She was naked, drunk, and she had a wine bottle in her hand. She placed the bottle on the dresser and fell on top of him. That woke him up quick enough.

"Fuck me," she demanded.

Harry was appalled. She smelled of sweat and booze. He could also smell the foul, fishy odor of her pussy. Even though his stomach was empty, he started to heave.

"I gotta go to the bathroom," he yelled. Iris rolled over slightly, enough to release him. He ran to the bathroom and locked the door. He managed not to barf, but he had to rinse his mouth with a mouthwash to get rid of the taste of his own bile.

He stayed there a very long time, but he knew that eventually he would have to come out. When he did, Iris was snoring away in his bed. He started to hyperventilate. He knew that he had to get out of there in order to save his life.

***

"What happened next?" Mr. Jancowski asked.

"There was a small suitcase under the bed. I grabbed it and just started filling it up with a few things. Suddenly Iris yelled at me, what are you doing?

"I'm getting out of here, I sobbed. Iris jumped out of bed. It was the fastest I'd seen her move in years. She ran out of the room. Seconds later, I felt her full weight on me. I could barely breathe. She rolled me onto my back, and I could see a kitchen knife coming at me, straight at my throat."

"What did you do next?" Jancowski interrupted.

"I reached up and grabbed her wrist. I was able to slow the descent of the knife, but not stop it altogether. She was just too strong, and I was having trouble breathing. Somehow I mustered all my strength and twisted her wrist. The knife was now aimed at her neck. I was running out of breath. With my last bit of strength I pushed up against her, trying to get a breath of air. As I did that, she seemed to lose her balance. She tried to weigh down heavier on me, and I pushed up harder. She was very drunk and unsteady, and somehow her head fell into the knife."

Jancowski waited a long time before speaking. The court room was silent. The jurors were trying to gauge the truth of what Harry had just sworn to. I'm sure they had a clear picture of a 400 pound Iris lying on top of his 150 pounds.

"I have no further questions," he said, and sat down.

The prosecutor approached the witness stand. He stood half facing the witness and half facing the jury.

"Isn't it true, Mr. Hampton, that you are homosexual?" he asked abruptly. Harry was stunned. He and Steve, and before that, he and Jimmy, had been very discreet. He knows nothing, and is just trying to trap me, Harry thought.

Harry still didn't think of himself as gay, and he answered, "No, I am not. You've seen her picture, sir. Don't you agree that she could have turned any man gay?"

The jurors roared with laughter. The prosecutor was not amused. "Isn't it true that you murdered your wife to be with a male lover?"

"No, it's not true. It happened just like I said," Harry mumbled with a sob in his voice. "If you want to know if she made my life a living hell, the answer is yes. But if you want to know if I planned to murder her, the answer is a resounding NO!" Harry looked at the jury. "No!" he repeated. The jury believed him, and the prosecutor knew it. He asked a dozen inane questions, but he couldn't shake Harry's story one iota. He finally looked at the judge and said. "I have no further questions for this pervert."

Jancowski objected, and the remark was stricken from the records, but it was enough to incense a good part of the jury. The prosecutor had just cooked his own goose.

"Mr. Prior," the judge fumed. "I will not permit that kind of talk in my court room."

"Yes, your honor. I apologize."

Mr. Jancowski then called a police forensic expert to the stand. He testified that the only finger prints found on the knife were Iris Hampton's. This was consistent with Harry's story that he never touched the knife. You could tell in cross examination that Mr. Prior had lost his steam.

"Could Mr. Hampton have wiped his prints off the knife and left only Mrs. Hamptons?" he asked limply.

The forensic expert actually started to laugh. "That would have been impossible without wiping off her prints as well. Besides, when the body was found she was gripping the knife so strongly, we had to pry it out of her hand. The defendant would have found it impossible to wrap her hand around the knife so tightly after her death."

Jancowski also called several character witnesses including Steve. Mr. Prior started to ask Steve if he was gay, but Jancowski objected, and the judge warned him "for the last time" that his question was inappropriate. His cross examination was tepid. All Steve had testified was that Harry was a kind and caring boss, and kept his home life to himself, never discussing it at work. There was little Prior could do to break down his evaluation about his boss.

The defense rested. Closing statements were made, and the jury began its deliberation. It took them less than two hours to bring in a verdict of not guilty.

Harry was in his own home that very night. In the front hall he found a basket with several bottles of wine and champagne. The accompanying note read: Congratulations. We never doubted you. Take a few days off and come back to the office when you are ready. We need you. Best regards, John F. Manning. John was the company's CEO.

Steve had arranged to have the bedroom cleaned of all the gory blood stains. He also had it repainted and recarpeted. Nobody could tell that anything so horrible had occurred here. The room was decorated with Steve's taste. After all, when a decent time would pass, he intended to move in with Harry.

***

He stayed there a very long time, but he knew that eventually he would have to come out. When he did, Iris was snoring away in his bed. He started to hyperventilate. He knew that he had to get out of there in order to save his life.

He dressed silently and ran out. He drove directly to Steve's apartment. It took a few minutes for his persistent knocking to wake up Steve. It took no longer to tell Steve what had happened.

"You left her in a drunken stupor?" Steve asked.

"As usual!" Harry said rolling his eyes. "I could go back in the morning. She won't even know that I'm gone."

"No," Steve said. "We're going back now. I'll follow you in my car, but I'll park a block away. Leave the front door open for me."

"What are you going to do?"

"You'll see."

They entered Harry's house silently and went into the kitchen. Steve put on a pair of rubber gloves that he had brought with him. He asked Harry where he kept the knives, and he removed a serrated steak knife.

They crept into Harry's bedroom. Iris was snoring away nearly at the edge of the bed. She was practically comatose. Steve got behind her and pushed her off the bed. She landed on the floor, awakened for a second, and fell asleep again. Steve placed the knife in her hand, and wrapped her fist around it. Strangely, she took a strong grip on it. Holding her wrist, he plunged the knife into her throat.

Harry watched the whole scene. He was aghast and frozen in place, yet he approved. Steve told him to lie on the floor. It was difficult, but he got Iris's body on top of Harry.

"Now wiggle her off of you. Give me five minutes to get on the road, and call the police. This is what you are going to tell them." He laid out the whole scenario. Then he took the suitcase from under the bed and put a few of Harry's items in it. Harry lay sobbing beside the body. He was scared to death. He waited ten minutes before he called the police.

***

Some people might complain that Harry and Steve got away with murder. Even though stories aren't supposed to end that way, just imagine how many people get away with murder every day.

Anyway, for what it's worth, Iris's murder was justifiable in my eyes. Think about it. If a person chooses to ruin and waste away her life, why should she be allowed to ruin the lives of everyone around her? It just isn't fair. In my opinion, justice was served.

End of the 14th Story

HANK BROOKS

FANTASY PLAY

Gay Erotica

Fantasy Play
By: Hank Brooks

I stood in front of the ten story high rise, and hesitated. I don't know why I hesitated. I wanted very much to go in and take the elevator to the fifth floor, to Apartment 5C. After all it was only a little sex I was after. *For God's sake*, I thought, *I'm forty two years old. I'm no virgin. Why am I shaking like this?*

Well, technically, I just lied. I am a virgin. It's nothing like the forty year old virgin, no sir. I have fucked so many women since I was nineteen that I have completely lost count. By the time I got married at twenty-seven, I had experienced enough casual sex to know that I wanted to be faithful to my wife. In fact, I had been faithful until this moment, and I could still turn and run. I wanted desperately to bolt back to my car, but I wanted to experience the forbidden fruit even more. My feet started walking toward the building. I opened the front door and entered the lobby. My heart was beating erratically. I was angry at my anxiety.

You see I have a little secret. And that was the cause of all my fears.

My name is Walt Digby. Of course in school I was often called Walt Disney. I really didn't care, but sometimes the kids overdid it. My first sexual encounter was in college   with Beth Bolling. Beth was the school slut. She had done every athlete on every team in the school. I was on the football team. It's true I was a second stringer, but still I was a team member, and therefore I had the privilege of being on Beth's to do list.

One day, shortly after my nineteenth birthday, Beth asked me to meet her in a park near the school. It was well wooded and had the reputation of being a trysting place. I knew what she wanted, and I was shaking like the virginal leaf that I was. It took her about a nano second to pull me into a bushy area and tell me to take my clothes off. The dear girl handed me a lubricated condom and told me to go to work. Apparently there was to be no kissing and certainly no preliminaries. I was merely to be another notch on her gun, if you will.

I was hardly aroused so I tried to think erotic thoughts in an attempt to get an erection. Much to my shock and horror, I began to fantasize that my football coach, Mr. Hutchins, had a big fat cock up my ass, and was fucking me hard and noisily. I had no idea where that came from. I never had a homoerotic thought before that moment, but it worked. I got rock hard, put on the condom and entered Beth. I came after only a few strokes and Beth cursed me for my premature ejaculation. To make up for it, she made me go down on her and I started to tongue her clitoris. I found it revolting, but I kept on going. Suddenly, inexplicably, I imagined I was sucking Coach Hutchins cock. Now it was even bigger and fatter than I had pictured it before. Beth began to grind her hips as her moans got louder. She came twice before she pushed me off of her.

"Not bad for a beginner," she said, and dressed as quickly as she had undressed. She disappeared before I had my jockey shorts back on, leaving me to ponder about my homosexual fantasies.

I didn't have to ponder long. Every time I fucked a young woman after that, and every time I whacked off, I imagined that I was fucking some hot male stud. Sometimes it was someone I knew, and other times I just conjured up a visionary Adonis. Suspecting full well that I was probably gay, or at least bi-sexual, I allowed myself to marry. Why not? I had successfully overcome any homosexual tendencies I had by fucking women. The beautiful thing about sex with my wife was that instead of imagining I was fucking a man, I thought about enjoyable past sexual experiences I had with her, and I became easily aroused. I remained totally faithful to Marian (Maid Marian I called her) and my two kids, until this very day.

I got married fifteen years ago. Shortly after we settled into our first apartment, we got our first PC. I knew that there were gay porn sites and gay chat rooms on line, and when my wife wasn't home I began to explore them. I was always a voyeur. When I was in a chat room, I would often get an IM from someone, but I never responded. I watched gay videos and perused nude photos of hot men posted on the internet. Over the years, my desire to have sex with a man grew exponentially.

Then two weeks ago, I was in a chat room, *M 4 M in Albany*. Suddenly I got an IM from someone whose screen name was hotbear. I had a thing for bears. Beefy men with hairy chests turned me on.

hotbear: *I just read your profile, sexy. I like your stats.*

Before answering I clicked on hotbear's profile. If he wasn't lying, he was just my age, hairy body, a seven inch cut cock, brown hair, blue eyes, 5'10", 195 lbs., a place to "entertain," loved sucking, rimming and fucking in both directions. I don't know what possessed me, but for the first time ever, I decided to answer the IM.

easyrider: *Your profile is much like mine*

hotbear: *I know. That's why I wrote to you. I live in Albany, NY. Do you?*

easyrider: *I'm from Albany also*

hotbear: *I'd like to get acquainted, but I hate IMing. Would it be OK to E Mail you?*

easyrider: *No problem. I'd like that*

hotbear: *You'll hear from me*

Hotbear signed off and I found myself literally shaking like a feather. Was it going to happen? After twenty-six years of lurid fantasizing, was it really going to happen? I hardly dared hope, but the next time I opened my E Mail there was a note from hotbear. It was long and chatty.

He was an audiologist, divorced for about five years, father of two teen age sons, loved being single, and loved entertaining men, the more the merrier. On and on he went. He loved Italian and Chinese cuisine but hated sushi. He couldn't abide the thought of eating raw fish. He loved theater, especially musical comedy, classical music, and opera.

He considered Albany to be a cultural wasteland, and often went to New York for theater weekends, and to enjoy the gay bars. He asked if I might consider going there with him one weekend. He also revealed his name: Ronald Naismith. He gave me his phone number and said to please call if I liked what he had written.

Hell yes, I did indeed. The man liked everything I liked, and I would love to go to New York with him if I could ever get away. To top it all off, he sent me a picture, fully dressed. He impressed me with the fact that he was too classy to send me a nude picture first time out. He was a handsome rugged looking dude. I could very definitely go for him.

I answered immediately telling him that I was married and I would call him on Tuesday evening when my wife played bridge. I asked him please not to call me. I told him that I taught Math at SUNY Albany, and had two teen age sons just like he did. I told him where I lived and asked where he lived and asked if we were far apart.

There followed three weeks of back and forth E Mails and telephone calls. I gave him my name, my profession, my home and office address, and an awful lot of personal information about me and my family. Ron had been honest with me and I was just as honest with him. We began to write lurid descriptions of what we would do to each other when we met. Now he felt it appropriate to send me a nude picture. WOW! I whacked off constantly to his picture and his letters, and avoided sex with my wife. I wanted to be with him so badly, I could think of nothing else. I became distracted while lecturing to my classes. Several times I had to turn to the chalk board and write something just to hide my tenting trousers. I was constantly on edge, and our letters and phone calls got hotter and hotter.

Finally, when I thought I would go insane, we made up a time to meet at his apartment. I told my wife that I had some heavy research to do, and I would be at the university library all day Saturday. I had always been a model husband and she bought my story without question.

And so here it was Saturday morning, and I was about to knock on Ron Naismith's door. My knees were buckling and my whole body was shaking. I could still turn and run, but instead I knocked on his door.

The door opened a crack and I could see a brown head of hair. An arm reached out and pulled me into the room. The other arm quickly closed and bolted the door. There stood Ron, naked as a jay bird, cock erect, and every bit as big as his profile and his picture had promised. His tool was throbbing and seemed to be bobbing up and down. He threw his arms around me and shocked me by kissing me. His tongue forced my lips open and we started French kissing. I had never kissed a man before, but I got caught up in the passion quickly enough, and my cock started to surge against my briefs, begging for release. I was pressed against him and involuntarily I started dry humping his willing body. Our cocks were humping together.

Ron pulled away and he started to undo my belt buckle. I was anxious to get naked, and I pulled down my zipper, so that when the buckle was undone my pants slipped down to my ankles. I kicked off my loafers and stepped out of my trousers. Ron immediately fell to his knees and he started chewing gently on my cut cock through my briefs. He took hold of the waist band with his teeth and slowly started to tug down my underwear using only his teeth. That made me wild with desire. I wanted to help, but thought better of it. While he was playing with my cock, I quickly removed my shirt. Now, when finally my briefs were down to my ankles, I was as naked as he was. I kicked off my briefs and took off my socks. Ron dragged me to his bedroom, and threw me roughly on his bed.

I was on my back and he lay atop my writhing body. We were kissing passionately, but suddenly he pulled away and started slithering down my body. My eyes were tight shut and I jumped when he inserted his tongue into one of my ears. He tickled that ear with the tip of his tongue and then started to nibble on my neck. I wondered how I could explain a hickey if he gave me one, but I was so lost in the moment that I decided not to worry about it until I had to.

From my neck, he worked his way to my nipples and started suckling them in turn. Why had I not known before how erogenous a man's nipples were? I thought that was reserved only for women. I was so worked up, I began to rub my hands gently up and down his back. The great amount of hair on his back was very sensual to me and I got even more worked up. I could only reach halfway down his ass cheeks, but for the first time I heard Ron moaning in delight. He moved further down and now he was darting his tongue in and out my belly button. I had to gasp to catch my breath. This was beyond all my fantasies, beyond my wildest dreams. He could have only one further destination going south and that was my genital area. I moaned loudly in anticipation, but I got a big surprise.

He bypassed my pubes, cock, and balls altogether and started licking up and down the insides of my legs. The area closest to my balls was the most erotic of course, but this was all a big tease, and I was a bit unhappy with Ron at that moment. I had no choice, however, but to go along with it. The final straw was when he began to lick my feet and each of my ten toes individually. The man was driving me insane. Then when I was certain he had to go to my cock, he surprised me again. He made me turn over onto my belly and he mounted me. I could feel his stiff cock find its way into my crack and he started dry humping my ass.

I wanted him to fuck me, but I thought, *Please don't fuck me until you have gone down on me and sucked my cock.* But I said nothing. He repeated the process of slithering down my body. This time when he was finished tickling my ears with his tongue, he slid right down to my ass. He kissed both cheeks and sucked all over them. He separated my cheeks with his hands and I could feel cool air attack my hole. When I felt his tongue start to lick up and down my entire crack, I actually whimpered. His tongue stopped at the hole and I could feel him trying to enter me with the tip. I realized then that I was crying. I had never had sex so intense, so gratifying, so satisfying, as I was having at that moment. I could not wait to reciprocate and give Ron the same joy, but first and foremost, I was praying that he wouldn't fuck me just then.

My prayers were answered. He rolled me back over, and this time he went for the part of me he had bypassed before. He took my balls into his hand and started to knead them gently. He bent over and started kissing and licking them. My tears were increasing. I was ashamed but I couldn't help myself. At the exact moment that I felt I could not bear anymore teasing he began to lick up and down the under shaft of my cock. When he reached the top, he skirted his tongue gently around my cockhead. I could feel the familiar sensation of a great orgasm building in my legs and working its way up to my balls, which were beginning to constrict. I was about to yell that I was cumming when suddenly Ron engulfed my cock in his mouth. Obviously I didn't have to say anything. His lips covered his teeth and he pumped them gently up and down my tool. His tongue was sliding up and down the underside of my cock as his saliva dripped from his mouth, wetting my groin.

When I exploded, I literally saw stars. There wasn't a doubt in my mind that this was the most intense orgasm that I had ever experienced, and that was when I decided that this was the answer to why God created man. Ron held me in his mouth until I began to soften. Then he lay fully on top of me and began to kiss me. He was sharing my cum with me. I was unprepared for it, but I quickly recovered and enjoyed the moment.

"Well my little virgin, what did you think?" Ron asked me as he snuggled close and pressed his hard cock against my thigh.

"I was wondering," I answered, "why the hell I waited so long. Why the hell was I so scared?"

"I used to think like that when I was married," Ron said. "After my first time, I knew that there was no going back. Have you got the guts to make the transition?"

I grew silent. I never thought about any transition. I figured I could see men on the side. "What do you mean?" I asked.

"Lots of guys stay married and play around on the side. If you want to do that, great, but find yourself other married men. No single gay man is going to put up with a part time lover, who is always looking at his watch, and constantly cancelling dates because something came up with the wife and kids."

Ron was right of course. I had never thought that far ahead. I didn't know what to say so I mumbled in his ear, "I'd like to go down on you now. I've been waiting for this for a very long time."

"No," he said emphatically. "You're the virgin and it's your day, or maybe I should say days. Next time I'll let you fuck me, and the third time we get together I'll let you suck me off and the fourth time I'll fuck you. You see Wally, I really like you. I'm very attracted to you, and this is my way of making sure I'll see you again. It's kind of like Scheherazade and The Thousand and One Nights. You had a good time, didn't you? You do want to see me again, don't you?"

I felt a shiver run through me. I didn't like the way Ron asked that. It sounded ominous, even threatening. The truth, however, was that I did want to see him again, and experience the full range of male to male sex. Today was only the tip of the iceberg.

"Of course I want more," I said, and I reached over and kissed him. He held me tight and we began a sword fight with our tongues.

"Good," he said. "The last guy I really fell in love with, got second thoughts. He went home and E Mailed me that he couldn't see me anymore because he wanted to preserve his marriage and his way of life. He admitted that he would never reach sexual gratification with his wife as he had with me, but he was willing to accept it."

"That must have hurt," I said. As I said it, the little bit of fear I had felt before, returned.

"Oh, it hurt all right. I waited until the next day when I knew he would be at work, and I called his house. His wife answered, and I told her what a faggot son of a bitch she was married to. She didn't believe me at first so I described the size of his uncut prick, and the little mole he had in his pubic area. I described how he sucked my cock and how I slipped my cock up his ass. That's when she hung up on me, but I fixed his goose. I waited a couple of days, and I called his office. They told me that he had taken a leave of absence. That made me feel really good." Ron started to laugh. "You would never do that to me Wally, would you?"

I was shaking and I started to get out of bed. "Of course not," I said. "I gotta pee and then I've got to get on home."

"No way," Ron said. "You told me that you had all day. Let's have lunch together before you go. It'll make us feel like we're an old married couple instead of a quickie trick."

All I could think of was getting home and never seeing Ron again. He had probably ruined me for all men in the future, but at that moment in time, I didn't care.

"Sure," I said. "Lunch will be great, the icing on the cake." I grinned broadly at Ron, hoping not to betray my true feelings. On the way out of the building, I told him that I had a phobia about elevators and preferred to walk up and down the five flights. In reality, I wanted to avoid security cameras. He said that it was good exercise and he joined me. We had lunch together, and I should have been nominated for an academy award. I smiled and squeezed his knee and thanked him over and over for the masterful introduction he gave me into the gay world. I assured him several times that he had given me the best sex I had ever had in my life, all the while I was quaking at the possibility that he might out me if I upset him. I was also thinking that I had told him one truth at least. It was the best sex I had ever had in my life and it was only a hint of what was to come. I was scared, true, but I wanted more, and I thought I could play along with him for whatever time it took for me to experience everything with him.

I took out my appointment book, and said, "My last class on Tuesday ends at 5 PM. It's the latest I teach, so I usually see students to answer their questions and discuss their problems after class that evening. I don't have dinner at home and I usually get home very late. It happens to be my wife's bridge night as I told you. How about I don't see students this week, and I give you my whole evening?"

Ron smiled and squeezed my hand. "You know what I said about part timers and clock watching," he said. "I really don't like it. But you're fresh, and I can put up with it. By the time I'm through with your instructions, you'll be begging me to let you live with me and you'll be leaving your wife."

When he said that, he must have seen me turn white, but I kept my composure. "That's an enticing idea." I said. "We'll see."

It was at that moment that I knew that when Ron had allowed me to experience everything he had in mind, there was only one thing left for me to do.

I HAD TO SILENCE RON NAISMITH!

* * *

I had an upset stomach all day Sunday and Monday. On the one hand, I couldn't wait to fuck Ron as he had promised. On the other hand, I was scared to death of him outing me to my family, my friends and my colleagues. He already knew where I lived, where I worked, and my phone number. If I didn't show up on Tuesday, he could ruin me. I decided to play along with him, and I stuck to my guns concerning retiring Ron from civilized society.

I had been very discreet. Nobody in the world was aware that I even knew Ron Naismith. I intended to keep it that way. On Tuesday evening I parked several blocks from his apartment building and walked over. As I walked through his parking lot and entered the lobby, I made sure to keep my head down so as not to be picked up by security cameras if there were any. Once again, I opted not to take the elevator, but walked up the five flights. Before knocking on his door, I made sure that I had regained my breath.

Once again he greeted me in the nude. For the moment I forgot my fears and I was consumed with lust. I didn't wait for Ron to undress me. I shed my clothes as fast as I could and then we wrapped up in each other's arms and kissed passionately.

"So do I get to fuck you tonight?" I asked expectantly.

"Absolutely, but I made us some dinner. Let's eat first." Dinner turned out to be tuna fish salad sandwiches and coffee. Needless to say, I had no appetite, but I ate just the same.

After dinner, I helped him put everything in the dish washer, and we went into his bedroom. We lay down on his bed facing each other and hunkered close. We began to kiss and fondle each other's cocks. When we were both good and hard, Ron rolled over on his back and placed a pillow under his butt.

"You'll find condoms and lube in my bedside table," he said. "Take them out of the drawer." I did as commanded.

"We're going to use plenty of lube, but the condoms are up to you. I don't care one way or another. I know you have no reason to believe me, but I'm clean."

I thought about it for awhile. I didn't know if I would ever have sex with a man again after I dispatched Ron, and I didn't want to cheat myself. "I think I'll go commando," I said. Ron smiled at me and kissed me. I think he liked my decision.

He instructed me on how to fill his ass hole with lube and how to spread it with at least two fingers inside of him. He told me to ream and stretch his ass so as to get it ready to receive me. Actually I didn't know there was that much preparation to it, and I was grateful for the instructions. When Ron was certain that his ass was prepared, he told me to lube my cock generously and place my head at his hole. He raised his legs and I clearly saw his well-greased tunnel. Hungrily I started my entry. I was expecting a lot of resistance, but I slipped in rather easily. When I was all the way in, I distinctly felt Ron constrict his muscles and tighten up around my throbbing tool. Without moving inside of him, I relaxed my body until I was lying on top of him. I could feel his hard cock probing my abdomen.

My lips found his and we started to kiss. I got more and more passionate. He pulled his mouth away and made some guttural sound which I took to be my go ahead signal. I began to pump inside him, gently at first. My only thought was that my wife's vagina was nowhere as tight, nor did it feel nearly as good. Ron began to thrust with me as I began to pump in and out of him. He began to make little moaning noises which heightened my lust.

"Harder, harder," he began to mumble and I started pumping harder and harder. Suddenly I stopped.

"Why did you stop?" he asked.

"I don't want to cum yet and I'm almost there."

"Cum, baby, cum," he said. "You'll have a million goes at it in the future. Let yourself shoot."

I was so lost in trying not to cum, I missed the significance of what he said. I began pumping slowly again.

"No," Ron actually yelled. "Pump hard." I had to obey him.

Seconds later I was shooting stream after stream of hot cum up his ass. Ron was whinnying like a horse. I collapsed on top of him and whispered in his ear, "I love you, babe." I didn't even realize that I had said that. I always uttered it automatically to my wife after I came inside of her. I didn't mean it with her, and I didn't mean it with Ron, but I said it nevertheless.

I lay on top of him as we kissed, until my softening rod fell out of him. Then I started to disengage myself from his sexy, hairy body. As I lifted myself up, I heard swishing noises and I felt a little stuck. I hadn't realized that Ron had cum and his juice had spread between us. I rolled over on my back so that we were lying side by side. I took his hand and muttered, "God, Ron that was so wonderful. I can't thank you enough."

"Lovers don't have to thank each other," he answered, and he rolled over to resume kissing me. "By the way," he added, "I love you too." Again I thought nothing of it. That's what people said to each other after they fucked. Wasn't it?

I wanted more that night, but Ron reminded me of his Scheherazade principle. He wouldn't let me reciprocate in any way. We agreed to meet again next Saturday. I said I would try to give him the whole day, and I asked if I could call him anywhere when I was alone in my office. He gave me his cell phone number and said to call between twelve and one any day, if I had the opportunity.

When I said that I had to leave, he scoffed. "Part time lover," he sneered. I wasn't sure if he was mocking me or being facetious. I didn't like it either way. No matter, for the next few days, I lost some of the fears I had, and I could think only of our next session of love making.

Nonetheless, I took the same precautions when entering his building and his apartment. I arrived before 9 AM on Saturday. All morning long he allowed me to make love to him. I tasted a man's cock for the first time. I sucked it as he had instructed me and I slobbered up his precum. I wouldn't let him cum. I wanted him to shoot up my ass.

"Don't you want to taste my cum?" he asked.

"I've tasted my own often enough," I answered. "Besides there will be a million other times," I said, mimicking his own words. "I'd so much rather get fucked."

Ron prepared my ass with three greasy fingers. He reamed and stretched until he felt I was ready. When at last he entered me, the pain was more than I could bear and I screamed out. I wanted him to pull out, but instead he pushed all the way in. I almost passed out from the pain. When he was all the way in, Ron lay perfectly still. The pain disappeared almost as quickly as it had begun. He started gently pumping and I started gently thrusting. At some point, I can't tell you when, he began to hit my prostate with each thrust. That did it. Now it was I who was yelling, "Harder, harder, please!"

When his cum squirted up my ass, I had the weirdest feeling. I felt like I was being fulfilled; it was like a vital missing piece of me was being put back into my body. I grabbed him and started kissing him profusely. I still feared what he could do to me, but I had to admit, I needed him to complete my life. I didn't care to start analyzing my emotions at that time. I just enjoyed the moment and once again I whispered. "I love you."

"Did you mean it when you said there will be a million other times?" he asked. I didn't answer him.

We went out for lunch. When we got back to his apartment, we spent the rest of the day making love. We sucked cock, rimmed ass, and fucked each other yet again. I never dreamed that I could be so aroused, and cum so many times in so short a span of time. When finally it was time for me to leave, Ron smiled. "Part timer," he chuckled. Only this time he said it with affection and I wasn't frightened.

As I was about to leave, he said, "You will be back on Tuesday, won't you? You know I could ruin you if you stand me up." I should have been frightened again, but strangely, I wasn't.

I ran my palm down his cheek. "I'll be back, my darling," I said. "If you truly love me, as I am beginning to love you, you won't ruin me. I could never forgive you for that. Let me make the transition you want me to make, in my own way and in my own time." I leaned over to kiss him and was shocked to see a tear rolling down his cheek.

"Of course, love," he said. "Just please come back to me."

Driving home, things turned weird. All the love and the lust I had felt just moments before began to leave me. I realized that there was very little difference between leaving my wife and coming out, and Ron outing me. I didn't think I would have a problem at work. Half the professors at the university were gay. I knew that some were even sleeping with male students. My fear was that of hurting my wife and my two very straight sons. I didn't think I could do that to them, and I renewed my resolve to do away with Ron. The problem I had now was that I had fallen hopelessly in love with him.

* * *

For the next few weeks I saw Ron as often as possible. Sometimes we had dinner out. He seemed to get a feeling of domesticity when we did. On Saturdays we sometimes had lunch out. Other Saturdays, we made love all day without eating. I needed him to fulfill my sexual needs, of course, but I was also taking the opportunity to study his habits, so that I would know the exact moment to dispatch him.

If only he could accept what I could give him instead of demanding a full time lover to live with him. I didn't want to eliminate him from my life, but his demands left me no choice. I also knew that I couldn't wait too long because he was getting more insistent as his patience was wearing thin. The more he pushed me, the more I knew I had to render him powerless to ruin my life. The problem was that with each new sexual encounter, I wanted him more. In fact, I loved him more.

I always fucked him while he lay on his back. From the moment I entered him, he kept his eyes closed. Even after I rolled off him to lie at his side and to catch my breath, he kept his eyes closed. I wondered what beautiful visions he was conjuring up. One Tuesday evening after I came, I told him that I was dying of thirst and wanted to get a drink of water. I asked if he wanted anything. "Yes," he said. "Don't take long."

I went into the kitchen and ran the water. As it ran, I opened the knife drawer and quietly removed one of the largest bread cutting knives. I wrapped my hand around it and ran into the bedroom. I am sure that Ron did not know what hit him because I plunged the knife into his throat so that he could not cry out, and he died instantly. I could not believe that I had really done it. I was cold and shaking like a leaf. I was glad to see that all the blood he shed was on the bed sheets. None of it had spurted onto the floor or the walls, like the gory scenes one often saw in the movies.

Suddenly I was freezing cold. I needed to dress, but my hand was bloody. "Out, out damned spot," kept running through my brain. I felt like I was in the middle of a Shakespearian drama. "The deed is done and cannot be undone!"

I went to the kitchen sink and washed the knife and my hands until there was no sign of blood. I wiped the knife dry and placed it back in the drawer. I used the dish towel as a glove, and put the knife at the bottom of the drawer, covering it with the other knives. I went back into the bedroom and tried not to look at the corpse, but curiosity got the best of me. Ron's eyes were closed. He looked very peaceful.

I got dressed and removed a small screwdriver from my hip pocket. I had placed it there for the sole purpose of doing what I was about to do. I unscrewed Ron's computer and removed the hard drive. I wiped the computer down with the towel to remove any finger prints.

I went through Ron's pants pockets and found his address book in his hip pocket. I took it out and put it in mine. I went to his cell phone and deleted my name from the phone log as well as all incoming and outgoing calls. I did the same with his land line, and then I went through the apartment wiping down door handles, drawer handles and anything else that I might have touched. I even got out the dust buster and vacuumed up any loose hairs I found lying on the bed or the floors. I emptied the contents of the dust buster into a plastic bag and put the hard drive and telephone book in the bag as well.

When I was satisfied that the apartment was clean of any of my fingerprints, I picked up the plastic bag and opened the front door with the towel. I peeked out. There was nobody in the hall. As soon as I was in the hallway, I wrapped the bag in the towel and ran down the hall without fear. I already knew that the only security cameras in the building were in the elevator. I walked down the stairs, and when I was sure that the lobby was clear, I left the building.

I drove home and stopped at an alleyway that I had previously scoped out. There were two huge dumpsters in the alley. I parked up the street and walked back to the alley. Once I was out of sight, I stomped on the hard drive. It shattered easily, but I smashed it until it was pulverized. I threw the towel and the plastic bag into one of the dumpsters. I removed some plastic garbage bags from the other dumpster and threw them on top of my plastic bag.

When I got home I was shaking with fear. I was extremely grateful that my wife was not home yet. I went into a hot shower and damn near scalded myself trying to cleanse myself. When she got home I pretended to be asleep.

I had been so careful. I was sure that I had committed the perfect crime, but I was arrested less than a week later. You see my wife had begun to suspect my infidelity because I avoided sex with her so often. She had gone to the university library one Saturday, and when I wasn't there, she hired a detective to follow me on Saturdays and Tuesday evenings. The detective had plenty of pictures of me walking through Ron's parking lot and entering his building. He had pictures of the two of us having lunch and one dinner together. He had even retrieved the plastic bag from the dumpster after I left the alley.

I received a fifty-year sentence which was as good as life to me. I could be paroled after thirty years. The only reason I didn't get the death penalty is that my lawyer was able to convince the jury that Ron was blackmailing me with threats of exposure. That got me some sympathy, and I suspected that at least one member of the jury was married and secretly gay.

How much better off I would have been to have left my wife to go and live with Ron, or even to have let him out me. My wife divorced me, my family won't speak to me, and my friends have disappeared from sight. I only have one friend left, and we have never met.

One day I got a letter from a fellow named Jay Castle. He told me that Ron had outed him to his wife and ruined his life. He thanked me for what I had done, and asked what he could do for me.

We began writing back and forth, and we have fallen in love through our letters. We are going to meet this Saturday for the first time, and we are both very excited about it. I am entitled to one conjugal visit a month. If everything goes well between us when he visits, and if Jay consents, I am going to put his name in to be my conjugal visitor. After all Ron instructed both of us in male to male sex, so it should be a very good match.

<h1 style="text-align:center">End of the 15th Story</h1>

Hank Brooks

Gay Erotica
SECRET DESIRE
A Foot Out the Closet

Secret Desire

A Foot out the Closet

By: Hank Brooks

Part 1

The first e-mail came from Bart.

Dear Harry B.:

I constantly read erotic gay stories on the internet, but I have never written to an author before. I can't tell you how much your story, Lost in Time, moved me. It was like you were writing about me. I related to every word. I too am in my very senior years, and still married to a woman. I wouldn't do anything to hurt her or my large family, but I constantly dream of being in a loving relationship with a man. The main character in your story is in the same boat as I am. Your words captured exactly what I feel. Thanks again for your sensitive and beautiful words.

Bart (retired school teacher) in California

Bart did not expect to get an answer. He was pleased and very surprised to get a prompt reply from Harry.

Dear Bart:

Thanks for your kind words. It's always nice to know that someone out there is reading my stuff and even enjoying it. It wasn't a stretch for me to write about a senior married man yearning to be in a gay relationship. I was that guy, but unlike you (I surmise) my marriage was from hell. I just walked out one day, gave my wife all my worldly goods (I figured my kids would get it someday anyway) and changed my life and my lifestyle forever. I don't recommend it for everyone, but my kids and grandchildren accepted it, and they are very fond of my partner. I have never been happier in my life. Where do you live in California? My elder son lives in Los Angeles. I am attaching a picture of me and my partner, Len. He's the skinny one on the right with the full head of beautiful silver hair. I'm the slightly pudgy one on the left. Can you send me a picture of you?

Harry in Florida

Bart answered.

Dear friend:

I live in a section of Los Angeles called Hancock Park. Do you know it? The houses are old and stately. I always tell people that Hancock Park was the Beverly Hills of LA before there was a Beverly Hills. Where does your son live? I must tell you that you and Len are very handsome men. I have begun to fantasize about the two of you having sex, and I get very aroused. Last night Len turned into me. You and I did it all, even anal. There is no way I could get hard enough to penetrate you, but it was my fantasy after all. You can't stop my fantasies, but if you prefer, you can tell me to stop telling you about it. I was able to stroke myself to climax imagining having sex with you. That hasn't happened in ages. My picture is attached. Be truthful.

Bart

Dear Bart:

EUREKA!!! First of all, I am being perfectly honest when I say, you are a knockout. I could easily go for you. There is no way I would not want to fantasize about going down on you. I would take all you have to offer whatever amount that is. Do you have any naked pictures? I am enclosing one of me. I am not big like the guys in my stories, but as Len kindly says, more than a mouthful is a waste. Feel free to keep on fanta-sizing about me and telling me about it. At our age, Len and I have no illusions about middle-class morality. We have freely taken someone to bed with us on rare occasions.

The second Eureka is that my son and his family live in Hancock Park at 153 McKinley Place. Is that far from you?

Hugs,
Harry

Early the next morning, Harry ran to his computer. Bart had not yet answered his last e-mail. Harry knew that because Bart was in the closet, he might not always be able to sneak away and answer his secret mail. Harry did not wait for an answer. He wrote:

Dear Bart:

Last night, I began to think about your fantasy and I got very aroused. I practically attacked Len in the middle of the night and we took good care of each other, so thanks. Wish you were here.

Hugs and kisses,
Harry

Later in the day, Harry received an e-mail from Bart.

Hi, handsome:

Your cock is big enough for me or anyone else. So what if it doesn't match all those fictional characters? Does anyone's? You aren't going to believe this, but your son lives right around the corner from me. This morning I was walking my great grandson in his carriage, and for fun walked by your boy's house. Since it was Sunday, I hoped maybe to get a glimpse of him, but if anyone was outdoors they were in the very private backyard. Your son must be wealthy judging by his house.

Now tell me how good a detective I am. There were three cars in the driveway. They either had company, or my scenario is that the third car belongs to a teen-aged grandson or granddaughter, since it wasn't a luxury car like the other two. Let me know how good I am. I must also tell you how pleased I am that I am the subject of your fantasies also. Now I don't have to feel guilty about fantasizing about you.

Love,
Bart

That night, after Len fell asleep, Harry went to the computer and booted up. He wrote:

Dear Bart:

You are a regular Sherlock Holmes. My son has two boys of his own, nineteen and fourteen. I'm sure the third car belongs to my elder grandson. He just dropped out of college and is applying for fire fighters' school. My son is a doctor and a complete over achiever. He must be very disappointed about Donald dropping out of school. Still, firefighting is a worthy and noble profession, and Donald is handsome enough to make the firemen's calendar in the near future. LOL…

Len is asleep. As I write to you, I am sitting at the computer playing with myself. I keep picturing you and me going at it. I am really aroused. I picture you between my legs sucking my cock. Then you stand up and put your cock in my mouth. I hope you are feeling the ecstasy as much as I am.

We usually go to LA every Thanksgiving. My son doesn't like for Len and me to stay in his house because of the two teenage boys so we stay in a hotel. (As if they don't know what is going on.) I wonder if you will be able to join us in the hotel for a few hours. I'll let you know our *plans as soon as we book the hotel and air flights. Oh man, I'm cumming. I had to go clean myself up just to write.*

With love,
Harry

Harry switched over to a gay story website and was reading some newly posted material, when after just a few minutes he got a note from Bart.

My very dear friend:

I will find a way to be with you guys. Trust me.

All my love,
Bart

Over the next few months, Harry and Bart wrote as often as possible. One time Bart wrote six times in one day. They described in graphic language, growing more lurid with each note, just what they would do to each other when they met. Harry admitted how much he loved to rim a clean, pink ass, and Bart said, he would do anything Harry wanted to do, just to make up for all his lost and misspent years. Harry actually began to think of ways to prevent Len from going on the trip with him. When he realized what he was thinking, he grew angry at himself and refrained from writing to Bart for three days. Finally, he got a desperate e-mail from Bart asking if something had happened and was he well.

Harry wrote back and told a little white lie.

Darling:

My computer crashed and I was out of touch for a couple of days. I suppose I could have gone to the library or to a friend, but I couldn't write what I write to you on a friend's computer or in a public place. This proves that we should exchange addresses and telephone numbers.

I promise never to call you except in a dire emergency and if your wife answers, I could say that I am someone who used to teach with you back when we were both working. But you, babe, can call me any-time you can find a moment...

Harry then proceeded to give Bart his address and mobile phone number. He himself wondered why he didn't give Bart his home number. It bothered him for a split second.

Not five minutes went by and he received a note from Bart with his address and phone number. Harry wondered if it was a cell phone. Bart concluded the note:

I hope you are near your phone. I am going to call you in just a few seconds.

Len was in the living room reading a book so Harry went out on their patio. As soon as he closed the sliding glass doors the phone rang. He looked at his caller ID. It said *Wireless Caller.*

"Hello," Harry said in a somewhat frightened tone of voice.

An equally scared voice asked, "Is that you, Harry? It's Bart."

"Oh Bart, my dearest darling, it is so wonderful to hear your voice but it's not a good time to talk. Look, Len will go bowling tomorrow from about 1PM to 5PM. On Tuesday, he will go to Bingo from about 6PM to 10:30PM. This is all Eastern Time, of course. If you can get someplace private and call me either of those two times, we can have wonderful phone sex."

"I'll manage both times," Bart answered. "I swear. I love you, sweetheart." Bart hung up.

The next day, at 1:15 PM, Harry's cell phone rang. He didn't even look at the ID. He was sure it was Bart.

"Hello," he said. His voice sounded inquisitive.

"Harry, it's me, Bart. Is Len gone?"

"Yes."

"Good, I'm totally naked in my bedroom. My wife is spending the day at some spa with a girlfriend. Get naked and talk to me, please. I'm bursting with anticipation."

"Hold on," Harry said as he put the phone down and stripped in record time. He lay down on his bed and picked up the phone. "Bart," he said. "I'm lying naked in my bed. I'm flat on my back and my erect cock is trying to reach the ceiling. Stroke it for me, will you?"

"Yes, darling. It will be my pleasure. Shall I stroke you gently or hard?"

"Gently, very gently. Make your fist into a feather duster."

"Whatever you say."

"Now, Bart, lie down next to me and I'll do the same to you."

"Oh yes, Harry. It feels so good. Make me cum."

They stroked themselves in silence for a few moments. Each could hear the other murmuring sighs into the phone. Now they were both as erect as they would ever get, as they imagined that they were stroking each other.

Harry broke the silence. "I'm leaning over you now, babe. I'm taking your big, hard cock into my mouth. My tongue is sliding up and down the underside of your shaft. Your pre-cum and my saliva are mixing and lubricating your manhood. Can you feel it darling? Can you feel it?"

"Oh, yes I can. I'm in heaven. I'm crawling around you now. I'm going to do the same to you as we play 69."

Harry waited a moment and then he said, "I can feel my cock in your mouth. It feels so good. I don't want you ever to stop. Suck my cock all day, baby, please."

Harry began to hear little mewling sounds on the line. The sounds grew louder, then a small screech. "I'm cumming," Bart informed him. Finally, a loud scream went through the lines and Bart was spent.

"That was wonderful," he said to Harry. "I can't thank you enough."

Harry was still stroking himself. He imagined Bart's cum coursing down his throat. "I'm not done yet. Suck me a little longer," he begged.

"Yes, yes, of course. I want to do that so badly. Can you feel my finger up your ass as I suck your cock?" Bart asked.

That did it. Harry could feel his orgasm building. When it went beyond the point of no return, he said, "I'm cumming, baby. Don't stop sucking. Aah, aah, aaaaaah!"

There was silence for a moment and Bart asked, "Are you OK?"

"Yes, I'm just mixing our cum and spreading it all over my cock."

"You're bad," Bart said.

Part 2

Day after day, Bart and Harry wrote to each other. Their mail grew more and more lurid, even pornographic. They talked of sucking, fucking and rimming each other. Nothing was out of bounds. Harry was able to write more often. Bart had to wait for opportunities. If Harry didn't hear from Bart for a day, he grew frantic. Once after a wait of 36 hours, he almost called California, but in the end he restrained himself. Bart called as often as he could on Len's Bingo or Bowling days, and they had phone sex. After awhile the phone sex did not satisfy either of them. They wanted the real thing.

At last Harry wrote to Bart.

We are arriving in LA on the Monday before Thanksgiving at 1:10 PM, PST. We are renting a car and checking into a pretty run down motel on Sunset Blvd. We never spend a lot of money on hotels, and this one is very clean and only about a ten-minute drive from my son's house. It's called The Sunburst, just off Western Avenue. We'll be checking out early the following Monday to make a 9:05 flight back to Ft. Lauderdale. The only day we are committed is Thanksgiving Day. The rest of the time we are on our own. Call me on my cell. You are welcome to our California residence whenever you can make it. Len is aware of your existence. I showed him your pictures, dressed and naked, and he wants to help make your fantasies come true also. He knows how you feel. He didn't come out until after his wife died. So you see, we are three kindred souls.

Bart answered almost immediately.

Dear Harry:

I have good news, bad news, depending on your viewpoint. My wife fell this morning and broke her hip. She is in the hospital. The doctors say she will be there for at least a week and then rehab for at least three more. She will definitely be in rehab during your stay. I will visit with her most of the day, but my evenings will be free. I am sure that one of my kids will want me to stay with him or her, but I can say no to them without arousing suspicion. It looks like we can meet often, even dine together. I am so excited. My only wish is that I could do this openly and not be so sub-rosa. Also, I must be honest and tell you that I wish Len was not in the picture. But after all these years, I shouldn't be so self-ish. Two cocks are better than one. I have been fantasizing the possibilities.

Dear Bart:

I showed Len your letter and he is sympathetic to your de-sires. He said that we could be alone the first time. He'll go to a movie or something. However, he wants in on the action after that. Agreed?

Dear Harry:

Agreed! But who knows? After I meet Len, I might want him there from the get go. Let's see how it all plays out.

Harry and Len checked into the motel and they were unpacking their suitcases when there was a knock on their door.

"Who the hell can that be?" Harry mused as he went to the door. He opened the door and there stood a handsome older gentleman, grinning from ear to ear. He looked familiar to Harry, but he couldn't quite place him.

"Harry?" the man asked.

"Yes."

"I'm Bart."

"Oh, my God!" Harry yelled. He grabbed Bart and pulled him into the room. Len discreetly closed the door. He was smiling as Bart and Harry embraced and kissed each other passionately, their mouths open, their tongues dueling. Harry pulled away and as if he and Bart were old friends, he said to Len, "Len, this is my friend, California Bart." Bart stuck out his hand, but Len grabbed him in a bear hug.

"Don't be so formal," he said. "We are going to be intimate friends. How long can you stay? Do you want me to go out for an hour or two? I can have a cup of coffee at the McDonalds across the street."

"Please don't leave," Bart said. "I only live ten minutes away. I was just in the rehab hospital with my wife. I told her that I was going to get some stuff at the supermarket for my dinner tonight, so I can only stay a moment. I just wanted desperately to see you both. I can come back about 6 PM. Would you, guys like to have dinner with me at a fine restaurant? My treat."

"Definitely," Harry said, and Len nodded.

"I gotta go," Bart said and he kissed Harry. Then he kissed Len and said, "Please be here too. You're gorgeous, especially those beautiful blue eyes."

"We'll both be here," Len said.

It was just shy of 6PM when Harry's cell phone rang. He heard Bart say, "I'm very close. Would you guys mind waiting outside? It's still rush hour and parking is a bitch in this neighborhood."

"Not at all. We'll be out front."

They went to a wonderful Mexican restaurant, but if the truth be told, none of them really enjoyed the meal. They were all nervous about what they knew was going to happen that evening. At the same time expectations ran high in all of them. Bart could not wait for dinner to be over, but to his credit, he did not hurry.

"Look, guys," Bart said, "There's nobody at my house but me. I have a huge king sized bed. How about we go there instead of the motel?"

"It sounds good, but are you sure that nobody will drop in on you?"

"One of my kids might call to check on me, but they wouldn't come over. They would have too long a drive."

"OK then," Len said, "but you'll have to drive us back afterwards."

"No sweat. It's not far at all."

Part 3

The three of them undressed and embraced in a group hug. They fondled each other's privates and kissed each other back and forth. Harry instructed Bart to lie down in bed on his stomach. Bart did exactly as he was told. Suddenly he felt a tongue licking his right ear and then the tip of the tongue entered his ear canal. What a strange feeling. He was titillated, but he was more fascinated by the warm, moist sensation. His wife had never done this to him, nor had the very few men he had ever been with. He wondered who was licking his ear.

He didn't have time to dwell on who when he felt a tongue running up and down his left ass cheek. His whole body shivered. For awhile one tongue played with his ears alternately, and the other licked up and down both his ass cheeks. Bart had never in his life been so turned on. Then the licking of his ears stopped. Deft hands separated his southern cheeks, and whoever was licking him down there suddenly began to lick his ass hole. The tip of the tongue was pushing into his opening. He was about to moan with pleasure but stopped himself when he felt another tongue licking his balls.

Now he did indeed moan loudly. The tongue stopped licking his ass hole and a greasy finger sought entrance. He wasn't sure but he thought someone whispered *relax* into his ear. He tried to do just that and the finger slipped in. Bart moaned louder.

"Turn over now," one of them instructed him. Bart rolled over, but still he kept his eyes shut. He had no idea why he did that, but it somehow seemed appropriate to do so. The two tongues went to work again. One tongue found his nipples and suckled and nipped at them. The other tongue went to work on his balls licking them all over, moving up to the shaft of his penis, teasing him unmercifully. His whole body began to writhe in pleasure and frustration. It seemed a very long time, but finally the tongue began to lick up and down his shaft, and finally it happened. His cock was sucked into a mouth. Irrationally, he hoped it was Harry's so he opened his eyes. Harry was sucking his cock and fondling his balls. Len was nipping at his nipples.

"I can't hold off much longer," Bart announced.

"Don't hold back," Len said as Harry continued to suck away. It was hard to say who was enjoying things more, Bart or Harry.

Suddenly it happened. Harry could feel Bart's balls constrict as he yelled, "I'm cumming."

He expected Harry to back off, but Harry sucked more feverishly, and allowed Bart's cum to trickle down his throat. Bart came with the loud scream Harry had often heard on the telephone. He held Bart's cock in his mouth until Bart begged him to release it.

"Well," Harry asked, "how did you enjoy that?" Bart answered by sitting up, grabbing Harry, and kissing him passionately. He was surprised to taste his own cum in Harry's mouth.

"It's my turn now," Bart announced. "You two lie on your backs and I'll go down on both of you." He positioned himself on his hands and knees between the two lovers. Leaning over, he took Harry's member into his mouth. It tasted as good as all his fantasies had promised. With one hand he fondled Harry's balls and with his other hand, he began to stroke Len's cock. He continued to do this back and forth. After nearly half an hour, he felt Harry's balls begin to constrict. By this time Harry was moaning loudly. Bart abandoned Len temporarily and did everything he could to bring Harry to climax. Harry came screaming as loudly as Bart had. Bart took Harry's cum, but refrained from swallowing. Instead he went down on Len with a mouthful of cum, using it as a lubricant. The squishy feeling was very erotic to Len and he too started to writhe and moan.

"I'm cumming," he yelled and spurted generously into Bart's mouth. This time Bart swallowed as much as he could, but there was enough for Harry and Len to taste when he kissed them.

The three men lay side by side in Bart's big bed. They were on their backs with Bart in the middle. Bart fondled both their cocks and they each fondled Bart's cock and balls. Every so often they turned their heads and kissed each other. Time passed as they basked in the afterglow.

"Let's wash and get dressed," Harry said, "and you can drive us back to the motel, Bart."

"Can we get together tomorrow?" Bart asked. He was actually pleading.

"My son is taking us out to dinner," Harry said, "but we can call you when we get back to the motel, and if you are up to it, you are more than welcome to come around."

"He means C-U-M," Len laughed.

"It's a deal," Bart agreed.

During that week they were able to get together four times before it was time for Len and Harry to leave. The best and longest session they enjoyed together was the night before their departure. Before he left the motel, Bart announced that he could now die a happy man.

On the flight home, Harry asked Len if he was really all right with what had happened in Los Angeles.

"Absolutely," Len asserted. "I know how it feels to be as tortured as Bart, and we really made his fantasies become a reality. I'm happy to have been a part of that. Anyway, I still have you, and that's all that matters. I know you wanted to have sex with Bart. If I had objected, you might have resented me."

Harry smiled at Len and squeezed his knee as the male flight attendant asked what they would like to drink. He saw Harry's hand on Len's knee and he smiled at the two elderly gentlemen.

Len and Harry wrote to Bart regularly and when possible they spoke on the phone. A few weeks before Thanksgiving, Harry sent Bart their flight and motel arrangements for their annual visit to Los Angeles. Bart didn't answer. After three days, Harry wrote again. His e-mail was returned. Bart's E-Mail address no longer existed.

On a hunch, Harry went online to The Los Angeles Times website. He searched the obituaries for the entire past week, and he found Bart's final biography. Bart left a loving wife, six children, fifteen grandchildren, and three great grandchildren. He took his secret to the grave.

Len and Harry regretted that they could not give Bart one more week of the love he so desperately craved, but they were happy about the week they had given him. That evening they raised a glass of wine to celebrate Bart's life, and to thank God for the opportunity He had given them to make Bart's fantasies come true.

End of the 16th Story

Gay Romance

Christmas in a Warm Climate

Horny Visitors

Hank Brooks

Horny Visitors

Christmas in a Warm Climate
By: Hank Brooks

I was neither born nor bred in Manhattan, but if there ever were such a character as a true New Yorker, you're looking at one. For many years, Gerry and I had subscriptions to both The Metropolitan Opera and The New York City Opera. We didn't subscribe to The New York City Ballet, but we attended often. We never missed an opening night of a new Broadway production. The opening of a new exhibit at The Metropolitan Museum of Art found us both in attendance. We ate most of our meals at home, but every Saturday night we went to whichever restaurant The New York Times was recommending that week. We lived in the greatest city in the world, and we took advantage of all that it had to offer.

Gerry and I met before we were out of our teen years. We were both freshman at Columbia University and living on campus. He was from a small town in Indiana, and I was from an even smaller town in Iowa. I left because I knew I was gay, and the atmosphere for gays in a small town in Iowa was hazardous to say the least. I didn't find out right away, but Gerry decided on a New York school for the same reason.

My first class on the official opening day of school, excluding orientation, was English 101. Gerry was in my class. The professor assigned us seats alphabetically by first name. He said that he could remember our names easier that way. Gerald sat in the middle of the second row. My name is Kenneth, and I ended up sitting right behind him in the third row. There were five rows of six seats per row in the class room.

We didn't speak to each other until the third class session. Professor something or other (I forget his name) was a little late. I was in my seat when Gerry came in. Our eyes met and we smiled. He looked quickly away, and I could tell that he was very shy. I also knew, without a shadow of a doubt, that he and I played for the same team. I'm not sure how it works, but my gaydar is practically flawless. Before he could sit down, I held out my hand and introduced myself.

"Hi. I'm Kenny, from Iowa," I said.

He shook my hand warmly. "Gerry, from Indiana."

"How do you like New York so far?" I asked trying to make conversation.

"I haven't gotten out much yet. I'm a little afraid to venture out on my own. I never saw so many people on the streets in my life."

"Me too," I lied. I had already discovered some great gay bars in Greenwich Village, and one on Columbus Avenue, but I didn't want Gerry to know. "Maybe you and I could explore the scene together this weekend." Gerry smiled, and his shoulders relaxed as if I had relieved him of some great burden.

This was our only class together that semester. We had no more sessions before the weekend, so I asked him what dorm room he was in, and I said that I would pick him up after dinner on Friday evening. He surprised me by saying, "Let's have dinner together Friday, and take it from there. What's your room number? I'll pick you up at 5:30."

After that Gerry was far from shy. On our first date that Friday evening, I steered him into a gay bar in The Village. As soon as he realized where I had taken him, he grabbed me, hugged me, and started to kiss me, but he thought better of it, and aborted the kiss.

I whispered in his ear, "My roommate lives in New Jersey. He went home for the weekend. If you'd like to continue what you were doing later on in my room, I would really love that."

"Do we have to waste the whole evening?" Gerry asked. "Can't we just go there now?"

"I thought you were shy," I said facetiously.

"I am," he answered, "but not with you. Listen to me," he said very seriously. "I'm a virgin, and I don't want to be one after tonight. Please be my first." I started to laugh.

"You find that amusing?" he asked, sounding very hurt.

"Yes, very amusing. I'm a virgin too." Gerry grinned from ear to ear.

"Let's get outa here," he said.

That was the beginning of a forty-two year relationship. I'm not going to tell you that neither of us ever cheated. We gave each other permission. We were both engineers, and there was a lot of travel in our jobs, so it was bound to happen. In the end it didn't matter. Gerry and I were soul mates. He's gone now, but I know we will meet again.

We were pretty awkward that first night. All we did was whack each other off, but after we recovered a little, I asked him if I could taste his cock. We were both uncut and pretty average in the size department, so neither of us was self-conscious about size. The result of my attempt to taste him was a bad game of sixty-nine. We both had to learn to keep our teeth tucked in. It didn't take us long to perfect our techniques, and neither of us was shy about swallowing our cum juices.

Anal sex came on the third week of our relationship. We discussed it at great length before we tried it. We agreed to use rubbers for cleanliness, and not because we were afraid the other might have a disease. It was a time long before the HIV virus reared its ugly head.

We waited until all our expenses for our senior year were paid in full by our parents; then we let them in on our little secret. I'd love to say how understanding they were, but they weren't. Neither of our parents ever wanted to see us again. We got through that trauma because we had each other to lean on, and we found strength in each other's love.

We each landed good jobs in different consulting firms in New York City, and we were on our way to successful careers. Lincoln Center was under construction. We bought a co-op apartment nearby, and set up household. We made many, many friends, both straight and gay.

Our favorite time of year in The Big Apple was Christmas time. We never tired of gazing at the gaily decorated shop windows, the tree in Rockefeller Center, and the tree in The Museum of Art, which was a work of art all by itself. We would wrap ourselves with warm scarves and put on gloves, and watch the ice skaters in the rink at Rockefeller Center, and the one in Central Park. Sometimes we would even go ice skating ourselves. I used to wish the holiday season would never end. The lights of the ornately adorned city just bedazzled both of us.

Our lives were full, professionally, privately and socially. I, for one, never thought it would end. And then one day it did end, and our lives were shattered. Even though neither of us smoked, Gerry was diagnosed with lung cancer. By the time it was diagnosed, the disease had travelled to his liver, and it was over pretty fast.

I became a leaf blowing in the wind. I went along with the crowd, but I had no idea what I was doing. My friends tried to keep me busy and occupied, and I appreciated them, but their efforts were futile. I would walk to a theater, and halfway there, I would forget where I was going. I'd miss performances that I had badly wanted to see. Forget about work. I couldn't even function, and I decided to retire at sixty-one. Now things were worse. I had even more idle time to get through.

Gerry and I had been very close to another gay couple, who were about ten years older than we were. They had retired to South Florida, and they kept begging me (bugging me, actually) to come for a visit, especially in the dead of winter.

The second winter after Gerry's death was particularly bitter cold and snowy. I had given up all my theater subscriptions, and I pretty much never left my apartment. I was becoming a hermit in our (my) apartment.

Early in December I received another invitation from Bob and his partner, Bill, to spend the holidays with them. I was miserable, and I knew it. I thought maybe a change of scenery would help, so I reluctantly decided to give it a try. How much worse could it be celebrating with well-meaning friends in Florida, than with well-meaning friends in New York?

I had never been anywhere in the world before, where winter wasn't winter, so I relied exclusively on my hosts' suggestions as to what to pack. I didn't even own a pair of shorts, but every department store in New York had a cruise wear section where I was able to buy some appropriate clothing. Originally I was going to book a ten day trip, but in the end, at Bob's insistence, I booked two weeks. I wasn't staying at a hotel so it would not cost me anymore. In addition, by leaving several days after New Year's instead of the day after, I saved nearly $100 on the air fare.

When the big jet took off at Newark Airport for Ft. Lauderdale on December 23rd, I was as frightened as a virgin on her wedding night. I could feel the butterflies buzzing around in my tummy. Bob and Bill were close friends. I was very fond of them, so I couldn't understand my growing anxiety. Then it came to me.

All my friends in New York were constantly trying to 'fix me up' with someone, and I was getting fed up with it. I didn't want to be fixed up. I was not ready, nor would I ever be, to replace Gerry. If Bob and Bill tried to fix me up, I swore I would leave on the first plane out. I didn't need their help to connect with a one night stand if I wanted to. The higher the plane flew gaining altitude, the more I realized that I was being very foolish, and I did indeed begin to calm down and enjoy the journey. In fact, I dozed off.

I dreamed that I was standing in front of The Pieta, in the Michelangelo Museum in Florence, Italy. Mary was holding the dying Jesus in her arms as she always did, but something was very different. Ah yes, these were not marble statues. These were flesh and blood people. Suddenly, the figures began to morph. Mary was turning into Gerry, and Jesus was turning into me. Gerry cradled me in his arms, rocking me gently.

"Don't cry," he said. "We are looking after you." What did he mean by 'we'? He, Mary and Jesus? I could only wonder. Gerry laid his hand on my chest, and for the first time I could see a huge hole where my heart should be. The hole was quickly filling with blood, and Gerry was trying to fill the hole with something to stop the blood from gushing. I couldn't make out what it was. He wasn't making any progress. The more he filled the hole with the unknown substance, the more it filled with blood.

"Sir, sir," I heard a voice say, and someone was shaking my shoulder. I opened my eyes. A handsome male flight attendant was looking at me with some concern. "You must have been dreaming," he said. "You were sobbing very loudly."

I was terribly embarrassed and apologized profusely. The flight was three and a half hours long, and I forced myself to stay awake. If I was going to have a break down, better to do it at Bob and Bill's apartment, than amidst a couple of hundred strange people.

The flight arrived at 5 PM. I picked up my bag at the carousel, and walked outside with my carry-on and my suit case. Bob and Bill told me they had a white Lexus, and would pick me up at curbside. My first impression was of the heat and humidity everyone talks about. Actually it was welcome. The temperature in New York, when I left, was 28°F. But still, it was winter in South Florida. I didn't realize at the time, but in an hour or so, when it was dark, the temperature might go down into the sixties.

Car after car passed me by, but finally I saw a white Lexus. It could not quite get to the curb. The front passenger window opened and Bill waved at me. Suddenly the trunk popped open. I put my bags in the trunk and jumped into the back seat. I should have been surprised, but I should also have expected it. There was a handsome, very distinguished looking gentleman, in the back seat.

I ignored him by greeting Bob and Bill profusely. When I could not ignore him any longer, I stuck out my hand. "Hi," I said, "I'm Ken."

"I figured," he said with a smile in his voice, so that I couldn't take offense. "I'm Bailey." I had to admit that Bailey was a good looking man. I thought he was in his late forties, but it turned out that he was in his late fifties, just a couple of years younger than I. How did he do it? I wondered if he had had any plastic surgery. He hadn't.

"We figured you'd be hungry at this hour," Bill explained, "especially since they don't feed you anymore on these airplanes, so we're going out to dinner, and we asked Bailey to join us." Bill said it like there was no plot, like they weren't trying to fix us up. That's a laugh.

"Don't look so unhappy, Ken," Bailey said. "These two guys have been trying to fix me up for over a year since my partner died. There's no discouraging them. I would say that you are their latest victim, but I'm not sure who the victim is here this evening." He broke out laughing, and I realized that he was treating this entire match making business as one big joke. I decided to treat it the same way, and let it roll off my shoulder. I even liked Bailey a little.

I had no idea where we were heading, but as I looked out the car window, I could see houses, office buildings, and lawns, which were decorated even more elaborately than in New York. The temperature was in the low eighties, and I couldn't process the ambiguity. Wherever I looked, I saw Christmas trees decorated with tinsel made to look like snow on branches. I imagined that all of it should be melting. I just couldn't get used to the whole idea of celebrating Christmas in such a warm climate.

The restaurant we finally arrived at was called Posie's. It was in Wilton Manors, which Bill told me was the so-called gay section of Ft. Lauderdale. A valet took our car, and the head waiter sat us at an outdoor table. In fact, most of the tables were outdoors. Once again I had to pinch myself to accept the reality of eating outdoors on December

23rd. The temperature had dipped to the mid-seventies, and I was glad that I was still wearing the blazer I had flown in. I looked around and there were plenty of diners in shorts and tee shirts. I felt like a wuss.

"This place is noted for its hamburgers," Bailey said. "You ought to try one." I took him at his word, and ordered a bacon burger with stewed onions, and a side of sweet potato fries. It was delicious.

The four of us chatted cordially, and I learned that Bailey's partner, James, had died of pancreatic cancer. We both had to agree that cancer was a vile disease, and we expressed an open prayer that someday it would be as extinct as polio. Somewhere in this world, I prayed silently, there must be another Jonas Salk.

When we arrived at the apartment building where Bob and Bill lived, I was surprised to see that Bailey got out of the car with us. He took my carry-on bag and said, "Here, let me help you with that." I panicked. Were Bob and Bill expecting me to sleep with Bailey that night? I think Bailey saw the look on my face, because he started to laugh.

"Don't worry," he said. "I live next door to the guys, on the fourth floor."

"Sorry," I said. "I'm getting paranoid about guys trying to fix me up."

"I don't like it either, but it doesn't bother me. My friends mean well."

When we got to the front door, Bailey dropped my bag, and said, "Well, I'll see you tomorrow evening. We're all going to church for Christmas Eve services. Have you ever been to a gay church, Ken?" Bailey asked. I had to admit that not only had I never been to a gay church, I hardly ever attended any church.

"Good night, guys," he said, and he kissed Bob and Bill on their lips. He kissed me on my cheek, and I wished he had kissed me on the lips also.

Bob and Bill's apartment was lavishly decorated for Christmas, and once again, I had a feeling of total incongruity, especially since I could hear the air conditioning purring away. Bob showed me to the guest bedroom, which had a guest bath room as well. "You'll have total privacy," he assured me.

I took advantage of the situation to take a long hot shower. I felt grungy from the long trip. In the shower I thought about Bailey and his handsome, manly, good lucks, and I was shocked to be getting an erection, so I whacked off to relieve myself. I hadn't done anything wrong in admiring Bailey's good looks, so why did I feel that I was desecrating Gerry's memory?

At least the orgasm, which I had just experienced, helped me to fall asleep rather quickly. Suddenly, my repose was disturbed by a bright light at the foot of my bed.

Gerry was standing there. He was smiling at me, and he was naked. I blinked my eyes to see if I was dreaming. I guess I was dreaming, because when I looked again, he was wearing a white flowing robe. Now, standing next to him, was a very handsome older man. He was at least ten years older than Gerry. He too wore a white flowing robe.

"This is James," Gerry said. "In life he was Bailey's partner. We are both very sad, Ken, that you and Bailey are so lonely, and won't allow yourselves to find happiness. You both have long lives ahead of you, and what you are doing to yourselves is just not right. We have to go now."

"Please, Gerry, don't leave me yet. Where are you going?"

"To visit Bailey and to deliver the same message. You two were meant for each other. I beg you not to throw your lives away."

The apparitions disappeared and I woke up. I was amazed to find bright sunlight streaming into the room. Where had the night gone so fast? I got out of bed, went to the bathroom, showered and shaved and did other things. I laid out the uniform of Ft. Lauderdale residents, i.e., shorts, T-shirt and sandals. I didn't bother with underwear. I figured I would change for church later in the day. It wasn't until I was dressing that I noticed the time. I glanced at my watch as I put it on. It said 4 o'clock in the afternoon. Impossible! It must have stopped during the night. I looked again. The second hand was turning at its usual rate of speed.

I ran out into the kitchen, where I expected to find at least one of my hosts. Nobody was in the house, but I found a note on the kitchen counter.

Dear Ken:

You were sleeping so soundly, we didn't have the heart to wake you. Bill and I went shopping for dinner tonight. We invited Bailey to eat with us before the Christmas service.

Help yourself to the contents of the refrigerator.

Hugs, Bob

I was still full from last night's dinner at Posie's, so all I did was heat up the coffee that was still in the pot on the coffee maker machine. I had just taken my first sip when the phone rang. I wasn't going to answer it unless the caller ID indicated that it was one of my hosts. It was neither. It was Bailey, so I picked up the handset.

He wanted to speak to Bill or Bob. I explained that I was alone, and I asked if I could help him. He said that he only wanted to know if he could bring something for tonight's dinner. I told him I didn't know, but asked him if he would like to come over and have a cup of coffee with me. He was over one second after we hung up.

I poured him a cup of coffee and as soon as we were both settled down again, Bailey said something that scared the hell out of me.

"I met your late partner, Gerry, last night. It was in a dream of course."

"And I met James in a dream."

We stared at each other, unable to speak. Finally, with great effort, I asked. "Did they say anything to you?"

"Yes, they said I should tell you about my dream, and to be happy, move on, and find a new person to share my life with. I think they meant that person to be you. What did they say to you?"

"Essentially, the same thing. They said that we were meant for each other."

Bailey put down his coffee cup, and laid his hand on mine. That simple act sent shivers through me, yet it was warm and comforting.

"I didn't want to come down here for the holidays," I confessed. "I swear I heard Gerry urging me on all the time. I got no peace until I booked the airline tickets."

"I never wanted to meet you at the airport or have dinner with you, but something in my mind kept insisting I do it."

"It's a miracle that we both had the same dream," I said, "but I don't know what to make of the rest of it. Let's not talk about it now. Let's just see what happens." We smiled at each other and sipped our coffee in silence.

We were too overwhelmed to make much conversation at dinner either, and I could tell how uncomfortable Bill and Bob were. I began to believe that they thought that Bailey and I hated each other.

There was a pageant at the church that night. In the vestibule, they had set up a living crèche. Over the crèche was a platform, and on the platform stood a group of angels protecting the baby in the manger. Bailey and I saw them at the same time. Gerry and James were among the angels. They appeared exactly as we had seen them in our dreams.

"How many angels do you see?" I asked Bailey.

"Including James and Gerry, I see six. Why are you asking?"

I didn't answer. I looked over at Bill and Bob who were staring at the crèche in admiration. "How many angels do you see?" I asked them.

They looked at me like I was crazy. Finally Bill found his voice. "What a funny question to ask," he said. "Obviously there are four. Why are you asking?"

Bailey and I looked at each other and smiled. "No reason, Bill," I answered. I took Bailey's hand. "Don't you think we should all go into the sanctuary and find seats?" I asked.

Both of us were filled with the love of the Christmas season. Bailey held my hand so tightly that it hurt, but I didn't want to discourage him.

"Do you believe in miracles?" he asked me.

"I didn't until yesterday. I do now."

"Do you believe in love at almost first sight?" he asked again.

"I do now," I said, and I leaned over and we kissed each other for the first time.

"Atta boy," I distinctly heard Gerry's voice. At the same time Bailey jumped.

"What's the matter?" I asked.

"I swear. I just heard James's voice."

When we got home Bailey invited us in for some eggnog and apple pie. We accepted. When it was time to go, I apologized to Bob and Bill, and told them that I was staying with Bailey that night.

You know what? They weren't upset at all. They went next door to their own apartment with the biggest smiles I had ever seen on their faces.

When we were alone, I whispered to Bailey, "Merry Christmas, Friend."

"Merry Christmas, Love," he whispered back.

We embraced, and I swear I heard singing, but I didn't know where it came from.

We then kissed, exchanging saliva for what seemed like a marvelous, wonderful, long-sought-after eternity. I noticed that Bailey's bulge wasn't up-tight and pushing forward like mine, but his was throbbing along his right thigh as it grew thicker and thicker and seemed to be sliding up the leg of his trousers.

"Get your pants off, and I'll do the same with mine," I said, hurriedly unbuckling, unzipping, stepping out, and grabbing a similarly naked, heavenly-sent partner-to-be for God only knows how long.

Again we kissed, and then we kissed some more, rubbing each other all over — as much as possible while still kissing — crushing his thicker-than-mine against my longer-than-his excited, throbbing member... oh, Hell! You know what I mean. I wanted him so much, and at that moment, Bailey said, "Let's not rush this."

He lovingly took me by the hand and led me down the short hall to the Master Suite of the condo. At the door, he asked, "Which of us carries the other across the ... threshold?"

I looked at the gorgeous hunk standing next to me, shrugged my shoulders, got a stupid look on my face, then looked down his chest and abs to his tempting "sausage" and put my hand around it. He understood my silent meaning, and he grabbed my only-slightly-longer "hot dog".

Together we walked into the bedroom, and turned toward the Queen sized bed to the left, and immediately stopped ... shocked at what we saw. His stranglehold on my cock was suddenly yanked to the side, and I very nearly fell to my knees.

We saw the impressions of two people lying there, a few inches apart. Slowly, the impressions began rising, as if the two would-be people were floating upward, and then suddenly the comforter was completely smooth — not an indent or depression of any kind.

But what WAS laid there were four roses — two white and two red —a white and a red, next to each other, but the two reds were nearer the center of the bed, and the two whites were nearer the outside edges of the bed. Each two was tied together with red and white curling ribbons, and beneath the stems was a folded piece of plain white paper on top of the comforter.

"From James and Gerry," Bailey said at the same time as I said, "From Gerry and James." Tears came into our eyes as smiles of the Season of Peace and Good Will crept across our lips.

I made my way to the right side of the bed, while Bailey made his way to the left side of it. Together we lifted the roses and smelled them. The reds smelled of cinnamon; the whites, of the same frankincense we had smelled at the midnight service at church.

We looked across the bed at each other. Our eyes were yet a little sad, but our smiles showed our new-found happiness —happiness radiating in more ways than one.

We each picked up the notes that had guarded the cut stems from dripping any of their mutual sap onto the comforter. Then we both moved to the upholstered bench at the foot of the bed, and sat next to each other. Mine had my name, Ken, on it, in Gerry's handwriting. Bailey's note had his name on it, and in James's handwriting, as I later learned.

Together, we opened them, and began reading aloud. *To my Dear Ken,* mine began. *To my Dear Bailey,* his began. Then we began reading aloud the same words together.

We thank God and praise the angels in the Highest that you have found each other; we've been hoping and praying that you would. Now you can both be happy with each other and stop worrying about us — neither of us has any pain at all, especially now that you're together.

We know that you'll never stop loving us, as we hope that you'll know that we'll never stop loving you. As you know ... Love ... True Love ... goes on forever ... and will never die.

Bailey and I stopped reading at the same point and looked at each other with silent laughter coming from our bellies and heart-filled-chests, enormous smiles that actually hurt, and with rivers of tears. We turned back to the notes and continued reading aloud.

The red roses are for the Love that you and I had, and the white ones are for the Sadness and Emptiness you've both experienced since we left. Now hold the roses in one hand as you intertwine your fingers with...

My note said, *Bailey's*; his note said, *Ken's*.

Know that from this day forward, you two will be as one, and also know that at some future date in your time (which is the same as today in our time), we four will be together as one, for eternity. You think you can put up with us that long?

Just remember — we'll always love you. And some one, or two, or more days, we might just stop in to see how you're doing. You probably won't be able to see us as you did earlier tonight, but we'll be there, and we'll see you.

And now, my Love ... the Light is getting stronger, and we're being called home. We can hear the angels singing; there's work to be done, both here and there — it's not all sitting on clouds around here, ya know, or continual singing of beautiful hymns, or cleaning off dusty angel's wings; no sir-eee!

And on that note of Gabriel's Horn, I'll just give you a final kiss........until we meet again.

I love you, Hon.

My note was signed, *Gerry*; his note was signed, *James*.

We were still naked, you may remember, and after crying a bath-tub of tears, we each got a glass of water, then showered, dried off, and got into bed about 2 AM. We held each other for the longest time, saying nothing, doing nothing, not getting erect, just absorbing everything we'd experienced since meeting at the airport.

"You awake?" Bailey asked in a whisper.

"Yeah. I was about to ask you the same thing."

"I've got to read that note again."

"Me, too."

We both jumped out of bed. Bailey's motion detector turned on the bedroom light. We hurried to the dresser across the room and looked at each other with furrowed brows.

"What happened to the roses, Bailey?" I asked.

"I don't know. Where'd you put yours?"

"I laid mine in the center of the fold of the open note. You?"

"I did, too. But there are no roses, and the notes are closed. What gives?"

Slowly, simultaneously, we opened the notes. The words were still there, but instead of the roses, some golden dust was strewn across a portion of each fold of the two notes. "Dust?" we asked each other, but as the days, weeks, months, and years passed, we began referring to it as our Angel Dust. We kept it safe.

* * *

As time passed, we showed our "notes" to fewer and fewer people. All they could see was white paper, but no words.

The notes became aged with handling, but Bailey and I could still read them, more often at first, but not quite so, as time and arthritis grew more quickly, or was it our minds that couldn't concentrate so well?

Now and again, Gerry and James stop by for a visit. We can't see them anymore, but we do feel their presence and we can almost hear their loving voices.

And here it is ... almost Christmas, once again.

What we do feel is that tender kiss to each of us as they leave us once more.

"Until then, my Loves," we both say to them. "Merry Christmas to you and the rest of the Heavenly Hosts ... Until then."

End of the 17th Story

HANK BROOKS

Things Aren't Always What They Seem

Doubtful Heart

Gay Romance Erotica

Doubtful Heart

Things Aren't Always What They Seem

By: Hank Brooks

So a friend of mine told me this story the other day. It reinforced an old adage…you know, the one about things aren't always what they seem. I found the whole thing to be a little unbelievable, but my friend swore it was true, and I have no reason to disbelieve him.

He started out by telling me about Bill and Ted…two handsome gentlemen now in their early thirties. It was difficult for him to describe their relationship, or to ascribe a name to it. They lived together, slept in the same bed, and had fantastic sex together, but they didn't think of themselves as a couple. They had never made any commitments to each other, and they were not monogamous by any stretch of the imagination. Either, or both, was very apt to come home with a trick. When that happened, they used the spare bedroom, but it was not uncommon for them to sleep three to the bed as well. Notwithstanding their somewhat strange relationship, they were best friends, who would trust each other with their lives.

They had known each other since they were born, just a week apart, Ted being the elder. They lived next door to one another. They went all through school together, right up to the day they both graduated from State U. They roomed together all through college, where they shared each other's bodies and others as well.

These days, Ted is a reporter for the local newspaper, and like all good reporters, he is trying to write the great American novel. Bill has been working in the accounting office of a major tool and dye manufacturer since he graduated college. He is now the accounting supervisor, and has a staff of six. Neither of the two friends ever came out at work, and they were very cautious about being seen in gay clubs, or gay events of any sort. This drew them closer together, both as fuck buddies, and as friends.

About six months ago, a young man, just out of college, was added to Bill's staff. Bill strongly suspected that Fred was gay. He made no moves on him, but continued to observe him closely. His observations were centered on learning what Fred's sexual orientation was, but in the process, he learned a lot more. He determined to enlist Ted's help in confirming his suspicions, and learning the truth about Fred Scott.

One evening, he and Ted were lying in bed, basking in the afterglow of some very memorable love making. After Ted had cum in Bill's ass, he never lost his seven inch erection, and was able to continue pumping until he came a second time. Not to be outdone, Bill came in Ted's mouth twice in quick succession also.

"You were really hot tonight, buddy," Ted said.

"Good enough to ask you to do me a favor?" Bill asked.

"Anytime," Ted shot back. "What can I do for you?"

"Are you up for a little detective work?"

"Sure…sounds like fun. Fill me in on the facts, just the facts sir," Ted mimicked Sgt. Friday from Dragnet, an old TV detective show.

"About six months ago, I hired a young accountant fresh out of college. His work is excellent, it really is, but there's something strange about him."

"In what way, strange?"

"Well, for one thing, I can't figure out if he's straight or gay."

"So what's the big deal? Are you hot for him or something?"

"I could be. He's really good looking, and I caught a glimpse of his equipment once in the men's room. Wow! Anyway, I wouldn't make a move on a co-worker. I'm in the closet at work."

"So what do you want me to do? Find out if he's gay?"

"That would be nice, but only incidental," Bill answered. "I can't figure him out. He hardly ever talks. If you want someone who'll listen to you, and never talk, he's the greatest. I also find him to be very snoopy. On the rare occasions that he does say something, he asks some really probing questions…way beyond the scope of an intern learning a new job. I'm really suspicious of his motives. Even my assistant, Julia, thinks he's a little creepy."

"I still don't understand what you want me to do."

"Well, last Friday after work, I stopped off at Skippy's for happy hour, and my weekly TGIF drink. The crowd at Skippy's is primarily gay, but it isn't strictly a gay bar. Plenty of straights go there too. That's why I wasn't afraid to be seen there, and it's near my office. When I walked in, the first person I saw was Fred sitting at the bar. His back was to me and he was talking to another guy. The other guy handed him an envelope and Fred stuffed it in his pocket. I high tailed it right out of there. I didn't want him to see me."

"That doesn't prove he's gay," Ted pointed out. "You said yourself straights hang out there too. Are you beginning to suspect industrial espionage maybe? This is like a fucking movie."

Bill ignored Ted. "I want you to wait for him to leave my office next Friday, and follow him. If he stops for a drink, I want you to cruise him. Please try to turn on all your charm, flex all your muscles, and maneuver him into bed, not ours, his. People talk too much when they are in bed with a lover. Maybe you can learn why he is constantly probing and asking crazy questions."

"And how will I recognize this lucky fellow who is about to enjoy my body?"

"I'll leave the building with him and wish him a nice weekend before I go in the opposite direction."

"You're mad, you know," Ted said with a snicker, "But this little caper could be fun." He turned over and kissed Bill. "I'd like to fuck some more, but I'm bushed. G'Night."

During the week, Ted got more and more excited about doing some sleuthing for Bill. He was a good reporter, but he rarely got a shot at investigative reporting. That gave him more food for thought. What if Bill's suspicions were correct, and there was a story in all this, one that could get him a by-line and an exclusive? He couldn't wait for the work week to end.

On Friday he stationed himself across the street from Bill's office, a good fifteen minutes before quitting time. He was glad the early spring evening was warm, because he waited almost a half hour before Bill and Fred emerged. There was a quick goodbye, and the two men went in opposite directions. Ted followed Fred right into Skippy's bar. It was the first time he had ever been there.

The bar was fully occupied, but there was a free area at the end, where the bartender took orders. Fred went there and Ted stood right behind him. There were two other bar patrons in front of Fred. Ted pretended that someone jostled him, and his sexy body rubbed up against Fred.

"Oops, I'm sorry," he pretended to apologize. "This place sure is crowded."

"It always is, especially happy hour on Friday night. I guess you don't come here often."

"Right. This is my first time. I don't work anywhere near here. I was supposed to meet a friend, but at the last minute he texted me that he couldn't make it."

"Well, I'm here alone too," Fred lamented. "Let me buy you a drink, and then neither of us will be wallflowers."

Ted could not believe his luck. Fred was coming on to him. This was going to be a piece of cake, and the bonus was that Ted was very, very physically attracted to Fred. He didn't seem 'strange' at all.

"Thanks," Ted said. "You're very kind."

Two drinks, and an hour later, all Ted knew was that Fred was seven years younger than he was, had graduated from State U, and worked in the accounting department at Bill's firm.

"I'm still at my first job after college," Ted told Fred, "and I love it. Most people hate their first job as much as they hate their first sexual experience. How about you?"

"I loved my first sexual experience, but I'm not crazy about my first job."

"How come?" Ted probed. "Tough boss?"

"Oh no. My boss is great. I just can't explain it. It's a story for another time." (Bill is going to love that, when I tell him, Ted mused.) Ted got excited. Even if there was to be no sex tonight, Fred promised him 'another time.' Then Ted's luck continued.

"What are you doing for dinner?" Fred asked.

"Well I was supposed to go out with my friend, so I guess I have no plans."

"I live really close by. Why don't you come home with me, and I'll whip something up."

Ted's groin was now fully atingle. "You don't have to get fancy," he said. "There's only one thing I'd care to eat right now."

Fred smiled, took Ted's hand and led him out of the bar.

As soon as they entered Fred's apartment, Fred removed his jacket, tie and shoes. His carpeting was plush and thick, so Ted removed his shoes also, and as an afterthought he removed his jacket. He was not wearing a tie.

"I've got some baked chicken breasts in the freezer," Fred said. "I'll defrost them, bake them, open a can of peas, and we'll have a meal. How does that sound?" Without waiting for an answer he said, "Come into the kitchen with me while I get everything ready."

"I need to pee first."

Fred pointed to the john which was at the end of a tiny hallway. Ted was surprised to see Fred's college diploma hanging in the hall. He glanced at it quickly. Something was wrong, but he didn't realize just what at first. When he came out of the bathroom, he took another good look at the certificate. Fred had lied to Bill. He told him that he graduated just before he came to work at Bill's office. The certificate clearly showed that Fred had graduated more than three years ago. If he had graduated a little over six months ago, he would probably be ten years younger than Ted, but he was only seven years younger. Maybe Bill had a right to be suspicious after all.

He returned to the kitchen, and he and Fred made small talk while dinner warmed and they set the table. As each minute passed Ted got hornier and hornier for Fred. Fred was hot to trot also, but he seemed more restrained.

When they finally started to eat, Ted asked, "What is it that you hate about your job? If your boss is great, that's ninety percent of the battle? Is it boring or what?"

"I can't really talk about it," Fred said, looking uncomfortable. "Maybe another time."

When they finished eating, they cleaned up and put all the dishes in the dishwasher. Fred took Ted's hand. "If you aren't in a big hurry, I'd like it if you stayed on for awhile, or all night, if you'd like."

"I'd like," Ted answered, and Fred steered him toward the bedroom.

They sat down on Fred's bed. "Don't do anything," Fred said as he started to unbutton and remove Ted's shirt. Ted made minimal movements, merely to assist Fred in taking off his shirt. When Ted was naked from the waste up, Fred began to play with his nipples. He rubbed and pinched them softly and then he suckled them as gently as a baby suckles his breast-feeding mother. Ted was amazed. Nobody, not even Bill, had begun foreplay so sensuously, so lovingly.

He had to say it, in between his moans of pleasure. "Do you do this to all your boyfriends?"

"No," Fred said, interrupting his suckling tongue, "only to the ones I really dig, and who turn me on." In that moment, Ted forgot his mission of detection, and became Fred's lover, completely and without any reservations. As he resumed playing with Ted's nipples, Fred rested his palm on Ted's crotch, which was still encumbered by clothing.

"I can't stand it," Ted yelled out. "Please, let's both of us undress fully."

"Yes, yes," Fred said, as he began to tear off his clothes. They both stood up to admire each other, and Ted found his heart beating so fast, he was afraid he might pass out. Standing before him was an Adonis of Olympian proportions. Fred stood six feet tall. He had short, tight, curly black hair that was truly Grecian. It lacked only a wreathed crown to complete his statuesque look. His deep blue eyes were accented by his pale complexion. His biceps bulged, and his abs were wavy and taut. Ted doubted that Fred had any extra body fat at all. His legs and calves were so muscular, Ted wondered if Fred was a dancer among his other talents. Finally Ted's eyes wandered to where they wanted to go all along. His eyes feasted on Fred's magnificent cock. It was erect, and at least nine inches at the time. But what Ted most admired was the girth. He wondered if he could get his entire fist around it. He reached out to try, and he made it, but barely. Fred was uncut, but his hard member was protruding through the foreskin, exposing a purplish-pink head. Ted could tell that Fred had very little foreskin, and he liked it that way. He loved a foreskin that only went as far as the piss slit, and allowed a glimpse of the slit. His own cock was like that.

"You are…" Ted started to say, but words failed him.

Fred was also staring at Ted. The man was in his early thirties, but his body was that of a twenty year old. Every inch of him was muscled, but not in an ugly way like a body builder's. His long, brown, slightly wavy hair covered his ears. His dark brown eyes were warm and sensual, causing Fred's cock to jerk. His butt was a perfect bubble, giving Fred very carnal designs on it.

They stared at each other for a very long time, until finally Ted weakened. He could stand it (nor stand up) any longer. He fell to his knees and took as much of Fred's cock into his mouth as he could. At the same time he played with Fred's balls, brushing them lightly with his fingertips, and occasionally with his tongue.

He could hear Fred's cries of 'aaahh' and his ecstatic moans. It was music to his ears. He knew it was not his imagination, when he began to feel Ted's cock growing even larger, and his balls growing smaller. Fred was about to burst his dam, and Ted steeled himself for it. He swallowed what he could, but Fred's cum production overwhelmed him. Most of it ran down the edge of his mouth. Fred stayed put for quite a while. Amazingly his cock was not softening, but eventually he pulled it out. Ted stood up and the two men began to kiss, sharing Fred's seed.

Fred reached into his nightstand and extracted a condom and a tube of KY Jelly. As he handed it to Ted, Ted said, "OK, but I want you to suck me a little first before I fuck you."

"Not a problem at all."

They shared a shower after the love making ceased, and while they cleansed themselves, Fred asked Ted to please spend the night. Until now Ted's life had consisted of a series of one night stands, but he never stayed the entire night. He came home to sleep with Bill. No commitment there! Now he hesitated. He desperately wanted to stay the night, but he was afraid to give Fred the wrong idea.

"Not tonight," he said.

"Maybe next time?" Fred asked, sounding a little hurt. Ted had mixed emotions. He wasn't sure he wanted another time. It wasn't his MO.

Even as he dressed to leave, Fred asked him once again to stay. He just shook his head. "I'll call you," he said and took his leave.

Bill was waiting for him when he got home.

"Well???" he asked.

"Shit, I'm going to kill you. You know fucking well, what."

"OK, slut," Ted said. "I learned two things. First off, he thinks you are a good boss. He actually likes you. He must be crazy." Bill gave Ted a really dirty look, in jest of course.

"The second thing is a little suspicious. You said he came to work for you a short time ago right out of college, but I saw his diploma, and he graduated over three years ago. It'll be four years in a couple of months."

"Did you fuck him?" Bill asked. "Next time, try to find out what the discrepancy is all about."

"I don't think there'll be a next time."

"Why not?" Bill demanded to know. "Wasn't he hot enough?"

"That's not the problem. The problem is I like him too much, and I'm afraid about what I might find out about him."

"You're being a jerk you know. A good fuck is a good fuck, nothing more, nothing less. Call him. Pretty please, call him for me."

Ted made the call, and they met at Skippy's the next evening. It was a Saturday evening and they both secretly hoped that they would spend the night together. Of course they did.

This time Fred fucked Ted, and Fred sucked Ted. As they lay in bed afterward, their legs and arms hopelessly entwined, their kisses sharing Ted's cum, Ted dared to ask, "Fred, honey, you told me that your job is the first job you've ever had after graduating college, but you graduated three years ago. What happened in between?"

Fred took a long time in answering. Finally he said, "My grandpa left me some money, and I decided to use it to see the world before settling down, so I backpacked across Europe and then South America, until I ran out of money, and had to go to work." That seemed plausible enough to Ted, but there was something unconvincing in the way Fred said it, so Ted tried one more ploy.

"I'm really glad to hear that," he said. "I thought maybe you were in prison or something." Fred started to laugh so hard that Ted had to kiss him to shut him up.

Fred and Ted continued to see each other a couple of times a week over the next month. Each time they dated, they met at Skippy's and Ted spent the night at Fred's. He learned nothing more from Fred, and he stopped suspecting that anything was wrong. One Saturday morning before Ted left to go home, the two men made a date for Monday night, and Fred dropped a bombshell.

"Don't meet me at Skippy's," he said. "By noon on Monday, I'll be out of where I am working. We can meet anywhere that's convenient to you."

Ted was shocked. Bill never said a word about Fred's leaving. "When did you decide to leave? Why? How much notice did you give?"

"I didn't give any notice," Fred answered. "I'm leaving under special circumstances."

"Please tell me what's going on. I'll never last until Monday night."

"Ted, honey," Fred said, "I really care for you. I've fallen in love with you, and now I'm scared."

Ted wasn't shocked by Fred's confession. He was more than certain that he loved Fred also. "Why are you scared?" he asked.

"Because I've been lying to you. I didn't want to, but I had to."

"Are you going to tell me what's going on, or do I have to torture it out of you?"

"The owners of the company that I have been working for began to suspect that someone was embezzling funds. My real boss is a private investigator. I've been working for him for three years. I get placed in various positions, so I can learn the truth about what's going on, from the inside. I wish I had known you sooner. I could have given you a few scoops over these years. You can have this one, if you want. I now know who is embezzling the funds, and how. On Monday morning, the cops will come to the office to take the suspect to jail, and I'll be on to my next assignment. It'll make the newspapers, but I'd like you to have the exclusive. It'll be my gift to you for having lied to you. Now that you know what I do for a living, I'll never lie to you again, I swear."

Ted jumped up and embraced Fred. He was blinded by the offer of a scoop, and he never thought beyond his ego.

"Where's your computer?" he asked. "I want you to give me all the gory details, so I can have the story all typed and ready to go the second they make the bust."

"Does this mean you're going to stay a while longer?" Fred asked and grabbed Ted's crotch.

"That's an affirmative," Ted laughed.

Before actually starting to type, Ted sat Fred down on the sofa and conducted a professional style interview. He got the whole sequence of events from his first day on the job to his point of discovery. Fred kept referring to the thief as "The Perp" and Ted asked him to explain how the crime was committed.

"The Perp," Fred began his narrative, "applied for and obtained a corporate name from the state. Then it was easy to obtain a federal ID number from the IRS. With that in hand, The Perp opened a corporate checking account, at a bank other than where the real business had its accounts. The thief printed invoices with the phony company's name and a PO Box address, and then sent invoices, in moderate amounts, for goods and services, to the legitimate business, on a regular basis. The Perp approved the invoices, and they went through the company's payment process. The Perp deposited the checks in the phony checking account. Every week on Friday, our suspect cashed a check made out to the phony company's president and wrote 'salary' in the memo section."

"How much do you figure he has embezzled to date?" Ted asked.

"What makes you think it's a man?"

"I just assumed," Fred stated.

"The auditors have pulled all the records out of the archives, and the first payment to the phony company occurred over five years ago. They estimate the fraud to be slightly over $750,000."

"Wow. Yes, this is going to be one hell of a story. Leave me alone for an hour, honey so I can write the story. I'll refer to the embezzler as The Perp just as you did, but when can I know who it is?"

"I'll let you know as soon as the bust is made. Then you can insert the thief's name and let the presses roll."

"So nobody in the tool and dye office knows anything about this yet?" Ted asked. "Monday's events will shock the pants off everyone, won't it?"

"It sure will. I know you are a reporter, Ted," Fred said, "but can I trust you to keep quiet about this until it breaks? I've already told you too much, and only so you could get a scoop."

"I would never betray your trust. Now will you get the fuck out of my hair so I can write the story? By the way, I love you."

Fred smiled broadly, kissed Ted on his forehead and left the room. Ted was dismayed. Did he really tell Fred that he loved him? The words just flowed out of him. It came out naturally, without any thought processes. He smiled to himself, finally admitting that it was true; he did love Fred.

He opened a new document in Fred's Word Program and started to write. About halfway through, a thought came to him. Between Fred and Bill, he was familiar with the full cast of characters in the accounting office. Assuming that the thief worked in the accounting office, and he figured that was probably the case, he believed that he should be able to identify The Perp.

So who could approve the phony invoice, and get it into the payment system, with as few people as possible seeing the invoice? Hell, it was a small office. Anybody could be the culprit. But then the light finally dawned. A few years ago, he went to Bill's office to pick him up after work. Bill's car was in the repair shop for a couple of days. When he got there, Bill was not ready for him. He asked Ted to wait a minute while he signed a few checks. There was a pile of about six invoices in front of him with paperwork and a check attached to each packet.

Bill carefully checked the invoice to make sure that the receipt date was stamped on it, and that someone in the receiving department had initialed the invoice indicating that the quantity of material noted on the invoice was correct. He made sure that the check was drawn for the correct amount after allowable discount rates were applied. He then placed the check, and a copy of the invoice in the mailing envelope provided, and put it in an outgoing mail box. Then he stapled together all the back up documents and placed them in a box for the file clerk.

It struck Ted like a lethal lightening bolt. The only one who could get all this through to the mailing process without arousing suspicion was Bill. He could sign the check without the necessary receipt documentation. Ted felt sick. He ran to the bathroom and vomited. All the evidence led to his best friend, his brother, his fuck buddy, the guy he would lay down his life for.

He cleaned himself up, and ran out of the house, leaving the unfinished story in a Word Document file. He knew that he couldn't go home, but he had no idea where he would go. Fred heard his front door slam, and ran around his apartment looking for Ted. He could only wonder what happened and where Ted had gone to. His stomach sank. He had confided way too much to Ted. Could he really trust him? Did he just blow six months of undercover detective work, because he believed that Ted loved him as much as he loved Ted? He wanted to scream, knowing that he had surrendered his professionalism to love, and that was a pretty dumb thing to do.

Ted ran to a nearby park, found a bench, and sat down in utter despair. The embezzler was his Bill. He knew it to be fact, but he could not believe it or accept it. He started to cry, but nothing came to his mind by way of a solution. If Bill was the culprit, what was he doing with the money and where was it all going? He wasn't living any differently, or high on the hog, than he ever had in the past. Ted's unhappiness was mixed with confusion. He didn't know what he could do or where to turn. He sat for hours on the park bench, and finally decided on a course of action.

With red and swollen eyes, he returned to Fred's apartment. Fred had given him a key to his place the week before and he used it to get in. He barged right in without knocking. Fred ran to the door and Ted was shocked to see that Fred's eyes were as red and swollen as his. The two men fell into each other's arms. They began to kiss and proclaim their love for each other.

"Why are you crying?" Ted asked.

"I was so afraid you would blow my cover prematurely. I'm so sorry I mistrusted you. But why did you run out like that, and why have you been crying?"

"Oh, Fred! You have every right to mistrust me. I have deceived you. I'm crying for a lot of reasons."

"You're not making sense. Please talk to me. What's going on?'

Ted took Fred's hand and led him to the sofa. "We'd better sit down and I'll explain." Just then Ted's cell phone rang. He looked at the caller ID. It was Bill.

"I need to take this call. I'll make it short." He opened the phone and said, "Hello." He listened for a second and then said, "Look Babe, I can't really talk now. I'm spending the rest of the weekend with Fred. I won't be home until Monday after work." He hung up.

Poor Fred was confused. Ted was talking to someone he called Babe. It sounded like Ted had a lover. Did he just make a fool of himself? No, he couldn't have. Ted kept telling him how much he loved him. All he could do was remain silent.

Ted started to cry again and Fred took his hands into his own, but he remained silent. Finally Ted regained his composure, and started to talk.

"That was my roommate," he stated in a very matter of fact way. "We have literally been friends since we were born. We are best friends, as a matter of fact. I admit we have sex together, but it isn't love like you and I have together. It's fuck buddy lust, and nothing more. I don't consider us to be lovers, but until today, I considered us to be best friends forever, the kind of friend you would lay down your life for." Ted hesitated, not certain how to continue.

"Fred," he said, "you are my life, my love. I can't conceive of going another day without you. Do you believe me?" Fred was confused. All he could do was nod, so Ted went on.

"A few weeks ago, my roommate told me that one of his staff was acting strangely in his office. He wanted me to get close to that person and learn what I could. Of course, I told my best friend that I would do that. How could I know that he was your boss, or that I would fall madly in love with you?" Ted broke out crying again, and Fred sat there with his mouth hanging open. He was still holding Ted's hands, and he didn't realize that he was squeezing them harder and harder by the moment.

"Are you telling me that Bill is your roommate, and that I am such a rotten detective that he got suspicious of me?"

"Well, I don't think you would have raised suspicion if Bill wasn't guilty."

"But that's the point, honey. Bill isn't the guilty one."

Ted's eyes grew to saucer size. "He's not?"

"No, he isn't, but your BFF has another fault that you may or may not be aware of. He's a very lazy man. He has been assigning more and more of his responsibilities to his assistant, Julia, over the past few years. One of the things she has been doing is reviewing the checks for payment. She would separate the paper work, and all Bill got was the mailing envelope and the check to sign. He's guilty of a serious breach of internal control. I've already spoken to the authorities. They'll give him a slap on the wrists, and admonish him to go back to doing his job description. He may even get passed up for his next raise, but he won't lose his job. I've put in a good word for him, and told them that he's a good guy, a talented guy, and a very loyal employee. I told you that I liked him."

Ted began to laugh hysterically. "You did tell me not to assume The Perp was a man."

"I can see now why you were so upset. Well you can relax now. Your BFF is a good guy. But tell me, how do I stand in your life now?"

Ted jumped up and grabbed Fred. He wrapped his arms around him and squeezed his ass. "You're at the top of the heap. How would you feel about surprising Bill and going over there? We'll tell him about us, but not what's coming down in the office on Monday. I'll need to start bringing my stuff over here, if we are going to live together."

"When did we decide that we were going to live together?" Fred asked.

"The moment I saw you at Skippy's. Anyway, respect your elders and don't argue with me."

"I wouldn't dream of it. Would it be alright if we went over to Bill's a little later? Right now, I have something more interesting in mind."

So, it's like I said at the beginning. Things are not always what they appear to be, and we should, all of us, stop making assumptions.

End of the 18th Story

HANK BROOKS

PLEASURE THIRST

Gay Romance Erotica

Pleasure Thirst
By: Hank Brooks

Jeremy Harmon:

This tale begins with Jeremy at sixty-three years old, living a life of hell in California. He was caught up in a quagmire, from which he saw no escape. He was in a marriage that ripped out his guts every day, hour by hour, until he wanted to cry out in pain so that everyone could know his suffering.

It started out well enough, but over the years, the marriage had disintegrated until it was just a shell, a sham, a pretense designed only to fool the outside world. Jeremy met Connie shortly after he graduated from college and had begun his teaching career. They were introduced at the home of a mutual friend. Jeremy was very good looking, and had plenty of success with the ladies. He was in no rush for a relationship. Besides that, he had lots of luck with the guys too, and he wasn't at all sure about his sexual orientation.

Connie overwhelmed him. She showed up wherever he went. At parties she was all over him, and his young cock responded to her not-so-subtle brushes against him. He couldn't even recall how it all came down, but before he knew it, they were making wedding plans, then honeymoon plans, and discussing their combined future. Connie made it quite clear that she didn't want any children. Jeremy didn't know what to make of that, but he went along with it.

After their marriage, Connie opened two day care centers and a home health care agency. Her income far exceeded Jeremy's. She insisted that Jeremy work for her. He stopped teaching and worked for Connie as the office manager. Eventually he worked for her part-time and went back to teaching. He returned without tenure, and had to begin his career anew.

Little by little over the years, Jeremy noticed disturbing changes in Connie. She began to smoke and drink heavily. Wine was her beverage of choice. She drank all day, through dinner, and after dinner.

Most of the time, she never made it to 'after dinner.' She would pass out at the dinner table and sleep for hours before stirring and dragging herself to bed. Often she didn't make it to bed. Jeremy let her sleep it off in the dining room. Sometimes he had to remove a lit cigarette from her fingers as she slept with her face on the table.

She became almost helpless and Jeremy had to wait on her hand and foot. All he ever heard from her was bring me this, go shopping for me, put gas in my car, etc. Every day she got fatter and fatter and did less and less for herself. Her feet began to look like elephant legs, and they were so swollen she could barely walk. Sex between them was a distant memory, barely recalled by either of them. Jeremy and her doctor warned her that she was killing herself, but she didn't die, and Jeremy went on suffering. He turned to the internet for solace.

The internet provided him with two means of temporary respite. He searched the gay chat lines and met some men who were also married. They didn't dare go to the bars, so this was how they met each other. He got together with one or another whenever he could, and they helped each other relieve their sexual frustrations. Some of his fuck buddies swore that they loved their wives, but needed more. He began to think he was the only one who hated his wife and his life.

After his wife passed out every evening, Jeremy would go into his den and close the door. He didn't dare lock it. She would certainly question that, should she happen to wake up. If he wasn't in the gay chat rooms, he would read gay literature on the many gay story sites he discovered just while browsing. Many of the stories were just slutty porn, and he would masturbate regularly while devouring the contents. But many of the stories were well written, with good plot lines. As an English teacher, he appreciated how they aroused him without always being explicit about sexual activity. Some were beautiful love stories that made him cry.

One day, he read a story that he particularly enjoyed. He searched the contents of the web site for other stories that the author had written. He started to read whatever he could find written by this author. He loved the way the author developed his characters and teased the reader into wondering would they or wouldn't they. The stories always had happy Hollywood endings, which Jeremy appreciated because his own life was pure hell. That's how he came across a story by this author which touched his very soul. It started with a footnote in which the author claimed that the story was true. It did not say that it was the author's own true story, but after reading a few lines Jeremy was convinced that it was autobiographical.

The author wrote under the pen name, Rock Androll. The story was called, A Soul in Anguish and it was about a man who was secretly gay, and whose marriage was a total sham. He lived with a shrewish wife, who caused his ulcers to bleed regularly. They hadn't had sex for years, and so the protagonist cruised the known pick-up parks for stolen moments of pleasure with other desperate men.

There came a time when the character met another man with whom he had an instant attraction. After having sex in a dark and deserted section of the park, they did something the man had never done before: he and his pick-up went together to a small café and enjoyed a cup of coffee together.

They bonded instantly, especially when they discovered that their marriages and their lives were similar. One man had no children and the other had two, but both were in college and adults. The two men began to see each other often, but now they took a hotel room.

They saw each other more and more and fell deeply in love, throwing caution to the wind.

Eventually the man's wife grew suspicious and she had a detective follow him to one of his trysts. There followed a bitter divorce which cost the man a great deal of money.

Now that he lived alone in a small apartment, his lover was a constant visitor. One day he just moved in, leaving his wife to wonder what had gone wrong in their marriage. The two men lived happily ever after, of course.

Jeremy read the story over and over. He wept bitterly each time he read it.

He had never written to an author before, but he was so convinced that the story was autobiographical that he decided to send the author a note. He wanted to tell Rock Androll how much the story had touched his heart and why.

Haley Bronson:

On one of those rare moments in time, when Halley's Comet was shooting across the night sky, a baby boy was born in Buffalo, NY. Fittingly, his parents named him Haley, Haley Bronson.

During Haley's youth, he began to realize that he was gay, but it was his secret to keep, and he kept it well, even to himself. He dated girls and dreamed about marriage. Like so many others, he believed that marriage to a good woman would cure him. The problem was that no girl he knew could turn him on, but when a good looking guy came into view, it was all Haley could do to hide his erection.

One evening in his junior year in college, he met Rhonda at a fraternity dance. She rubbed against him and he tried to pull back a little so that she couldn't feel his hard cock, on which her rubbing had done its magic. He was amazed that a girl was actually causing him to get an erection. Rhonda was very persistent and continued to rub up tightly against Haley's body. Pulling away was becoming awkward, so Haley thought *what the hell,* and pushed back against Rhonda. His hard cock rubbed against her belly, and she pulled them closer together.

"Thank God," she whispered in his ear. "I thought there was something wrong with you."

That night, the aggressive child-woman took Haley's virginity in the back seat of his father's car, and Rhonda conceived a child. In fact, she conceived twin boys. Abortion was out of the question in those days. The couple got married quietly and with the help of both sets of parents, Haley finished college. He majored in business and became a CPA. He provided well for his family and everything seemed to be just what he wanted.

But as so many before him had discovered, his actual sexual nature could not be suppressed forever. One of his clients had a young and handsome male bookkeeper who was out at the office as well as in his private life. Jody and Haley had to work closely together. One day they stayed late at the client's office in order to finish a project, because Haley's busy schedule did not permit him to return to this client another day.

Haley never knew what hit him. Jody was intoxicating him and clouding his judgment. He wanted to have sex with him so badly, his gut was churning. Still the two men maintained an outward decorum. Haley was bursting with sexual desire and tension. Not caring about the consequences, he suddenly threw his arms around Jody and kissed him full on the lips. He didn't know what to expect, but he certainly didn't expect what happened. Jody kissed back and forced open Haley's lips in a passionate, sexual, inviting kiss.

They finished the project quickly and hurried to Jody's apartment. When they got there they undressed in record time. They took a moment to admire each other's bodies, especially their tools. They were both about 5'10" with hard bodies that obviously proved that they worked out a lot. Neither had much chest hair but both had thick bushes of pubic hair. They were both uncircumcised and about six inches erect. *Just average,* they both thought and sighed with relief.

"Shower with me?" Jody asked. Haley's heart was beating so fast he could only nod, and Jody led him into the shower. It was probably the longest shower either of them had ever taken. They soaped their cocks and asses over and over. As each soaped the other's ass they would insert a finger then two, until finally Jody screamed out over the cascading water, "Give it to me, Haley. Please give it to me."

Jody put his hands against the shower wall, and jutted out his ass, enticing Haley to enter. It may have been Haley's first time, but he didn't hesitate. He positioned his soapy cockhead and began to push. He slipped right in. Obviously it wasn't Jody's first time. It had been nearly a month since Haley had sex with his wife and he came rather quickly. As he felt his orgasm growing, he reached around and took Jody's cock in his hand. He began to stroke, not too delicately. Jody came seconds after Haley.

They remained in the shower even after Haley slipped out. They cleaned themselves thoroughly, but stayed in the shower, kissing and fondling each other. The time came when the water was cooling significantly, so they stepped out of the shower and dried themselves off. Back in the bedroom, Haley began to dress.

"Do you have to leave?" Jody asked.

"Yes," Haley answered. "If you would like, I'll try to arrange for us to get together soon when we can spend more time together."

"I'd like that a lot," Jody answered.

A few days later, after consulting with Jody, Haley told his wife he was going to an important tax seminar in Miami from Monday to

Friday in two weeks. Jody arranged to take that week off. Haley got two round trip plane tickets leaving Sunday afternoon from Buffalo and Friday evening from Miami.

At the Miami Airport they rented a car and found a cheap motel outside the city on the north side. Haley wanted to visit Ft. Lauderdale also. The two young men made love all day, but in the evening they checked out the gay night life in Miami and Ft. Lauderdale. The hardest thing they ever did that week was to check out of the motel.

They continued their clandestine romance for several years. During that time, Haley became more and more impatient with Rhonda. They rarely had sex and she became more and more demanding and shrewish. He spent more and more time at the office and with Jody. Jody listened patiently to Haley's complaints about his home life and kept urging him to move out and move in with him, but Haley couldn't bring himself to do it. "I can't leave until the kids are out of the house and Rhonda can care for herself," he told Jody.

Then one day Jody called Haley and asked him to meet him for lunch at a coffee shop near Haley's office. It was there that Jody delivered his Dear John address.

"I can't live like this anymore," he told Haley. "I don't want to live in the shadows, and I don't want to make love to someone who constantly looks at the clock to see how much time he has left." He hesitated but continued. "I've met a great guy. We can be there for each other full time and we want to be together. He has his own house so I'm moving out of my apartment at the end of the month and I'm moving in with him."

Haley was devastated, but he looked lovingly at Jody, and said, "I understand, sweetheart. I can't blame you, and I certainly won't try to stop you. All I can do is wish you the best." Jody reached across the table and squeezed Haley's hand. "Let me ask you," Haley went on, "if I was free, who would you chose, me or him?"

"You," Jody said, and he ran out of the coffee shop.

After that, Haley had no sex with Rhonda and practically no male sex either. He grew more and more unhappy and Rhonda became more and more bitchy. This went on until Haley sold his practice and retired. The kids were grown and living on their own by then. Haley began to plan an escape. He went to a lawyer and arranged to have most of his assets transferred to Rhonda's name. He left himself one IRA account and with his forthcoming social security check, he felt he would be all right. He could always seek employment with another CPA if need be. He gave Rhonda the lion's share of his assets.

One evening, when Rhonda was playing cards with her girlfriends, Haley loaded his car with his personal things and started the long drive to Florida. He left Rhonda a note telling her that she would have plenty of money, but he wanted out of the marriage. She could divorce him or not. It was her choice. He didn't plan on getting married again so he didn't care. She divorced him within a year.

Haley found an apartment in Ft. Lauderdale. It was one bedroom and tiny, but he didn't care. He was so happy that it seemed like a palace to him. He bought some thrift shop furniture and began his new life. He even got a part time job with a local CPA and after two weeks, he felt like he had been there forever.

As soon as he hooked up his computer, he hit the gay chat lines, made contacts and had sex at least three times a week. In a couple of months he didn't need to have anonymous sex. He began to make real friendships and he established a stable of fuck buddies.

He began to read gay erotica on the internet. The stories were hot and held his voyeuristic attention, but most were so badly written that it actually offended him. He was sure he could do better, so he wrote a short story about a gay author who falls in love with his characters. He dreams of having sex with them, and it is totally real to the author. After awhile the author is lost in a world of his own creation. He doesn't know the real world from the fictional world he created. He submitted the story to his favorite erotic gay site and it was published. He was shocked to receive a slew of favorable fan mail, so he wrote more and more. He even wrote full novels, and was getting E Mail from around the globe. He wasn't making money at it, but he was having the time of his life and writing was becoming his hobby and consuming much of his leisure time.

He took the time to send a thank you note to everyone who wrote to him. Sometimes he would exchange two or three letters until the correspondence stopped. One day, he got a letter from a fan which absolutely broke his heart. He wrote a long letter back, and it led to a continuing string of letters until the two men felt like old friends.

Jeremy and Haley:

The first letter read:

Dear Rock: You don't know how much your story, A Soul in Anguish, touched my heart. It was as if you had bared my soul, and were writing about me. I am living in hell. My wife has grown fat and slovenly. She smokes and drinks and passes out at the dinner table every night. We never have sex anymore, nor would I want to. The only relief I get is in an adult book store. I stop on my way to work, rent a DVD and go into a booth. Most of the time someone joins me in the booth. We go down on each other and then go our separate ways. I need to get out of here, but I don't know how and I am scared stiff. Thank you for your beautiful story. Bill.

Usually Haley would respond with a short thank you note, but he just had to write to this guy.

Dear Bill: I know exactly how you feel. Your situation is worse than mine ever was. Leaving my wife was easier than I thought it would be. I just walked out one day. My kids are grown and living on their own. I didn't give a damn about what they would think. I didn't even care that I had barely enough money to survive. All I cared about was my freedom and my sanity. I'm not saying you should walk out and do what I did, but I can assure you, I have never been happier in my life. Please feel free to write and cry on my shoulder. I will advise you as best I can. Haley Bronson, Ft. Lauderdale, FL (my real name and home)

Hi Haley: My real name is Jeremy Harmon. Even though we never had kids, I can't just up and leave, as much as I would like to. I live in a community property state, and I need to walk away with enough assets to stay above water. My wife fell asleep at the dining room table again tonight. For all I care the cleaning lady can find her that way in the morning. I'm not dragging her upstairs again. She's just too fat. Before she fell asleep she started yelling at me, blaming me for everything that went wrong in her day today. I don't know how much more I can take. Looking at her has become a bad dream. Listening to her spout venom at me is a fucking nightmare. Jeremy.

Dear Jeremy: Just reading your words breaks my heart. If it's any consolation, a vast majority of my gay friends were previously married. I think it was a common thing to do before the gay rights movement got into fourth gear. Some of them had good marriages, but could not deny their nature. Other marriages were bad, and these guys didn't just divorce, they escaped. Like me. The price of freedom for me was costly. I just gave her everything, drove away, and started a new life. I moved to a gay Mecca, made many friends, and my life is better now than even I dreamed it would be. I can't understand why you allow yourself such physical and emotional abuse. Hugs, Haley.

Dear Haley: She was so drunk tonight that she asked me to help her stand up after dinner. It's getting impossible for me to raise her up these days, but tonight she was stuck between the arms of the chair, and I couldn't budge her. She started yelling at me, saying that I was an incompetent fool, and she threw a dinner plate at me. I might have caught it, but there was food on the plate and it slipped out of my hands. Fortunately our dining room floor is carpeted and it didn't break. Whatever the slop was that she served for dinner, I couldn't eat it. After she passed out, I just drove down to Burger King for a hamburger. This is my life. Thanks for listening. Thanks for caring. Jeremy

Jeremy: We need to talk. Please call me anytime you can at 954-555-3377. You are a victim of domestic abuse, and you should not tolerate it any longer. Get your affairs in order and see a divorce attorney. You must get out of that house. You can stay with me until you decide where you want to go and what you want to do. I realize that we are at opposite ends of the country, but you could stand getting as far away from her as possible. Surely you need a long vacation and plenty of respite. Your friend, Haley

Dear Friend: I'm sorry I haven't written in a few days, but I have been really busy this past week. I went to see a lawyer, and showed her all my assets. We discussed how it could be equitably distributed in a divorce settlement. She didn't split every last item in half. For instance, I want my wife to have the house. It is debt free, and for that I *asked for certain other concessions. The lawyer was satisfied that it was a fair fifty-fifty split, and didn't feel that my wife had a cause of action in challenging it. I told her that I was going to leave the house on Friday, June 5th. That's the last day of the school year and the beginning of my retirement. She said that she would arrange to have the divorce petition served on Connie about 6 PM that evening. I gave her my power of attorney concerning all matters in the divorce proceedings. I feel so much better knowing that I just have to ride out ten more weeks. She is going to a bar with some of her friends tomorrow after dinner (if she doesn't pass out). As soon as she leaves, I'll call you. It will be late because of the time difference, but you said I could call anytime. Love, Jeremy*

Jeremy: I didn't think you would do it. I am so proud of you and so happy for you. I'll be sitting by the phone waiting for your call. Please don't worry about a thing. I'm here for you. I'll help you get settled and I'll introduce you to my friends. You'll have an instant family to support you also. Love, Haley

Haley sat in his lounge chair watching television. He dozed off right after the 11 o'clock news began. At 11:30 his telephone woke him with its shrill, persistent ringing. He muted the TV and grabbed the phone, not bothering to check the caller ID as he usually did.

"Hello," he said hoarsely. His nap was still upon him.

"Haley?" the voice at the other end asked. "It's Jeremy."

It is always easier to write down your thoughts than to speak them. Their conversation was awkward and hesitant. Jeremy could only repeat his anger and frustration about his fat slob of a wife, and his lack of sex with men. Haley could only listen and occasionally mutter, "Poor man."

In the end Haley became quite strong in declaring, "She's killing you. You have to get out of there." After they hung up, Haley could kick himself for his lack of skill in advising Jeremy, but he couldn't do anything about it now. He just went to bed.

In the morning, he checked his e-mail. He usually got so many fan mails it took him quite a while to send thank you notes and sometimes make a few comments. There was a letter from Jeremy among the others. Haley opened it first.

Dear Haley: I know you mean well, but you don't know me, and you don't know the million other things going on in my life. I don't think I can just walk out like you did. I have many other considerations. I know I have to leave but I don't know how I will do it or when. Jeremy.

Haley feared that this letter was a kiss off and he would never hear from Jeremy again. He responded immediately.

Dear Jeremy: If it seemed like I was pushing you to leave your wife, I sincerely apologize. That's your decision to make, and only yours. Of course I don't know all about you, but I know enough about your situation to know that it is slowly killing you. I know it's crazy, but I think I am falling in love with you. Maybe I'm pushing you for selfish reasons, but even if I am, it's for your own good. By all means, do it right. Do it in your own time, but do it. Love, Haley.

Days went by and Haley did not hear from Jeremy. He regretted having been so aggressive. It really was none of his business, but he had projected his own situation on Jeremy, and he knew now that it was the wrong thing to do. Obviously Jeremy wasn't willing to give up as much as he had. He wished he had done it differently. Well, there was nothing he could do now so he tried to put Jeremy out of his head. He considered writing a letter of apology, but he concluded that might make a bad situation worse.

Then almost a month after his last note, Haley heard from Jeremy.

Dear Haley: I am sorry I haven't written to you in such a long time, but my life now is in a greater turmoil than ever. The night I heard from you last, Connie not only passed out at the dinner table, she went into some sort of coma. I had to call 911. It turned out to be a diabetic coma. She was in the hospital for a few days and is now bedridden. I have become her caregiver. I knew it would come to this someday. I get help from her own health care personnel, but I won't have them very much longer. Her business is on the verge of bankruptcy. I couldn't live with myself if I walked away now. She is more helpless than a newborn

*baby. She still smokes and she keeps wine on her bedside table. Conse-
quently she is drunk most of the time and I have to keep a constant eye on
her for fear that she will harm herself and burn the house down. She is
less active than ever and her body consumes most of a queen size mattress. I couldn't share a bed with her if I tried. Please don't give up on
me. Although she defies all the odds, and continues to live, I don't know
how long this can go on. I may have to put her in a nursing home, if they
will take her, and if I can afford it. I know I can't take care of her forever. Forgive me for laying all this crap on you. I am so miserable and
your letters and your friendship help more than you know. Love, Jeremy*

*Dear Jeremy: My heart cries for you. You can lean on me. Call
me whenever you would like, and write as often as you want to. Let me
be your sounding board. When I hadn't heard from you for such a long
time, I was afraid you had wished to cut off our friendship. Thank God, I
was wrong. Love, Haley.*

Two more weeks went by before Haley heard from Jeremy. Haley attributed it to his being a busy caregiver.

*Dear Haley: I have decided that Connie is play acting this dia-
betes thing so that I will continue to wait on her hand and foot. I have
reason to believe that she is not as helpless as she would like me to believe. I don't think she is considering that her business is going down the
tubes. She is perfectly well enough to take care of herself. She just
doesn't want to. I was at my lawyer yesterday and I signed a million
papers. School ends on Friday and my retirement begins. I intend to
pack my car Thursday evening. She'll never know. She never gets out of
bed. I'll leave directly from school, and be on the road by 4 PM. I have
a map laid out to Ft. Lauderdale, but I'll need directions to your apartment. I'll call you along the way, and more often as I approach Ft.
Lauderdale. I can't believe I'm doing this. I hope that Connie will get
hold of herself, and start living again. I am so excited. Love, Jeremy*

*Dear Jeremy: Bravo. I am as excited as you are. I can't wait to
see you, to hold you in my arms, to kiss you, and well, you know the*

drill. Drive carefully. Come home safely. Love, Haley.

Jeremy drove about six hours before pulling in to a motel. As soon as he was settled in his room, he pulled out his cell phone and plugged in his charger. He was just about to dial Haley, when the phone rang. It was Connie. He decided to answer since she could not abuse him so many miles from home.

"Where the fuck are you?" she yelled into the phone. "I got served with divorce papers. The aide had to go to the door. You know I can't go down the stairs. I want you home immediately. I'm starving, and I want you to make my dinner."

Jeremy hesitated a long time before he said very calmly, "You can reach me through my lawyer. I'm out of your life forever. From now on you can make your own meals and look after your own house and your own business. I'm done with it." He hung up and dialed Haley.

"I'm on my way," he said. "I expect you to make a party when I arrive."

"You're on," Haley answered. "First we'll have a party for two, and when we have thoroughly exhausted each other, I'll make a bash and introduce you to your new life."

It took Jeremy almost five days to cross the country. He didn't rush, just wanting to enjoy the peace and quiet with nobody around to nag him. He called Haley at least twice a day. As instructed, Jeremy called Haley from a certain point, which Haley figured was about a half hour away. He gave him directions to his building. Twenty five minutes later, he went to the parking area and moved his car into a guest spot. He had instructed Jeremy to park in his assigned spot, B102. He sat in his car and waited. His heart was beating wildly.

A few minutes later, a late model mini van pulled into his parking space. It was a tan Chrysler Town and Country, just as Jeremy had described. Haley jumped out of his car and ran to the mini van. He stood back as Jeremy exited the car. God, the man was an Adonis. He had graying blond hair, blue eyes, maybe a few extra pounds, which looked good on the six-footer. Besides, Haley enjoyed squeezing love handles when making love.

A few seconds later, Jeremy spotted Haley approaching him. He stared at the man, who was so different than he was. Haley stood 5'10".

He had black hair which was now salt and pepper, hazel eyes, and a very lean body. Jeremy liked what he saw.

"Haley?" he asked.

"Yes, Jeremy I presume."

The two men hugged, but did not kiss.

"Let's get all your stuff inside," Haley said. "Then we can relax."

Haley had donated to charity much of the clothes he never wore anymore, and he had made room for Jeremy's stuff in the closet and dresser drawers. It would be a little tight in a one bedroom, one bathroom apartment, but they could consider a larger place *if things worked out.* It took them almost two hours to put all of Jeremy's stuff away. By the time they were finished, it was lunch time, and Haley got an idea.

"Come," he said. "I'm taking you out for lunch." He took Jeremy's hand and held it as they walked to a restaurant just two streets away. "We are in the heart of gay Ft. Lauderdale," Haley said, "and you are going to dine among all gay men and maybe a few women."

Jeremy gripped Haley's hand tighter. "You're making my dreams come true," he said in a raspy voice. Summer heat and humidity had not yet invaded South Florida on this beautiful spring day. They ate outside amidst gently flowing cool breezes and delightful eye candy. After lunch they sat and chatted for awhile. Jeremy kept ogling the tight bubble asses as they passed their table. Finally he got bold and buried his nervousness. "I think I'd like to go home and get better acquainted," he said.

The two men almost ran home. Once inside the apartment, they embraced and kissed for the first time. Their tongues began a passionate duel, and they kept kissing as they began to undress. They had to stop kissing to get totally naked. They stood facing each other. Their dicks were hard and hungry as they gave each other the eye.

Jeremy was about two inches taller than Haley. Neither was circumcised, but their purple cockheads pushed out way beyond their foreskins. Haley was now about six inches and Jeremy about seven. They stood immobile, just staring at each other until Jeremy could stand it no longer. He fell to his knees and enveloped Haley's cock in his eager mouth. He ran his tongue all over the shaft as his lips pumped up and down. Occasionally he withdrew and licked Haley's balls and even ventured towards Haley's crack. Haley pulled Jeremy's head closer into him, not because he wanted his prick deeper into Jeremy's mouth, but because he needed to steady himself, lest he should fall down on the floor.

Haley's moans grew to a roar as he exploded into Jeremy's mouth. Jeremy was trying to swallow all that he could, and barely heard Haley murmur, "Save some for me." They lay down side by side on Haley's bed, which was now their bed. Facing each other, they continued their kissing duel. Haley began to fondle Jeremy's unfulfilled dick. When he felt that he could breathe again, he leaned down and took Jeremy into him. He sucked until he felt that Jeremy was about to cum. Then he stopped and let the feeling subside. Reaching into the drawer of his bedside table, he extracted a tube of lube. He coated Jeremy's cock generously and then his own ass hole. He straddled Jeremy and slowly sat down on Jeremy's cock, guiding it into his man hole amidst sighs of pleasure from both of them. Haley rode Jeremy gently until he felt Jeremy start to cum, and then he let loose, pumping hard. He was so lost in his own rapture; he almost missed realizing that he was cumming for a second time. He could not remember a time before this, when he had come twice in one session.

This day was their wedding day. Their future days were spent enjoying their companionship. Their nights were filled with social events and making love. They didn't always reach Nirvana, but in bed, they would kiss and fondle until they fell asleep. Jeremy and Haley lived the life that once they could only long for, but it was better than either of them had ever dreamed of, because they had each other. Their union was never dreamed of in their original fantasies; but being together made the fulfilled dream perfect.

End of the 19th Story

Hank Brooks

Fountain of Dreams

Gay Romance Erotica

Fountain of Dreams
By: Hank Brooks

Saturday night!

The joint was jumping. The gay bar was generally frequented by men in their twenties and thirties. 'The Far Side' was a noisy place, where disco music was blaring nonstop, so it was rare to see anyone there who was older than forty.

Three friends in their late twenties were crowded together around the bar. They tried to talk to each other but it was so noisy that they finally surrendered to being silent, and they just listened to the ear-blasting music. Finally one of them screeched.

"Where's Danny?" Alex yelled to Davie.

"I don't know," Davie screamed back.

"He called me this afternoon," Steve joined in, trying to be heard. "He said that he'd be here tonight and he had a big surprise."

After that they gave up trying to be heard for a little while more. It wasn't long before Danny came in with a big grin on his face. "Come with me," he said. "I need to talk to you, and it's too noisy here."

The foursome left and wended their way to a straight bar a street away. The atmosphere was intimate, dark and quiet. They found a table in a corner, and sat down.

"What's the big news, Danny?" Steve asked.

Danny's grin returned to his face. "You know the wishing fountain in Roosevelt Square in the center of town? Everybody says that if you throw in a coin and make a wish, it'll come true."

"Bull crap," Alex said adamantly.

"It worked for me first time I did it," Danny insisted. "I guess you gotta believe in it for it to work. I threw in a quarter three days ago, and I asked to win the lottery."

"Fuck, you didn't," Davie said.

"Well, I didn't win the big one, but I had five numbers and I won $5,700.00. That's serious bucks, folks."

They all started to whoop and holler, disturbing the quiet demeanor of the bar. They found themselves being stared at, and Danny said, "Let's go back to 'The Far Side' where we can make noise. Besides, I feel like dancing."

Alex

Early the following Monday morning, before the busy streets began to fill and before the dawn of the day, Alex stood at the fountain. A sign fastened to the brick wall surrounding the fountain informed the public that all proceeds from the fountain were donated to various charities. He reached into his pocket and took out all his coins: a dime, two nickels and three quarters. He threw them into the fountain, closed his eyes, and made a wish. Watching him from a distance was a young college student.

The young man had started to approach the fountain to feed it and make a wish, but when he saw Alex, he drew back into the still-dark morning. He didn't want to disturb a man making a sacred wish. But Alex saw him.

When Alex was done, he did something crazy. He crossed himself, without a clue as to why he should do so. Members of his religion did not cross themselves. Besides, he hadn't been inside a church since high school. Instead of leaving, he too disappeared into the shadows. He wanted to see what the young man would do.

As would be expected, the young man did exactly what Alex had done. When he was finished, and he started to back off from the fountain, Alex scared the daylights out of him by approaching him and asking, "Do you think we'll get our wishes?"

As soon as he recovered from being startled, the student started to laugh. "I sure hope so," he said. "Just last night one of the guys in my dorm was telling us all about getting his wish. He has been coming here every day after school for a month, and wishing the same wish. It actually came true for him."

"Oh, and what was his wish?"

The student laughed again. "Well it seems that he was a virgin, and he wished that he would meet a lovely girl, and that they would fall in love, and she would want to make love to him as much as he wanted to make love to her. It came true for him. He met a girl right after his first coin toss, and last night they consummated their love."

"I hope you wished for something more unattainable," Alex cautioned. "That sounds like a coincidence to me."

"Maybe."

"You live in a dorm?" Alex asked. "Are you a student?"

The young man nodded. "Yes. I'm a senior."

Alex stuck out his hand, "My name's Alex," he said.

"Jason," the student responded, shaking Alex's hand.

"Hey, it's way too early for me to go to work, or for you to go to a class. Would you have breakfast with me? It's my treat."

"Thank you, Alex. I'd like that a lot. Actually I have no classes today. I work part-time over at The Emporium. I don't have to be at work until 2 PM."

"Fantastic!"

Alex took Jason to a coffee shop which was located around the corner from his office. He usually skipped breakfast, but he had lunch there almost every day. They both ordered the breakfast special: two eggs (any style), potatoes, choice of bread and coffee for $3.79.

"It's great you have a part-time job," Alex commented. "Jobs are tough to get these days, especially part-time jobs. By the way, what's your major?"

"I'm majoring in accounting, and for your information, if I didn't have the job, I couldn't make it. I'm paying my own way through."

"That's tough. Are your parents dead?"

"No, they are very much alive. It's just that they have disowned me."

"That's pretty cruel. It happened to me also, so I know how it feels. Why were you disowned?"

Jason didn't answer the question. Instead he said incredulously, "You were disowned too. What a coincidence. Why were you disowned?"

"I asked first," Alex sounded a little uncomfortable.

"I told them that I was gay. That might not sound like a big deal to you in this day and age, but my father is a Baptist minister."

Alex was silent and Jason was sure that he was going to ask him to get out, but finally Alex got his senses back. "You're kidding me, aren't you?"

"No, it's the truth. Don't you believe me?"

"Frankly, it's hard for me to believe anything right now. It may be a coincidence that we met making a wish in the same fountain, and it may be a coincidence that we were both disowned, but it's unbelievable that we both got disowned for the same reason. By the way, my father is a Methodist minister."

Jason was speechless. Eventually he said, "Wow!"

"Maybe meeting each other wasn't such a coincidence. Maybe it was a miracle," Alex reflected.

"What do you mean?"

"Now that I know you're gay, I can tell you this. When I first laid eyes on you, I thought that you were so fucking hot."

"Thanks, Alex. You're pretty hot yourself."

"Are you ready for another miracle?" Alex asked with a smile on his face.

"Can I stand it?"

"I sure hope so, Jason. I'm a CPA. I just struck out on my own a few months ago, and I could sure use some part-time help around the office, especially while I'm with clients. I have an answering service, but I'm sure my clients would appreciate a sexy male voice answering their questions, instead of waiting for me to get around to it. I guess you can figure out that the majority of my clients are gay."

"Wow!! I'd sure rather be interning with you than selling socks at The Emporium," Jason said, looking really excited.

"What are they paying you at the store?"

"Minimum wage."

Alex laughed. "I'll pay you fifty percent more."

"I could hug you," Jason said, "but we are in a public place, a coffee shop, and all these people are having breakfast. I wouldn't want to gross them out."

"Well, Jason, if we went up to my office, we'd be the only two people there, and you could hug me without anyone seeing you do it."

"What a great idea."

"By the way Jase, what did you wish for?"

"When it comes true, I'll tell you. I don't want to put a hex on it."

Davie

That evening, on the way home from work, Davie went a little out of his way, and he found himself standing at the fountain. He reached into his pocket and retrieved two quarters. He tossed them into the fountain and made a wish. Then he stood silently in front of the fountain and said a few silent prayers. Just as had happened with Alex, a man started to approach the fountain with similar intent, but when he saw Davie, he turned and walked quickly away.

Davie took a bus home. When he entered his lonely apartment, he was struck by a deep feeling of loneliness and solitude. Sure he had lots of friends and he partied a lot, but for all that, he went home to a lonely apartment. When he got together with his friends, he usually met them at some watering hole or at a movie house. There didn't seem to be any socializing in anyone's home, at least not for him.

Every evening when he wasn't going out, which was most of the time, he would make himself a frozen TV dinner. While he ate, he would do the crossword puzzle from that morning's newspaper, which he never had time to read in the morning. Then he would strip naked and sit in his easy chair and watch TV. He wasn't a big fan of TV, and more often than not, he would insert a porno disk into his DVD player. He would begin to stroke his cock as he got aroused, and finally he would bring himself to a very unsatisfying orgasm.

He would then clean himself up and go to bed, dreaming all the while that he would meet his Prince Charming on the very next day.

Steve

Steve approached the fountain, and saw Davie throw some coins in. He was shocked and very embarrassed. He didn't want his friend to see him succumbing to voodoo, even if his friend was doing the same thing. He quickly retreated and waited for Davie to leave. When Davie was out of sight, he went back to the fountain and rashly threw in every piece of change he had, which came to $1.10 in nickels, dimes, and quarters.

When he was ready to make his wish, he looked around. There wasn't a soul in sight. He made his wish in a whisper, but it was certainly audible.

"Please God," he whispered, "Give me the strength to tell Davie how much I love him and how much I want to be with him. I know he just wants to party all the time and not settle down, at least for now, but I must tell him how I feel. If I don't, I'll go crazy. He may want to stop being my friend, but I'm willing to risk it. Dear God, I am so lonely. I can't stand going back to my apartment any more. It's forbidding and empty, and I hate the solitude."

Steve started to cry, and he ran all the way to his bus stop. When he got there, his bus was just approaching. He never knew why he did what he did next. He let the bus go by, just as he heard some inner voice whisper in his ear, "God helps those who help themselves."

The next bus to come along took a different route. It was the bus Davie took to go home. In fact, Davie had just taken the previous one. After he got seated on the bus, Steve took out his phone and called Davie.

Davie was surprised to get the call. He rarely got a call at home. If his friends wanted to make some arrangements to meet somewhere, it was usually done during their working hours. They hardly ever called each other just to chat. He glanced at the caller ID and answered the phone.

"Steve," he said. "What's up?"

"Hi kiddo," Steve said brightly, hiding his depression. "I was wondering. Did you start dinner yet?"

"No. I just got in. I haven't even taken off my shoes yet."

Steve steeled himself. "I can pick you up in a few minutes. Would you like to go out to dinner with me? I feel like talking. What I don't feel like is spending another lonely evening alone at home." He couldn't believe he had said that. Steve expected Davie to laugh at him. He did not expect the answer he got.

"Steve," Davie said. "That's the nicest question anybody has ever asked me, and the greatest invitation. I don't want to be alone tonight either. I'll be ready when you get here."

Alex and Jason

Alex put a key into his office door, and he and Jason tered. Alex locked the door behind him. He led Jason through a small reception area. There were two doors in the room. One was on the left side, and the other was behind the receptionist's desk. The door on the left was open, but the other door was closed. Jason looked into the open room. One side was lined with file cabinets, and the other side was lined with office supplies. Between the two sides, on the far wall, there was some office equipment, which appeared to be a copy machine and a fax machine. There was no window in the room. Jason thought that maybe it was just meant to be a storeroom.

Alex opened the door behind the receptionist's desk. "This is my office," he said. Jason looked around. The office was sparsely furnished. Alex's degrees and his CPA certificate hung on the wall behind his desk. There was a large window on the left side, and underneath the window was a sofa. Two comfortable chairs faced the desk. Along the right wall there was a computer station.

"You can hug me now," Alex advised Jason.

Jason removed his knap sack and wrapped his arms around Alex, but Alex had other ideas. He grabbed Jason's cock and started kneading lightly. At the same time, his lips found Jason's, and Jason's hand found Alex's package.

"How am I doing as a boss so far?" Alex asked.

"Pretty damned good. I've never made love to a boss before."

The two men began to strip. When they were fully naked they stared at each other, sizing themselves up, as is the habit of all men. They were both tight skinned and muscular. Alex was a 5'10", blue-eyed blond. He had a straight nose and a square chin. His cock was cut and about four and a half inches flaccid, but now it was hard and nearly seven inches, Jason was 5'9", had brown hair, blue eyes, a pug nose, a few freckles, and was as cute as a button. His cock was about the same size as Alex's, but he was uncut.

Jason fell on the sofa and lay on his back. Alex fell on top of him and they continued to kiss and fondle. Alex began to crawl up Jason's body until he was able to present his cock to Jason's mouth. Jason did not hesitate to take as much of Alex's cock into his mouth as he could, but he didn't neglect Alex's balls and inner thighs. His wandering tongue made Alex whimper and purr. Alex came gushing into Jason's mouth and Jason swallowed it all.

"I'm sorry," Alex said. "I didn't mean to cum so fast. It's been too long."

"No need to apologize," Jason laughed. "I came before you did."

Alex got up and got some tissues. First he used a finger to capture some of Jason's spunk, and the two men lapped it up greedily. Then he wiped Jason clean with tissues. They got dressed and sat on the sofa holding hands.

"You made me very happy," Alex said. "Do you think that this might be more than a one night stand?"

"Definitely."

"Do you think you might want to move out of your dorm and into my apartment?"

"I'm graduating in a couple of months, so that's no problem. You'll have to take the rent out of my wages."

"Deal! Now are you going to tell me what you wished for?" Alex asked.

"Actually I asked for two things. First I asked for someone to love me, and then as an afterthought I wished to be offered a job in accounting so I could stop struggling when school is over. Now you know, so tell me what you wished for."

"I wished for my ideal guy to sweep me off my feet. I turned around, and there he was. There you were."

Davie and Steve

Steve bounded into Davie's apartment. He was excited and he had a big grin on his face. He wanted desperately to wrap Davie up in his arms, but he restrained himself.

"I am so glad you came over tonight," Davie said. "I'm in the mood for company, and a quiet dinner for two."

"I couldn't agree more. I came directly from work and don't have my car. Is there a nice place nearby?"

"My car is in the garage below the building. We can use it if you have a specific place in mind. Otherwise there's a great little eclectic neighborhood restaurant just around the corner."

"That sounds fine," Steve said. "It's not the food I crave. It's your company." Steve said 'your company' instead of 'the company.' It was a little bold, but he hoped that Davie would get the subtle difference. The more time that Steve was alone with Davie in the restaurant, the bolder he got. While they were waiting for the entrée, he even dared ask. "How come we never made it together?" He didn't know what kind of reaction that would get from Davie, but he was desperate.

"I dunno. Maybe it's because we've been just good buddies for so long."

Both of them had placed their folded hands on top of the ble. Steve put his hand on Davie's. It was now or never. "Davie," he said, "I care for you a lot. In fact, I love you. I've wanted to tell you that for such a long time."

Davie just stared at Steve. He couldn't believe what he had just heard. He didn't know what to say or how to respond, so he just stared at Steve in silence.

Finally, he said a single word. "Fuck."

Steve was devastated, but nothing more was said because their entrées were served at that moment.

When the waiter left, Steve said, "Maybe I should leave now."

"If you dare leave this table, I'll track you down, lasso you, and drag you back to my apartment."

"What? What are you saying?"

"I'm saying that I feel the same way. I've been too chicken to say anything to you. Whenever I'm with a guy, I can't get into him because no guy ever measures up to you. Steve baby, I went to the wishing fountain tonight and I wished for you."

It was Steve's turn to remain silent. Finally he uttered, "Fuck. I wished for you."

They were too happy and excited to eat. They left most of their meal, paid, and left. They ran all the way home. No two people undressed quicker. When they were naked, things got a little awkward as they went through the checking out process. They could have passed for brothers. They both had light brown hair, dark brown eyes, Roman noses, square chins, muscular bodies, and cut cocks. They were both erect and measured about six and a half inches. They both stood about 5" 10" tall.

Finally, they fell into each other's arms and they grabbed the other's cock. They made love all through the night, and they both called in sick to work the next day. They were together every night for the rest of the week.

Epilogue

On Saturday, the three friends met at The Far Side. Alex brought Jason along, and introduced him as his first associate in his growing practice. He didn't mention their growing relationship.

Davie and Steve announced that they were moving in together.

Nobody mentioned the fountain in Roosevelt Square until Danny came running in, and announced that he had four numbers in that week's lottery. He had been visiting the fountain almost every day. Then they each related their amazing stories.

Danny proposed a toast, and they all drank to the fountain and to their good fortune. Nobody chalked up what happened to them as mere coincidence. They all gave credit to the wishing fountain.

"You just gotta believe in the fountain of dreams, and the dream will happen," Danny said after concluding their toast.

"Amen," said the other friends.

End of the 20th Story

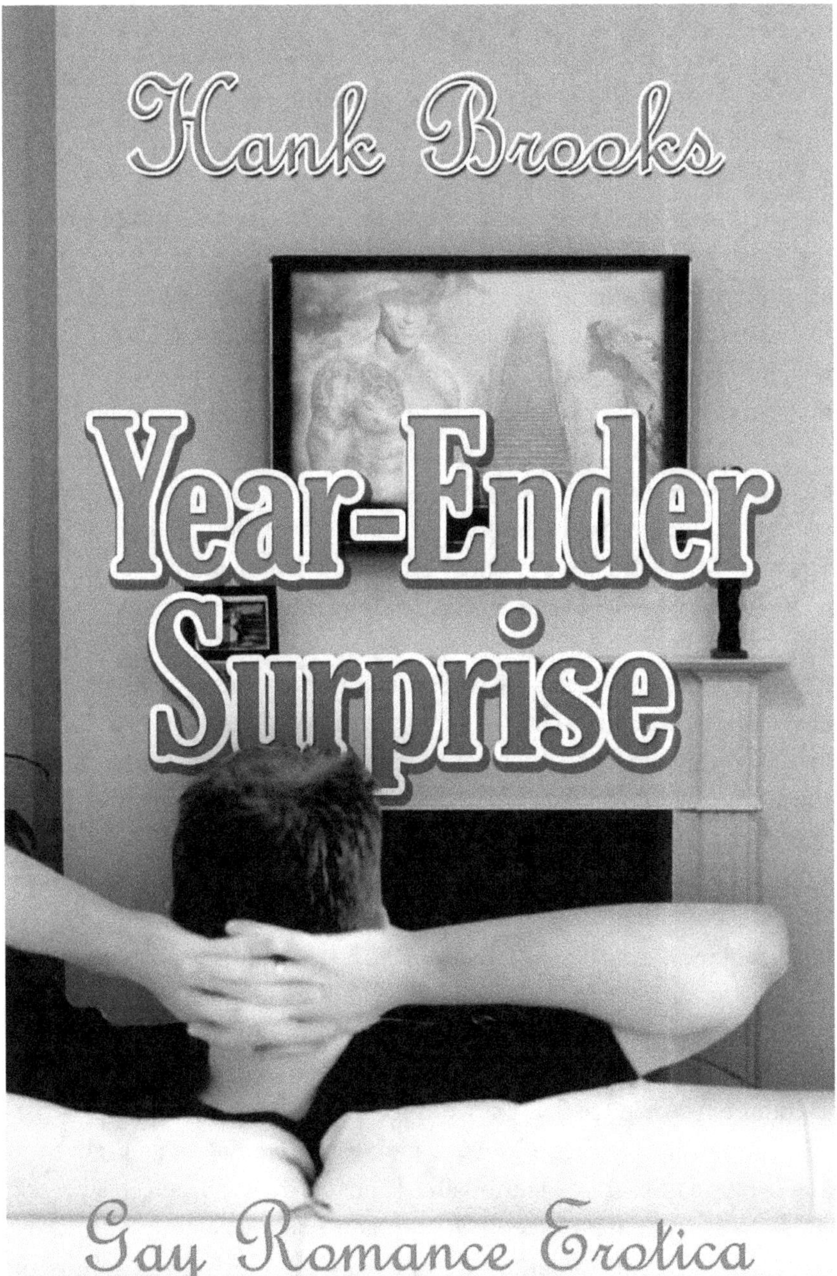
Hank Brooks
Year-Ender Surprise
Gay Romance Erotica

Year-Ender Surprise
By: Hank Brooks

It was New Year's Eve. The year 2000 was about to begin. We had finally reached the millennium, and according to informed experts, all the computers in the world would crash at midnight. Indeed, the world might even come to an end, since it could no longer function without computers. Well, if the world was going to end, I wanted to be in the comfort of my own bed, and not partying in some night club.

That wasn't very likely to happen anyway. Rog and I never went out on New Year's Eve. Even when we were very young, we preferred to stay home, light a fire in the fireplace, and watch the ball drop in Times Square. We would have a small glass of wine at midnight, and then make love in the new year, before cuddling snugly in bed, and sleeping until late the next morning.

Roger, the love of my life; now it's more than four years since he died and left me alone. I still ache when I think of him. He was my first love, and the only man I was ever intimate with. I have been celibate since he died. I could have had many men, but I'm just not interested. I've resigned myself to being a fifth wheel when I go out with friends. I must abandon humility and tell you, that even in my early sixties, I am a very handsome man. I have been cruised often by very good looking guys, but like I said, I'm just not into sex anymore, not even lustful one night stands. The thought of making love to anyone but Roger disturbs me. I keep telling myself that Rog is dead, and I should seek my own happiness. I even rationalize, and tell myself that it's OK to compromise and 'settle', but I still feel nothing.

On January first of 1999, I took early retirement, and moved to South Florida the following month. I moved from Buffalo, New York, and believe me, I appreciated that I wouldn't be freezing my ass off that winter. It was hard to believe that it was New Year's Eve (my first in Florida), and the low temperature tonight was expected to be 75°F. It was 74°F on Christmas Eve, practically a cold snap. That's really wonderful, but hard to get used to. I suppose I will in time.

I was not lonely, and had made many good friends here. I had several invitations to join them that night at some bar, or in someone's home, but I had no desire to leave my recliner and my TV set. I had already poured the glass of wine I'd toast the New Year with, if I could stay awake that long. I put out some cheese and crackers on the coffee table and turned on the TV. It was exactly 6 PM, and I found an old, sappy, holiday movie. I don't know how many times some character in it said, "Nobody should be alone on New Year's Eve."

At first I paid no attention, but after awhile I began to imagine that the character who said those words looked like Roger, my Rog. I concentrated harder on the screen, and sure enough the actor did not resemble Rog. He was Rog. I rubbed my eyes. I needed to make sure that I saw what I saw.

Suddenly, there was a commercial running. In fact, the commercials never ended. I switched from channel to channel and all I could get were commercials. I even switched to PBS and even they were showing nothing but commercials. That's impossible. I grew truly frightened.

It occurred to me that maybe it wasn't a good idea to be alone on New Year's Eve after all. Maybe I was going stir crazy. It was then I made the boldest decision of my life. I showered, dressed as sexily as I could, and left my apartment on the most dangerous night of the year. Or was it the loneliest night of the year? Or was it both? I headed to Charlie's, a nearby gay bar, where I knew some of my friends were having dinner and spending the evening.

I spotted four of my friends at a table in the dining room. They were coupled, but there was a fifth man with them, and they were seated at a table for six. Kevin spotted me and waved at me.

"Where the hell have you been? We were afraid you weren't going to show up, and we were about to order. Why didn't you answer your phone?"

I was stunned. I had never agreed to have dinner here with these men, and for sure my phone hadn't rung. Once again I chalked it up to being stir crazy, and I was suddenly glad to be out socializing, and not alone on New Year's Eve.

"I got a whole slew of calls from friends in Buffalo," I lied. "I guess I lost track of the time, but here I am at last." I flashed my gorgeous smile which always made everything all right.

I sat down next to the stranger and Kevin said, "Greg, I'd like you to meet my friend Jason. He's visiting from Columbus, but he hopes to be moving down here before the end of 2000." Jason and I shook hands, and I gave him the once over. I couldn't tell how tall he was because we were both seated, but our eyes were level, so I figured that he was about my height, 5'11" tall. His eyes were dark brown. Mine are a lighter brown. We both had salt and pepper hair (once brown) and strong chins. Jason had a pleasant, friendly face and I liked him immediately. I think he liked me too because he directed all his attention to me.

He asked me about myself, and for the first time in four years I had no trouble talking about myself, and of course, about Roger. Instead of getting teary, my body grew warm and happy, remembering back to all the good and bad times we had together in thirty-five years, and how much I had loved him. This prompted me to ask Jason to tell me something about himself.

"I'm a widower too," he said. "It's funny. His name was Greg also. We weren't together as long as you and Roger, only twenty-one years. Nevertheless, we were wildly in love. On his fiftieth birthday, I took him out for a celebration dinner. In the middle of the entree he just keeled over and died. He had had a massive heart attack. I found out later on that he had suffered degenerative heart disease since he was a youngster. He never told me. I guess he didn't want me to worry."

There were tears in Jason's eyes. I was very moved, and without thinking, I put my hand on his. He looked up and stared into my eyes. We found ourselves smiling at each other.

"You have a beautiful smile," he said. Then looking down at my hand on his, he said, "Thanks for comforting me."

All I could do was smile back at him. We were oblivious to the other people at the table until Eddie, Kevin's partner, yelled, "Hey you two, break it up. The waiter is trying to take your order."

Eddie kept on yelling and I heard a pounding in my head. No it wasn't in my head; it was my front door. Eddie was pounding on it, and now he was yelling, "Greg, are you OK? You're scaring me. Please answer me."

I was seated in front of my TV. I had fallen asleep and dreamt the whole New Year's Eve scene. I ran to the front door completely forgetting that I was totally naked. I threw open the door, and Kevin and Eddie, Trevor and Ryan, rushed in, and immediately started laughing. It was Ryan who said, "That's a nice package you've got there."

I wanted to reach for my robe, but by that time it was not necessary. The Narcissus in me was flattered by the appreciative stares I was getting. Foolishly I looked to see if Jason was with them. Of course not.

"To what do I owe the pleasure," I asked.

"To friendship, and well-meaning, but pesky friends," Trevor said.

"We aren't going to leave you alone on New Year's Eve," Kevin added. "You have no choice in the matter. Now put on a jock strap, and let's get out of here. We're going to Charlie's for dinner. I made the reservations."

"As much as I'd like to go in a jock strap, do you mind if I get dressed?"

My friends were all wearing long jeans. This was my first full winter in Florida. I was used to the sub-freezing Buffalo weather. They all thought I was crazy when I put on shorts and a tank top and, as I left the apartment, I slipped into flip-flops.

"I hope you don't freeze, "Kevin said, "especially since you didn't even put on underwear."

"I gave up underwear, or I should say long-johns, when I left Buffalo. By the way, thank you. I should have said yes about going out in the first place."

One of them slapped me on the back. I don't know which one. "That's what friends are for," he said.

We lived walking distance to the restaurant. I was glad to walk. I could not get enough of this weather. Reservations or not, we had to wait forty-five minutes for our table. We headed for the bar. There were no bar stools available, so after we got our drinks, we huddled together in the lobby waiting for our table to be ready.

I thought I heard my name being called, but it was so noisy I couldn't be certain. I heard it again, louder this time. I looked around and I saw who was calling me. It was Jason from my dream, but of course it wasn't Jason. It was Jeremy Smith. In my former life I had taught American History at the University of Buffalo, and Jeremy was one of my colleagues. He was a couple of years younger than I. We were friendly enough at school, but we never socialized. I didn't have a clue that he was gay.

When he finally got to me, he embraced me in a bear hug. "I had no idea you were gay," he said, "or are you just slumming?"

"I'm not slumming," I said. "I had no idea that you were gay. I'm having dinner here with some friends. Let me introduce you."

Now you have to know Kevin. He's a hopeless romantic. He and Eddie are always trying to fix me up. Trevor and Ryan are content to let me be, and I appreciate it. When I introduced Kevin to Jeremy, I could see hearts being reflected in Kevin's eyes.

"Nice to meet you," he said to Jeremy. "Are you here alone?"

"Yes, I'm unhappily alone. I taught history with Greg at UB. I'm down here on winter break. I hate the thought of going back. Buffalo had another six inches last night. I've got three years until retirement and then I hope to join you guys."

"Do you have plans for dinner?" Kevin persisted.

"I figured I'd do fast food. I hate to eat alone."

"Nonsense, have dinner with us. They'll probably put us at a table for six anyway, so I'm sure it's not a problem. I'll go tell the maître d'." I was suddenly very uncomfortable. I liked Jeremy. He was very handsome, but I didn't like Kevin's not so subtle attempt at matchmaking. I wasn't ready for it, and I never would be.

"So there." I hadn't realized that I said that out loud and everybody was staring at me.

"What?" Ryan asked.

"Nothing," I laughed. "Just day dreaming."

I turned to Jeremy. "Where are you staying, and when are you returning to Buffalo?" I asked. Then I realized he might think I was hoping he would leave soon, and that I didn't want to see him again, so I quickly added, "Do we have time to get together, and reminisce before you leave?" I didn't imagine it, Jeremy did look relieved.

"Classes resume on January 14th," he said. "I'm flying home on the thirteenth."

"That's too long to stay in a lonely hotel room. Why don't you move in with me tomorrow, Jeremy? I have a guest room with a private bath, and I won't charge," I smiled at him. To this day I don't know why I offered Jeremy the invitation. I hate having strangers and guests in my house. I feel like I have given up my privacy when that happens.

Jeremy took my hand, much the same as I had taken Jason's in my dream, and suddenly I was glad I had tendered the invitation. "That is so generous of you. Are you sure?"

"I'm sure," I smiled back at him. "In fact, we all live in the same building, walking distance from here. Come back with me tonight, and tomorrow I'll drive you over to the hotel to check you out."

"That would be wonderful," he said. He smiled at me and I conceded that his smile was even more winning than mine. Something strange was happening to me.

Just before midnight, we filled our champagne glasses and stood up. We knew that we would all be kissing each other at midnight and we were just getting ready. The whole restaurant started chanting the countdown at number ten. Since the world didn't end at midnight, we all yelled, "Happy New Year" and took a sip of our champagne. We laid our glasses on the table and went around kissing each other. I kissed everyone chastely, even though it was on the lips. And then Jeremy and I stood staring at each other. I bent in to kiss him, but he grabbed me around the waist and pulled me to him.

"This is the happiest New Year's Eve of my life," he whispered in my ear. He put his lips against mine, and began to kiss me passionately. His tongue parted my lips, and the moment that I began to tickle his tongue with mine, I could feel our stiff cocks rubbing hard against each other. I knew without a shadow of a doubt that I was going to get laid that night after a four year drought. I was to find out some hours later that I didn't get laid. I got loved.

By the time we reached my apartment, about two in the morning, Jeremy knew everything I could tell him about Roger. He told me that he had been in a few relationships in his life. None of them had lasted very long, and the one true love that he always dreamed of still eluded him.

Neither of us were big drinkers, and we hadn't overdone it at the restaurant. I poured both of us a glass of red wine and we sat down on my sofa. At first there was an uncomfortable silence between us. I finally said, "I had no idea you were gay. As far as I was concerned, you were as straight as the proverbial arrow."

"Me too, I'm still shocked to find out that you aren't straight. You always talked in the plural...we did this...we did that, and I thought you were married."

"I was married in every sense of the word, but not to a woman. If Rog was alive, and we were still living in Buffalo, we could get legally married now."

"Would you?"

"I don't know. I'd probably leave it up to Rog. I was 100% committed to him. A Justice of the Peace couldn't improve on that number."

We grew quiet again. This time Jeremy broke the ice. "Since the day I met you," he began, "I've had the hots for you. I should never have accepted your invitation. Right now, I'm fighting the urge to pounce on you and devour you with my kisses and my love. Greg, I'm scared."

I was truly not surprised by his confession. Suddenly all my resolves to stay celibate and honor Roger's memory were sucked up by some powerful cosmic vacuum cleaner. I was tired of jacking off. I wanted to have sex with a warm body, and sitting alone with me was a willing partner who admitted to desiring me. Neither of us had said or thought about the word 'love' yet.

"Don't be scared," I begged Jeremy. I put my arms around him and offered him my lips.

"Is this your answer? Is this your final answer?" he asked jokingly.

"It is," I said, and I forced my tongue into his willing mouth. We kissed for what seemed, at the time, to be forever. Our hands groped our crotches and we had to stop kissing long enough to drop our trousers. Neither one of us was wearing underwear. I was holding him so tightly, I didn't realize that he wanted me to release him. Finally he was able to push me away. Before I could react, his mouth was buried in my crotch. He was bathing me in very wet comfort.

His educated tongue was all over my pubic area, my balls, and finally my cock. It had been so long since I had felt such passion in me and in my partner. I was about to tell Jeremy to turn around so we could play 69, but it was too late. I was past the point of no return. All I could yell was, "I'm cuuumming." Jeremy sucked me dry and finally sat next to me on the sofa. We were both breathing hard.

When I could breathe again, I said, "I want to suck your cock Jeremy, but stop me before you cum. I don't have condoms, but I don't care. Just unload inside of me and fill my guts."

"Don't think ill of me, but I always carry condoms in my pocket. It's an act of wishful thinking. They are so old, I hope they don't split."

I started to laugh. "Are you telling me that it's been a very long time for you too?" Jeremy nodded. "Well then maybe we can skip the condoms, if you have always used them in the distant past." We both laughed. Jeremy was still laughing when I leaned over and started to suck his succulent cock. He stopped me a lot sooner than I would have liked. I went to the bathroom and got a jar of Vaseline. I greased his cock generously and then I greased my ass. While I was doing all this, I studied his beautiful, cut, eight inch cock. It had been about five inches before he hardened. I am about the same size, but I am uncut. I don't have a lot of foreskin. The head of my penis peeps out of its sheath when it is flaccid.

We were ready now. I stretched out on my sofa, flat on my back. When Jeremy climbed on top of me, we started to kiss. We kissed so long, we almost forgot our ultimate mission. Finally Jeremy placed his cock at the opening of my love canal, but he didn't move.

"What's wrong?" I asked.

"I'm waiting for you to tell me when you're ready."

"I'm ready. I am so ready." It had been so long, I feared that he might hurt me. Foolish me. Roger had been just as long as Jeremy, but he was much wider around. I was well stretched, and to my delight, I hadn't shrunk. Jeremy entered me easily. In fact, after he was all the way in, I had to flex my ass to make it good and tight for him. I guess I did well. He started to groan and moan. Suddenly his moaning gave way to a blood curdling scream, and I felt him deposit his seed high up my guts.

"I'm glad we didn't use a rubber," I said.

Finally he fell out of me, and I suggested we shower.

"Before we shower, I've got to say it. I love you Greg. I've loved you since I met you in Buffalo too many years ago. I don't expect you to love me as much as I love you. I realize that you will never stop loving Roger, but can you love me enough to share your life with me? Surely meeting you like this in a distant place, after so many years, is a good omen."

I was dumbstruck, but not so much that I couldn't think straight. I knew for sure, after making love to Jeremy, that I didn't want to be a hermit anymore. I didn't want to sleep alone anymore. I wanted love, I needed love. My matchmaking friends were in for one hell of a surprise.

"Yes, yes," I answered. "I do want to share my life with you. I want that very much."

"Then I think we should shower together."

For the next three years, I spent my summers in Buffalo with Jeremy. I even managed to teach some summer courses at the university. He came down to Florida on every school break. Our frequent separations would have been hard to take, but we knew we would be together soon…forever, and we were able to bear it.

The longest and loneliest night of the year had come and gone, and I was no longer lonely. I truly think Roger had a lot to do with that, and if his love for me carried any merit with the gods that be, I was destined never to spend another New Year's Eve alone again.

End of the 21st Story

Hank Brooks

Love Me If You Can

Gay Romance Erotica

Love Me If You Can

By: Hank Brooks

Joe Gordon woke up on his fortieth birthday alone in bed. That was certainly not unusual for him. The handsome, nearly young, executive was used to waking up alone. If he had sex in the evening at someone else's place, he left as soon as he could, and if someone had sex with him at his apartment, he made it quite clear that he was not welcome to spend the night. He enjoyed playing the field and he wasn't going to let himself get *involved*. To that end he always avoided over nighters.

Joey had a counterpart in the non-commitment department. Yuri Stigorian grew up in Athens to an Israeli mother and a Greek father. He moved to New York to attend Columbia University. After school, he remained in the big apple, where he opened an American branch of his father's designer clothing manufacturing business.

Yuri's mother was a tall exotic looking model who came to Athens for a runway show to promote Israeli fashion. There she met Yuri's handsome father and she never returned to Israel. Yuri inherited his mother's beauty and his father's athletic body.

His maternal grandparents had immigrated to Israel from New York City when Yuri's mother was a baby. He had spent every summer of his boyhood visiting them in Israel, and as a result he spoke Greek, English and Hebrew like a native. He also enjoyed American, Israeli (through his mother), and Greek (by birth) citizenship. He had no problem attracting handsome young studs to his bedroom, but like Joey, he made it quite clear that they could not spend the night.

Joey was vice president and principal buyer for a chain of boutiques, which sold high end designer clothing. One morning he had an appointment with Yuri to view his current line of designer clothing. The line included the works of some of the top designers in the world. The two men were immediately attracted to each other and slept together that very night.

On the night before his fortieth birthday, Joey had dinner with Yuri, with whom he had been tricking with off and on for the past six months. Yuri was five years younger than he, but they both looked to be in their late twenties. If he was honest with himself, he enjoyed sex with Yuri more than anyone else he could remember. Even the time they spent together, before and after sex, was relaxing and casual. They would sip wine and talk about nothing in particular. Yet everything Yuri said, all the small talk, seemed to be so intelligent and important to Joey.

Last night Yuri fell asleep after their second sexual encounter of the evening, and rather than wake him and tell him it was time to go, Joey cuddled up to him, wrapped his arm around Yuri's torso and he too fell asleep. He could not remember sleeping so well in years. When he awoke, he was terribly disappointed that Yuri was gone. *He probably left in the middle of the night,* Joey thought. That was what he always demanded of his tricks, so why was he disappointed?

He wanted to roll over and get another forty winks, but he had to pee badly. Instead he got out of bed and headed for the bathroom. He thought he smelled something, and so he took a deep breath and inhaled deeply. He was not mistaken. The apartment was filled with the pleasant aroma of bacon frying on a griddle. He stopped to pee, only because he had to, and then headed to the kitchen. There was Yuri at the range, as naked as he was.

"Good morning, handsome," Yuri said, "Your breakfast is almost ready. Pour the juice and butter the toast, please, while I finish the bacon and eggs."

Yesterday, or maybe last week, Joey would have been angry to have Yuri stay over. This morning he was delighted. The domesticity of the scene did not escape him, but he brushed aside the feeling of entrapment and decided to enjoy the moment. Joey had never consciously decided that it was time to settle down, but seeing Yuri making breakfast for both of them, so overwhelmed him, that he thought that maybe he and Yuri could make a life together.

Easy guy, he thought. *You have no idea what Yuri thinks about all this.*

Joey went over to Yuri and put his arms around him. His cock pushed up against Yuri's ass as he kissed Yuri on the neck. "I'm glad you didn't run away," Joey said. "Today is a big birthday for me and I really need someone to share it with. I guess I really mean that I need someone to console me."

"I know," Yuri said. "I didn't fall asleep on you last night. I only pretended. I wanted to be with you on this very special occasion." Yuri turned around and kissed Joey on his lips. "Happy birthday, young man," he said.

They ate breakfast in relative silence. Joey's parents were long dead. He had no other family, and since his childhood, Joey had never eaten breakfast at home with another human being. He really was at a loss for conversation. His mind was working overtime. He still believed that he didn't want any involvements, but he was feeling things for Yuri that he was totally unused to.

They rinsed the dishes, and placed them in the dishwasher. All this was done in silence. To be honest, both men were confused about their feelings.

"Let's shower and get back in bed," Yuri suggested. "I want to make love to you all day long as a birthday present."

"I like the way you think," Joey said. He took Yuri's hand and led him into the bathroom. He started the shower and waited for the temperature to be at his satisfaction level. Then the two entered the stall. Once inside they wrapped their arms around each other and hugged tightly. Their cocks rubbed together and they both began to get hard.

I love this man, Joey thought, *but I don't dare tell him. Shit!*

They made love most of the day, and in the evening Yuri took Joey out for a gourmet dinner to celebrate his birthday. Joey didn't even protest when Yuri picked up the tab. They parted after dinner and days went by before they spoke again. Neither wanted to be the one to admit how much he missed the other. More strange was the fact that they both remained celibate during this time of confusion.

Finally one morning, Yuri had to call Joey on business. That broke the ice.

"It's been too long," Joey said. "Let's get together tonight."

"You're on," Yuri said. "I have a slew of appointments this afternoon. I'll be running late so come on over to my place about 6:30 and we'll decide on what to do."

"Sure," Joey said, but what he really wanted to say was *let's skip dinner and fuck our brains out.* "I'll see you then," he concluded as he hung up.

It was only 3 PM, but just then his secretary came in to inform him that she was leaving, and to wish him a Merry Christmas. Joey had completely forgotten that it was Christmas Eve and his office was closing early. He was not close enough with anyone to have made holiday plans and for the first time in his life that bothered him. He actually felt remorse. He figured that Yuri was in the same boat since his folks were in Greece. He was glad he had invited Yuri to spend the evening with him, and he could have kicked himself for being such an asshole for not having called Yuri sooner.

He had about three hours to kill before going over to Yuri's apartment. He decided to buy Yuri a Christmas present. He was the last person in the office so he locked up and headed for Bloomingdale's. He bought Yuri a handsome pair of kid gloves, which he had gift wrapped. He thought several times about it, and in the end he enclosed a card which read, "Affectionately, Joey." He still had a couple of hours to kill so he dropped in at a cocktail lounge which was located a short distance from Yuri's apartment.

The lounge was empty except for an elderly man at the bar. Most people had left work early and had headed home to be with their families. Joey seated himself at the bar and ordered a scotch and soda. He could see that the man sitting a few seats down from him was an exceptionally handsome older man, about 65 to 70 years old, holding a beer in his hands. The glass was full and the beer had no head. Obviously the man had not drunk a sip of the brew. Suddenly he put his arm on the bar, placed his head on his arm and began to cry. His whole body heaved with the force of his sobs.

Joey rushed over and put his arm around the man's shoulder. He looked up at Joey, and Joey gasped. The man looked like an older version of himself. He was the same height; his eyes were the exact same color; his hair was speckled with gray but the original color was the same as his. The man was still sobbing, but as his crying abated he said, "Thanks for caring Joey."

"How did you know my name?" Joey asked. The man didn't answer him, and an uncomfortable silence followed. Finally Joey asked, "Why are you crying, fella? Is there something I can do to help?"

"No one can help," the man said. "Here it is Christmas Eve, and I'm all alone. There's not a soul on earth I can share the evening with."

"Surely a good looking guy like you has at least one girlfriend to be with tonight," Joey tried to console the guy.

"First of all, Joey, I'm gay, and I don't even have one boyfriend to share this evening with either."

"That's hard to believe," Joey said. "Have you been living on Mars for the past twenty years?"

"I might just as well have been out of this world," the man said. "I have pushed away every man that ever wanted to be close to me. I was afraid of a relationship. I only wanted to have one night stands. I couldn't bear the thought of committing to anyone. I just wanted to be fancy free, and I am. Now that I'm old, *older*," he corrected himself, "here I am, a lonely man. I was a jerk."

His words stung Joey to his core. Wasn't that what he was doing? Wasn't he forty and still alone? Didn't he push all his loves out of his life? No wonder the stranger was crying. Suddenly Joey felt like crying with him.

The man looked at Joey accusingly. "You're doing the same thing. Aren't you, you fool?"

What right had this stranger to say these things to him? He had no cause to call him a fool even if he was one. Joey was getting more and more uncomfortable. Not only did this man know his name, but he seemed to know all about him.

"You have no right to say these things," Joey answered back. "I love my life and I don't want to complicate it. Anyway, whether I do or not, is none of your business. Now I suggest you stop sniveling and I'll buy you a fresh beer."

"I'm sorry," the man said. "I guess I overstepped my bounds. I'd like a fresh drink, thank you."

"You have me at a disadvantage. You seem to know my name, but I don't know yours," Joey said.

He expected the man to tell him his name, but instead the stranger said, "It's not important for you to know my name." Obviously he had no intention of giving Joey that information.

"Have it your way," Joey said. "I'll just call you Rumpelstilskin." Joey turned to the bartender and ordered a fresh beer for Rumpy and a scotch and soda for him. He then turned back to the older man and asked, "How is it you know my name and so much about me? I'd really like to know."

"I can read it in your face. You are basically a lonely man, Joey. You have few friends and except for Yuri, you never see a trick twice. I can see it all just by looking into your eyes."

"There you go again," Joey said. "How do you know about Yuri?"

"None of your business," the stranger answered, and now Joey was beginning to get frightened.

"Yuri is the best thing that ever happened to you. I just know you'll let him slip away and you'll end up a lonely old man like me."

"Nonsense," Joey said. "I have plenty of friends and I'm not lonely, nor will I ever be."

"Why do I have to repeat myself?" Rumpy asked. "You know damn well that you have a few acquaintances, but no real friends. If you had half a brain you would see that Yuri is a good friend. Why he even stayed overnight with you so you wouldn't be alone on your birthday. You surely know that went against his philosophy also, but he did it for you. And if that isn't enough, he's the best lover you ever had. When he sucks your cock, you envision that Paradise must be like that. Don't even try to deny it."

Joey got up to leave. He had enough. "You're crazy old man and I don't have to listen to this garbage."

"Don't bother to leave," the stranger said. "I was just ing. Thanks for the drink." He got up and left so quickly that he left Joey stunned. He took a sip of his cocktail and tried to make sense of what had just happened. As he was musing, another older man shuffled in and sat down in the spot vacated by the stranger Joey had been talking to.

"A martini," the man ordered. Joey looked at the man and did a double take.

My God, he thought. *That's what Yuri might look like in about thirty years.*

The man took a sip of his martini. Then he laid his head down on his arm and began to sob. Instinctively Joey wanted to console him just as he had tried to console Rumpy, but after his recent experience, he decided against it.

After some time passed, the man raised his head and looked at Joey. "What kind of man ignores a crying man on Christmas Eve?" he asked.

"The kind of man who doesn't give a shit why you are crying," Joey answered, making his voice sound as cruel as possible. "I see that you are going to tell me, whether I'm interested or not, so OK. Why are you crying and can I help?"

"No you can't help, but I'll tell you why I am so sad. It's Christmas Eve and I am all alone. There's not a soul in the world I can share this magical evening with. When I was your age I was just like you. I refused to get involved. I never slept with the same man twice. Then I met someone and I fell madly in love with him. Unfortunately, he didn't want involvement either, so I was afraid to tell him how I felt about him, and after awhile we stopped seeing each other. I continued my wanton ways until my youth and beauty faded, and now I'm practically celibate. I don't care so much about that, but I care that I am so damned lonely."

"My heart bleeds for you," Joey said facetiously. The truth is that the man was too close to the truth of his own life, and Joey was distinctly uncomfortable. "I can understand that you didn't get involved with anyone, but why don't you have any friends?"

"I was so busy avoiding a relationship, I failed to realize the difference between a friend and an avaricious lover. God, I was such a fool," the old man said. "You seem determined to follow in my footsteps, you jerk," the man accused Joey.

"Hey, stop it! You have no right to talk to me that way," Joey hissed at the man.

"I have every right, you moron," the man said. He got up and left without paying his bar tab.

"Did you see that?" Joey asked the bartender. "That guy left without paying his bill."

"What man?" the bartender asked.

"The guy I was just talking to," Joey shouted at the bartender.

"No need to yell, dude. There has been nobody in here but you and me since you came in. I just served you your last drink. I think you have had one too many."

Joey was about to protest when a voice inside him seemed to tell him to cool it. He took what remained of his drink to a small corner table and tried to make sense of what had just happened to him.

I have just met two guys who could be me and Yuri 25 or 30 years down the pike. They are old and miserable and very, very lonely. Is this an omen, a portent of how our lives will be someday? No, no, it can't be. It's too sad. I don't want to be like those guys. Dear God, don't let me end up like that.

Joey felt his shoulder being shaken vigorously. He had fallen asleep.

"Look buddy," he heard the bartender say. "It's almost 8 o'clock. We're closing for the holiday. I'm going to have to ask you to leave."

"Oh God," Joey whined. "I've missed my date with Yuri. Please God let him still be home." He paid the bartender and ran out and towards Yuri's building. When he got there, he rang Yuri's apartment and Yuri buzzed him in through the front door.

Thank God he's home, Joey thought. When he got to Yuri's apartment, Yuri was standing at the door waiting for him.

"I was so worried," he said. "What happened to you? Why didn't you answer your cell phone?"

Joey wasn't sure how he could explain what happened to him so he removed Yuri's present from his coat pocket, and threw his coat on a chair. His eyes met Yuri's and he began to cry like a baby. Yuri wrapped his arms around his crying friend.

"What's the matter, sweetheart?" Yuri asked.

Sweetheart!!! Yuri called him *sweetheart.* Joey cried even harder. Yuri held him tighter.

It took Joey awhile to get control of himself. "I can't explain anything," he said, "but I have something to say to you. After I say it, you can kick me out if you'd like, but if I don't confess something to you, I'll never forgive myself."

Joey was still clutching Yuri's gift in one of his hands so Yuri took his other hand and led him to the sofa. The two men sat down.

"It sounds very serious," Yuri said. "Go ahead."

Joey did not mince any words. He was afraid he would lose his courage if he did. He took a deep breath and said, "Yuri, I love you. I haven't been with anyone else since my birthday. I don't want to be alone any more. I want to be with you. I want to go to sleep with you, and wake up with you and make love to you every single day and night for the rest of my life. I need you so much to share my life with me. Even if you don't feel the same way, I'm glad I told you."

Yuri was still holding Joey's free hand and he squeezed it hard. "You jerk," he said.

He's rejecting me, Joey thought. *No! The old man who looked like Yuri, he called me a jerk also.*

"I guess you'd like me to take off and disappear forever," Joey said.

"No, you moron, (the old man called Joey that too) I want you to stay. I want you to stay with me forever. I feel the same way you do, but I thought that if I admitted it to you, you would run away, and I didn't want to risk not ever seeing you again."

"I feared the same thing," Joey said. He wanted to embrace Yuri but he still held Yuri's Christmas present in his hand. He thrust it at Yuri. "Merry Christmas," he said.

"I got you something too," Yuri said. He ran to the server in the dining room and retrieved a package. It was identical to Joey's and also came from Bloomingdale. They both ripped open their packages and broke out laughing. Each had given the other an identical pair of kid gloves. The note in Joey's gift read, *With affection, Yuri.*

Finally they embraced and both started sobbing. "What gave you the courage to tell me that you wanted me forever?" Yuri asked.

"I'll tell you all about it in the morning, after we've made love a hundred times."

"That's a deal," Yuri said. "I didn't think there would be any restaurants open this evening, so I made us dinner, but I think it's spoiled by now."

"I know a Chinese restaurant close by that's open really late. I'll bet they don't close on Christmas Eve," Joey said. They grabbed their coats and ran to the restaurant which was still open and very crowded. They were seated in the last remaining booth and the waiter handed them menus. Service was a bit slow so Joey took the opportunity to look around. Seated at a small table, in a corner of the restaurant, were the two men he had encountered at the bar. They were smiling at each other and were not embarrassed to hold each other's hands in public. They looked over at Joey and smiled. One of them mouthed the words, *thank you.* Then they both disappeared and the table was empty.

Joey wanted desperately to tell Yuri about his Christmas miracle, but he figured this was not the time. All he wanted to do was eat dinner and make love to Yuri all night long, and all day tomorrow, and every day after that, forever and ever.

End of the 22nd Story

A ROAD TO NOWHERE

Gay Romance
HANK BROOKS

A Road to Nowhere

By: Hank Brooks

How often had the man heard the expression, *A Road to Nowhere*? It had never really sunk in. After all, it was nothing more than a poetic expression. Roads can't go 'nowhere.' They usually have a beginning, a middle section and an end, wherever that end may be. *Just like the yellow brick road*, he thought.

So where was he going? He was thoroughly lost. But isn't that what he wanted all along? To be alone. Wasn't that the entire reason for this trip? In spite of the fact that there was no light at the end of the road, so to speak, he had no choice, but to trudge right along. He could not go back, and he was reluctant to get off the road. He had to believe that every road had some destination at the end, after all.

In a short while he came across a fallen tree that had been pushed to the side of the road. *That would make an excellent bench to rest on*, the man thought. He removed his knapsack and laid it down near the tree. Then he sat down and his thoughts wandered back to a month earlier, and to the events which brought him here.

James Bannerman was an account executive at one of Madison Avenue's largest and most successful advertising agencies. The pressure on him was enormous. Long hours and constant deadlines had taken a toll on him. His wife of only one year had walked out on him. The first night, or I should say the first early morning, he returned to an empty home, he suddenly started to hyper ventilate. He could not breathe. Lucky for him, he was able to call 911 before he passed out.

Even luckier, the heart attack was very mild and little damage was done. It was a strong warning to him to stop abusing his body. He was discharged in a mere four days with strict orders to take several weeks off and get plenty of rest, relaxation and recreation. The agency wasn't happy but they gave him an eight week sabbatical.

His sister was a travel agent, and the two of them poured over travel brochures, and a myriad of escorted tours. He rejected them out of hand. He definitely wanted to be alone and away from people. He did, however, examine the pictures carefully, and he fell in love with Scotland, or at least, the look of Scotland as pictured by the travel industry. With a little bit more research, Arlene booked a bed and breakfast for him, miles from the nearest large city. After arriving in Edinburgh, he would have to rent an auto and travel almost forty-five miles to the inn. That was exactly what he wanted.

The inn was everything he dreamed it would be. It was small, quaint and remote. It was surrounded by English gardens and was picture book pretty. There were only two other guests, a honeymoon couple from London. He barely saw them, even at breakfast.

He spent his days sitting on the veranda with a blanket wrapped around his legs and a good book in hand. He was happy and content for about three days, then boredom set in, and he decided to take a hike. Right after breakfast the inn keeper packed him a picnic lunch, and he started up one of the several paths that led away from the inn.

The early autumn air was crisp and a bit blustery. He loved it. It felt so invigorating. He walked for about two hours, taking deep breaths of the refreshing air. He didn't notice that the path had ended, and he was walking in a small clearing surrounded by groves of trees. For a second he panicked. He had paid no attention to the direction he was walking in so even if he could use the position of the sun to establish the direction of his return route, he didn't know what that direction was.

He tried to remember if the sun had been in front of him or to the rear, to the right or to the left, but no memory was afforded him. All he could do was to turn around completely and start walking in a reverse direction. He walked for hours, through clearings and through groves, but he never found the path he had been on. Finally, as twilight was upon him, he stumbled on a paved road, just wide enough for one auto going in one direction.

If I follow the road, he thought, eventually I will come to some civilization. Suddenly he started to laugh. Maybe he'd be lucky enough to find Brigadoon and marry Cyd Charisse. The thought warmed and amused him, but he had to make a decision in which direction to start walking. For no reason at all, except for a hunch, he turned right and renewed his trek until he came upon the tree trunk.

He decided that he had rested long enough on the make shift bench. His food was long gone and it was time to move on. He put his knapsack back on and continued on his confused way.

According to his watch, it was ten o'clock at night when he saw something up ahead. He was certain he saw a light, but then it seemed to disappear. He hurried his step, and there it was again. It was definitely a light, but this time it was brighter and did not disappear. As he got closer, he could see that the light came from a small cottage. *Thank God*, he thought. I'll be able to call the inn from there to come and get me.

As he drew nearer and nearer to the cottage, it became prettier and prettier as far as he was concerned. Surely kind souls dwelt there. He sprinted the last one hundred yards to the front door. *Thank goodness the lights are still on*, he thought. A beautifully carved knocker adorned the front door and he began to knock.

The door was answered by a tall, very lean, very distinguished looking gentleman in his late thirties. Bannerman thought that he was probably five to seven years older than he was.

The man smiled at James. "Don't tell me you're lost," he said. "If you are, you'll be the second lost tourist this week. He broke out into a hearty laugh. "Come in, come in," he said, waving Bannerman in.

"Take off that knapsack and get comfortable," the man said. He extended his hand. "I'm Ian MacBeigh," he said. "Are you hungry? I've got plenty to eat and drink."

"I'm James Bannerman and I'm starved," the wanderer said, "but mostly I am so damned thirsty."

"Would you like plain water or a little wine?" Ian asked.

"Water please," James responded. Ian went to a small refrigerator and removed a pitcher of water. He poured a generous amount for James, and the two men sat down at a small table. Everything in the cottage was small.

"I can give you a ham sandwich with cheese if that will do." Ian told James.

"Oh my, yes. That will do just fine."

"Are you staying at the Olde Wayside Inn?" Ian asked.

Bannerman nodded. His mouth was full.

"I'm afraid I have no phone. The road back is partly paved, partly dirt and partly grass fields. It's too dangerous to negotiate in the dark. I can drive you back in the morning, and I can only offer you my hospitality and shelter for the night."

"That's more than kind of you," James said gratefully.

"Have you ever slept with a man before?" Ian asked.

James looked aghast. "Wh.. what?" he asked.

Ian broke out laughing. "I meant that in the literal sense. I only have one bed, but it's big enough for both of us." James relaxed and joined Ian in laughter.

"It's not too late," Ian said. "I'm starved for company out here. Would you join me in a little conversation over a mug of beer before we turn in?"

"I'd be delighted," James said.

After the beers were poured, the two men sat on two easy chairs in the front room. "You look like a very urbane American," Ian said to James. "What in the world brings you to our remote part of the world?"

For some reason James found Ian easy to talk to and he found himself relating the whole story. He told him how his wife had walked out on him, about his mild heart attack, and how he had chosen this region for the sheer beauty of the pictures he had seen. "Now you look too young to be retired so what brings you here?" James asked Ian.

"I was afraid you would ask," Ian said jokingly. "I teach English Literature at the University of Edinburgh. About six months ago my world was turned upside down and I had a nervous breakdown. I was forced to take a year's sabbatical. This cottage was my weekend getaway, but for now it's my home for another few months."

"I wouldn't mind spending a few months here. It's the closest thing I've ever seen to Paradise," James said.

"That would be wonderful if you could," Ian said. "At one time I had someone to share this Edenic spot with, but now I'm alone." Ian grew quiet, and James allowed him his moment of reflection.

"If you don't mind my asking," James said. "What was it turned your world around?"

"It's funny," Ian said, "until now I had not wished to speak of it, but you are so easy to talk to, and I feel like getting it off my chest, so here goes."

Ian poured some more beer in each of their glasses and began: "First of all, James, I can tell you this because you can't run away, and you're stuck here for the night. I'm gay." He stopped to see James's reaction, and looked at James inquiringly.

"Relax, friend," James said. "I'm in advertising. I interact daily with gay male models, gay photographers, gay copy editors and so on. I figured you were gay the minute I got here. For a straight guy, I have excellent gaydar."

Ian did indeed relax and he continued. "I met Fergie (Evan Ferguson) in college. I was majoring in English Lit and he was into mathematics. We began studying together, and it didn't take long for us to discover that besides both of us being gay, we had fallen hopelessly in love with each other. I know you here about promiscuity in the gay community, but Fergie and I knew each other for nearly a year before we made love. He was my first and my only. I will never forget that first night with him as long as I live.

"We were both very lucky in procuring teaching positions at the University. We bought a house together and were as happy as the proverbial pigs in shit. We both had the jobs we wanted, the lover we wanted, and the house we wanted. We had it all, but Jamie my man, don't ever get too complacent. One day, returning from work, Fergie was hit broadside by a very drunk teen ager. He was killed instantly. I was a useless bag of shit after that, and the University ordered a year off for me."

Ian buried his head in his hands and broke out sobbing. James was never a touchy, feely person and he wasn't even consciously aware of what he did next, but he got up, went over to Ian and put his arms around him. Ian put his arms around James and sobbed on his shoulder.

James took Ian's beer glass and his own and washed them in the sink. When he returned to the living room, Ian was still crying. He stood him up and said, "Let's get you to bed."

When they entered the bedroom, James began to laugh.

"What?" Ian asked.

"Am I the first guy you have slept with since Fergie?" He said it with a smile, hoping to lighten the mood and perhaps get a smile out of Ian. It worked. Ian looked at him and said with a wide grin, "In the literal sense, yes."

They both stripped to their boxer shorts and Ian pointed the way to the bathroom. James went first and then Ian. When Ian got back to the bedroom, he found James standing there.

"Why aren't you in bed yet? I promise you are safe if you want to be."

James had the good grace to laugh. "I was just waiting to see which side of the bed you wanted."

"How kind of you," Ian said. "I always slept on Fergie's right side," he said.

"Then so be it," James said. He crept into bed and Ian followed. As he got into bed, Ian turned off his bedside light and the room was in darkness. Although their bodies never touched, James was in a state of utter nervousness. Ian fell asleep immediately, but it took James quite a while.

James had no idea what time it was when something woke him. As soon as he got his bearings, he realized that Ian had rolled over and thrown his arm around his chest. In so doing he had nested against James, who literally froze. He thought that maybe Ian was dreaming, and thinking that he was Fergie. He wanted to give Ian that pleasant dream so he didn't push him away. Besides, there was no harm done if another man held him. In fact, it was kind of comforting. He and his wife made love and then turned away from each other. They had never held each other like this and James kind of liked it. He liked it, that is, until he felt Ian's erection against his thigh.

Once again he panicked, but soon relaxed. Nothing was going on and nothing was going to. The problem was that his own manhood was as stiff as a steel rod.

Ian went on sleeping soundly, so that after a while James relaxed enough to fall asleep also. Ian's arm was still thrown around James.

Ian awoke first. He was surprised and a little upset to find his arm over James's chest. James was still sleeping and Ian didn't want to disturb him so he decided not to move. Lying still, he dozed off again. He dreamed that he was nesting against Fergie. His hand wandered down to find Fergie's very hard cock. He began to caress it playfully.

In his sleep, Jamie began to moan. Someone was doing wonderful things to his cock. He felt an orgasm coming on. It was going to be a good one, he could tell. He not only felt it in his groin, he felt it all over his body. His wife was smothering his body and playing with his cock like she never had before. At last she was making love to him, not just having sex.

He came all over Ian's hand, his underwear, his own thighs and the bed linens. The two men woke with a start. Jamie was still euphoric from his orgasm, but Ian realized immediately what had happened.

"Shit, shit, shit," he yelled. "I am so sorry." He jumped out of bed to get a towel, but James grabbed his hand.

"Easy man, relax. I needed that badly and it was great. There's no need to apologize and don't panic. I loved it." He let go of Ian who ran to get the towel. When things were somewhat dried up and cleaned, James found himself without underwear, lying naked in bed. He motioned for Ian to join him. Ian removed his boxers and got into bed with James.

"That was fun," James said. "Let's play some more. Jamie liked it."

The two men faced each other. Their bodies rubbed against each other. Ian's erect cock was grinding into James's groin, and James's flaccid cock was getting hard again.

"This is incredible," James sighed. "I never knew." Ian leaned over and kissed James. At first James wanted to recoil, but he didn't and moments later his tongue was playing dueling swords with Ian's. He was shocked to learn that he was enjoying kissing a man.

When Ian felt that James was hard again, he leaned over him. Ian's tongue began to explore James's neck, then his nipples, then his navel and finally his inner thighs. James was moaning and tossing his body around. Ian wrapped his tongue around James's cock head and then down his shaft. James had gotten a few blow jobs in college from girls, but never anything like this. Much to his very temporary dismay, Ian removed his mouth from James's cock and began to suck up and down his crack, occasionally inserting his tongue into the hole. James was moaning and screaming and Ian knew what to do. He took as much of James's seven inches into his mouth as he could. He ran his tongue up and down James's shaft, and it didn't take long before James had another pulsating orgasm. This time Ian swallowed all of it.

The two men lay back exhausted. "You taste so good," Ian said to James. "I have missed Fergie so. Do you think that you would ever want to do any of that stuff to me?"

"It can be arranged. I'm certain," James answered and leaned over to kiss Ian. He tried to repeat everything Ian had done to him, but he hesitated before each new maneuver. He thought it would be disgusting and that he would think it was gross, but a whole new world was opening up to him. He couldn't believe how good Ian's cock tasted or his cum or his ass hole crack. James was walking on air, or at least floating on the bed.

"When I was in college," Jamie began to confess, "I had some gay friends. All of us, straight and gay, had many drinking sessions together. When we had too many beers in our bellies, we guys would relate some of our sexual activity to each other. The gay encounters aroused me more than the straight stories, and when one of the gays tried to get into my pants, I refused to act on it, no matter how much I yearned for the experience. You have helped me rediscover an aspect of my life I had buried, and like I said before, Jamie likes it."

"I'm pleased," Ian said, and the two men went right on exploring each other's bodies and their sexuality."

Eventually they showered and dressed. After breakfast Ian drove James to the inn, where he packed up and moved out. Of course, he moved in with Ian.

The next day, they drove to Edinburgh for food and other supplies. Ian took James to see his city apartment. There he showed him pictures of Fergie. "God he was so good looking. What do you see in me?" James asked.

Ian laughed. "Crazy man," he said. "You're much better looking."

When they left the apartment, Ian took James for a walk around the neighborhood. While the two men idled away the time window shopping, Ian asked James, "Since advertising is so stressful, if you could do something else, what would you do?"

James looked up and down the busy little street they were on. "I think I'd like to own one of these little shops along this street," he said. I'd get to know everyone in the neighborhood and get home at a decent time to a restful place with a loving mate. My God, look!" James pointed to a sign in the window of a small tobacco shop. The sign read, "For Sale."

There was a sweet smell of tobacco emanating from the shop. In the window the shopkeeper had dozens of beautifully carved pipes for sale. The shop was more of an antique pipe shop than a tobacco shop. They went inside. The owner had exotic pipe tobaccos from all over the world. James was getting heady from the aromas.

"This place is fantastic," he said to Ian. I want to buy it and live with you forever. If I go back to what I was doing, I'll be dead in a short time. Besides, I don't ever want to be too far from you. I love you."

Ian ran out of the store. James ran after him. He worried that he had moved too fast and Ian would hate him. Ian was sobbing. James put his arm around him. "I'm sorry," he said. "I'm too impulsive."

"Shut up, you crazy man. Buy the damned store, if you can afford it, but don't apologize for loving me. I love you too."

James had his sister, Arlene, ship him all his clothes and a few personal things from his Manhattan apartment. He paid his landlord to break his lease, and asked him to donate his furniture to charity. He became a resident of Edinburgh. He never lost his New York accent and the residents referred to him as that crazy American. Ian even got him a job at the University teaching Foreign Advertising three hours a week. After a while he found himself teaching advertising on a full time basis. He had to hire a young lad to run the shop for him.

No life is ever stress-free, but James came damn near close to it. As far as he was concerned, he had visited Scotland, traveled a road to nowhere, and found his Brigadoon. Furthermore he now preferred Ian MacBeigh to Cyd Charisse.

End of the 23rd Story

HANK BROOKS

A COMFORTABLE SORROW

GAY ROMANCE EROTICA

A Comfortable Sorrow

By: Hank Brooks

Part One

The Blackest Friday Morning

It all came down on January 6th, two days after my 27th birthday. That day turned out to be the worst day of my life, and because I am relatively young, I hope I can say the same thing sixty years from now. I never want to have another day like it again. Let me tell you about it from the beginning.

First of all, it was a Friday. I woke up feeling pretty good. I was looking forward to a great weekend. I was planning on keeping warm by spending a good part of it in bed with my boyfriend Colin. Colin and I only saw each other on weekends. We didn't see each other during the week because we didn't want to bring stress to our respective work places by getting in late, or day dreaming about the evening to come. We both felt that our jobs were not secure enough. I, for instance, had flunked the bar exam once, and was awaiting the results of my second try. My firm only allowed three attempts, and then you were out of there if you failed to pass after the third try.

I stepped out of bed and expected to find Peaches running up to me with expectations that I would take her for her walk before I attended to myself. Peaches was a present to me from my folks on my ninth birthday. She was a cuddly puppy then, but quickly grew into the massive Labrador Retriever that she was. She had now reached the ripe old age of 18. In human years she was well over 100, and I knew I wouldn't have her for much longer. I attributed her longevity to my love for her and to the good care I gave her. When she didn't come to my side, I called for her, but there was no response. I even failed to hear her heavy breathing. With trepidation I went into my living room and found my precious companion dead on the floor.

I cried and tried to revive her, but my efforts were futile. I was holding her in my arms, rocking her gently back and forth, when my phone rang. It was so early in the morning that I feared more bad news. I was right.

I picked up the phone wanting to share my grief with whoever was on the other end, but I didn't get past hello when I heard Colin's voice. "Hey Franklin," he said quickly, "we're off for this weekend. I'm going skiing with Ron. Seeya." He hung up before I could say a word. I got the distinct feeling that Colin had just dumped me.

I dressed quickly and wrapped Peaches in a big plastic garbage bag. I put her body in my car and drove to my vet. I arranged for her cremation and forked up $250 which I could barely afford.

Then I called my office, and told them that my dog had died, and I needed to take a personal day. We all had three personal days a year, and by January 6th I hadn't taken any yet, so that was no trouble. When I got home from the vet, the mailman had just finished sorting the mail in my apartment building's mail boxes. I ran to my box and opened it. There was a telephone bill, an electric bill, and notification from the state that I had flunked the bar exam again.

I picked up the morning paper which was lying at my front door. I went into my apartment, threw myself on my bed, and cried like a baby. Finally, I thought about my parents. They had always been my number one support group. They lived 500 miles away, but they would want to know about Peaches. After all she had spent her early years in their home and they loved her also. I crept out of bed and punched in my parents' phone number.

My mother answered and she sounded like she had been crying herself. She could barely talk. "What's wrong?" I asked.

"Your father and I haven't been getting along lately. He left me last night and I haven't heard from him since. I don't know where he is. This has been coming on for a long time and I don't know if I am glad or sad. I can't talk now, darling," she said. "I'll call when I hear from him."

I never did tell her about Peaches. The day was getting progressively worse and I had deluded myself into believing that I had reached rock bottom. I vowed not to allow myself that deceit again. Good thing I did. My phone rang again and this time I trembled as I answered it. It was my father.

"I don't want you to hear this from your mother," he said before I could even say hello. "We've split up. I couldn't take another day with her. Over the past few years she's become a perfect bitch. All she does is criticize me and find fault with everything I do. As soon as I get my head together, I'll call you." He hung up before I could say one word.

I was really depressed now, but my tears were for the loss of Peaches more than for any of the other tragedies that had beset me that day. I needed to mourn for her, and find some closure, but I didn't know what I could do all by myself. I couldn't even rely on my parents for comfort as I had always done. They had been a constant source of support, even when I came out to them.

Finally I thought of what I might do to alleviate my pain and depression. It was a crazy thought then, and it became crazier and crazier as I made plans to act on it. I decided to go to a wake and pretend the wake was for Peaches. Could I get any crazier? Can you see how badly my mind was functioning, or rather, not functioning?

I grabbed the morning paper, and checked the obituaries. The closest funeral service scheduled for that day was at 10 AM, in a funeral parlor about a half mile from my apartment. It was for a Jonathan Hayes, 87, who died peacefully in his sleep. I imagined that Peaches had died peacefully in her sleep also, so that was a good omen. I forced myself to shower and shave and dress appropriately. I even drank a little juice before I left home. On my walk to Jonathan's funeral, I stopped at a coffee shop where I fortified myself with a bagel and a cup of much needed steaming hot coffee.

Part Two
A Ray of Light

I entered the establishment of Briggs and Sons and signed the guest book. I intended to avoid greeting any members of the family and realized that I didn't see any. Then I remembered that Jonathan's obit did not mention any family survivors. I walked directly into the chapel. I took a seat in the back row, whipped out a handkerchief and started crying profusely for my beloved Peaches. There were a handful of men of various ages seated up front. I didn't see any women, which surprised me. It also surprised me that I was the only one crying.

The service began, but I heard very little of it. I did gather that there would be no graveside service because Mr. Hayes was being cremated. The minister relinquished his microphone to two or three of the mourners who said a few words about their deceased friend. The last gentlemen to speak really got my attention.

The minister introduced him as Smitty, so I gather his name was Smith. He was a tall, handsome man, probably six feet, three or four inches, which is about four inches taller than I am. I'd say he was about thirty five years old. He was slightly overweight, which I find appealing. I hate skin and bones. His hair was very black, ebony you might say, and very straight, parted on his left side. His eyes were blue and soft, and very friendly looking. His nose had a very slight hook at the bridge and his chin was manly and square. I could definitely go for this guy. Smitty's eulogy was short and sweet. You could tell how difficult it was for him to speak, and I finally began to pay attention the moment he outed himself.

"Fifteen years ago," he started, "I arrived in this town fresh from the farm, literally. As a gay youth I was abused and despised by my family. The first thing I did was to try to get a job. I checked the papers and found myself applying for a job in Jonny's machine shop. I was really good with my hands and with machines, from working on the farm. The first thing Jonny did was hit on me. I was flattered, but I said no. He gave me the job anyway, and he was more than my boss. He became my mentor and my support system. He taught me city ways, and cried with me through my many romances and many breakups (the listeners smiled) so now that Jonny is gone, I am feeling alone again, and very vulnerable, I shall miss him dearly." Smitty emitted a little sob and sat down.

When the service ended, I was still crying for Peaches in the back row. I wasn't even aware that the service was over. Suddenly I felt an arm on my shoulder. I looked up and had trouble focusing through my tears. It was Smitty. He smiled down at me and said, "Hi. My name is David Smith. I'm afraid I don't know you, but a few of us are going back to Jonny's place. I've arranged for a luncheon and we are going to celebrate his life. Since his partner died five years ago, I'm afraid that we are the only family left to mourn for him. Would you please join us?"

I told you I was crazy that day. I could have sworn that Smitty had invited himself and some of his friends to join me in mourning Peaches and celebrating her life.

"I'd really like to," I said, "but I don't have transportation."

"Not a problem," Smitty said. "You can ride with me and I'll get you home after lunch." I accepted immediately and followed Smitty out of the funeral parlor. It didn't even occur to me to concoct some crazy story about how I knew Jonny, and why I was crying so loud.

Jonathan Hayes had lived in an upscale neighborhood, in a spacious two bedroom condominium apartment. A terrace, situated off the living room, afforded a glorious view of the city. My entire little three bedroom apartment would have fit neatly in the dining room. When we arrived, the dining room table was laden with luncheon meats, salads and rolls. On the server there was a bucket of ice, and assorted bottles of booze and soda. The caterer Smitty had hired was standing by to serve us. 'Us' turned out to be Smitty and me, and two other elderly gentlemen. I assumed the older men were Jonny's friends since they were his contemporaries.

Smitty introduced me to Gary and Dick, who turned out to be partners. We filled our plates and headed for the living room. I sat on the sofa with Smitty, and Gary and Dick sat on the two chairs facing the sofa. That way we could all use the coffee table which was between us. I thought that Smitty was sitting closer to me than was necessary, and I didn't mind at all. However, I did mind, and I had a moment of panic, when Dick asked me, "How did you know Jonny, Frank? I can't recall that he ever mentioned you." Now check out my answer for sheer brilliance.

"My widowed grandmother used to live in this building. She died a couple of years ago and she and Jonny were somewhat friendly. When I came out, she introduced me to him. She told me that I was too full of angst, and she was sure that Jonny could advise me. Well, he sure did. He gave me a sense of self-esteem that I had never had in my life before. It hurts me a lot that after my grandmother passed, I lost touch with him. It's a good thing I have a nasty habit of reading obits or I wouldn't have known he had died." I finished and lowered my head. The guys apparently bought my story. I should be a screenwriter.

After that, the three others reminisced a little about Jonny and after an hour or so Dick and Gary got up to leave. They told me how nice it was to meet me, and left Smitty and me alone. We resumed our places on the sofa as the caterer cleaned up. He packaged all the food that was left over, and at Smitty's instructions he placed everything in two shopping bags.

"Take a bag home," Smitty insisted. "I live alone and will probably have to dump most of this anyway."

I'm alone too," I said, "and I'll probably have to get rid of some of this also."

When the caterer left, Smitty asked me, "What do you do for a living?" and that's how we passed the next two hours, telling each other all about ourselves.

Jonny gave the machine shop to Smitty when he retired and Smitty still ran it. It was doing very well, and Smitty had an apartment on the floor above this one. I could only wonder if he knew I was a fraud, since I had created a resident who never lived here and never even existed. He was just like me, in and out of romances, unable to connect. He was eight years older than I, so of course his heart had been broken more often than mine. I really liked Smitty, and I was sort of over the crazy state I had been in before the funeral. I decided to tell him the truth and then take a cab home, certain that he would toss me out.

"Smitty," I began, "I have a confession to make. I never knew Jonny."

"I know," he replied softly. "Jonny and I shared everything, and I know he would have shared his acquaintance with you. He was also a hopeless romantic and he would have wanted to hook us up."

"When I first saw you at the funeral, and you sat down in the back, I was suspicious. I could tell you were hurting, and needed a friend. That's why I asked you to come home with me. When you told me about your grandmother I was certain you didn't know Jonathan. I've lived in this building for eight years and I never knew such a grandmother as you describe. Do you want to talk about what's bothering you?"

I broke out in one big loud sigh and told him about my morning and my mourning, how great the day started out and how it deteriorated bit by bit. I tried to explain how I needed to go to a wake to complete my mourning of Peaches. That was the hardest part to explain because it was so crazy. I ended up with my head buried in my hands crying like a baby. I didn't realize that Smitty had taken me in his arms, and was gently rocking me. I put my arms down and rested my head on his chest. He began to rub a hand up and down my back. When I realized that he was comforting me and how good it felt, I was filled with guilt. Smitty was hurting too, and I wasn't doing a damn thing for him.

I pulled my head off his chest and looked up into his sad eyes. We stared at each other for a moment and then Smitty leaned down and kissed me gently. It felt so good. I responded by parting my lips a little and his kiss became more passionate.

Part Three
Full Sunshine

In just a few moments we were naked and locked together on the sofa. We began to make love, not because we were in love, but because we both needed the comfort which making love would give us.

We were both crying and kissing the tears off our faces as we fondled our cocks. I couldn't even describe Smitty's cock. All I could tell was that it was a fistful, at least seven hard inches. It was uncut and his foreskin seemed always to be in the way. We stroked each other and we both came in each other's palms. Afterwards, we held ourselves as close together as possible. We rubbed our bodies together and cried like two little infants. I don't know how long we clung to each other, but neither of us wanted to let go.

Finally, after what seemed like hours, Smitty said, "Frank, I think I have fallen in love with you."

My heart began to beat faster. I was beginning to feel the same way. Never before had I held a man so long, just held him, without wanting to let go. Something was happening here, but I answered him by saying, "I'm sure that what you feel is simply pity."

"No," he answered. "If it isn't love, I know for sure it isn't pity either."

I was so confused. I stood up and my flaccid five inch cut cock was now dangling in front of his nose. He grabbed my ass and pulled me to him. Before I knew it he engulfed my cock in his mouth, and it began to engorge. His hot, wet mouth, his tongue and his lips were doing their jobs. In just moments, I had another awesome climax, and I collapsed back on the couch. Smitty resumed kissing me and I tasted my own cum.

"Not pity," he said again. "I swear it is love."

As bad as that day had been, every day after that got better and better. Smitty and I began to see each other more and more. I slept over in his condo apartment several times a week, until finally I moved in with him, and gave up my rental.

He had inherited Jonny's apartment, and before he could put it on the market, my father leased it with an option to buy. When Dad left my mother, he decided to retire and move as far away as he could and make a new start. So now my father lived in my building, which had its good points and bad. I felt weird when I saw him with a woman. Dad was still virile, and good looking and women often stayed over in his apartment. Like me, he seemed to be getting younger and happier every day. That made me sad for my mother and glad for him.

Before meeting Smitty I had been a party animal, but Smitty was older and more level headed than I. He would take none of my nonsense, and he made sure that I studied a little bit every night for the bar exam. I was antsy to party at first, but I soon fell into a disciplined study routine. My performance at work began to improve and I found myself being handed more and more responsibility. I almost looked forward to the next bar exam. I aced it! I could not believe how my life had gone from utter despair to a glorious present and an even more promising future in less than nine months.

The night I passed the bar exam Smitty took me and Dad out to dinner to celebrate. He wanted to go to his favorite gay bar and restaurant, and my father said that it was all right with him. Before dinner we had a drink at the bar. Smitty introduced Dad to some of our friends, and more than one, thinking he was gay, came on to him. I couldn't believe it, but Dad showed an interest and flirted back. I wondered if he didn't swing both ways, or if he would switch teams, if the right guy came along. If so, we lived so close, I would surely find out. Thinking about my own happiness with Smitty, it would be OK with me if he did switch, or at least try it out for the fun of it.

Part Four

I Get Company in the Sunshine

Shortly before my 28th birthday, my father paid me a visit at work. "I know it wouldn't be ethical," he began, "for you to represent me in my divorce from your mother, but maybe one of your associates could."

I knew that my father had provided my mother with much more than any law required, and so I turned him over to one of the firm's partners with instruction not to take a hard line with my mother. In fact, my dad was willing to give her a little more if it was not unreasonable. His visit gave me the opportunity to take him to lunch and spend a little quality time with him. He had taken my place as the chief party goer in our city, and he had precious little time to give to his now serious minded and very reformed son. He requested we go to a quiet restaurant because he wanted to talk to me about a very confidential matter. I had never seen him quite so serious and it frightened me. I was afraid that he might be very ill.

"Frank, I have to tell you that I have never been happier in my life," he began.

"I can tell," I answered, but I'm afraid I said it kind of facetiously. "Every day, I see a new broad going in or out of your apartment. For God's sake Dad, some of them are younger than Smitty. In fact some are even younger than I am."

Dad raised his eyebrows and looked at me quizzically, which prompted me to add, "Come to think of it, I haven't seen a lot of that lately."

Dad smiled and the light went off in my head. "Of course," I said, "You are seeing someone seriously. Good for you, Dad. When do Smitty and I get to meet her?"

"You don't get to meet her," Dad said. I must have looked like he just slapped me in the face, but he started to laugh. "Hear me out," he pleaded. "You know, son, that I have always been your biggest fan. I have always supported you and had your back. I didn't give a shit when you told your mother and me that you were gay. All I cared about was that you were happy, and I supported your living a lifestyle which would assure your continued happiness. I love you unconditionally." He then laid one of his hands on top of one of mine. "Can I ask you to return the favor and love me unconditionally also?"

"My God, Dad," I said. "That goes without question. Why would you even ask?"

"Because the person I am seeing seriously, as you put it, is not a she. He's a he." He paused to let it sink in, but it didn't sink in right away. Then I remembered the night at the gay bar when he flirted back at the guys who were coming on to him.

"It happened the night we celebrated my passing the bar, didn't it?" I asked. "Smitty and I should never have taken you to that place. I should have known that your good looks would get a lot of reaction."

"No! No!" he said emphatically. "Don't blame yourself. It happened a long time ago. Would you like to hear about it?"

"You were about ten years old the first time," Dad said, and he looked at me knowingly when he said, 'the first time.' "A fellow salesman passed away suddenly. His funeral was in a city about 200 miles away. I had to go, but your mother didn't know him and she chose to stay home. Besides you were too young to leave alone. I drove there with another salesman from my office. He's married and you know him, so I won't mention names." I nodded knowingly.

"Anyway, we shared a hotel room the night of the funeral. As soon as we settled in we went to the bar and tied one on. I honestly don't remember everything that happened that night, but my friend seduced me. The thing of it is, when I think back on it all, I am always amazed that I was so easily seduced. I guess I have a couple of gay genes in me. I don't have to tell you what a revelation it was for me. I tasted cock and semen for the first time (I winced) and it was wonderful. Every time my friend entered me in the mouth or the ass (I winced some more) and when I entered him, I never felt so connected to another human being." He paused here and studied my face. He was trying to gauge my reaction. I tried to show no emotion so he continued. "My friend and I continued to have sex until I left your mother last year and moved away. He wanted to visit me for a weekend, but I wouldn't let him."

"Because I'm available and he isn't. Besides that, I'm seriously involved." Again he paused, waiting for me to say something.

"Can you tell me who he is and something about him? Is he at least old enough to be my step daddy?" I asked with a sneer. Immediately I was sorry I asked that. My father looked so sad, and I had promised to support him no matter what. If he wasn't sitting across the table from me, I would have put my arms around him and embraced him.

"I'm sorry, Dad. I didn't mean that. If Mr. Wonderful makes you happy, I'll accept him. The only reason I'm worried about an age issue is that I don't want some youngster to bilk you out of your hard earned retirement money. Smitty and I do well on our own, so I say this out of concern for you, and not out of greed."

"Do you remember how many guys hit on me that night we first went to the bar? Honestly Frank, did you think I could be interested in any of those twinkies? If I settle down with someone I want him to be my companion. I want him to like and want to do all the things that I like and want to do, even if it's staying home and watching the tube. I started to go to gay bars without you and without your knowledge. I finally found one place where the clientele tend to be, shall we say, more mature men. That's where I met Richard. He likes to be called Rick. Frank, son, he's two years older than I."

I was over my initial shock and I finally stood up and threw my arms around my father. "Does he make you as happy as Smitty makes me?" I asked. My dad nodded vigorously. "Great, so when do we meet him?"

"I'll bring him around tonight," Dad said, "and I am going to exercise my option to buy Smitty's apartment. You see, Rick just left his wife nine months ago and has been living in a rented room. We'd like to make my rental into a real home where we can grow old together."

"Stop," I yelled. "You'll make me cry." I hugged my father harder and said, "I love you, Dad. I love you unconditionally. Of course, I support you, and I am very happy for you."

That night, after Rick and my Dad retired to 'their' own apartment, Smitty and I lay in bed wrapped up in each other's arms. We began to play the "what if" game.

"What if Jonny and Peaches hadn't died at the same time?" I started.

"What if you hadn't exercised a crazy urge to mourn for Peaches at a human funeral?

"We would never have met," we said simultaneously.

"What if we hadn't taken your father to a gay bar?" Smitty asked.

"His gay genes might not have kicked into gear and he might not have met Rick," I concluded.

"That's scary too," Smitty said. "Did you see how happy they are together?"

"I guess we can conclude," I said sagely, "that Peaches and Jonny played Cupid for us and we played Cupid for my dad and Richard."

"Or as Shakespeare so wisely concluded," Smitty said, "All's Well That Ends Well." That having been said, he rolled over on top of me and added, "But I much prefer beginnings. Let's get started."

He grabbed my cock and started stroking it. When my body began to writhe in pleasure, he bent over me and took all of me into his mouth, and that was the beginning of something wonderful. I gushed into his mouth, and he gushed into my ass. We were insatiable, and we made love all night.

End of the 24th Story

Gay Romance Erotica

ELMWOOD LANE
Secrets

Hank Brooks

Elmwood Lane Secrets
By: Hank Brooks

One

The foothills of the Ramapo Mountains lie along the New York, New Jersey border northwest of New York City. Nestled snugly along these foothills are a number of small, quaint bedroom communities which many New York commuters call home. Most of these towns look like time passed them by. It is hard to imagine that a short bus ride into Manhattan can catapult you forward a whole century and more.

One of these timeless communities is Suffern in New York State. And in this town there is a dead end street called Elmwood Lane. One enters Elmwood Lane from a secondary road and the street ends facing a thick, overgrown forest. On the other side of the forest is the equally quaint town of Mahwah in the state of New Jersey.

There are five Victorian style houses on each side of Elmwood Lane. They were built between 1849 and 1865 and have been designated landmarks by the town. The residents are allowed to make all the improvements and upgrades they want on the inside of their houses, but they can do nothing to the outside without adhering to strict historical society rules, and receiving permission from the town elders.

There is practically no turnover on Elmwood Lane. The homeowners are a close-knit, extended family. During the summer months, they have block parties every Sunday, and during the winter they pool their resources to assure quick snow removal from the street. If someone is in trouble he can always count on his neighbors to help out. Most of the men and some of the women commute daily to Manhattan, and they carpool to the bus depot.

In the middle of the 1980's, two of the houses on Elmwood Lane turned over. It was the first time in fifteen years that a change had occurred. The sellers of these two homes were brothers who lived next door to each other. They had both raised their families on Elmwood Lane, but recently they had both lost their wives, and their children lived great distances away. As much as it hurt them, they decided to sell their homes and retire to Florida.

One of the houses was purchased by Matt and Bernice Grover. They had son Terry, six, and daughter Kaitlin, four. The other house was purchased by Brad and Melissa Brenner. They had twin six-year-old sons, Tommy and Cory. The sellers arranged for both closings to be held at the realtor's office on the same day, and both couples arranged to move the following day.

The two families met for the first time at their closings and became instant friends, especially the men. They were both thirty four years old and they were both investment managers who worked for different brokerage firms. They were delighted to learn that they would be commuting to work together. The kids were even happier knowing that they already had friends on the block.

The next day, after their moving trucks left, both families were welcomed by some of the other residents of Elmwood Lane, and they were reminded that there would be a potluck block party the following Sunday.

Moving is stressful and strenuous. That first night in their new homes, Matt and Brad kissed their spouses lightly on the lips and rolled over hoping to get some much needed sleep. They would not be "baptizing" their houses by making love for at least another day. Bernice and Melissa fell asleep immediately, but Matt and Brad tossed and turned for hours. Being in a new environment had nothing to do with their restlessness. They couldn't sleep because each one was fantasizing making love to the other. They both harbored the same dark secret. Each secretly hungered for men, but both had married to avoid the stigma of living a gay life. Before moving to the suburbs each of them would work late at least one night a week. They knew places in New York where they could pick up a trick and have a quickie in some hotel where they rented by the hour. Fortunately (or some might say unfortunately) they had never run into each other. It would be much harder to do this now, since the last bus to Suffern left The Port Authority Terminal at 10 PM.

It was no use. Neither man could sleep. Each finally got out of bed, went to his bathroom and brought himself to a messy conclusion, fantasizing all the while that he was fucking his next door neighbor.

The two families soon melded into the extended family on Elmwood Lane. The children grew particularly close since they were the only kids their age on the street. The two families were so close they began to think of themselves as a single family unit. Matt and Brad grew very close indeed. Not only did they commute together to The Port Authority but they were the only Elmwood Lane commuters who then shared a subway ride to the financial district downtown.

They sat together on the bus and their thighs usually touched. Neither ever made a move to separate, because neither was even aware that they were touching. Often during deep conversation, one or the other would make a point and lay his hand on the other's knee. This action was welcomed by both of them.

They never got a seat on the overcrowded subway train and often their bodies were crushed together by the rush hour crowds. On more than one occasion they could feel the other's semi erect package. Making no move to "pull away," they would pretend not to notice. Rapidly, their lust for each other was growing, but neither dared make a move on the other.

Finally Matt got an idea. He suggested to Brad that they join a gym in their community and work out a couple of evenings a week and on Saturdays. Brad jumped at the chance, hoping to shower with Matt after the workout, and finally get to see his secret love in the nude. Neither one considered the fact that they might not be able to hide their erections which were bound to sprout up. On the first night at the gym that's exactly what happened.

They worked out vigorously, and were both ringing wet with their manly sweat. In the locker room, they had to help each other peel off their tee shirts which clung tenaciously to their torsos. Soon they were naked and were able at last to check each other out. They could not hide their growing hardons and didn't even try. Neither was embarrassed. Each hoped that the other would get the hint.

Matt was five feet, eleven inches. He had straight black hair which he kept quite short. It was almost a buzz cut. He had a straight Roman nose and sky blue eyes. His body fat was near zero if that's possible. He had played football in college and his muscular body was still intact. He was cut, and in his erect state he was about seven very thick inches.

Brad stood an inch taller than Matt. He too had blue eyes, but they were darker than Matt's. He wore his straight ash blond hair long, almost covering his ears. He had a pug nose which made him look a lot younger than Matt. He wasn't as muscular as Matt, but still he was firm. Maybe he had a couple of extra pounds which did not mar his beautiful body. Ah, but he had a magnificent cock. Like Matt, he was circumcised. He wasn't as wide around, but he was at least an inch longer. Without shame, both men stared at each other smiling. Finally Matt said, "You have a beautiful body, bro."

Brad answered, "I'd trade mine for yours any day."

They were happy to see that there were no walls separating the six shower stations. They were good enough friends that they felt that they could ignore the unwritten rule of every other shower and every other urinal so they stepped under side by side showers. They were alone in the room at that moment and something happened. A sixth sense took over their powers to reason. The two men were too full of lust to think straight. They stared into each other's eyes and they both instinctively knew. They grabbed each other and began to kiss passionately, all the while stroking the other's cock. They both came after just a couple of strokes.

Still holding on tightly, Brad whispered in Matt's ear. "I have dreamt of this moment since we met. I have no regrets."

Matt whispered back, "I have no regrets either. I love you Brad."

For twenty years they continued to love each other. They loved each other more every day, and every day was more torturous than the day before. Each stolen moment that they could spend together was precious. Gym nights practically ceased being workout nights and became fuck nights. They drove their car into the woods and found remote spots where they could make love. They went fishing together. They took afternoons off and went to one of the hourly hotels they had scoped out before they had ever met. They went to baseball fantasy camp and shared a room. They went on camping and fishing trips together. They did what they could, but there was one thing they never could do, nor would ever do. They never left their wives for each other.

When Kaitlin Grover and Cory Brenner announced that they were getting married, the two families were overjoyed. Brad and Matt split the cost of the elaborate wedding right down the middle. When Terry and Tommy announced that they were going to Massachusetts to get married, (New York had not yet come around) both their parents were shocked. Nobody had suspected a thing. They assured the boys that they loved them, and would stand behind them, and everyone went to Boston for the celebration. Secretly Brad and Matt expressed their joy that their sons would never have to go through what they went through every day. They could openly and joyously express their love for each other.

About a year after Tommy and Terry were married, a letter was published in Grandma Ellie's advice column. It read:

Dear Grandma Ellie:

I have kept a secret all my life and I hope I can keep that secret until I die. I am not writing to ask your advice on anything, although I would welcome any you have to offer. It's just that I can't hold in my secret any longer, and I want to let it out via this public forum. I pray that you will publish this letter and not judge me. I know many of your readers will condemn me, and tell me that I got what I deserved, and that it is God's will. I refuse to believe that.

Last week I lost the love of my life. He was returning home late from a business meeting. A drunken teenager ran a stop sign and plowed right into him at very high speed. My lover was killed instantly. It is destroying me that I can't mourn him properly. I must act merely as a bereaved friend and offer what condolences I can to his wife and children. But in fact, I want to rend my clothing and cover myself with ashes like they do in the bible. I have a wife and children of my own. My whole attitude toward them has changed. I am indifferent to their needs. I no longer care if I live or die. My life is over.

Mourning secretly in upstate New York.

Grandma Ellie answered:

Dear Mourning:

Nobody can advise a person how to handle the deep grief you describe, but I do know that life goes on and you must move ahead with it. Your friend would want you to take care of his family, and certainly he wouldn't want you to ignore yours. Hard as it may be, you must find the strength to care for two families now.

Grandma Ellie's column did not appear in the local papers, but was published daily in The New York Post. Matt was sure that none of his or Brad's family would ever see the column. Kaitlin and Cory were now living in London, England, to where Cory had been transferred. Tommy and Terry lived in Manhattan, but he knew that they didn't even subscribe to a newspaper. They preferred to get their news on their smart phones. They didn't even answer or check their e-mails any more. They considered e-mailing to be a dinosaur form of communication. They rarely used their cell phones for conversation, preferring only to correspond via text messaging. Matt concluded that he had better learn how to text them or risk losing touch with his sons.

A year after Matt's letter appeared in Grandma Ellie's column, Bernice told Matt that she and Melissa were going to England for the month of July to visit their kids. Immediately Tommy and Terry implored Matt to spend the month in their spare bedroom so that he wouldn't have to commute during that time or go home to an empty house. He was very tempted, but he declined their offer. Time had helped heal his hurt a little and his sexual juices were flowing strongly within him. He figured that he could visit his old haunts (if they still existed) and maybe pick up a one night stand. He was still a handsome, muscular looking man. He did have a hint of a belly but it was almost unnoticeable.

The first night after the ladies left, Matt went straight to a gay bar that he used to visit in Greenwich Village before he gave himself to Brad. It was an eye opening evening. He was approached by plenty of good-looking young men, but they were all hustling him. He wasn't about to pay for sex. Looking around, he saw that there were no men in the bar who looked a day over twenty-five. He smiled inwardly, realizing that these young men probably saw him as a sugar daddy. He was about to leave when he spotted a table with newspapers and magazines. He checked the contents of the table and came across The Gay Yellow Pages. He thumbed through and found three more gay establishments within a few blocks of this one. He wrote down their addresses and left.

This time he was much more cautious before entering. He stood in the doorway of the first of the three bars and scanned the faces. Most of the patrons looked as young as the men in the last place, but there was a smattering of more mature men. Matt figured that he could always come back, so he went to the second place on his list. This was more like it. The bar was populated by men who were more or less his own age. It wasn't that he wouldn't have had sex with a younger man, but they all treated him as a meal ticket. He went in and headed straight for the men's room.

It was a Friday night and he had left his attaché case in the office because he knew what his plans were for the night. He removed his tie and stuffed it in his pocket. Unfortunately he had no place to leave his jacket and this was as casual as he could get. He peed and returned to the bar. He was pleased to see that many of the men still had jackets on and some still wore ties. These are my people, he thought with a chuckle. The place was mobbed with TGIF patrons, but Matt edged his way to the bar and ordered a scotch and soda. Two male bodies crushed up against him on both sides and he was reminded of his subway rides with Brad.

He decided that life was too short to be coy. Neither of the two men leaning up against him seemed to be with anyone. He glanced at them both and did a double take when he saw the man on his left. He didn't look anything like Brad, but in many ways he reminded Matt of his dead lover. He was shorter than Brad, but he had the same color blond-gray hair. His eyes were blue and he had Brad's pug nose. The resemblance ended there.

Matt turned to his left and he held out his hand. "Hi," he said. "I'm Bill." Matt wondered why he couldn't tell this stranger his real name. Matthew is a common enough name. Happily the man smiled back and said, "Nice to meet you. I'm Walt, and thanks."

"Thanks for what?" Matt/Bill asked.

"Well, I'm usually too shy to approach anyone and I appreciate that you broke the ice for us. I was wondering how to introduce myself to you. Let's get away from the bar and over to the rear. It's less crowded there and we can hear each other talk."

"Sounds like a plan," Matt answered and he followed Walt to a relatively quiet corner at the rear of the bar. It struck Matt that Walt was being anything but shy. Matt may have made the first move, but Walt was now leading the way, figuratively and literally. There was a ledge running the length of the rear wall of the establishment. It was intended to hold patrons' drinks. They put their glasses on it, and leaned against the ledge.

"Keep your eyes open for a table to free up," Walt ed. "It would be nice to sit for a change and get to know each other." Matt thought that Walt was moving too fast in a direction that he did not want to go. All he wanted was to get laid, to have sex with a man, to feel someone's cock besides his own. He had loved Brad and he loved Bernice. He didn't need any more love in his life.

"Look, I haven't had sex in over a year," Matt half lied. He meant sex with a man. "All I want is to get my rocks off," he continued. "If you are so inclined also, that's great. Otherwise, let's not waste time."

Walt looked disappointed. He gazed into Walt's eyes. The face he saw was kind and loving and belied his harsh words. "You must have loved him very much," he commented to Matt.

"What do you mean?" Matt asked suspiciously.

"You're trying to act tough, but I can see in your face how much you are hurting."

Matt dropped his eyes and began to sob silently. "You are very astute," he said to Walt. He looked up to see Walt smiling at him, and Matt's heart softened. If he was going to luck out and get laid that night, why not with someone as wise and compassionate as this guy? Then when Walt could sense that Matt had stowed his tough guy persona, he put his arm around Matt's shoulder.

"I'm sorry if I have opened old wounds," Walt said. "If you still want to get laid," he continued, "I live only minutes from here. Would you like to come up to my place, Bill?"

"I'd like that a lot, but I have a confession. My name isn't Bill, it's Matt."

Walt did not look surprised. "Thanks for being honest," he said. "It shows that you are beginning to trust me a little. In case you are curious, my real name is Walter Davis."

"I'd love to go to your place Walt," Matt said.

Two

Walt had a small one bedroom apartment in a high rise. It was cozy and tastefully furnished. It was a bit too cluttered for Matt's taste, but it wasn't overdone or messy looking. When they entered the living room, Walt took off his loafers and tossed them aside. He invited Matt to do the same.

"Have a seat," he said pointing to the sofa. "I'll make us a couple of drinks." He made two scotch and sodas and sat down next to Matt on the sofa. "Do you want to talk about your loss?" he asked sympathetically.

Matt did need to talk about it, just as he had cried his heart out to Grandma Ellie, but he said, "Another time, maybe." Walt brightened at the words, "another time."

After a couple of drinks, Walt leaned over in an attempt to kiss Matt. This surprised Matt. He wanted to get laid, and had no thoughts of kissing or making love. He wasn't quite sure how to handle the situation but he didn't want to blow his chances, and he did like Walt a lot. He turned to Walt and their lips met briefly. After another sip or two Walt turned again to kiss Matt and Matt started to kiss Walt. This time Walt parted his lips and Matt parted his. Nature took over. They began to kiss passionately and their tongues pushed hard against each other. Matt was fully aroused. He closed his eyes and he could feel Walt pinching his nipples through his shirt, so he began to undo the buttons and Walt began to help.

Moments later Matt was naked from the waist up. His erection was pushing hard against his pants. Walt began to suckle his nipples and lightly nip at them.

"Please get undressed," Matt pleaded with Walt. When Walt stood up to disrobe, Matt finished undressing and they bared themselves to each other. Walt's cock was smaller than Brad's but it was beautiful and uncut and inviting. Matt could not restrain himself. He fondled Walt's balls in his hand and took Walt's hard member into his mouth. Walt gushed into Matt's mouth after just a few seconds.

"I'm sorry," Walt apologized. "I didn't want to cum so fast, but it's been a long time for me too. My lover died six months ago. I've been cruising the bars, and you're the first man I have wanted to go home with."

"Please," Matt cried, "don't get any ideas about me. I'm not an eligible bachelor. I have more to confess. I'm a married man with grown children. My late lover was married also. We made love for twenty years in secret, but never in shame. I don't want to go through that again. I won't ever leave my wife and hurt her. I love her, but I need to have sex with men. It's an uncontrollable urge."

Walt started to laugh. "What's so funny?" Matt wanted to know. He sounded angry.

"Don't be angry," Walt said. "I'm married too. I rent this place under an assumed name so that I can have use of it. My late lover was married too. This bed (he pointed into the bedroom) hasn't seen any action in a very long time. I was going to give up the apartment, but I decided to hold on for awhile and now I'm glad I did." He leaned over to kiss Matt again, but Matt turned away.

"I don't want to get involved with another married man. It's too hard," Matt said. "You understand that this is a one night stand."

"If that's the way you want it," Walt said, sounding very disappointed. He fell to his knees and took Matt's cock into his mouth. Matt almost swooned. He hadn't had a blow job since his last time with Brad. Bernice never offered him oral sex. He had never asked her to do it, and he wondered if she would. Walt's tongue and lips were working miracles, and Matt lay prone on the sofa enjoying the moment. He felt his orgasm coming on. It was much too fast, just like Walt's.

After Matt came, Walt lay on top of him and the two men kissed passionately. Finally Matt said that he had to leave to make his bus home. He knew that he didn't have to go, and that there was nobody at home waiting for him, but he didn't want Walt to get the wrong idea.

"My wife is visiting her folks in Kansas for a couple of weeks," Walt said. "She left this afternoon. I don't have to go back to Scarsdale. I'll be staying in the city for the two weeks she'll be away. I'd like it if you could come again."

"Maybe," Matt said, knowing that he wouldn't. He dressed quickly in order to make the last bus home.

As he kissed Walt goodbye, Walt handed Matt a card. "This is my business card," Walt said. "I've written the address of this apartment and the telephone number on the back. I would really like to see you again, but if you should throw the card away after you leave here, and then get second thoughts, I've rented under the name of Walter Smith."

Matt laughed inwardly. That's just what he had intended to do, throw the card away. Instead he put it in his wallet and left hastily. He made the last bus home.

He lay in bed that night trying to picture making love to Bernice as he stroked himself, but only Walt came to mind. When he thought of Walt he got hard and aroused, and he was able to stroke himself to climax. He hadn't cum twice in one evening since Brad had died. He felt good and slept like a log. Against his better judgment, he called Walt at the apartment the next morning. It was a Saturday and he felt that Walt would not be working.

Walt was out and Matt left a message giving Walt his cell phone number. About an hour later Walt called back. He sounded very excited and expressed to Matt how pleased he was that Matt called him. They made up to meet for dinner at a fine restaurant in Greenwich Village and then to hang out for awhile at The Village Place, the bar where they had met. They didn't discuss what would happen after that, but they each hoped that they would spend the night together.

At dinner the two men opened up to each other. They spoke of their lives, careers, and their families. Then with great difficulty they spoke of their secret lives and their lost loves. They both cried and they comforted each other. They were bonding and growing close.

Later at The Village Place, their moods lightened and Walt asked Matt if he would like to dance. "I've never danced with a man," Matt answered.

"You can lead," Walt said and he hauled Matt to the dance floor for a slow dance. They held each other tightly and both men could feel the other's hardness. They smiled at each other and kissed lightly.

Two young men were standing at the edge of the dance floor. They were the youngest people in the bar. They preferred to come here rather than to other places because neither could stand the amped up music and the loudness where younger people of their generation hung out. They preferred the quieter, more romantic music of this place. They were both watching Matt and Walt closely. Suddenly one of the observers grabbed the other's arm and they ran out of the bar.

They stood outside for a moment trying to catch their breaths. Tommy asked Terry, "Did you see what I saw? Tell me it was a mirage."

"No mirage," Terry answered. "What are we going to do about it?"

"We're going home for a brainstorming session."

Three

It was late Sunday morning. Matt and Walt were wrapped up in each other's arms in Walt's hideaway bedroom. Since coming home the previous evening, they had made love three times, twice orally and once anally. They were both feeling like young men again. They were fondling, licking, and tickling each other, and generally acting like a couple of kids when Matt's mobile phone rang. He answered it reluctantly.

"Hi Dad," he heard Terry say. "I want you to pack an overnight bag and come into the city today." Obviously Terry thought, or he was pretending, that his dad was at home. "Tommy and I are taking you out to dinner tonight and you can sleep over. We aren't taking no for an answer."

"Gee, Terry," Matt sounded chagrined. "I have dinner plans with a friend tonight."

"I'll give you two choices," Terry said with a laugh. "Either cancel your friend or bring him along. The four of us will have fun. I promise you." Matt was forced to accept the invitation with trepidation. Although Terry was laughing, there was something ominous in his tone. Matt didn't like this at all.

It got him thinking. Getting involved with Walt was a really bad idea. He had a loving wife. He had cheated on her only because of his deep love for Brad. He didn't love Walt in that way. He liked Walt for the sex he could provide and nothing more. No! It was time to stop seeing Walt before things got out of hand. Matt had used his fist before and he could use it again. He decided to go to Tommy and Terry's apartment by himself.

He jumped out of bed. "I've got to go," he said. Walt was clearly disappointed. "My son needs me," Matt lied.

"You'll call?" Walt asked. Matt nodded.

He dressed and literally ran to The Port Authority. Unfortunately the bus line was on a Sunday schedule. He had a long wait for a bus. When he finally arrived home, he picked up his car at the depot. He drove to his house, showered, shaved, packed a bag with clothes for work the next morning, and just made the last bus back to New York. He felt like a cheat, and he didn't like the feeling. He had never felt that way with Brad. He took a cab to his sons' apartment.

When Terry opened the door, he looked beyond his father and he was clearly disappointed. "You didn't bring your friend?" he asked.

"Why should I?"

"Just asked," Terry sulked. He really had hoped to see his father's lover.

It was early for dinner so the three men sat around chewing the breeze over bottles of beer. It was Tommy who finally erupted. He couldn't maintain his silence any longer. "Dad," he blurted out, "we saw you last night at The Village Place with a rather good looking guy, and you two were dancing and kissing. Is there something you would like to tell us?"

Matt's world collapsed in a second. He turned ashen and began to hyperventilate. Both of his sons got concerned, and Terry put his arms around Matt's shoulders. Matt could not believe what he had just been asked. All these years he and Brad had kept their secret, and had been so careful, but now, because of his lust, he had been exposed. He didn't know what he could say, how he could explain, but one thing was for sure, he would leave Brad out of it.

Matt composed himself and took a deep breath. He stood up, pushing Terry's arm off his shoulder. He looked back and forth at the two young men who were so dear to him. He started to say something but only a strange croaking sound came out. He cleared his throat and started to speak again. Tommy and Terry looked at him expectantly.

"I'll be as brief as I can," Matt said. "I've been gay all my life. I thought I had done a good job of hiding it until now. So you two know at last. I'd better leave."

He got up to get his overnight bag, but Terry said, "Sit down, Dad. You aren't going anywhere." Losing his resolve, Matt sat down and started to sob. "When we saw you last night," Terry continued, "it wasn't the biggest surprise in the world. Tommy and I have been conjecturing about you and his dad for years now."

Matt wanted to get swallowed up by a sink hole. "What in the world are you talking about?" he asked, feigning innocence.

Terry looked at Tommy as if to ask, should I tell him or do you want to?

"I'll tell him," Tommy said. "It was just after our sixteenth birthdays. We had just gotten our drivers' licenses. You and my dad had gone to the gym in your car. Terry and I decided to drive to the gym in my dad's car to surprise you and hit you both up for a malt after your work out. When we got to the gym, we couldn't find your car and you weren't inside, so we got worried. We waited until you went to the gym next time and we followed you. We shut off the car lights and stayed a safe distance behind you. We saw the two of you get out of the front of the car and go into the back. We actually didn't want to see more, but it didn't take a rocket scientist to figure out what was going on. After that we studied your behavior, how you spoke to each other, and how you interacted. Maybe if we weren't a gay couple ourselves, we wouldn't have noticed a thing, but it was very obvious to us that you two were in love."

"What was your reaction to all of this?" Matt asked.

"After we got over the initial shock," Terry answered, "and after we had a chance to determine how much you guys loved each other we began to accept it. We also began to take comfort just realizing how much love you gave each other. I think maybe I can safely say that we were a little bit jealous. If anything, it strengthened our love." Terry looked at Tommy and they kissed.

"Didn't you hate us for cheating on your mothers?" Matt wanted to know.

"We were angry at first," Tommy said," but when we saw how much love you guys gave our moms and us kids, we got over it. We knew that you could never reveal your secret and we had to accept it. We even vowed to cover for you if anything should happen which might expose you." Tommy put his arms around Matt. "I could even tell that you were hurting more than my mother when my dad was killed. A thousand times I wanted to hug you and tell you that Terry and I were there for you, but we couldn't say a word."

Matt was crying softly. Wisely Terry and Tommy said nothing until Matt regained his composure. Tommy spoke first. "There's this great little restaurant in the Village. It's on a side street and really off the beaten path. We're going there for dinner and after dinner we're going to The Village Place to listen to the music. Are you sure you don't want to invite your friend Dad? It's on us."

"I don't know," Matt answered honestly. "We just met. He's married also and his wife is away for a couple of weeks. He maintains an apartment in the city that he and his married lover used. But his lover died six months ago. He was going to give it up, but now he wants me to share it with him. Leading a double life is just too hard. I don't think I want to go through it again. Maybe I should just let sleeping dogs lie."

"Dad," Terry said, "never say never. Think about it. An available gay man would begin to resent that you can only be a part time lover, but another married man might be perfect."

"I was thinking in terms of one night stands to avoid that problem," Matt explained.

"Not in this day and age," Tommy said with authority in his voice. "It's too dangerous. Why don't you keep an open mind? Invite him to join us and see how it plays out."

"Go ahead," Terry urged. "It's no fun being a third wheel."

Matt took out his wallet and found Walt's card. He pushed in the numbers of the apartment telephone. Half of him hoped Walt was out and the other half hoped that he was in. Walt answered on the third ring.

"Hi Walt," Matt said. "It's Matt." There was no question that Walt started to cry on the other end.

"I thought I'd never hear from you again," Walt said. "Thank God you called."

"My sons want to take me out to dinner tonight. They asked if you would like to join us if you are free."

"If I wasn't, I would free myself up," Walt sobbed. Matt started to cry also. He handed the phone to Terry.

"Tell Walt where and when to meet us, please," he was struggling to talk.

Walt was at the restaurant when the others arrived. He wanted desperately to embrace Matt and kiss him until he couldn't breathe, but both men showed more restraint than Terry and Tommy. They both kissed Walt on the lips when Matt introduced them.

Before leaving the restaurant to go to The Village Place, Terry and Tommy went to the men's room and Matt and Walt were alone for a few minutes.

"My boys think we should have a go at it and see how it plays out," Matt said. "What do you think about that?"

"I think that's the best idea I have ever heard."

Four

They developed a routine. Once a week they "worked late" and whenever they could manage it, they met for "lunch" at Walt's apartment. Walt seemed content with the status quo, but Matt was definitely missing what he had with Brad on Elmwood Drive. He came up with the idea of having dinner with the wives and seeing a show on a Saturday night. They would tell the women that Walt was a good client of Matt's. It made sense since Walt was a very successful attorney and Matt was a financial advisor.

Patricia Davis was polite and cordial, as was Bernice Grover, but there was no real chemistry between them. Nevertheless Matt pressured Bernice into having the Davises for dinner one evening because Walt Davis "is one of my best customers." The evening was pleasant but no sparks were generated to start a fire. Then of course, Patricia had to reciprocate. At the insistence of the men, these back and forth dinners became a routine.

About a year after Bernice's visit to London with Melissa, Matt made an announcement at one of their mutual dinners. "Bernice and I are going to London next month to visit our daughter and son in law. How would you two like to take a holiday and go with us?" Walt knew that the announcement was coming, but the women were surprised, flabbergasted and speechless. As the idea sunk in, the women began to view it as a great idea. During the past year, Melissa Brenner had sold her house and moved to Florida to care for her aging parents. She still went to London, but it was for quick trips and Bernice did not go with her. As close as they had been, they were losing touch.

Things changed between Patricia and Bernice after that. They were on the phone constantly planning the trip and their sightseeing itinerary. They were beginning to enjoy each other's company and of course their husbands were overjoyed. The trip to London brought them almost as close as they had been with the Brenners.

The Davises lived in a huge six bedroom house across the Hudson River from the Grovers. They had recently become empty nesters, and they were looking to scale down considerably. About that time a house became available on Elmwood Lane. It was a charming little bungalow at the end of the street, abutting the forest. It had two bedrooms, but an enclosed patio had been added along the way, and it made an ideal media and rec room. The Davises bought it before it even went on the market, thanks to the Grover's inside information.

After the Davises moved in, and were welcomed into the tightly knit community, Matt experienced a great sense of serenity and peace. The part of his life that he had lost with Brad's death was his again. He and Walt were deeply in love, and Matt stopped comparing this love with Brad's. He loved them both and that was enough to end comparisons. The men now had more opportunities to have sex. Walt joined Matt's gym, and they were able to make frequent trips to the woods that had served Matt and Brad so well.

The joys of Elmwood Lane were restored to Matt, and all was well with the world once again.

End of the 25th Story

Gay Romance Erotica

Sensual Bet Rendezvous

Hank Brooks

Sensual Bet Rendezvous
By: Hank Brooks

They met in college and were an item for a couple of years. As sexual partners they had fun, but they didn't date exclusively. They both considered monogamy to be a dirty word. Nevertheless, when the sex stopped between them, and after they graduated, they remained close friends. They hung out together at gay bars, but they usually left separately. Both men were very handsome and neither had any trouble scoring a one night stand. When they were both staring thirty in the face, each began to wonder what it would be like to settle down with one guy, but neither did anything about it, and they certainly didn't discuss it with each other.

One Friday evening after work, they met at a local restaurant for happy hour and a bite to eat before hitting their favorite gay bar. There was plenty of action waiting for them at the bar on a TGIF night. They each ordered a hamburger deluxe and a beer. The waiter served the burgers with two beers, a happy hour special.

Tony looked at the waiter as he was serving them. The young man barely looked at either of them. He was about twenty two and cute as a kitten. When he left the table Tony asked Hal, "Is he or isn't he?"

"Is he or isn't he what?" Hal asked'

"Gay, jerk," Tony responded.

"Never," Hal stated emphatically. "This is a straight establishment, and he's as straight as an arrow."

"Wanna bet? My gaydar never lies," Tony retorted smugly.

"Yeah, I'll bet," Hal said. "What are you going to do, ask him directly?"

"Nope!" Tony said. Now he was being smug. "I'm taking him home with me tonight."

"Fat chance," Hal started to laugh. They bet $5.00.

Half way through their dinner, and after one beer was consumed, Tony saw the cute waiter standing on a side. He was keeping an eye on his tables to make sure that everyone was satisfied and did not need his attention. Tony got up quickly and walked over to him. Hal couldn't hear what they were talking about but the waiter kept smiling at Tony.

Tony returned to the table and sat down. "You owe me five bucks," he said. "I'm picking him up at 10:30 when the restaurant closes." Hal grinned, handed him $5.00 and Tony added it to the tip.

"I've got to hand it to you." Hal said. "I would have bet anything that the boy was straight. Hey, you didn't offer him money, did you? This isn't a gay for pay situation, is it?"

"I swear," Tony answered. "It's a freebie."

That incident gave rise to an ongoing competition between them. Wherever they would spot some good looking guy, one of them would bet the other that he could bed the guy that night. Tony had a success rate of about 85% and Hal was right behind him. The game added spice to their sex lives, and both thoroughly enjoyed it, especially since they were breaking even. They enjoyed the game until Ken came into their lives.

They were at the bar one Saturday evening, when Ken edged his way up to the bar and accidentally jostled Tony. Tony turned to berate the man, but he did a double take instead. Standing beside him was the man of his dreams, every gay man's dreams. Ken was mature, about thirty-five. He was at least six feet tall. He had black wavy hair and a pale complexion. His eyes were blue. His chin was manly.

Tony smiled at him. "Hi," he said, "I don't recall seeing you here before." Tony grimaced internally. *What a terrible pick up line,* he thought.

"Right," Ken said. "I just moved here from Phoenix. It's a job transfer. I was told that this was a good place to meet guys, especially on a weekend. I'm really just hoping to make friends," he added as an afterthought.

"Just friends? I hope you have nothing against sex," Tony laughed. He stuck out his hand and said, "I'm Tony and this here's my buddy Hal." He said buddy so Ken would have no doubt that they were just friends.

Ken shook both their hands as he said, "I'm Ken." After he got his drink, he stepped back a little and stood between Tony and Hal. They made a tight little circle. The three gabbed for a little while and then Ken said he had to go to the john.

"Save my place," he said jokingly.

"I'll bet you...." Tony started to say after Ken left.

"Not this time buddy," Hal answered. "I want him."

"Bullshit!" Tony answered. "I saw him first."

"Honest," Hal said, "I'm thinking more than a one night stand."

Tony sneered. "Sure you are," he said. "I'll bet you a thousand bucks that I can win him first."

Hal said. "He's just the guy I've been looking for. I'll take your bet."

"You're on," Tony said, "but this will take some work. The deed doesn't have to be for tonight. You claim that it's for the long haul anyway, so the winner is the one who gets him into bed first." They shook hands on it just as Ken returned. He saw them shaking hands and wondered what that was about.

"Have you had dinner yet?" Hal asked Ken.

Ken shook his head and before Hal could invite him to dinner all by himself, Tony said, "Have dinner with us tonight and we'll all get better acquainted." Ken was delighted to accept.

At dinner he told Tony and Hal that he had been in a monogamous relationship for about ten years in Phoenix. When he was transferred to New York, his partner refused to go with him. He told Ken that he had been sleeping around and preferred it that way. He wanted to be free to be with other guys. Ken admitted that he was very hurt, and now he just wouldn't allow himself to get into another relationship. Hal and Tony grunted inwardly, but this wasn't going to stop either of them. It was going to be tougher than they thought.

Over the next few weeks Hal and Tony encouraged Ken's friendship. They often met at the same bar they originally met in. The three usually left with a trick, and never together. Hal and Tony began to call Ken individually and ask him to go somewhere. They neglected to tell the other. Even being alone with Ken made no difference. He had no trouble going home with one night stands, but he could not be seduced by the two guys he considered to be his closest friends.

One Friday evening as the three friends were enjoying a twofer beer together, Tony announced that he had to go to London on business and he would be away for two weeks. "You two better behave yourselves while I'm away," he said. That remark meant little to Ken, but it was an open invitation for Hal to disobey Tony.

The first thing Hal did, when Tony was gone, was to invite Ken to his apartment for a home cooked meal. Ken accepted immediately, especially after Hal told him that he was a gourmet cook.

Ken was used to meeting Hal directly from work, so he would be rather dressed up. Imagine his surprise when he arrived at Hal's place with a bottle of wine in hand. Hal was barefoot, wearing tight cut-off jeans and a muscle shirt. There was a bulge in Hal's crotch that Ken could not overlook. It announced loud and clear that Hal was not wearing underwear.

"Wow," Ken said, "I feel overdressed."

"Feel free to strip," Hal said. "I've been dying to see what hangs between your legs." He took the wine from Ken, set it on the dining room table and then embraced him. Usually Hal kissed Ken on the cheek, but this time he kissed him on the lips. He didn't dare use tongue, and Ken did not seem to react one way or the other.

"I'll take you up on your offer," Ken said. He removed his shoes and socks so that he could enjoy Hal's heavily carpeted floors, but his jeans and T shirt remained on his body.

"What's on the menu?" Ken asked. "Shall we enjoy a glass of wine now or would you rather serve it with dinner?'

"Let's have a glass now," Hal said. "We can have more with dinner. Don't be afraid to drink all you want. I have plenty on hand." Hal went to a cabinet and took out two wine glasses which he put on the coffee table. Then he uncorked the wine Ken had brought. He sat down next to Ken on the sofa and poured two glasses of wine.

"Here's to us," Hal toasted, and they had there first sip of wine.

"Don't let me have too much," Ken instructed Hal. "I really don't have a lot of tolerance for alcohol. I'm sure you've noticed that I never have more than two beers, or one cocktail, or one glass of wine when we are out together. That's my limit."

Hal could not help wonder that if Ken got a little drunk would he let loose some of his reserve? "I'll be your monitor," Hal promised.

"So what's for dinner?" Ken asked. "You haven't said."

"Don't you want to be surprised?"

"No," Ken answered. "I hate surprises. When I get a surprise I feel like I'm not in control of myself anymore."

"What's the big deal? Don't you want ever to be a little out of control? I find it fun to abandon my inhibitions and just go with the flow sometimes. For one thing sex is always better," Hal said.

Ken laughed. "I prefer to stay in control," he said. "I don't want to get hurt again."

"Did you ever consider that if you don't allow yourself to face harm's way, you may never love again?" Hal tried to look like a wise old professor, but the smile on his face betrayed him.

"That's something to think about," Ken said. "Now what's for dinner?"

"No," Hal said, "this is my ball game and I will surprise you whether you like it or not." He looked at Ken's wine glass. Both his and Ken's glasses were more than half empty and he topped them off. Ken did not seem to notice. In fact they had three glasses before they sat down to dinner.

Ken did not seem too steady on his feet, when he sat down. Before serving the appetizer, Hal opened a fresh bottle of wine and poured them both a glass. Ken took a sip immediately. "That's good," he slurred.

Hal served a Caesar's salad to start. He put out a basket of sliced Italian bread to go with it. Ken gobbled up the salad, two slices of thickly buttered bread and the rest of his wine glass. He acted ravenous. "This is nice," he kept uttering. "I can't thank you enough, Hal. You're a real sweetheart." Hal smiled and brought out a standing rib roast with roast potatoes. He cut two generous slices for each of them, and refilled the wine glasses. Ken immediately took a couple of sips of wine before attacking the roast.

He cleaned the plate and Hal served him seconds. For dessert Hal served apple pie ala mode. He had intended to make a pot of coffee to go with it, but instead he refilled Ken's wine glass. By the end of the meal, Ken was slurring his words badly. Hal sat him down on the sofa facing the TV. "You take it easy," Hal said. "I'll clean up and then I'll put a movie on."

"That's nice," Ken grinned. Hal cleaned up and loaded the dishwasher. He opened a cabinet below the TV and took out a DVD. He put the DVD into the player. It was the raunchiest porn film he had. He lowered the lights, and sat down next to Ken on the sofa.

The film totally aroused Hal. He placed his palm high up Ken's thigh and started working his way crotchward. Ken did not resist him. Encouraged, he began to fondle Ken through his trousers. Ken was flaccid but the fondling had an effect. Hal could feel Ken getting hard. Unhappily, Ken was not doing anything in return to let Hal know that he was interested. Hal looked at Ken's face and started to smile. Ken was fast asleep and he looked like an angel.

"Come with me, Angel," Hal whispered in Ken's ear. He stood Ken up and walked him to the bedroom. He undressed Ken to his bare skin and laid him in the bed. Hal sat at the edge of the bed. He caressed Ken's cheek and stared long at his body. The rest of him was as beautiful as his face. His cock was cut and about five inches in its flaccid state. His balls were tight and invitingly tasty. Ken had a purple birthmark on his abdomen about the size of a quarter. Hal leaned over and kissed the birthmark. He avoided contact with the object of his desire.

He thought that Ken was fast asleep again, but he was only three quarters gone to Morpheus. "I love you," Hal whispered in Ken's ear. "I have loved you from the moment I laid eyes on you. I swear I would never hurt you." He covered Ken's naked body, got undressed and lay down next to his sleeping beauty. Ken had turned on his side and Hal nested up against him. His hard cock pushed against Ken's buttocks but he made no attempt to take advantage of the inebriated Ken. They slept that way well into the night.

Ken awakened about three in the morning needing to pee badly. He had just been awake enough before falling asleep to know what had transpired. He disengaged himself from Hal, got out of bed, and stood gazing at Hal for a moment. After he relieved himself, his first thought was to dress and leave, but he really didn't want to go. He kept gazing at Hal and a very warm glow enveloped him. He felt emotions he thought had died in Phoenix.

Hal had been a perfect gentleman and did not even try to take advantage of him when he was not in control of his thought processes. That was an act of someone in love. Someone in love! Suddenly he remembered what Hal had whispered to him before he fell asleep. He climbed into bed, and this time it was he who nested against Hal and pressed his hard cock into Hal's buttocks. He made no attempt to enter his friend, but he put his arm around Hal and rested his palm on Hal's cock. He just left it there and did not move it. He didn't want to wake Hal, at least, not yet.

Before he fell asleep again he whispered in Hal's ear, "I love you too."

Harsh Sunday morning sunlight penetrated the bedroom and woke them up. Hal turned to Ken and smiled. "Good morning, handsome," he said. I wish we could wake up this way every day."

"Me too," Ken answered, "but I'm afraid."

Hal put his arm on Ken's shoulder. "I'm not that jerk in Phoenix," he said. "Besides, I've already sowed my wild oats. I have just one desire now, and that's to settle down. I can't think of anyone I want to settle down with more than you. In fact, I'm so in love with you, that if it isn't you, I'm afraid it might never be anyone."

"I know that it shouldn't be a problem, but for some reason it is. I love you also, but I can't help feeling fear," Ken sobbed. He took Hal's hand off his shoulder and kissed Hal's palm.

"I can't think of how I can convince you of my fidelity except to relate a story, a story that I know will make you angry. It's not necessary for me to reveal this, but I want to tell it to convince you of my sincerity," Hal said. "The night we met, Tony wanted to bet me that he could bed you before I did. I told him I wasn't interested, that I looked at you as someone for the long haul, someone very special. He insisted on betting a thousand dollars. I didn't want to, but he kind of forced me. Well, I kind of bedded you first. If I collect my bet would you please give the money to your favorite charity?"

"That's what I am, a bet?" Ken did indeed sound angry.

"No my love, never. I never honored that bet in my mind. I wanted to sleep with you, sure, but not to collect on a bet. I wanted to sleep with you so I could show you how much I love you."

"For someone who wants to show me how much he loves me, you talk an awful lot and act very little," Ken remarked. "What do you say we brush our teeth and shower and make love all day?"

Hal's eyes filled with tears. "Yes, yes," he said, "let's do that."

For a while there it looked like they would never get out of the shower. They fucked each other twice using soap as lubricant. Finally they exited the stall shower and made themselves a bit of breakfast. Then it was back to bed. They cuddled for a while until they were recovered, and then they twisted into a sixty-nine position. They both came yet again. Now they really needed recovery time. They cuddled close, ground their cocks together and fell asleep.

Hal woke first and he started to tickle Ken's nose. Ken woke up smiling. When Hal saw the smile on Ken's face, he whispered in his ear, "I love you; I'll love you forever." Ken responded with a passionate kiss with lots of tongue.

Then Ken smiled again. "It's my turn to confess something," he said. "Last night I wasn't as drunk as I wanted you to believe."

"Scoundrel!" Hal yelled and he began to wrestle with Ken in the bed.

"Let's go out for a five star dinner tonight to celebrate," Ken said suddenly.

"It's a deal," Hal said, and he began devouring Ken with kisses.

When Tony returned from Europe, and his friends told him that they were moving in together, he grew insanely jealous. It wasn't that he cared one iota for Ken, but he did desperately want to have sex with him. He thought he could kibosh the deal, so he asked Hal in front of Ken, "Do you want the thousand in cash or will a check do?" Then he looked at Ken and said, "Don't get too flattered good looking. You are nothing but a bet between us."

Imagine Tony's surprise when Ken said, "You can write the check to United Way. Hal told me from the get go about your bet. Did you think that I would love him less?"

Deflated, Tony asked in all sincerity, "Do you two guys really love each other?"

"Madly," Hal said.

"Beyond belief," Ken said.

"Then I envy you and wish you the best," Tony said. "I can only hope I meet someone as great as you two."

"Don't work too hard at it, and don't get desperate," Hal advised Tony. "There is someone out there for you and he'll come into your life when you least expect it."

"Do you really think so?" Tony asked.

Ken looked directly into Tony's eyes and said, "Wanna bet?"

End of the 26th Story

Hank Brooks

A Commuter's
OBSESSION

Gay Romance Erotica

A Commuter's Obsession
By: Hank Brooks

Part One

My partner Doug and I bought a small bungalow in Oceanside, New York. I do mean small. It was very expensive real estate, as it was only one block from the ocean. It cost us a pretty penny, but it was worth it just for the view and the serenity alone. Doug is a teacher, and he was able to get a job teaching science at Oceanside Senior High School.

I work for a prestigious Wall Street investment firm, which had once been headquartered in the World Trade Center. Thank God I had just started college that terrible year. The firm lost too many good men in the inferno. Doug, of course, no longer had to commute to work, but I did. I didn't mind at all. As I told you, it was all worth it. Every morning I took the same Long Island RR train to Manhattan, and then I took the subway down town from Penn Station.

I had been commuting for just under a year, when it happened to me. It was the day I lost all my senses, and I allowed my world to be turned upside down by an irrational obsession.

It was a hot September day, the day after Labor Day. I always sat in the most forward passenger car, because it was closest to the subway upon arrival. I think that is why it was always the most crowded car, and seats were always scarce. At the Valley Stream station, which is the next stop after mine, a young man got on the train. He was about six feet tall, blond hair and blue eyes. He was wearing a tee shirt, cargo shorts and sandals. The tee shirt read New York University. His muscles were mounds of pure hardness, and my crotch started to tingle at the sight of them. From the bulge in his crotch I reckoned that he wore no underwear. He was carrying a couple of text books in his hand.

He came through the doors and looked around. I was smitten. I could only lament that the seat next to mine was occupied. He found a seat just two rows in front of me, and I was able to view his beautiful blond head. I could also swear that I could smell his after shave lotion, which intoxicated me. That, of course, was practically impossible. The aroma must have come from the man sitting next to me.

I kept my eyes on him when we got off in Manhattan. I reasoned that if he attended NYU downtown, he might actually take the same subway train as I did. But if he went to NYU uptown, we would part ways at Penn Station. How foolish I was. Just wearing a New York University tee shirt did not necessarily make him a student at that institution. Why did it matter to me anyhow?

He headed for the Uptown Train platform. I was devastated and could not get over my irrational behavior. All day long I was distracted at work. I could not keep myself from thinking of him (and wanting him). I prayed he might be on my home going train. I searched the platform and waited until the last minute to board the train. I did not see him.

The next morning, as my train approached the Valley Stream station, my whole body went on the alert. I felt like a hunter seeking prey in the jungle. He boarded the train and my groin grew warm at the mere sight of him. I wanted to jump up, embrace him, grab his package and kiss him until we both passed out from lack of air. Of course I didn't. He looked around at the seat situation, and found one at the head of the car. I relaxed when he did, because I was afraid he might have been forced to go into the car behind us.

I closed my eyes and began to fantasize that I was in bed with the beautiful young man. We were naked and his cock was uncut. It looked more like a baseball bat than a prick. I grabbed hold of it and began licking it all over. It was too big for me to take in my mouth. Then I mounted him and began slowly descending on him as his massive tool entered my ass. As big as it was, it didn't hurt at all. I was awakened from my fantasy when the train lurched to a stop at its destination. I did not see Adonis (that's what I named him). He must have gotten up and darted off the train as soon as the doors opened.

I love Doug, so where was all this erotic Adonis fantasy coming from? Fat chance that my fantasies about him could ever come true. First of all I am about eleven or twelve years older than he is. I am only five feet, seven inches tall, and at least twenty-five pounds overweight. As I approach my thirtieth birthday, I am balding at a rapid rate. I am far from ugly, but nobody would look at me twice. Doug is about as average as I am, but maybe not as much overweight. We are just as average in the cock department and we are both cut. Still, in spite of all that, we are very popular. We both have the reputation of being the life of the party, and we have a very busy social life. Off the record, our sex life as a couple is fantastic, so why was I being so irrational in my lust for Adonis?

Adonis continued to ride my train, and my car, for weeks. I continued to fantasize about him, but that was it. What more could there be? I missed him terribly on school breaks, but he always returned. One day I tried something, and to my delight it actually worked. Instead of taking the window seat, I took the aisle seat. This successfully discouraged others who got on in Oceanside from crawling over me. When Adonis got on in Valley Stream it was one of the few seats available. He excused himself and stepped over me to take the vacant seat. I smiled at him and he smiled back. My heart stopped working for a beat or two.

I tried to make conversation with him. "Are you a regular commuter?" I asked.

Without looking at me, he muttered something which sounded like, "Uh huh." He opened one of his textbooks, and I took it as a sign not to bother him. About halfway through the trip he closed his book. He took out his cell phone, and reached someone by speed dial.

"Mornin' beautiful," he said. "Wanna meet me at the coffee shop? I don't have an early class this morning......Terrific, I'll see you there." He hung up. I wanted to cry. He has a girlfriend. So what? I have a boyfriend.

Sitting next to him like this aroused me, and I started to erect. Thank goodness it was late autumn now, and I was wearing a coat which would cover my embarrassment. We didn't talk at all after that, and I even dozed off a bit. He was very impatient about getting off the train and he almost knocked me over. Who cares? He actually touched me.

I tried the same ploy again the following morning, and the seat remained vacant until Valley Stream. Adonis got on, spotted the seat, and made a bee line for it. I figured he wanted that seat because I had not tried to make inane conversation the day before, so I intended to try to keep it that way. This time, as he crawled over me, he said good morning. I gave him my most ingratiating smile as I pulled my coat over my groin. For whatever reason, those two seats eventually became our seats. It reminded me of our seats in church. They were not assigned, but everybody always gravitated to the same pew and the same seats. It's a really strange phenomenon. My bingo playing pals tell me that the same kind of seat habit occurs at the bingo halls also.

I could go on conjecturing about this seat fetish for hours, but all I really cared about at the time is that we got to sit together every morning. We spoke very little, but eventually we introduced ourselves, and I knew that his name was Steven Ross, and he knew that I was James Hicks. Slowly, little by little, we began to have short conversations. He was majoring in Management Information Systems. He had just turned nineteen and he had a beautiful girlfriend. He showed me her picture, and as he beamed, I got sick to my stomach.

One day he dared to ask me if I was married. I half lied when I told him that I wasn't. I asked him why he wanted to know, and he said that there was no reason. The next morning when the train arrived at Penn Station, he shook my hand and said goodbye. I looked confused and he said that his freshman year was over, and he hoped to see me again after Labor Day. My world fell apart. When I got to work, I told everybody that I felt sick. I left the office and I returned home. I went to bed and stayed there for two days.

Doug and I went on vacation the last two weeks of July. Imagine my surprise the first day back at work, when Steve got on the train at Valley Stream and took his "assigned" seat.

"Good morning," I said. "I didn't expect to see you for another few weeks."

"I'm going into the city to meet my girlfriend. I figured I'd take this train and say hello."

"You flatter me, but I am also very pleased."

Then I got a real shocker. He asked me, "Do you have to rush right to work? Do you have time for a cup of coffee with me? I really would like to talk to you."

Without answering him, I took out my cell phone and dialled my office. I left a message with the still unmanned switch board. I said that something had come up and I would be a little late.

"Thanks," Steve said.

We found a table in a quiet corner of a coffee shop just outside the station. Steve wasted no time. He looked me in the eye, leaned into me and whispered, "I'm going to ask you something. I hope you won't get insulted if I'm wrong. You're gay, aren't you?" I was stunned. I didn't want to scare Steve away, and I had never confided that information to Mr. Macho Man. "And you have a partner," he continued. It was a statement rather than a question. I finally found my tongue.

"Yes I am, and yes I do, but how did you know? I thought I was pretty good at hiding my sexual orientation. I'm in the closet at work, and I don't think anyone there even has a suspicion."

"Don't be so sure," he asserted. "You act masculine enough, but you slip up. The first time I suspected that you might be gay, was when you talked about escaping from the city and buying a home on Long Island. You said "we" several times, but you told me you were single. Another time you said that "we" never had more than coffee and a roll for breakfast. If you want to hide who you are, you should learn to watch those little slips and use the singular."

I started to laugh. If I didn't laugh I would surely have cried. I asked, and not too kindly, "What's your point?"

"I broke up with my girl yesterday. One of the reasons is that I failed to get it up for her several times lately. Recently I met a really nice guy in my accounting class, and I gave into temptation. I let him seduce me. Besides the fact that I had no trouble getting and staying hard with him, the sex was fantastic. It satisfied me in such a way that I knew I had to be gay."

"Do you think that you may have something going with this guy?"

"No, I just wanted to experiment with him, and see how I felt. Besides, he missed home too much, and he transferred to the University of Michigan for next year."

"We are almost strangers," I said. "Why are you telling me all this?"

Steve merely shrugged his shoulders, so I continued without an answer from him. "You know that I am the last person in the world you should be telling all this to. I am happy as a lark and very much in love with my partner, Doug, but at the same time I am so hot for you, I am holding back from pouncing on you."

"I know," Steve sighed. "That's another reason why I'm sure I'm gay. I've been picking up on how you felt about me. If I was straight, that would never have happened."

"I guess you're right about that," I reasoned. Then I added, "Surely you can't have any sexual desires for a fat pig like me."

Steve jumped on me. "You're not fat," he said. "At worst you are pleasingly plump. You are fun to talk to and to be with, and yes, I could have feelings for you."

I was more than stunned. "Where is this leading to?" I asked.

"To a bedroom, I hope"

"I'd be cheating on Doug. I've never done that."

"No, not at all. You would not be cheating. Look at it as you're being a mentor to me, breaking me in, and teaching me how to be gay, so to speak. I am sure that eventually I'll find my other half, just as you have found yours."

Irrationally, at that moment I could swear I heard Doug yelling at me to wake up. For a moment I was filled with confusion. Suddenly I felt my shoulder being violently shaken. "You'll have to move mister, so I can get out. We're here."

I roused myself from a deep sleep, and swung my legs around so that my seat companion could get out. When I came back to reality I realized that it was Adonis, not Doug, who woke me. I was back to the first day he sat next to me, and I had dreamed our entire growing relationship. I realized that I didn't even know his name, and that I had created a fantasy name for him.

I came to a bitter conclusion. I was losing my mind, and I had better erase Adonis from my thoughts, if I ever hoped to get back to reality. Then, just as if I had never resolved to forget about him, I made a fateful decision. It was too late for today, but I vowed to follow him if he was on the train the next day.

Part Two

My little ploy did not work the next day. Someone started to climb over me at the Oceanside station. I just sighed, moved over, and saved the man the discomfort of squeezing between me and the seat in front. I could barely breathe until I saw Adonis get on in Valley Stream. He found a seat somewhere behind me, but I knew he wouldn't get off until we got into Manhattan.

The trains were always so crowded this time of day, and I lost sight of him in Penn Station, but I headed toward the uptown train tracks. I spotted him just going through the turnstile, and I followed him closely. I was secure in the knowledge that nobody ever noticed me, and he wasn't going to be an exception. I even stood close to him in the over crowded subway car. He actually glanced my way a couple of times and our eyes met. As I suspected, he didn't seem to recognize me at all.

I was surprised when he got off at the station before the NYU stop. I almost didn't make it out of the car before the doors closed, but I saw him ascending the stairs and going out into the daylight. He crossed the street rapidly and went into a corner coffee shop. I discreetly peered in through the shop windows. A beautiful young woman sat at a table for two. When she saw him, she jumped up and they kissed with way too much passion for a public place. I grew insanely jealous. If I had a weapon I would have killed the girl. When I realized what I was thinking, I became aware of my growing insanity. I ran to the subway, and took the train down town to work.

After that I calmed down for a few days, but about a week later I followed Adonis again. This time he went right to school. I was shocked. He went to Columbia, not NYU. There was another male student waiting for him at the main gate. They smiled at each other, hugged and went on inside. My curiosity was aroused. I whipped out my cell phone and called in sick to my office. Like the idiot I had become, I waited in very cold weather for them to exit the building. There were any number of exits they could have used besides this one, but I waited anyway. I knew that I was becoming more and more irrational, but I was unable to stop myself.

I skipped lunch, and I was rewarded for my patience when they came out together at about 1 PM. They headed for the subway station, and to my great surprise, they walked toward the uptown track. I was following them too closely, but I was sure that I was remaining, as always, the cellophane man.

They exited somewhere in The Bronx. We were in an area I was totally unfamiliar with. They walked two short blocks, and went into an apartment building. Every erotic bone in my body was tingling. Could Adonis be having a rendezvous, perhaps a sex session, with this handsome young man? Suddenly I was struck with three thoughts.

The first was ordinary enough. Should I continue my vigil, or should I go home and try to relieve myself of this ridiculous obsession? My obsession had rendered me incapable of a rational decision, and I knew I would never leave.

The second was still sort of ordinary. I suddenly realized that I was acting as obsessively as von Aschenbach in Thomas Mann's classic novel, "Death in Venice." I was stalking Adonis just as von Aschenbach had stalked the beautiful young boy, Tadzio? I wondered if I was committing a crime. Worse yet, the similar circumstances in the novel did not make for a happy ending.

The third was pure conjecture and came out of left field. Could my dream be coming true? Was this other young student the one from Adonis's accounting class, the one who was at this very moment readily seducing him? The idea was truly absurd, and a pure case of wishful thinking, but it did help me decide whether I should stay or go home. I stayed.

About two hours later, Adonis came out of the building. I needed to pee so badly, I was about to wet my pants. I followed him to the down town subway tracks, and gratefully used the filthy, smelly facility provided by New York Transit. We got on the same train and although there was an empty seat next to his, I took a seat a little away from him, but where I could easily keep an eye on him. We got off at Penn Station and I followed him on to the same train to Valley Stream and Oceanside. We were among the first to board the train. I scooted in behind him and took the seat next to his. This time I was determined to make conversation with him.

From the moment he had emerged from his friend's apartment, I could see a difference in him. His face had always seemed rather sad, sometimes it even looked surly. Now his face was flushed, and there was a Mona Lisa like smile on his face. Maybe he had enjoyed male sex after all, and had finally admitted his sexual orientation to himself. I hoped that he would be more inclined to make conversation with me, than he had been the other time we sat together.

After we were comfortably seated, I turned to him and said, "Hi, I've seen you on my morning train. I think we even sat together once."

To my surprise and utter joy, he turned to me. He was smiling and said, "Yes you do look familiar." I had extended my hand to shake his, and he took it and said, "My name is Steven Ross." Needless to say, I grew pale and nearly passed out.

"Are you OK?" he asked.

"Yes. I'm fine. My name is James Hicks."

We said very little after that. I was too stunned to say anything. Instead I put my brain into overdrive. What if my dream had been more than a dream? What if it had been a prophecy? I grew bold. "Are you a college student?" I asked.

"Yes I go to Columbia. Don't be misled by my NYU tee shirt. It used to belong to my brother. What do you do?"

"I'm an investment manager. What's your major?"

"Management Information Services." By now I was not surprised that my dream was becoming a reality. In fact my spirits were buoyed by it.

"Does your firm ever hire summer interns?" he asked.

"As a matter of fact we do. Would you like me to get you an application?"

"Would I like it? I'd love it."

"I get on in Oceanside," I informed him. "I know you get on in Valley Stream. I'll try to save you a seat next to me tomorrow, and we can talk about the internship."

Steve smiled at me. His teeth were so white they sparkled. "I am so glad we *finally* met," he said. This is my lucky day."

What did he mean by *finally* met? Had he noticed me ogling and stalking him after all? Was there a glimmer of a chance that he was attracted to me? Was my dream coming true in the best way possible? I grew light headed and nearly passed out.

Part Three

The following morning, I was able to save Steve the seat next to me by telling a few people that the seat was taken. After a few days, when other passengers saw that we always sat together, they just naturally left the seat for Steve. It did indeed become "our seats."

I gave him an application to intern at my office, and he filled it out. When I brought it to Human Resources, I asked Mr. Sawyers to put the application at the top of the list as a favor to me. He was more than willing. Nepotism is a beautiful thing.

One day, I asked Steve, "How come a handsome dude like you never talks about his beautiful girlfriend, and then whips out pictures of her to show everybody?"

Steve began to laugh. "Funny you should ask," he said. He took out his wallet and showed me a picture of the beautiful girl I had seen him kissing at the coffee shop. This time I wasn't jealous at all. "This is my girlfriend. Actually, we used to be a very hot item, but lately not so much. We are growing apart. I think my interest in her is waning."

"Why so?" I asked. I was hoping for the answer I had gotten in my dream, but Steve just shrugged his shoulder as if to say, "Who knows?"

In my dream, we had lost touch with each other, for a short while, at the end of the semester, but now we shared a morning and an evening commute to *our* office. Doug and I did go on vacation the last two weeks of July. We made love constantly, and I fantasized that I was making love to Steve. Doug actually had to tell me to take it easy. "You're acting like a tiger," he chided me. Usually vacation trips are over too soon, but I was so anxious to be with Steve that this vacation seemed endless.

At work, I invited Steve to lunch as often as possible. One day he invited me to lunch, and I dared hope that this would be the time when he would come out to me. He had different news, but it was good news none the less.

"Sawyers has offered me a part time job when school begins. I gladly accepted. We'll set my hours as soon as I have my class schedule."

He was so happy, and I was even happier for many reasons. My hand was on the table and he placed his palm on my hand. "I'll be forever grateful to you," he said." Thanks James." It was a moment when we should have kissed, but I had to restrain myself.

"Nonsense," I said. "You earned the job because of your talents."

We engaged in a little office gossip after that, and I finally got up the courage to ask, "How are things going with your girlfriend? Any better?"

Steve sighed. "No, it's over. We don't see each other any more."

"From what you have told me, it's probably for the best. Are you seeing anyone else?" I tried to be cagey.

"Off and on. Nobody special."

I decided to change the subject. "Steven," I said. "Next Thursday is my big three-o. My roommate Doug is making me a little party Saturday evening. Just my sister and a few close friends will be there. I'd very much like it if you came by." Steve jumped up and said, "That sounds great. We'll talk about it later. Right now, we better get back to the office before we are both fired."

I realized that I was probably about to out myself to Steve, but what the fuck. My prophetic dream was basically streaming itself out like a previously seen movie being downloaded to a TV set or a computer. I was willing to risk it. The few close friends I had referred to, were all gay, and my sister had become a bit of a fag hag thanks to Doug and me. There would be no doubt in Steve's mind about me, when he came to the party. I wished he would ask me directly about my sexual orientation, just like in my dream, but so far it was not to be.

On the trip home that day, Steve not only accepted my invitation, but he insisted on coming over on Saturday to help us with preparations for the party. He wouldn't take no for an answer. Right then and there I decided I had to come out to him before he walked into our house.

"Steve," I almost whispered, "I have something to tell you." He looked at me quizzically so I continued. "Doug isn't just a room mate, we're partners."

"No kidding. Do you guys have a business going on the side?" How naïve could he be? Or was he toying with me? I ignored his remarks.

"No, Steve, we're life partners, we're a gay couple, and we're lovers." There I said it. I stared straight ahead, waiting for a reaction. Suddenly I felt Steve taking my hand in his. I turned to look at him and he was smiling at me.

"Did you think I didn't know?" he asked. "I was just waiting for you to tell me." I guess he had been toying with me after all.

"You don't mind?" I asked. "It won't ruin our friendship will it?"

"So, you think I'm naïve? You take the prize. Did you think I didn't see you following me around? You were there the day I practically broke up with my girlfriend, and you were waiting at the building when my fuck buddy Larry took my cherry. It doesn't take a rocket scientist to see how hot you are for me. And for what it's worth, James, you have become my best buddy, and I wouldn't mind a little hanky-panky between us. Do you and Doug have a monogamous relationship?"

I couldn't answer at first, because I was having too much trouble processing all this information. Finally I said, "Kinda."

"What does 'kinda' mean?"

"Doug and I occasionally savor the joys of sex with a third party, but only if we do a threesome."

Steve's eyes lit up. He beamed a huge smile. "How about I hang around when everybody else leaves Saturday after the party?"

"I'd love it, but I'll have to bounce it off Doug." Doug, of course was all for it.

After the party, Steve, Doug and I cleaned up all the garbage, and packed the excess food for the freezer. All the while Doug was groping Steve, and I was getting annoyed. At some point I grabbed Steve's hand and took him to the shower with me. Doug was forced to use the guest bath.

At last the three of us were laying on our king sized bed. We placed Steve between us, and began an oral exploration of every part of his body. His fully erect cock was about seven inches, and average size around. He was uncut. My restraint gave out and I pounced on his cock. Doug began to sensuously rim the eager boy. While Doug continued his rimming, I jumped up, greased my ass and Steve's cock, and began to sit down on him. When he was in my ass to the hilt, I had to notice that I had no pain just like in my dream. When Steve came gushing up my ass, I wanted to suck the rest of his stuff out of him, but as I pulled away, everything went black. In the darkness I could hear Doug yelling at me to please stay awake.

I woke up the next morning and Doug was hunkering up against me. His erect cock was dry humping my thigh. We were alone in the bed.

"Where's Steve?" I asked.

"Who's Steve?"

"The hunk that slept with us last night, dummy. Are you trying to be funny?"

"Go back to sleep. You're hallucinating."

"He helped us with the party last night. Are you trying to gaslight me?"

"What party?"

"My thirtieth, numbnuts."

"Now I know you're crazy. Your thirtieth birthday is four months away."

I panicked, I had dreamt a pure fantasy about Steve once before. Could it be happening again?

I jumped out of bed, and although it was Sunday, I called Dan Sawyers at home. I didn't realize how early it was. It was obvious that I woke the poor man up. I could tell that he was still in bed, but what was shocking was that I distinctly heard a voice ask, "Who is it, honey?" and that voice was a deep baritone. I didn't have time to think about it, when I asked Dan if we had an intern working for us whose name was Steven Ross.

"No, James," he yelled. "Now let me go back to sleep."

I then called every Ross in the Valley Stream phone book. I came across plenty of Stevens, but not one of them fit the description of a Columbia University student. Finally, I opened the front door, took in the Sunday paper, and checked the date. Impossible. It was last Labor Day weekend. I gave out a blood curdling shriek, and Doug came running.

It was right after Labor Day that I first spotted Steve entering the train, so I was shaking like a leaf when my train stopped at Valley Stream on the Tuesday after Labor Day. There were no seats available, and that presented a problem, but not for Steve. He came aboard, looked around and leaned against the door after it closed. He took out his cell phone and got lost in some conversation.

I don't know where I got the balls to do what I did next, but I asked the guy sitting in the seat next to me if he saw that good looking young man leaning against the door, and talking on his cell phone.

"What guy?" the man asked. "I don't see anyone."

"That's the story Dr. Grayson," I told my shrink. "When I got off the train, I did not go to work. I came right here, and I want to thank you so much for squeezing me in. Please, can you help me?"

"I'm sure there is a simple explanation. I'm going to begin by using a specialty of mine…hypnosis." Moments later I was sound asleep.

When I awoke, I found myself in a hospital bed. My left arm and left leg were in a cast, and I was heavily bandaged all over. I opened my eyes to see Doug hovering over me like a mother hen. He looked a little fuzzy to me, so I fluttered my eyelids in an attempt to clear my vision.

Doug gave out a loud, heart breaking sigh. "Thank God. You're awake," he sobbed.

"Where am I? What happened?" I asked in a raspy voice. I smiled inwardly. Those questions were so stereotypical, I thought.

"Some switchman made a terrible mistake, a fatal mistake, on the day after Labor Day. He accidently switched your train on to the wrong track, and there was a head on collision with a freight train. Both engineers and thirteen passengers were killed outright, and dozens of others were injured, some seriously, and others less so. You've been in a coma for two days, honey. You started to come back to us a couple of times before, but you slipped away again. Please stay with us this time, baby, please!"

"Where did the accident happen?"

"Right after the train left Valley Stream and reached full speed."

At this moment in time I declared myself to be officially crazy. My first thought was of Adonis or Steve or whoever he was. "Is there a list of the dead?" I asked.

"Yes, honey. I saved all the papers. I knew you would want to see them."

Doug went over to my bedside table. With my peripheral vision I could just about see that there was a pile of newspapers on the table. He removed the top one. It was Newsday. This one is from the day after the accident. It not only lists the dead, but it has pictures of all of them.

Doug sat me up in bed a little so that I could see the newspaper. He opened it to the page with the pictures of the fifteen dead. There were three columns and five rows of pictures. I looked closely and there he was, my Adonis, top row, middle picture. Underneath the picture there was a small caption, Norris Lipton, 18, Valley Stream, CCNY Student. The article contained a little blurb about each of them, and declared this to be the worst disaster in the history of The Long Island Rail Road.

My recovery was slow. I didn't return to work for another two months. I will never be able to explain the strange obsession I had with the youth who got on the train minutes before his death. These days, when I am commuting to Manhattan, I still see him getting on the train in Valley Stream. Sometimes he smiles at me, and other times he totally ignores me. It's almost like he is teasing me with his sexual charisma. I am grateful that the only time I fantasize about him these days is on the commuter train. Off the train, the only sexual fantasies I have are about Doug, and all the wonderful things I am going to do to him in bed tonight.

Rest in peace, Norris Lipton, and please allow me the same pleasure.

End of the 27th Story

HANK BROOKS

The Second Time Around

Gay Romance Erotica

The Second Time Around

By: Hank Brooks

I crept quietly out of bed and stepped into my slippers. I was trying to be as quiet as possible. My robe was lying on the arm of my boudoir chair. I removed it cautiously and put it on over my naked body. When I reached the bedroom door, I glanced over my shoulder. Ron was fast asleep on his back. He looked like an angel. Somehow he had thrown the covers off. His right arm lay across his forehead and his left rested on his crotch. I smiled at him and went to the bathroom.

As I peed, my morning woodie began to recede. I brushed my teeth and took a quick shower. I always shave in the shower, but I had shaved the night before at Ron's request so I skipped it this time. After drying myself, I put my bathrobe back on and went to the kitchen to start breakfast. On the way, I passed the bedroom door and glanced in. Ron continued to sleep, but he had rolled on his side. His ass was round and inviting. I wanted to kiss it, but I went on into the kitchen instead.

I set the table and got the coffee maker ready. All I had to do was push the start button. I could have awakened the sleeping beauty, but I decided to let him sleep a little longer. Instead, I sat down at the kitchen table and started to reflect on my current state of being. I was definitely in a place I had been trying to avoid for the past two years.

This was the third night in a row that Ron and I had slept together. Two nights ago I had slept in his apartment, and the night before that, he slept with me in mine. The last thing in the world I wanted was a relationship. Before Ron came home with me last evening, I wanted to tell him that three times was way over my limit for having sex with one guy, but I didn't, and I knew that I wouldn't. Damn it, I was already looking forward to tonight. Hell, it was Monday. I would love to stay in bed and suck and fuck all day, but we both had to go to work. We would have to wait until tonight.

***

I got married at twenty-one to my high school sweetheart. Sharon was a dream wife. I was going to the University of Michigan when we married, and we took a small apartment off campus. She got a job waiting tables at a nearby restaurant and helped pay my way through the remaining two years. She even helped me get my MBA at Wharton. She never complained once, nor did she ever indicate to me that she herself wanted to get a higher education.

I got my first job as assistant to the CFO in a publicly listed company with headquarters in Philadelphia. I could now support us and support us very well. We bought our first home and went about trying to get pregnant. It never happened, even though the doctors said that there was nothing wrong with either of us. I offered Sharon the option of going back to college or adopting, but she turned both down. Instead she went to a business school for a short while, and afterwards she got a job as a secretary in a small company. I was happy for her and thought that would make her happy too. How wrong I was.

She changed after that. She complained all the time about how miserable she was. She hated her job, her life was boring, and she was verbal in regretting *the years that she had wasted* putting me through school. It upset me enough that she felt that way, but her bitterness was all directed against me. No matter what I did, she was displeased with me for one reason or another. Little by little, the verbal abuse increased and her bitterness manifested as a 24/7 event.

We had less and less sex. I found myself whacking off every day, either before bedtime or in my morning shower. It was the only relief I had. At the time I was barely thirty. I guess that's why I was so vulnerable and allowed what happened to happen.

I hired a young man to join the team in my office. He had not yet graduated college, but he was well on his way, and he was taking classes two nights a week. He was twenty-one and very handsome, with a sweet personality. I found myself wanting to be with him more and more. I made excuses for him to work on projects with me. Our friendship grew. We began to have lunch together, and when we worked late we had dinner together. I never rushed our evenings together. Sharon couldn't care less when I came home, or if I came home.

One night Mac (George Mackenzie) and I stayed late to work on a proposal. It took much less time than we both expected, but Mac asked if I would have dinner with him anyway. I gladly accepted, not wanting to go home to Nagville.

"I've got plenty of leftovers from a Chinese restaurant," he informed me. "Why don't you come to my place and I'll heat it up, that is, if you don't mind leftovers?" I realized that I would be alone with Mac for the very first time. The strangest feeling came over me. I knew it was a feeling I had experienced before, and I probed my mind for an explanation. I suddenly identified that it was the same feeling I used to get when I anticipated having sex with Sharon in the good old days. That totally confused me. I had always accepted without question my heterosexual nature. At that moment I wasn't actually thinking about having sex with Mac. The feeling I was experiencing was merely a feeling of the expectation of sex. I dismissed the thought and gladly accepted his invitation. I had already told Sharon I'd be home late so I didn't even think of calling her.

Mac lived in a studio apartment not far from the office. It was small, but neat, and very clean. He had a tiny table with two chairs that would seat the two of us. His meager kitchen was set back from the room, and hidden by a curtain. Besides that there was a sleep sofa, coffee table, dresser, and bedside table. It was cozy to say the least.

As soon as we were in the apartment, Mac removed his suit jacket and tie, and undid his two top shirt buttons. He hung everything on a clothes rack. Apparently there was no closet in the place. Without asking, he started to remove my jacket and he told me to get comfortable. I removed my tie as well and he hung my stuff up next to his. It struck me as an act of intimacy and I smiled at such nonsense.

"I'll get the food out of the fridge and start warming it," he said. "Then I'll make us a drink and we can talk while we're waiting."

"Sounds good," I said. I sat down on the sleep sofa and watched Mac put the dinner in pots to warm. He set the table, and then went to a cabinet over the stove. He retrieved two glasses that he put on the coffee table, and took a bottle of white wine out of the fridge.

"Is this OK?" he asked. I nodded and he poured us each half a glass of wine. He sat down on the sleep sofa. When he did, his knee touched mine and I was distinctly uncomfortable, but I did not move away. I was sure it was an accident and I didn't want to draw attention to it. Mac raised his glass and I raised mine.

"To us," he said and he took a sip. I followed suit.

We sat in silence for a moment and then I said, "Nice place you have here. It's warm and cozy."

"It suits my needs," he said, "at least until I graduate."

We made small talk for a while. I was still amazed at how easy and relaxed I was around Mac. Every second with Sharon put me on edge. I never knew when she would attack me for something. Suddenly Mac stood up. "I think everything should be ready by now."

I stood up too. "I need to pee and wash my hands," I said. "Where's the…"

Mac pointed to a door I hadn't even noticed before. It was painted the same color as the surrounding wall and blended right in. I went into the bathroom. It was small too, but it had a stall shower, a small sink and a commode. Of course, the seat was up. I unzippered my fly and took out my cock. I was always proud of that cock. It was cut and five inches flaccid. When erect, it got to seven or eight inches. It varied with how aroused I was. I was partially aroused at the moment, but I couldn't think why, so I attributed it to having to pee.

As my water flowed I saw that there were magazines on the tank. I picked one up, and gawked. Then I examined the others and gasped. The magazines all contained nude pictures of men in various stages of arousal. There were even pictures of men in various positions having sex together. I should have been revolted, but once again, I was shocked to realize that I was becoming aroused. I put the magazines down and shook my cock dry. I even dabbed the slit with a bit of toilet paper. I stood there taking deep breaths until at last my cock began to go down. When I was finally in control of myself, it hit me like a balloon full of water. My dear friend Mac was gay. I had to steel myself to leave the bathroom.

When I got out, I saw that we each had a bowl of wonton soup sitting in front of us. A platter on the table held a variety of Chinese dishes. We need only help ourselves. Mac motioned for me to sit down.

I sat down and we ate in silence for awhile until finally I could restrain myself no longer. "That's an interesting batch of magazines you've got in the bathroom," I remarked as casually as I could.

Mac looked like I had just tasered him. "Shit, shit, shit," he kept repeating over and over again. "I forgot all about it." He jumped up to run to the bathroom to remove the offensive reading material. It was way too late. I grabbed his arm to stop him.

"Relax," I said. "I've never seen stuff like that, and I found it kind of arousing." Mac seemed to relax somewhat when I said that, and he sat down.

"Oh, Jim," he said. "I really am sorry. I didn't want you to find out this way. I wanted to tell you in my own way and in my own time."

"Why would you have so much trouble telling me? I thought we were good friends. Good friends don't have secrets." I smiled my best smile at him to let him know that I was still his friend, and probably I always would be.

"Really, Jim," he stammered. "I usually don't hide who I am and if someone asks I tell the truth. But with me it's, *if you don't ask if I am gay, I won't tell you.* Anyway you're the last person in the world I would tell that I was gay."

I was definitely hurt by that remark. "Why?" I asked.

"Because I'm in love with you." He said that quickly, as if he would lose his nerve if he hesitated.

"I guess you want to leave now?" he asked.

Actually a part of me did want to run, but instead I said, "I'd rather stay and talk about it. This is a shock to me, and I need time to absorb it."

Mac looked at me. There were definitely tears in his eyes. "Thanks for not running out on me," he said. "I know we can never be intimate, but just sitting here alone with you, is wonderful for me. It's the best I can hope for."

I have no idea why I did what I did next, but I did it. I stood up, took my handkerchief out of my pocket and wiped away his tears. As I did so, Mac took my hand and kissed the back of it.

A warm sensation swept through my body. It settled in my groin and I smiled at him. My cock was rising and it was right in front of his nose. There was no way I could hide it, so I blurted out, "Please don't make anything out of it. I'm just perpetually horny. My wife and I hardly ever have sex anymore."

"I'm sorry," was all Mac could manage to say.

"Don't be sorry for me. I whack off once or twice a day, and it keeps me going."

Mac started to laugh, and I got my shackles up. "You find that amusing?" I asked, not too sweetly.

"Oh no," he said. "It's just that I do the same thing. I know that most straight people think gays are promiscuous, but that's not true, at least, it's not true for me. I'm practically a virgin."

"Wow," I said. "I guess that puts us in the same boat." Mac stood up just then and I put my arms around him to comfort him. It was an unconscious act, and I thought nothing of it until Mac started to squeeze my waist, and then he laid his cheek against mine. I knew I should have pulled away, but I didn't want to. I hadn't had a warm cheek lie against mine since college days. I liked how it felt. Mac was the one who finally pulled away and looked in my eyes.

"Let me make you happy," he said. "You don't have to do anything to me, and I promise it will be our secret."

My almost fully erect cock was dripping precum and wetting my underwear. It needed relief and Mac was willing to take care of it for me. "Yes, yes," I mumbled. "Make me happy."

He released me and ran to the sleep sofa. He opened it up to a queen size bed. I just stood like a stone statue. I was uncertain what to do. "Undress," he directed me. As he said so, he started to take his clothes off. Seconds later he stood in front of me totally naked. I had to admire his body. It was lean and muscular. He had no hair at all, except sparse pubic hair. I stared at it and I was certain he kept it trimmed. (I did the same). I hesitated before I allowed my eyes to gaze upon his fantastic cock. It was uncut and fully erect when I first saw it. It was at least a half inch longer than mine and somewhat thicker.

I had never been aroused by a man's cock before. I had seen my share in locker rooms, but never erect. For some reason, his hard tool sent shivers through my body. I wanted to grab it and sense what another man's cock felt like, but I knew I would never do that. I diverted my attention by stripping myself. By the time that was done, Mac was in bed. He motioned for me to join him. I tried not to touch his naked body, but he slid close to me, and put an arm around my torso. I faced him and did the same. It had been years since I had been intimate with another human being, and I admit Mac's naked body felt wonderful next to mine. He hunkered into me and I felt his cock pressing hard into me.

"May I touch it?" I asked.

"You can touch any part of me," he answered and suddenly I felt him stroking my cock, and then my balls. He went back and forth and I can't tell you how good it felt.

"Are you OK with this?" Mac asked.

He was being considerate, and I screamed out, "Please don't stop," just to let him know it was all right. Because of this diversion, I had forgotten to touch him, so I reached down and enveloped as much of his tool in my palm as I could. I started to stroke even more gently than he was doing. He moaned softly and I knew he liked what I was doing. I had to admit, his cock felt really nice in my hand.

Our faces and our lips were inches apart. "Jim, I want to kiss you," Mac said. "Please let me. If it grosses you out, I'll stop. I swear."

I was confused. I never kissed a man before and I didn't know if I could, but at that moment, sex with Mac was becoming so rapturous that I simply whispered, "Yes."

He placed his lips on mine, making no attempt to use his tongue. He felt so good. It was actually I who forced my tongue into his mouth. Our tongues caressed, and my cock in his hand throbbed. Then Mac started to do something I didn't expect. He started kissing his way down my body. When he nibbled, sucked and kissed my nipples, I nearly jumped off the bed. I never knew that a man's nipples were so erogenous. He lingered there for the longest time before continuing his downward journey. After kissing my pubes for awhile, I anticipated my prize, but again he surprised me. He bypassed my cock and balls and started kissing down the inside of my thighs. He kept going and when he reached my toes, he started to suck them one at a time.

I could bear it no longer. "I need to cum," I begged him, and at last I felt his tongue on the underside of my shaft. He licked up and down and onto my balls. Occasionally he licked under my balls just at the top of my crack. I moaned loudly so he would know what pleasure he was giving me.

"Please," I begged again, and he started bathing my cock in earnest. His spittle slobbered around the head and his tongue stroked up and down the shaft. I cannot explain the pleasure I was feeling. I wanted to warn him that I was cumming but I couldn't catch my breath to speak. I exploded into his mouth and he kept on sucking and swallowing until I had to beg him to stop. He slithered up and resumed kissing me and I could taste my own cum in my mouth.

"Do you think you could ever do that to me?" he asked.

Without any hesitation, I answered, "You bet I can, and I will." I had never felt as close to, or as connected to another human being as I felt to Mac at that moment. I didn't just go down on him, I pounced on him. I was overwhelmed at how sweet his cock tasted. I tried to emulate how he had sucked me and the pleasure it had given me. I must have done something right because Mac was moaning and twisting his body in what was obvious sexual rapture. He never warned me when he was cumming, so I was shocked when he began to scream and unload into my mouth. I was about to pull away, but his thick juices tasted like honey, like the nectar of the gods. Instead of pulling away, I swallowed every drop and licked any excess off his diminishing cock.

I rolled over and we lay side by side. Mac took my hand and asked, "Do you hate me? Are you grossed out? Should I not bother to come to work on Monday?"

I started to laugh. "Jerk," I said. "You just gave me the best sex I have ever had in my life." I rolled on top of him and started kissing him passionately. When we came up for air, Mac said, "There's a lot more we can do."

"I know," I answered. "Will you teach me?"

After that night, I never slept with a woman again. For the next two years, Mac and I got together as often as we could. He and I experimented with anal sex, and after a time we decided that I was a top and he was a bottom. Nevertheless we were able to go both ways for variety. To his credit, he never pressured me to leave Sharon, even though he told me continuously how much he loved me. As for me, I made a terrible mistake. I never told him that I wanted to leave Sharon and live with him. It just never occurred to me that it was an option.

I attended his graduation, and expected to celebrate in our usual fashion, but first, I took him out for a fancy graduation dinner. It was over dessert, that he dropped his bombshell.

"I'm leaving next week for Seattle," he said. "I don't see much growth for me in your company, and I was recruited on campus as controller and office manager for a small electronics firm in Seattle."

I was stunned. "What about us?" I asked.

"I don't see much future for us either. You'll never come out of the closet, and I doubt you'll ever leave your abusive relationship. I need to think of me and my future for a change. I love you, but I realize I can't ever be with you. After dinner I'd like you to get up and leave before I change my mind."

I started to cry. I knew Mac was right. I didn't wait for the check to arrive. I went up to the cashier, paid the check and never saw Mac again.

I stayed with Sharon for another eight years. We had a sexless marriage and she constantly let me know how miserable she was and that I was the cause of it. Mac never tried to contact me in all that time. Then fate stepped in.

On the day before my fortieth birthday, the CEO of my firm called me in to his office. "Jim, he said, "I have a great proposition for you. We are opening a new market and establishing a presence in South Florida. Our demographic guys have located a perfect building for a warehouse and offices in Ft. Lauderdale. I'm sending Jackson out to run the operation, and I'd like you to be our CFO. You'll have to relocate, of course, so speak to your wife, and get back to me in a day or two. If you don't want to relocate, I'll understand and I'll have to recruit from the outside."

"What about salary?" I asked. Ordinarily I would not have asked such a question, but I had a plan brewing in my head.

"You'll receive a substantial increase, of course." He smiled at me. "I hope you will accept," he said. "You're the best man for the job."

I had been planning my escape from Sharon's bitching for months. Now I knew exactly what I was going to do. I would load my car with my personal things, and simply drive south. I would leave Sharon a note telling her she could divorce me if she wanted to. I didn't care one way or the other. I was out of her life and that was that. Over the next few weeks, I went to my broker and transferred more than half my assets into her name. I had my lawyer draw a quitclaim deed, and I gave her the house. The mortgage was almost paid up, and I made a final lump sum payment so the house would be free and clear. I took some of the funds from our joint checking account and opened a separate account in my name only, in a bank that had branches in Ft. Lauderdale. I tried to think of everything I could do to help Sharon get through the trauma of my escape, and I consoled myself by convincing myself that she wanted this as much as I did. I hated her so much, that I took particular joy in knowing that she didn't have a clue that I was being transferred.

One happy Saturday morning, she went to the mall, and I knew that she would be there for hours. It took me one hour to pack the car. I left her my note, and headed for the interstate and my new life.

***

I had been doing my homework, and before I took off, I looked on line for a rental apartment in the gayest section of Ft. Lauderdale. I didn't want to buy a condo until I was familiar with the city, and I was certain of where I wanted to live. I saw three apartment buildings that looked promising. I called the numbers listed and made three appointments all on the same day, morning, noon and mid afternoon. In the meantime I had booked a room in a nearby motel.

I arrived at the motel the day before my house hunting was to begin. After unpacking, I drove directly to my new office. Larry Jackson, the operations manager, had arrived the day before. We greeted each other as old friends and he showed me to my office. It was going to be my job to link our computer accounting systems to the main network, and I had two weeks to do it before we officially opened for business. I was more than up to the challenge. I told Larry that I had to look for an apartment the next day, and since it was temporary housing, I wouldn't be fussy. I assured him I would start work the day after that.

That evening, I consulted the gay yellow pages on my laptop, and found a slew of gay bars along one thoroughfare. I dressed in shorts, a muscle shirt, and sandals, and I headed out for the evening. I looked sexy in my skimpy garb. All the hours I had spent in the gym in order to avoid Sharon had paid off. After I had a light dinner at a restaurant near the motel, I went to one of the bars. It was still happy hour and I got myself two beers for the price of one. I sat at the bar and the bar tender noted that he had not seen me before. I explained that I was moving down, and had just arrived earlier in the day. We introduced ourselves, and he spoke to me whenever he had a free moment.

There was an animated conversation going on between the two guys sitting next to me on my right. They turned to get my opinion on something, and I suddenly found myself part of their conversation. They were both a little older than I am, but the one sitting closest to me was very handsome. He reminded me a little bit of Mac and what Mac might look like at his age.

After a bit, he turned away from the guy he was talking to and directed all his attention to me. He introduced himself. "My name's Ken," he said extending his hand.

"Jim," I responded. "It's a pleasure to meet you." After a few minutes of conversation, I found out that he lived walking distance from the bar. I asked him about the three locations I had appointments at, and he immediately gave me the pros and cons of each place. I was just finishing my third beer when Ken asked me if I'd like to see his place. That was the best offer I had since Mac left me. I really wanted to go with him, but I said, "Ken, I'd really like to, but I drove most of the night and I am just exhausted. Can I take a rain check?"

"Sure," he said. He took out his wallet and handed me his card. "Call me as soon as you settle in," he said.

"You bet," I answered him and headed back to the motel.

There was not much difference in the three apartments I looked at, so I took the first one because I could get possession in three days. I immediately bought a dinette set, a bedroom set, and a living room suite, and arranged for delivery on Saturday morning. I had to stay in the motel until the morning of delivery. I also bought some linens, and bathroom and kitchen accessories, which I stored at my office. I brought everything over to my apartment Saturday morning and waited for my furniture to be delivered. By Saturday night, I had everything in the apartment organized. I looked around and decided that all I needed were some wall hangings and I was all set. I would have to wait to get a Florida driver's license until after I linked up the computer system and could afford to take a few hours off.

Until I could have a land line hooked up, I used my cell phone for all my calls. Late Saturday, I phoned Ken. When he answered I could hear a lot of noise in the background. The number he had given me was his cell phone. He asked me to wait a minute while he went outside. He was at the bar where we had met. He begged me to come on over and he would introduce me to some of his friends.

When I got there, I was surprised at how busy the place was. I had been there last on a weekday, but the joint was jumping on Saturday night. Ken spotted me when I came through the door and came over to fetch me. I was shocked when he greeted me with a kiss on my lips. It was a rather chaste kiss, but I didn't expect it. We went to the bar and he insisted on buying me a drink. He introduced me to three of his friends. His friends, this time, all seemed to be a little younger than I. They welcomed me to Ft. Lauderdale and assured me that I would love it here. Little did they know that I loved every minute away from Sharon's nagging. I could have been anywhere in the world and been very content.

There was an active piano bar that night and we all stood around the piano, listening to the singer. Ken was behind me and I felt his arm encircling my waist. He whispered in my ear, "Are you ready to see my place tonight?"

I turned to him and smiled. "I'm ready when you are boss."

His hand crept lower and encircled my crotch. "I guess you're ready," he said. "Wanna go?"

That night I began my new life. I couldn't get enough sex with Ken. I was so love starved, I wanted more and more. Even when he told me that he was solely a top, I let him fuck me, protected of course. I guess, I knocked him out, because he fell fast asleep after cumming twice. When he did, I got dressed quietly, and crept out. I wanted to go home, where I was the king of the castle, and nobody was there to order me around.

I had sex with Ken again after that on a few occasions, but I did not want to get involved with any one. My twenty year adventure with Sharon had made me wary of any kind of commitment. I had no problem making contacts, and I enjoyed a one night stand two or three times a week. I was happy and content. The business Larry and I were sent to get going, was doing well also. Occasionally I heard from Sharon's lawyer, but I had provided for her and she didn't bother me much. After the first year she divorced me, and that made my life even simpler and much happier.

For more than two years I led this idyllic life, avoiding relationships and commitments. I was making lots of friends and I felt like a fixture in the local gay community. The only thing that wasn't on schedule was buying a condominium for myself. My apartment was small, but cozy, and easy to maintain. I just couldn't get up the incentive to make the next move.

***

One Friday night I was sitting in one of my favorite gay bars talking to a friend. This handsome guy came sauntering in looking very lost. He sat down right next to me and ordered a gin and tonic, which just happens to be my drink of choice. He looked around and seemed a little lost. When he got his drink the bartender commented that he had not seen him here before and I had a sudden vision of myself on the first day I came into this bar. I remembered how Ken had helped me break the ice so I turned to the guy, stuck out my hand, and introduced myself.

"I'm Jim," I said. "Are you visiting from out of town?"

"No, I just moved down from Chicago a couple of days ago. I'm staying at a motel until my load arrives. I've rented a place a few blocks from here." He stuck out his hand to greet mine. "Ron's the name," he said.

When we shook hands I felt a hot flash run through my body. I had never experienced anything like it. At first I got scared that maybe something bad was happening to me, but I felt too good. I was just simply attracted to this guy. He was so handsome, and when I looked into his eyes, I saw a gentleness and kindness that was awesome. I needed to know him better.

"I live close by here too. Where's your place?" I asked only to keep the conversation going. He gave me the address, and I flipped. He was in my building.

"What apartment?" I asked. "I'm in 3C."

"I'm in 4C. Ain't that a hoot?" he responded.

"I sure hope you don't walk around in high heels," I quipped.

"No," he answered seriously. "I'm gay, not a drag queen."

I put my hand on his knee without thinking. He didn't move away. "I think we are going to be great friends," I said. We talked for hours. I don't know where the time went. His life story was the same as mine, a bad marriage, a conversion by a best friend, and a transfer by his company. We marveled at how alike we were. As the evening wore on I asked if he would like to come home with me.

"It's a tight fit as you know, but it will be better than sleeping alone in a motel room," I assured him.

He took my hand. "I'm sure you're right," he said.

A few minutes later we were in my apartment. We were too old for coyness and we both began to undress rapidly. I took a moment to admire his fit body, and when he saw me gawking, he said, "I spent hours in the gym to get away from my wife."

"Me too," I said, and I dropped my boxers. We stared at each other. We were both cut, and we were fully erect. I guess we both measured the same, about seven inches. I couldn't stand there just staring at him any longer. I dropped to my knees and began to suck his cock. He pulled away.

"I like to make a little love first," he said, and he leaned into me and we began to kiss. We ended up rolling in my bed, kissing and fondling and giggling like virgins. Through it all I was aware that Ron made me feel different than any *other* of my one night stands. He made me feel warm, cuddly and wanted. If I wasn't so intent on avoiding a relationship, I might have recognized that I had fallen in love at first sight.

"It's OK now," he said. I smiled at him and went down on him. It wasn't long before I realized that he was about to blow. He pulled away. "Not yet," he said. "Jim, honey, I'm a bottom, if you want to...."

He called me honey and he was a bottom. I nearly cried. In fact, maybe I did. I retrieved the condoms and lube from my dresser drawer and got us ready. When I entered him, I was so overwhelmed by a feeling of connection that this time I did cry. I entered him too easily. It was as if my cock was the perfect size for his conduit. From the very first stroke he screamed in pleasure. He came long before I did, and his cum squished between our bodies. It only served to turn me on even more, if that was possible.

After we had both satisfied ourselves, we lingered in bed, kissing and fondling. We did have to get out of bed eventually and shower. He washed and soaped me, and I returned the favor. When we were dried off, Ron wanted to get dressed and go back to the hotel. I was the one who usually asked my guests to leave, so when I said," Please stay the night," I was shocked at myself. Ron did stay, and we slept in each other's arms. I hadn't done that with another human being since my honeymoon with Sharon.

Ron's furniture came early the next morning. After the delivery, we drove to his motel. I helped him pack and check out. Then we went back to his apartment and in a very short time, we had him unpacked and looking like he had lived there all his life.

"Will you help me christen the apartment tonight?" he asked. I panicked. Two nights in a row was not my style, nor my intent, but that's not what I said to Ron.

"Only if you allow me to take you out to dinner tonight as a Welcome Wagon gift."

So I spent the second night with Ron in his apartment fucking my brains out, and last night we were back in my apartment for more of the same. Now here it is early Monday morning and I am making breakfast for a sleeping beauty. We both have to go to work so I better wake him up.

***

Ron and I have not spent a night apart for a year now. We have virtually been living in two apartments, going back and forth between them. Whatever we suffered in our past lives, we have more than made up in this one. Our lives are filled with love every day. We have good friends, good jobs, a very substantial dual income, and lots and lots of sex. I never thought I would want to share my life with anyone again. Ron is my miracle. It is definitely true that love's more wonderful the second time around.

I managed to locate Mac in Seattle and I contacted him. I told him about Ron, and he was thrilled for me. He has a partner too. They have been together for over seven years. We promised to visit each other. I'd like that to happen but I don't have high hopes for such an excursion. Still, one should never say never.

Ron and I gave the building manager notice that we will be moving out when Ron's one year lease expires. We bought a lovely two bedroom condo in the next street. The fact that we own it together bonds us even closer. I guess there is a moral to this story.

No matter how you may resist getting 'involved,' if the right someone comes along, resistance is futile.

End of the 28th Story

Hank Brooks

Another Chance
of
Delight

Gay Romance Erotica

Another Chance of Delight
By: Hank Brooks

Conrad Jones was sixty-six years old when his partner of forty-two years died of a massive heart attack. Joshua Steiner was shoveling snow off their driveway in Astoria, Queens, New York. It was still snowing, and it was cold and blustery outside, but he chose to ignore his partner's advice to wait until the snow stopped.

"It'll be too heavy then," Josh explained. "I'd rather do two or three light loads than one heavy one."

Josh had just celebrated his seventy-first birthday the day before, and was determined to prove to himself that he was still fit, and full of piss and vinegar. He had never been sick a day in his life. Suddenly, in spite of the frigid weather, he got hot and clammy all over. The world began to spin, and he was beset with terrible nausea. The last thing he remembered was that he began to vomit up his recently eaten breakfast.

Connie was in a daze for weeks. Somehow he got through the funeral. Settling Josh's estate, and completing all the paperwork, dragged on for almost a year. During that time, he could barely function, so he sold his CPA practice to a young associate, and retired.

The first anniversary of Josh's death dawned similarly to the year before. It was January 5th, and it was snowing just as heavily as on that day. Connie made a bowl of oatmeal for himself, and ate it at the kitchen table. He was wearing his warmest, heaviest bathrobe, and as he spooned down his cereal, it occurred to him that he looked and felt like an old man. Suddenly he sat bolt upright in his chair. He could hear Josh yelling at him. "Damn you, Connie. It's time for you to start living again. I never meant for you to die with me."

Connie wasn't sure if he actually heard Josh's voice or if he imagined it, but the message was clear. He made a decision then and there. It was something he had been mulling over in his mind for weeks now, especially since the winter air began to chill his bones.

Josh and Connie's best friends, 'Ace' Gallo and Jimmy Romano had moved to a beautiful two bedroom condo in Deerfield Beach, FL just two years earlier. The apartment was on the third floor, and faced the ocean. Their view was tranquil, and very beautiful.

Alfred Gallo was nicknamed Ace, by his friends, because his garage was so full of tools, that they were convinced he had more gadgets than Ace Hardware. When he moved to Florida, he sold almost all of his precious tools, and made enough money to pay for the move, and then some.

Ace and Jimmy tried desperately to get Connie to spend some time with them after Josh's funeral, but he kept turning them down because he was so busy. This snowy morning, after hearing Josh yell at him, he decided to take them up on their offer. He called them quickly, lest he lose his nerve. He got their answering machine, and left a message. They didn't return his call until late afternoon.

"Where have you been?" Connie asked, not because he was nosy. He really wanted to know what two retired seniors did all day, on a week day, no less. He was really curious because his own life had come to a screeching halt.

"We spent most of the day at the beach," Ace answered. "We had breakfast at a coffee shop first, and then we had a hotdog at the beach. We are still debating if we should go out for dinner or stay home tonight. But enough of that! How are you doing, and when are you finally coming down for a stay? I hear it's snowing in New York right now."

"It sure is," Connie answered. "It started during the night and isn't expected to let up until tomorrow. Is your invitation still open?"

Ace gave out a little screech. "It sure is. You can stay until spring if you like, or stay forever. That will be up to you."

Since he had no idea how long he would stay, Connie booked his trip that day, with an open-ended return ticket. Two weeks later, Jimmy was at the airport to meet his friend. As Connie walked toward baggage claim at Fort Lauderdale/Hollywood International Airport, he was amazed. It seemed bigger and busier here than LaGuardia. For some idiotic reason he expected the airport to be a Quonset hut, surrounded by acres of open fields. He never expected it to be the typical airport of a large metropolitan city.

Connie picked up his two large suitcases, and struggled his way to get out of the terminal. Finally outside, he was hit with such welcomed warmth, as he had not felt since last summer. He took a deep breath and sighed.

His friends said that he should look for a red Hyundai Sonata; they would pick him up at curbside. There were so many people and so many pick-up cars, that Connie began to get frazzled. He thought that he was a fool to have come here, and to have left the comforts of home.

Finally he heard a honking horn, and looked out to see the red Hyundai. It was practically in the middle of the road, unable to get anywhere near the curb. Connie schlepped the suitcases toward the car, and the trunk popped open. He put his luggage in the trunk with Jimmy's help. Jimmy got into the driver's seat, and Connie occupied the front passenger seat.

"Where's Ace?" he asked.

"He decided to stay home and make us one of his fabulous, gourmet Italian meals instead of going out this evening. We figured you'd be tired and want to relax," Jimmy answered.

"You are so right. Thank you both for reading my mind. We'll have lots of time to run around, but tonight I just want to relax and get some sleep. I've been so apprehensive about this trip, I haven't been able to sleep for days."

Jimmy grew a bit upset. "Why would a visit to your two best and oldest friends bring on such anxiety?"

"It wasn't you guys. It was the hassle of travel. I don't do travel very well anymore." The car grew silent, and the two old friends hardly talked the rest of the way home.

Connie was grateful for two things that evening. First off, Ace and Jimmy had not invited a fourth for dinner in a vain attempt to fix him up. Secondly, they were content to stay home his first evening in Florida, and they didn't make a fuss when he retired early.

But his friends had different ideas for the rest of Connie's visit, however long or short that would be. They were determined to bombard Connie with the joys of retirement in Sunny South Florida.

The next morning when Connie came into the kitchen for breakfast, Ace and Jimmy were wearing swim suits. Connie was surprised to see them packing a picnic basket. Ace said, "Go change into a swim suit. We're going to the beach after breakfast."

"Wow! We're going swimming in mid-January. It'll take me some time to get used to that idea."

"You'll be getting used to a million lovely ideas," Jimmy said.

***

Forty-three years ago, on Thursday, July 3, 1970, twenty-four year old Conrad Jones was on his way to Fire Island on a ferry-boat. He and his buddy Jimmy Romano had split the cost of a hotel room for the holiday weekend. They agreed that if they didn't hook-up with someone, they would enjoy sex together. They were good friends, who had never had sex together, but as Jimmy so aptly put it, "I'm not spending all this money and not getting laid, so if it must be you and me, then so be it." Fortunately Connie agreed.

The hotel boasted a pool and a private beach, which were both clothing optional. The young men were well hung and uncut. They were always stared at in the bath houses in New York, and they had no trouble scoring there. They couldn't wait to get settled in their room, and then out to the nude facilities.

Standing not ten feet away, staring expectantly over the ship's rail, was a more mature gentleman of twenty-nine. Josh Steiner was also looking forward to a weekend of debauchery. He had major commitment problems, and therefore he was alone, but the hotel had matched him with another single. He and someone named Al Gallo, who was twenty-six, would be sharing the room. Josh was a physical fitness aficionado, and accordingly, was built like the proverbial brick pizzeria. He hoped that Al would not be a pimply-faced nerd. His and Al's room was adjacent to Connie and Jim's. In fact, they had an adjoining door.

As soon as the four men were unpacked, they all put on bathing suits. The hotel prohibited nudity in the hotel proper. They grabbed towels and headed for the beach. Leaving their rooms, they literally ran into each other. They introduced each other properly, and when they found out that they were all headed in the same direction, they went together.

By the time they reached the beach, they were laughing and joking like old friends. They couldn't wait to shed their suits, so that they could check each other out. Connie and Jimmy knew they were well hung, but as it developed, both Josh and Al were hung like donkeys.

Ingenuously, Connie gawked at both men and yelled, "WOW!"

"Knock it off," Josh told him. "You're pretty substantial yourself. Besides, I'm the one who should be self-conscious. I'm the only one of us who is circumcised. That's the burden life hands out to little Jewish baby boys."

Maybe it was because they were both of Italian descent, but Al and Jimmy were drawn to each other. They put their towels down side by side, and ran to the water. Josh and Connie just sat on their towels, and settled down to enjoy the eye candy. After about fifteen minutes, Josh asked Connie if he would like to go into the cool and very inviting ocean. Connie nodded and Josh jumped up. He extended his hand to Connie to help him up. When their hands clasped, it felt so good, that they both smiled at each other.

Al and Jimmy were grab-assing in the water. As soon as he got into the water, Connie started towards them, but Josh grabbed his hand and pulled him in another direction. "Let them be," Josh said. "I think they are getting something going here."

When Josh pulled on Connie's arm, their bodies brushed together. Connie never held back from speaking his mind. "Maybe we have something going too. I'm hard as nails."

"That's interesting," Josh said, and he reached under the water to attest to Connie's hardness. As soon as his palm enveloped Connie's cock, he felt it jerk, and Connie whimpered, "Shit. I just came."

That evening at dinner, the four men sat at the same table, and really got to know all about each other. They couldn't know it at the time, but a life time friendship was growing. After dinner they went to the hotel ballroom and danced most of the night away. Of course, Josh danced with Connie, and Al danced with Jimmy. The two couples slow-danced, and could not have pushed their stiff cocks any closer against each other.

"Will you sleep with me tonight?" Josh asked Connie.

"I thought you'd never ask."

Just then Jimmy came over and asked Connie if he would mind camping out in Josh's room, because he and Al wanted to sleep together. Josh and Connie doubled over from laughing so hard.

***

"I have to warn you," Ace said, "we're going to a gay, nude beach in Ft. Lauderdale. It's not like the wild old days on Fire Island, but it's wild enough for us old farts."

"You'll forgive me if the best I can do is eye the candy," Connie said.

"Of course. That's all that we do also." They packed the picnic basket, towels and beach chairs in the car and headed south toward Ft. Lauderdale on I-95. They had to park in a parking garage a couple of streets from the beach. The three of them managed to cart everything onto the sand. They set up the beach chairs, and stripped.

"Remember the first time on Fire Island?" Jimmy asked Ace. "I couldn't stop staring at your humongous dick."

"It was all yours the moment you started grabbing for it in the water, Babe."

Connie just smiled at them. Suddenly he missed Josh so much, he wanted to cry, but he controlled himself.

Jimmy and Ace sat for awhile viewing the array of varying body and cock sizes. After a time, Ace asked if anyone wanted to go in the water for a swim. Jimmy jumped up but Connie declined. "Go have fun," he said, "while I simply soak up this glorious weather."

His hosts weren't gone a minute when Connie heard a voice ask, "Was that Jimmy and Ace that just went into the water?" He looked up to see a handsome, tall, slightly chubby man, who did not look like he was more than fifty or so years young. He set up a beach chair right next to Connie.

"Yes," Connie answered simply.

The man leaned down and held out his hand. "Jerry Atkins," he said. "I'm a friend of theirs. We live in the same building. In fact, I'm right above them on the fourth floor. They like to kid me about being a top."

"Are you?" Connie asked.

"Am I what?"

"A top?"

"Let's say, I'm versatile. The guys told me that they were expecting an old friend from New York. Would that be you?"

"Yes. Where are my manners? I'm Connie Jones."

"Welcome, Connie Jones."

The two men smiled at each other and Jerry began to strip. Connie did a double take. It was déjà vu, and he was transported back to Fire Island when he first saw Josh's magnificent naked body. Jerry was as big as Josh and he was circumcised.

"I don't mean to pry," Jerry said, "but tomorrow is Sunday. Ace, Jimmy and I always go to church together, and then we have lunch out. It's sort of a Sunday ritual. I don't know what your religion is, but will you be going with us?"

"I'm Lutheran, and my late partner was Jewish. We didn't attend any church really. Jimmy and Ace are Catholics. I'm not sure I want to go to a Catholic mass."

Jerry smiled. "The church is non-denominational Protestant. It's a gay church. If you're gay, or if you can't stand discrimination against gays, or anybody for that matter, I promise you, you will be comfortable there."

"I guess I'll be joining you then."

Suddenly Connie had a disturbing thought. "Did you know that we would be here today, or is this truly a chance meeting?" he asked Jerry.

"I assure you," Jerry smiled. "I had no idea you would be here today. It's a total surprise and a very pleasant one. If I did know, I would have tagged along in one car, and saved the parking fees." He smiled at Connie and melted Connie's reserves.

They sat without talking for a little while, just enjoying the tranquility of the beach, and then Jerry said, "I think I'll join the guys in the water. Would you like to come with me?"

"Yes, I'd like that a lot."

***

They all went out to dinner that evening to a gay bar and restaurant in the gay section of Ft. Lauderdale. It was a wonderfully festive evening, but all Connie could think about was what happened on the beach. Once they were in the water, Jerry kept fondling him, until he could resist no longer and he fondled Jerry right back. Dammit. Jerry felt just like Josh; huge and cut. At first Connie wanted to cry. Then he wanted to stop fondling this perfect stranger, but he couldn't discipline himself enough to do so. Instead he began to stroke Jerry seriously. Jerry pushed against him, and whimpered in his ear as he came.

Immediately Connie sobered up. He ran out of the water and back onto the beach. The four men spent another three hours on the beach, and neither Jerry nor Connie mentioned the incident. Connie kept kicking himself for running away. He was sure that Jerry would have done as much for him if he hadn't chickened out. He sorely needed to have an orgasm. He was convinced that his balls were blue, but he didn't dare look.

At the dinner table Jerry kept reaching for Connie's hand, but Connie kept taking his hand away. Jerry kept smiling at Connie, but after awhile, he began to wonder what was going on with Connie. As for Connie, he couldn't imagine what Jerry saw in him. He was at least fifteen years older and pretty long in the tooth.

In a not so subtle effort to point out their age differences, Connie asked, "How old are you, Jerry?"

"Sixty-two."

"No way. You don't look a day over fifty."

"Well thanks, old man," Jerry said and broke out laughing. For some reason that confession made Connie feel better, but he was still convinced that he wasn't ready for a relationship, at least, not yet.

The piano player began to play a slow number, and Ace and Jimmy got up to dance. Jerry stood up also, and offered his hand to Connie. On the dance floor the two men wrapped their arms around each other's waists, and began to gyrate to the music. Instantly Connie was transported back to Fire Island and his first dance with Josh. He could feel Jerry grinding his erection into his flaccid cock.

Suddenly Connie gripped Jerry harder to keep from falling. This encouraged Jerry to rub harder against him. Connie grabbed tighter onto Jerry because he nearly fainted when he distinctly heard Josh's voice once again.

"Remember how good it was? I want you to have it all again. I love you, Babe, but you must move on. Give Jerry a chance. He's a good guy, and just right for you. He's going to try to kiss you. Let him."

When Connie felt that he could finally stand on his own legs, he looked into Jerry's eyes. Jerry was smiling and he pulled Connie in for a kiss. The kiss lasted at least a minute, and got more and more passionate. Now two erect cocks were rubbing together.

"We'd better stop," Connie said, "or I'll cum right here on the dance floor."

"Will you sleep with me tonight?" Jerry asked.

Connie got faint again. Those were Josh's words exactly as he had spoken them on Fire Island so many years ago. The words came out of Jerry's mouth, but the voice that spoke them, belonged to Joshua Steiner.

Connie was incapable of speech, so he just held Jerry closer if that was possible. Once again, Jerry leaned his face into Connie's and smiled at him, before he began to smother him with kisses.

When the four friends left the restaurant, they drove straight home. Connie stopped at Ace and Jimmy's apartment, and gathered up some toiletries and clothes for the next day. They agreed to meet for a light breakfast at a nearby coffee shop before going to church, and Connie went upstairs with Jerry. He was nervous and shaking like a leaf. Jerry was aware of Connie's state of agitation. He kept assuring him that their finding each other was fated, and that all would be well.

They hadn't waited for the elevator, but decided to climb the stairs. On the way up, mixed with Jerry's soothing voice, Connie distinctly heard Josh's voice yet again. "This is what I want for you, darling. Don't fight it. Give yourself totally over to Jerry. He will love you as much as I did, and you will love him in return."

Connie fell against the banister, and held tight to it to keep from falling. "What's wrong, Connie?" Jerry asked as he grabbed hold of the stricken man.

"Nothing is wrong. I need to lie down for a minute or two. I'm just overwhelmed by all that's happening."

"Of course, of course! I understand," Jerry said sympathetically. "I'm amazed myself at how fast all this is playing out. If I didn't know better I would say that we are being propelled by cosmic forces."

"If so," Connie conjectured, "it's a good thing that we are going to church tomorrow."

***

When they reached Jerry's apartment, Jerry helped Connie undress and he laid his new love gently on his bed. "We don't have to do anything tonight, Darling. Just get a good night's sleep. I'll be content just to lie next to you."

It occurred to Connie that he knew nothing about Jerry, but all he did was talk about Josh to Jerry. That could not have made Jerry very comfortable, he thought. "Have you ever been in a relationship?" Jerry, he asked. "Long or short?"

"Oh yes; very long. I had a lover for thirty-five years. We lived together from the time I was twenty-three years old. Bobby owned a convenience store in Merrick, Long Island. One night, he was robbed. He foolishly resisted the freaks that robbed him, and was rewarded with a bullet to his head for his efforts."

Jerry started to cry, and Connie put his arms around him to console him. He went on. "He left me more money than I knew he had, so I took early retirement and moved down here. When Ace and Jimmy moved in a couple of years ago, there was instant chemistry among us, and we became good friends. Without their friendship, I don't think I would have made it. At one point I even contemplated suicide." He started to cry again.

Connie hugged him harder. The two men held each other tightly, all the while rocking back and forth. Eventually they fell asleep that way, without ever having made love. It was enough that they were kindred souls, and they had found each other.

Things were different in the morning. About four o'clock in the morning, Jerry woke up. He had to pee badly, so he risked waking

Connie by unraveling himself. While he was peeing, he heard Connie say, "I need to take a leak also."

"I'm almost done."

When they had both peed, they brushed their teeth, and went back to bed. They were naked, just like at the beach, but somehow they both seemed more repressed.

"I need to tell you something," Jerry said. "For the past few days, I have imagined that I heard Bobby's voice. He kept telling me that I was going to meet somebody, and I would fall in love. He begged me not to repress my feelings, and to actively pursue that person. He even told me that the someone would be a visitor from New York. When Jimmy told me about your impending visit, I actually grew afraid. This situation could be considered paranormal by some people."

"Good God! The only reason I'm here at all is because I kept hearing Josh's voice urging me to come for a visit. When you showed up, I heard him practically begging me to pursue a relationship with you. I'm scared, Jerry. What do you make of it?"

"I'm not sure what to make of the situation, but I sure would like to make love with you." That having been said, Jerry started kissing his way down Connie's body. He couldn't know of course, but Connie was very ticklish. He began to giggle, and Jerry suckled even harder. They were going to have a great time.

When Jerry began to suckle Connie's nipples, Connie gave out one great big sigh, and before he even realized what had happened, Jerry was sucking his cock. His strokes were firm, but gentle. Connie was unable to control himself, and he came quickly, gushing down Jerry's gullet.

Afterward, they lay side by side and recuperated. "I haven't tasted cum in a long time," Jerry confessed. "God, it tasted so good."

"It's been a long time for me too," Connie said. He didn't wait for preliminaries, but bent over and took all of Jerry's massive cock into his mouth.

"Wait, I have something to tell you first," Jerry said. "I've had my prostate removed. I orgasm but I don't ejaculate."

"Then I'll have to be content just to suck a fat cock, and in the future don't be so selfish. Share my cum with me." Connie then resumed where he left off.

Their next encounter occurred in the shower. Jerry brought his jack-off lube into the shower and laid it on a shelf. Although both men were in their sixties, they still got hard as a rock. Love making had been so long ago for both of them that they had no trouble fucking in the shower and bringing each other to a glorious screaming conclusion. When Connie could not feel any semen filling him up, he was very disappointed, but of course, he would never tell Jerry that.

Connie stayed in Florida until after Easter. Jerry went back to New York with him to help him pack up his house, and hopefully to sell it quickly. The morning they left, Jimmy drove them to the airport, but they would drive back in Connie's car.

The house sold in June with a late August closing date. Connie managed to push the closing date back to after Labor Day, and he and Jerry spent the summer in New York. It wasn't any cooler than in Deerfield Beach.

The delay in closing gave Connie plenty of time to decide what he could bring down to Florida with him. Since he was moving in with Jerry, he had sold the house furnished, except for a few precious, must have, memories.

The first night they were alone in his house, Connie was very candid with Jerry. "I wouldn't feel right making love in Josh's bed. Please forgive me if we use the guest room."

They had made love often enough in Jerry's bed, but it was a bed he bought in Florida, and Bobby had never slept in it. He was about to tell Connie that he understood, when suddenly he heard Connie gasp. As clear as if Josh was in the room with them, Connie heard Josh's voice. "Don't be a complete dunderhead," the voice said. "Our bed was made for loving, and I want to see it used that way."

When he heard Connie's gasp, Jerry grew concerned. "What's wrong?" he asked.

"Nothing is wrong. Everything is wonderful. Let's sleep in the master bedroom, in our bed." Connie embraced Jerry, and leaned up to him for a long and passionate kiss.

"Please fuck me tonight," Connie directed. "And don't make it gentle."

On their last night in the house, they packed the car, and went to bed early to get an early start on the road. They did not make love. The alarm went off at 4:30 AM. They showered together, packed their overnight bags and left the house for the last time. Before getting in the car, Connie turned around and silently said goodbye to Josh, and all the happy memories he had in this house.

As tears flowed down his cheeks, he heard Josh's voice again. "Don't cry, my love. I'll always be with you, and someday we'll be together again."

Connie got behind the wheel and Jerry got comfortable in the passenger seat. They headed the car to Manhattan and on to New Jersey for the trip south.

Connie never heard Josh's voice again. In time, much as he hated to admit it, he came to doubt that he had ever heard Josh at all. Fortunately, Jerry was there to remind him that he had heard Bobby's voice; they both could not have imagined it. They made a pact never to talk of it, but Connie believed again.

End of the 29th Story

Hank Brooks

Backdoor
Getaway
Romance

Gay Romance Erotica

Backdoor Getaway Romance
By: Hank Brooks

He was a married man. Very married. Thirty years worth of married. Three grown children, all married. No grandchildren yet, but the kids were still newly-weds.

He lay in bed every night, thinking, fantasizing about all his "might have beens." He lay on one side of the bed, as far to his end as possible, and his wife lay on the other, as far to her end as possible. Two people could sleep comfortably between them in the king size bed. They had not had sex in almost five years, and he pleasured himself often in the shower. She claimed that her arthritis was too painful and that he hurt her when he touched her. Every night, when she went to sleep, she pushed their pillows as far apart as she could, hoping that he would not accidently touch her in his sleep.

His first fantasy every night was always the same. It wasn't a fantasy at all. It was a remembrance of a true experience in his life, and a lost opportunity.

He was in the navy, nineteen years old, still a virgin (that was his secret). One day, one of his buddies asked him to go on liberty with him. He had a date, and the girl asked him to bring a friend for her girlfriend. His buddy assured him that it was a sure thing. He wanted so much to get laid, but his stomach was turned in knots. He feared that he wouldn't be able to get it up. His sexual dreams were about men, not women. He knew what was going on with him, but he refused to admit the truth to himself. He believed that one day the right girl would come along and he would marry her and lead a 'normal' life.

He and his friend went to the restaurant where they were to meet the girls. He secretly hoped that they would get stood up and in fact, the girls never came. They waited for more than an hour and finally left the restaurant. They were too young to drink in this state, which had a minimum drinking age of twenty-one, so they waited outside a liquor store and asked a young customer to buy them a bottle of booze. The customer was glad to help out these two young and very handsome service men.

They took the bottle, safely tucked in a brown bag, and got a room at a nearby sleazy hotel. Once inside they opened the bottle and proceeded to chug-a-lug directly from the bottle. "Let's strip," his buddy said, "in case we get sick. We don't want to vomit all over our uniforms." They stripped down to their skivvies, and got a little drunker.

"I sure am horny tonight," his buddy said. "What a shame the girls stood us up. What do you say we whack off. I never can do it in the barracks with all those guys around."

"I wouldn't mind," he answered. "It's been a long time for me too."

They removed their skivvies. Both were hard as rocks. They began to jerk off and his buddy said. "Do me and I'll do you." By now he was quite drunk and happily agreed. He never did know exactly what happened next, but he was aware that out of curiosity they tasted each other's cocks, and then fucked each other using only their spit as a lubricant. Each sailor came in the other's ass.

He awoke in the morning and glanced at the dresser. The entire bottle of booze had been consumed. He knew what they had done the night before, but he had been too drunk to remember if he had enjoyed it. He wanted desperately to take his sleeping friend's cock in his hand and resume the activity of the night before, but he was scared shitless. If they were caught they would be dishonorably discharged. Their lives would be ruined.

Eventually they rose, freshened up and vacated the room. The incident was never spoken of again.

It wasn't until years later that he began to suspect that his buddy had seduced him, and that there never were any girls. He regretted not pursuing this event further and he called this incident one of his 'lost opportunities.' Lying in bed he would then fantasize that the two sailors resume making love in the morning, cold sober. They suck each other to orgasm and fuck each other over and over. The experience is wonderful and after that they go on liberty together as often as possible, and make man love until the navy separates them by assigning them elsewhere.

If he wasn't sleeping by the end of this fantasy, he began to remember other lost opportunities to be with a man. Many opportunities had presented themselves to him over the years. But always his fears had prevented him from acting upon them.

One other lost opportunity often came to his mind. He was thirty-two at the time:

A young college student worked as an intern in his office. He was pretty sure that the boy was gay, but he did not know any gay buzz words and had no real way of finding out. One day the boy mentioned that he was moving into an apartment of his own and needed to buy some wall décor. His wife was out of town with his kids visiting her parents. He told the boy that he had a few pieces of art in his basement that he was throwing out and invited him over after work to see if he could use any of it. The boy came over after work one day and chose a rather large landscape.

"This will be tough to hang without help," he said.

"No problem, I'll go over to your place and help you hang it," the man answered. "In the meantime, would you like a cup of coffee and a donut? We haven't had any dinner."

"That would be great," the young man said. So they sat around sipping coffee and eating donuts, when he steered the conversation to sex.

"I envy you being a bachelor," he said. "Married sex sucks. My wife refuses to go down on me. Nobody ever has, and I want it so bad. I'd give it to get it."

There was no reaction at first and then the young man said, "I sure would like that myself."

"How about it then?" he asked.

"If you go first," the boy said.

"Ha, ha, very funny," he said, and they both laughed. The matter was dropped.

Then the fantasy would pick up where memory left off. "Sure, I'll go first," he says. He goes down on the boy and soon they are playing sixty-nine. They have wild, passionate male sex all night. In the morning they go to work together. After the boy moves into his own apartment, they see each other as often as possible. They suck and fuck and give each other more pleasure than he ever could have dreamed.

And that's how he spent his nights, fantasizing, until he fell asleep. In the morning he would lock the bathroom door, and whack off while taking his morning shower.

The years passed and then a miracle occurred. He bought his first PC and went on line. He learned quickly how to find gay chat rooms and enter them. The thought of going to a gay bar had always been out of the question. The internet was a new opportunity, hopefully not a lost one. He hoped against hope to make contact with some gay man with whom he could at last have man sex with. He prayed that his contact would live nearby and that they could meet and make love.

Most of the time, he didn't understand the repartee going on between the men in the chat room. He would have sent a message if he knew what to say. Basically, he was a voyeur at first, and then one evening it happened. He received an instant message from one of the inhabitants of the room, "Sixty Something in Ft Lauderdale."

Hotguy1: *Hey man, your profile sounds just like mine.*

Cutesr: *Really! I'll have to read it. Hold on a minute.*

He found Hotguy1 and clicked on his profile. After reading the profile as fast as he could, he realized that he was chatting with another married, mature man. "Discretion required" was a dead giveaway.

Cutesr: *You're right. We sound like clones. How old are you?*

Hotguy1: *61*

Cutesr: *Bingo, I'm 62 and that's a real number.*

Hotguy1: *Are you as horny for a man as I am?*

Cutesr: *I don't know. How horny are you?*

They continued to chat back and forth for almost an hour, teasing each other, promising each other heaven knows what, and then........

Hotguy1: *Are you alone? Can you call me?*

Cutesr: *Yes, I'd like that. My wife is out playing bridge and won't be home for at least two more hours.*

Hotguy1: *I'm alone right now too. Please call me.*

He gave Cutesr his telephone number and they both signed off. His fingers shook as he pushed in Hotguy1's number, but then a voice answered. It was not what he expected. He expected some raspy, old sounding voice, but the voice he got was sexy and kind sounding.

"Hello," he heard. "Is this Cutesr? Hi, this is Hotguy1, better known as Jim Spalding."

"My name is Ralph," he said. He wasn't quite ready to offer his surname. "Where do you live?" he asked.

"On the 300 block of Sycamore," Jim said. Unlike Ralph, Jim had no trouble offering personal information.

"I'm on Pine, just two streets over in the 200 block."

"Wow," Jim almost yelped. "It's a beautiful night. Why don't you take a walk toward me and I'll walk to you. We can meet at the corner of Reed and Third Avenue. I'm wearing jeans, sneakers, and a blue sport shirt."

"This is exciting," Ralph said. "I'm wearing denim shorts, sneakers, and a red tee shirt. See you in five." He hung up and literally ran out of the house and up the street. His heart was pounding and he got a little dizzy from excitement.

Neither man was exactly running when they spotted each other, but they were approaching at a fast pace. They both liked what they saw. Jim was about five feet eleven inches with grey hair, and blue eyes. Ralph was about six feet with salt and pepper hair, and warm, brown eyes. They were both well built, very little extra weight and no bellies.

They stood facing each other for a moment, not knowing the appropriate thing to do. Finally Jim extended his hand and they shook hands cordially. Ralph didn't want to let go, and held on way too long. When he finally let go he said, "Do you want to go to Morey's Diner on Second and have a cup of coffee with me? We can talk there."

"Yes, good idea."

They turned toward Second Avenue and started walking. At first they said nothing and then Ralph said, "This is my first time. Honest, I'm scared shitless."

"I only did this once before and it was a disaster," Jim commented. "I literally ran away from the guy. We never did have sex, so I go on fantasizing."

Ralph laughed. "We'll have to exchange and compare fantasies. I've given up believing that any of my dreams will ever come true."

"I know what you mean. Most of the time I feel like I'm tied to a stake and being tortured." Jim does look tortured, Ralph thought. I wonder if I look that way too. They had reached the restaurant and when they entered they both scanned the room. "There's a nice quiet table in the corner over there," Jim said, and they headed toward it.

They each ordered coffee and a toasted English muffin.

"I have fantasized being with a man for as long as I can remember," Jim started. "It only happened once when I was nineteen. I was so scared I couldn't enjoy it."

"Who was it with?"

"My cousin, who was visiting us. He was about twenty-two at the time. God, years later he married and had a slew of kids. One day he just disappeared, leaving his wife and kids. I can only guess why and where he went, but he told me that day that if anyone ever found out he was gay, he'd kill himself. I'd give anything to find him."

"Geez," I said, "and I thought that I was tortured. I've only had one experience myself. It was with a navy buddy. I was so drunk I can't remember if it was good or bad."

Jim looked around and could see that nobody was watching them. He put his hand on top of Ralph's, whose first impulse was to pull away. But he didn't, and it felt really good.

"If ever I wanted to lose my cherry," Jim said, "it would be with you. You're a good-looking dude, man."

"Thanks. The feeling is mutual."

"Would you like to *get together?*" Jim asked Ralph pleadingly.

Ralph looked into Jim's eyes. Yes, he could definitely make love to this man. He was hungering even as he sipped his coffee. All he could do was nod.

"I've dreamt about this forever," Jim said. "I know just the place. It's a motel, not far from here, and they rent by the hour. I'm in real estate. I can always tell my wife that I'm showing property to someone. Just tell me when you can make it."

"Every Thursday my wife goes into Miami. She found a quack there who treats her for her arthritis. She lies on a bed for about four hours, while a slow drip of some shit enters her body. Frankly I think it's a placebo. Anyway she leaves about nine in the morning, and makes a day of it. She gets home about 6:30. Do you think Thursday would be good for you? I'm retired. Any day is good for me."

"Thursday is perfect for me. It's tomorrow."

"Of course, I forgot. Could you pick up some condoms and lube, just in case?" Ralph asked.

"You bet. No problem. Now Ralph, do you think I might get your full name and address so I can pick you up at about 9:15 tomorrow morning?"

They both laughed at that and it pretty much concluded the coffee and muffins. Before leaving the restaurant they went to the bathroom together. Neither had to pee, but when they saw that they were alone, Jim pulled Ralph to him and kissed him full on the lips. At the same time, they each grabbed the other's package and sighed. As they fondled each other, their lips parted and their tongues found each other.

"I've died and gone to heaven on the express," Ralph said.

"I'm in the same railroad car," Jim echoed.

When he got home, Ralph's wife was already there.

"Where were you?" she asked. "I was worried."

"It was such a lovely evening that I decided to take a walk."

"You could have left me a note," she said as she climbed the stairs, heading for the chaste bedroom.

The next morning Ralph did not whack off. He was saving it for Jim. He couldn't wait for his wife to leave. She seemed to be taking forever this morning and indeed she left about ten minutes later than usual. She was only gone a few minutes when Jim drove up. Ralph locked the house and bounded into Jim's car. When he sat down he leaned over and kissed Jim, who kissed him back. Then he put on his seat belt.

Ralph was a little worried about the check-in process, but he needn't have. Jim just signed one name in the book, John Smith, even though the two of them were standing there. The clerk didn't even look up. This was an everyday occurrence for him.

The room was small, but it was so clean that it was antiseptic. You could smell the bleach in the worn out sheets, but neither of the men cared.

"Jim," Ralph said, "I've been fantasizing about having every opening in my body invaded by a fat cock so don't be afraid to ask me to do anything. I swear I won't say no to you."

"God Ralph, so have I. So have I."

"Let me tell you how my fantasies go," Jim said. "I undress with my lover and take him by the hand into the shower. We soap each other good and wash every part of our bodies. We tease each other in the shower, but don't cum. We save that for the bedroom."

"My fantasies usually start in bed, so you lead the way."

They undressed slowly, never taking their eyes off the other. They both worked out and they had tight, muscled bodies with very little fat. As the undressing progressed each could feel himself getting hard. When they were down to their briefs, Jim said, "Let me take that off for you." He approached Ralph, got down on his knees and pulled Ralph's briefs off with his teeth. In the process, he allowed his lips to brush Ralph's cock and balls. Ralph restrained himself from crying with joy. "Let me do that to you," he said.

When they were completely naked, they smiled at each other. They were both about seven inches of hard, uncut manhood. Their pricks were throbbing and bobbing up and down. They embraced each other and rubbed their cocks together as they each moaned softly.

In the shower, they soaped each other good. It was nothing for them to stroke the other's cock with a soapy palm, but when Jim started to insert a soapy finger up Frank's ass, Frank let him do it, but he whimpered.

Jim stopped. "Did I hurt you?" he asked. "Why did you cry?"

"You didn't hurt me at all. I was crying for joy. Please let me do that to you."

They were working themselves into a frenzy, but finally they stopped, dried off and went to bed. In bed, they pressed their bodies together as their cocks ground hard, one against the other. They kissed passionately, but at this point each was afraid of taking the first step. Finally Jim rolled Ralph over and moved his kisses from Ralph's lips to his neck, and then down to his nipples, his navel, his inner thighs and then at last he began to suck Ralph's balls. All the while Ralph was making little whining sounds of pleasure. When Jim took Ralph's cock in his mouth, he screamed, "Oh Jesus, what did I do to deserve this joy?"

After a few strokes of Jim's tongue along the underside of Ralph's cock, Ralph exploded into Jim's mouth. When he recovered enough to think about it, Ralph realized that Jim had swallowed all of his cum.

They lie side by side as Ralph caught his breath. "How did it taste?" he asked.

"Like honey, like ambrosia, like everything I ever dreamed of," Jim answered, now beginning to cry. "I'm so happy," he sobbed.

Ralph leaned over and kissed Jim. Then his lips began a slow descent down Jim's body, bathing him with his tongue and teasing him. He suckled him until Jim begged for mercy and then he swallowed Jim's prick down his throat, as far as he could get it. Jim came almost as fast as Ralph had, and Ralph swallowed every drop of Jim's cum.

Lying side by side, Jim asked, "When we get hard again, let's fuck each other."

"You bet," Ralph mumbled, and he cuddled up to Jim.

They gave up the room at 3 PM so that they would each be home in plenty of time. Before they said goodbye, they made plans for their next meeting. Of course, they would meet every Thursday, but Ralph's wife played bridge two evenings a week, and Jim's wife played canasta one night a week. Happily one of the bridge nights coincided, and they made plans to meet that night also.

Occasionally, they could break away and have lunch together, and on rare occasions, they managed a dinner. They were happy. Their tortured souls were eased at long last. But too much happiness has its consequences.

As they fell more and more in love, and as their need for each other grew exponentially, their marriages suffered.

Ralph's marriage deteriorated rapidly. His wife was a bit of a shrew, but in the past he had never answered her back. Suddenly he began to rebel against her ordering him around. She found fault with everything he did, and he facetiously asked if he ever did anything right. Their dinner dates were always with her friends, and he could barely tolerate them. He started to balk at going out to dinner so often, and with people he disliked. She wept, telling him that he was spoiling her social life, and she asked him what it was he wanted. She even began to ask him if he wanted to end the marriage. He never answered her, but he wanted to scream, "Yes, a thousand times, yes."

Jim's wife was a heavy drinker and an even heavier smoker. She reeked of tobacco and was usually so high, he couldn't bear to be in the same room with her. They fought constantly. He wanted desperately to leave her, but he was too loyal, and he felt so bad for her that he could not do such a thing.

One day he came home from work to find her lying in the hallway. Her lifestyle had finally caught up with her, and her heart had rebelled. At first he blamed himself. He should have been a better husband and been more there for her. After the initial shock of her sudden death, he realized that she had tried AA, rehab, hypnosis and therapy. He had supported her through all that, and he concluded that he would not blame himself ever again. Fortunately during his mourning period, Ralph was there for him, and the two became even closer if that was possible.

In the days that followed, Jim was always available to be with Ralph, but Ralph was still restricted. One day his wife spent hours on the phone. When she came out of their bedroom, she proclaimed triumphantly, "I have just filled up our calendar for every night for the next month. The next two evenings we are going to the same restaurant. I know you won't mind because you love that restaurant."

Ralph remained silent. He stared at her in disbelief. The next Thursday when she left for Miami, he loaded his car with his essentials, and drove to Jim's house. He gave his wife everything he had, in payment for his freedom. He even went back to work to support himself. At first Jim said that he was acting hastily and he should go home, but Ralph wouldn't budge.

There was much unpleasantness at first with lawyers and the divorce, but Ralph gave his wife everything she asked for, and the agony didn't last too long. The serenity, happiness and peace that prevailed in Jim's house, more than made up for the brief period of unpleasantness.

One evening they lay in bed, holding each other tight after having made love. Ralph said, "I had just begun to accept the fact that I would never make love to a man, and then you came into my life. I must have done something really wonderful for God to have rewarded me like this."

"It's funny. I feel the same way," Jim said. "I lived in hell, not only because of my wife's addictions, but because I couldn't express love in the way God intended for me. Then you came along and changed my whole life. Thank you, sweetheart."

"No need for thanks. Just go on loving me, please," Ralph begged.

"For always," Jim assured him.

~~The End~~

Here is a sample from another story you may enjoy:

WARNING! *This collection of stories contains Anal Sex, Gay Romance and Light Bondage. If Military Gay Sex offends you, DO NOT read. Otherwise, enjoy!*

These gay men in uniform tread the line between duty and desire in 7 tales of sex and romance:

>> Young Pvt. Conner is in trouble in **"Boot Camp Demands,"** when a morning alone at the barracks lands him in the arms of Sgt. Adams... just as the company commander walks in on them.

>> In **"Drilling a Soldier,"** 18-year-old Benny tries his luck in the army while his new roommate Danny, a gay man, tries his luck with Benny.

>> **"Keeping Him Inside the Quarters"** continues the story of Benny and Danny, as more men enter their lives - and their bodies.

>> **"Losing Hope for Pleasure"** follows Air Force hotshot Johnnie, whose charmed life gets even better when he falls in love with Will, a crippled man. But Will knows falling for a star pilot means Johnnie can go on missions with no guarantee of return.

>> Carter gets the first big break of his career in **"Promotional Desire."** His posting is less-than-ideal, but he doesn't mind a short stint if it paves the way for a promising future. He's got his mind set and he thinks nothing can change it... until he meets Devin, a deck hand.

>> In **"Underground Soldiers,"** 18-year-old engine room apprentice John finds a kindred spirit willing to "indulge his perversions" when he meets Military chief Sam in the most awkward way: naked, legs spread, waiting for someone else!

BONUS!
This collection comes with a **free** Gay Romance story of 'a few good men' out of uniform in **"Burying the Past,"** where Dave returns to his childhood home to bury his father. But as he returns, he longs for, but will he ever have, closure with Rick, his former best friend and the secret love of his life...?

* * * Excerpts * * *

From **"Boot Camp Demands:"**

     I bent over the bunk with a wary look over my shoulder, to see Sgt. Adams getting something out of his pocket. I didn't know what it was, but I knew it was meant for me. What I didn't see was Lt. Jacobs squatting down behind me. Then I got the surprise of my life. I felt his hot breath seconds before I felt his tongue sliding up the crack of my ass, right over my asshole.

"Aaawhhhh!" I moaned with surprise, tossing my head back. "Ohh, Sir, w-what're you d-doing!"

I heard them both laugh.

"He's making you want what you think you don't want," Sgt. Adams said.

"Let me show you," Jacobs said, and went back to rimming me.

"Ohh, ohh, my god!" I moaned. "Oh, geezuss, sir… Ooohhhhh!"

I couldn't help it; I started twisting and moving my ass up and down to the tune of his tongue. I never felt anything like it. I didn't even know I had feelings in my ass, and it scared me that I did. Scared me because maybe they were right; I might want what I said I didn't want if they kept doing things like this to me.

From **"Keeping Him Inside the Quarters:"**

"You got a place planned for me to fuck you or do I bend you over the hood of your car?"

Soo felt himself tremble at Benny's tone. "I got us a spot," he said with a slight quiver in his voice. He got out of the car, saying, "It's just up this way. Follow me."

He set off down one of the trails, Benny following. About two hundred yards in, he stepped off the trail and led them to a clearing open to the water.

Benny pounced on Soo, pawing at his clothing and forcing his hands into the Asian boy's pants. For his part, Soo succeeded in pushing Benny's shirt off (thank gods it was still too cool for many bugs to be out). In an instant, Soo was naked except for his shoes and Benny's pants were around his ankles.

Benny pushed Soo to his knees and shoved himself balls deep into his gullet. Soo slurped and sucked at Benny's rod, and stroked his balls and pucker. Benny turned around and forced Soo's face into his crack; soon enough, Soo was lapping and slurping away at Benny's butthole like it was some manner of delicacy.

Benny gave his encouragement and approval in the nastiest language he knew: "Suck that shit, you fuckin' pussy ass bitch," and "Tongue fuck me like you want me to fuck your Asian boipussy," and

"Oh yeah, suck my ass you fuckin' whining little nasty bitch—I am so gonna fuck your boycunt until you beg me to cum."

From **"Losing Hope for Pleasure:"**

He was perfect, they were perfect.

I loved the reaction as I licked the crease where his bottom finished and his legs began, then I licked up his crack until I hit his rosebud which I alternately licked, kissed and sucked on. He came twice while I did that and I had my first ever no-touch orgasm.

Well-slicked fingers then, one at a time, I gradually opened him up until he was almost going ballistic.

"Please, Johnnie, please put your cock in there. I can't stand it much longer. Roll me over, I want to watch you as you enter me."

I did and was almost in shock when I saw his eyes. They were oozing lust, I had never seen anything like it. I put Vaseline on my cock and slid some into him with one finger before hooking his legs over my shoulders and positioning my cock head at his anal entry.

To purchase the book, look for **Passion and Loyalty**.

WANT FREE COPIES OF 4FUN BOOKS?
Just visit the blog and download free copies of 4Fun books:
http://4fun-gay.awesomeauthors.org/

If you enjoyed any of 4Fun books then please share the love and promote the books in Amazon.

Amazon Author Central - http://www.amazon.com/4Fun-Publishing/e/B00FOR7HCS

One Last Thing, For Kindle Readers...

When you turn the page, Kindle will give you the opportunity to rate this book and share your thoughts on Facebook and Twitter. If you enjoyed our writings, would you please take a few seconds to let your friends know about it? Because... when they enjoy they will be grateful to you and so will we.

Thank You!
4Fun Publishing

You may also like the books by these authors:

* * *

An Inter-Generational Love Story

A Love Found

Dick Parker

We were making out hot and heavy. The bed was creaking and our legs and arms were wrapped around each other. Our crotches were together and we were humping one another.

"What's wrong down there?"

"I don't know," I said.

"This happens a lot. I'm beginning to think you're not into me."

"Oh I am. I'm just tired."

"Tired! You were tired a couple of days ago. You were tired when we spent the day on the beach last weekend. Your dick seems like its tired all the time."

"I'm sorry, babe. I just don't know what's going on," I said.

I rolled over on my back. My dick was limp and lying across my leg.

"Are you gay, Alex?"

"What?" I asked.

"I'm asking you. Are you gay?"

"Connie, I love you. We've been dating for almost a year."

"Alex, you can't get your dick hard most of the time, but I've caught you jacking off half a dozen times. Why does your dick get hard when you jack off and not when we're naked together?"

I had no answer for her.

"You need to pack up your stuff. I want you out of here."

I was dumbstruck.

"Honey, please. It's just a phase. I'll be okay."

"Alex, I want a boyfriend who loves me and makes love to me. I'm twenty-six years old and not at the age where I want to give up sex."

"Connie, I'm just having problems right now."

"It's over, Alex. Get out by the weekend."

She got up and put on her clothes and left the bedroom. I lay there and didn't know what to do. I knew she was right. When we first met, we had pretty good sex, but now there was something wrong. She had a beautiful body and was hot as hell in bed but I had no desire anymore. As much as I didn't want to admit it, I thought I knew the reason. And it scared the hell out of me to think it.

I found a small apartment near the campus a few days later and moved my stuff in on Saturday. As much as I tried to get Connie to let me stay, she'd made up her mind and it was over. I resigned myself to the fact and decided to start over.

The building was one of four apartment buildings that were built around a patio and pool area that was shared by all of the buildings. Each building had four floors with four apartments on each floor. While they weren't brand new, they were well maintained and clean. The people living there, from what I could see, were pretty much everyday types who worked and went to school. The local college was nearby and many of the apartments had students in them. Being thirty-four, I felt a little old for that crowd.

I parked as near the entrance as I could and carried up an armful of boxes to my third floor apartment. I sat them down and left the door open and went back for another load. The apartment came furnished so all I had was my personal stuff.

As I walked out of the door toward my car, a kid came walking up to the building. He looked young, maybe seventeen or eighteen and smiled when he saw me. I looked him over and he was a handsome kid. He was as tall as I am, about six feet and very slim. He had medium brown hair, cut kind of long, and ice blue eyes. His teeth were very white and perfect.

"Moving in?"

"Yeah, I'm on the third floor."

"Cool, need a hand?"

"Hell yeah," I said. "I'm Alex."

"I'm Will," he said.

We each grabbed some boxes and carried them up the stairs. He was ahead of me and I got a good look at his ass as we climbed the steps. The kid had a nice butt on him.

"What? Why would I think that?" I said to myself.

We put the boxes down and headed back down to the car. We got the last of the stuff in one more trip.

"Thanks, Will," I said, as we put the last box down on the floor."

"Hey, no problem. I'm always happy to help."

I reached into my pocket and pulled out my wallet.

"Oh you don't need to pay me, Alex."

"Which apartment are you in?"

"I'm right below you, on the second floor."

To purchase the book, look for **A Love Found**.

* * *

WILD GAY EROTICA

CARIBBEAN FUN

DEXTER CHASE

"What's your name, boy?" I said, looking at the white boy.

"I'm Abraham."

"Well Abraham, in this house you'll be called Abe and you'll be punished if you ever talk to me again without addressing me as 'Sir.' Do you understand?"

He looked a little terrified but answered me correctly, "Yes, Sir."

"And what about you?" I said, looking at the black man.

"I'm Zeke ————— Sir."

I smiled at the long pause before the 'Sir' came out.

"Alright Zeke and Abe, I want you to put your hands on your sides and then turn around slowly for me until I tell you to stop."

They looked at me a little oddly before complying. When I was satisfied, after I had them both imprinted in my brain, I told them to stop and started questioning them.

Abe was eighteen, an illegal resident who had outstayed his visa. Zeke was a local, twenty-two years old, too lazy to work so took to crime. Both were well put together physically and during the next six months would look even better. My property was a working estate, producing good quality tobacco. I staffed it with local labor and treated them well, but Abe and Zeke would be treated as slaves. I told my overseer to do the same when they were working with him.

"Now, I want you both to get erections so that I can see what I'm going to be playing with for the next six months."

Abe looked shocked, Zeke looked belligerent, neither moved until I picked up the controller again, then they set to with Abe blushing and Zeke whining that this wasn't right.

Job done and I noticed Abe's cock first. It was interesting. Uncut, but when he pulled his skin back it looked circumcised, about six inches long. It was pretty like the rest of him with his medium-length, fair hair and blue eyes. Zeke took my breath away and made Abe's eyes come out on organ stops when he saw it. It was about twelve inches long, with nice thickness, and rigid. Both had pleasant ball sacs that I knew I would take pleasure in playing with. I was going to question them about their sexuality but not together.

Accommodation was the next thing to think about. Most of my workers lived with their families in the nearby village. The few that lived on the plantation had comfortable accommodation in a block close to the main gate so that they could wander into the village without a long walk. The only place I could put my two slaves was in a woodshed behind the house which was off to one side among the trees. I made them clean it out then we brought up two spare beds from the workers' block and I connected a hose to the water spigot.

"You'll eat in the kitchen of the main house except when you are working with the field gangs. If you give cook any trouble, I'll banish you to your shed and you'll eat the scraps that cook would normally throw away. You will always be with the working gang or in your shed unless I tell you otherwise, except of course for your meals. Disobey me and you will suffer the consequences that I can assure you will be very painful. Also, you will remain naked at all times."

That last one got the response I expected from Zeke. So, purely out of annoyance, I zapped him again with a 3. It soon became clear to me that Abe was in this position because he was easily led and had become a natural subservient to Zeke's demands. That however didn't result in any sexual contact, I found out later.

Both young men appeared to be heterosexual, but in Abe's case was a perception rather than something he had tried. Zeke boasted of his exploits with the ladies and I took it with a pinch of salt. What I decided though was that Abe was going to do Zeke first. I intended to have both of them frequently and provided that Zeke became less aggressive and more compliant, I wanted to feel his monster in my love tunnel sometime. It looked amazing.

To purchase the book, look for **Caribbean Fun by Dexter Chase**.

* * *

People can change in a matter of seconds, forbidden desires you never knew was inside can erupt when you give in to the hunger and leave inhibitions behind. What starts as lust can turn you into something else. Better or worse…

Freedom is taken away by lies, and love and innocence is lost or willingly given. Cages become a sanctuary or a nightmare. Deals are struck but ulterior motives arise. Choices are made but consequences prove more than what the body can take and weaknesses are taken advantage of. These are the stories of the men that are faced with intimate experiences that can break a man but choose to go on and push themselves to their limits and submit to the heights of pleasure. Their hearts are sad but their body enjoys every minute of it and craves for more. Things never felt so good to be at the **wrong place at the wrong time**.

This collection of stories includes:

Tremors In The Interrogation Room
Prisoner Of His Heart
A Trade For A Trade
Payback Scandal
Erotic Expense

To purchase the book, look for <u>**Wrong Place. Wrong Time by Chris Johns**</u>.

* * *

BAD SHERIFF

REDNECK SPEED TRAP

GAY HARDCORE
ANGUS MACGREGOR

Arlo Givens took a long drink of coffee and slid down further into the front seat of his patrol truck. He turned the radio down to a lower volume than he kept it normally. He closed his eyes and held the radar gun lazily in his left hand. He was backed into one of his favorite spots, behind a large billboard promising homemade fried pies at Ethel's Kitchen. From here, he could see all the way east and west on Hwy 69 that ran through the backwater town of Lone Pine. This was his domain, his kingdom, and he loved it.

The big man stretched out and lazily scratched his sack, feeling his bull-sized balls roll against his fingers through the polyester tan uniform slacks that gripped his big ass and package like a glove. His cock stood out like a Fletcher's corn dog from the State Fair in the thin pants, like a goddamn bratwurst with a fat mushroom at the top. He squeezed his cock and felt it grow thicker in his hand. The crisp white t-shirt under his uniform shirt covered a thick mat of chestnut brown hair that carpeted his barrel chest and beer gut that drifted over the leather Sam Brown gun belt. He patted his belly and grinned. Not too bad for forty-five, he thought. He was stronger than an ox and fast as lightning on his feet if he ever had to chase someone, which was pretty much never, these days. His hand bumped against his Glock sidearm. He tried to remember the last time he had to unholster his weapon except at the firing range. Things like that didn't happen a lot in Lone Pine.

The village of Lone Pine was known for three things: fried pies, the Lone Pine Okra Fest in September, and speed traps. The three mile stretch of Hwy 69 that ran east–west through the city limits was posted with plenty of signs reminding travelers of the 25 mph speed limit. The short school zone was marked at 20 mph. The place was notorious for absolute rigidity in regards to the speed limits and tickets were handed out like Halloween treats to the offenders. Sheriff Givens was the municipality's one and only law enforcement officer. He and his good friend, Judge Ezekiel Crow, held court once a week for the few idiots that attempted to talk their way out of their speeding ticket. They had a snowball's chance in hell of getting out of it. In fact, the court was just as likely to slap on additional sanctions for wasting their time when visitors attempted it.

Arlo and the traffic citations accounted for almost fifty percent of the annual revenue for the small town, sometimes even more. The high school kids that learned to drive were particularly careful to not break the rules, not wanting to face the wrath and monetary punishments. In fact, it was so rare to have an incident involving the youth of the town, Arlo rarely thought about it at all. No, the main preys that fell into his speed trap were college students headed to and from Stephen F. Austin University in Nacogdoches, and out of state drivers from Louisiana and Arkansas that were foolish enough to not believe the speed signs. They rarely made the same mistake twice. It was told that many in the area would go out of their way and take other routes to complete their travel to avoid the traps. It mattered very little to Arlo. Like a Venus fly-trap, he sat in his patrol truck and simply waited. In no time at all, another juicy fly would spring the jaws of the trap shut. They could cry and complain all they wanted and he would still write the ticket, especially to the women. In fact, nothing made him angrier than a woman who tried to use her gender or femininity to try and get out of the ticket. Over the years, he had been flashed, bribed, and threatened. He had watched women dissolve into tears, put on lipstick, slide a skirt up so high you could see her twat and he would snarl and hike the fine up ten percent more.

boys understood their bodies and encouraged them to masturbate as often as they wanted.

The horned up Givens brothers took him at his word and ended up jacking off so much his ex-wife called almost monthly to complain her wash cloths and hand towels were constantly found under their beds, crusted and stiff with boy batter.

Arlo just listened and replied, "Boys will be boys. They ain't hurtin' no one Justine. Better to squirt off on your towels than in some trailer trash teen twat." Usually, the phone would hang up at that point and he would howl in laughter.

These days, the idea of hooking up with another woman didn't fill him with much excitement or arousal. He knew it was unfair to only focus on the bad parts, but damn, she was such a harpy. Maybe someday he would find a nice lady and try it again. But for now, he had found another outlet for his libido and it was working just fine.

The whine of the radar gun woke Arlo from his daydream and he locked in like a hawk on the display.

"47 in a 25. Fuck me sideways, I love my job." Arlo flipped on the red and blues and burned out of his hideaway.

To purchase the book, look for **Bad Sheriff by Angus MacGregor**.

* * *

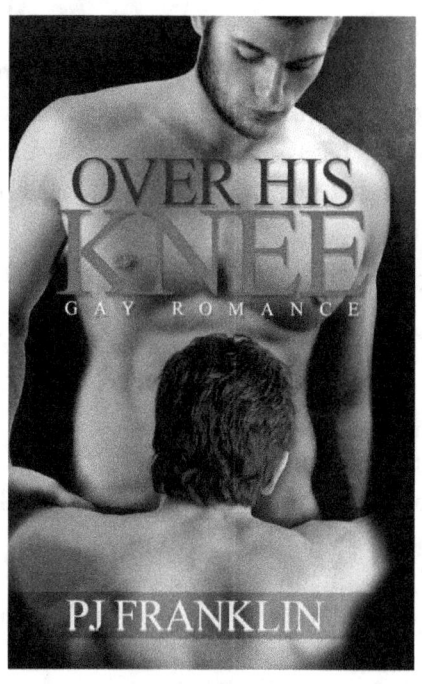

The place was jammed with men mostly in their middle to older ages, very few as young as Cody. All body types were represented, all heights. Facial hair ranged from none to full beards, obviously so-called "daddy bears," a few dressed in traditional black leather outfits. Cody liked older men at least in fantasy, but did not feel immediately attracted to anyone in near sight.

Just then Cody felt bumped into by somebody bigger and taller than his just under six-foot height. "Nice ass, kid. Here to get it spanked by Caldwell?" he grinned and gave Cody's backside a very gentle smack.

Cody's hands both flew back to guard his rear end without even thinking about it. The man's touch didn't feel ordinary or meaningless like a smack on the seat from his Little League coach from years before. It felt somewhere between deliciously risqué and an unwanted intrusion, Cody was not certain.

"Spanked? Me? Um, well, no, I was just here to … " and just then another man bumped him forward and then another as each unintended physical encounter propelled him deeper into the mass of humanity.

By the time Cody navigated the sea of men to the back wall, he wasn't sure he would ever get to do what he came to do in the first place. Just about then the crowd quieted a little to listen as the loud and rapid spanks from Caldwell's big bare palm on bare ass filled all of their ears. Cody's ears told him that there obviously was much more to the event than just book signing.

"Please, sir, not so hard!" the man finally begged and the crowd raised their drinks and roared with approval.

Cody had no idea that men were actually going to be spanked for real by the author. He could barely see Buck's head, just not his body or the man he was spanking; but he certainly could hear it and just that alone threatened his cock to get really hard. It got half-hard anyway. A hard blush nonetheless made him wonder if he could be arrested for public lewdness in a place like this.

Then Cody saw many others around him pawing at their own obvious arousals. He even saw men casually groping at other men's crotches and nobody seemed to mind. Only then could Cody relax a little, listen to more of the man's pleas and even dare to fantasize himself getting spanked over his favorite author's knee.

Buck finally stopped and the man jumped up. "Holy Jesus mother of … that was hot!" rubbing his spanked rear and the crowd roared with approval once again.

"Who's next?" Tom grinned into the mic and the next man came forward.

Cody was beginning to feel a little more confident now. He had heard stories of what might go on in gay bars, ignoring recent memories of his father's taunts that gay bars were "wicked places deserving of God's wrath." Cody had never seen public groping before, but even to his inexperienced eye God must be pretty squeamish if groping was such an awful sin.

Suddenly he felt his ass groped, felt up really hard this time. "Hey, little fella. Ain't seen you here before. How about you and me bust this place and have a nice fuck, you a virgin? I'll even spank your hot little ass if that's your thing."

Cody felt like looking around himself for a sign on his back that said, "Virgin meat, free for the taking," and in any case the unsolicited attention felt intrusive, so much so that the desire to have his book autographed by Buck Caldwell quite suddenly fell to the wayside.

"No sorry, I really gotta go," and Cody started to push himself into the crowd and headed for the front door not caring that on this, his first gay bar experience, that he was leaving sans a drink of anything.

Years of experience in bars had taught Buck to miss nobody and nothing and the first moment that the barely legal looking cute boy had entered into the mass of men crowding into the bar's otherwise dark and inviting atmosphere, Buck took notice. The boy looked skittish and unsure of himself just by the way he moved, his shoulders hunched, forehead furrowed and eyes darting.

"Newbie," Buck had muttered to himself. "Never take on a newbie" was Buck's new philosophy having been burned time and time again and yet the kid looked kind of, well, not like the rest, whatever that meant. So when Buck saw Cody start to leave, it was easy to figure the kid had been spooked.

"Too bad," Buck chuckled to himself. He might have at least talked to the kid and almost looked away too soon to see that as he darted out of the bar's front door, something dropped to the floor from the kid's back pocket, a paperback book by the looks of it.

Buck quickly excused himself and rushed for the door, but too late. Buck picked up the paperback. It was an older volume of his oldies and he poked his head a little outside of the door, but no longer could see the kid.

Letting the door close, Buck then looked more carefully at the paperback's well-used condition. The cover itself as well as many dog-eared pages showed ample evidence of a dedicated reader.

Buck then opened the front cover and inside was scrawled a first name, "Cody." Buck felt bad now. The kid was a fan, a real fan of his books and maybe not just one looking for a quick fuck or worse, to fall in love with him like some of the others. Buck pocketed the lost volume and went to find bar owner Tom McNeil.

"Loser! Stupid loser!" Cody roundly chastised himself during his journey on foot and bus back to his Aunt Nadine's house. "You should have stayed, you idiot! Why did you even bother to go? Now look what you've done, you've gone and lost the book!" Cody bitched himself out.

As Cody finally opened the home's front door, there stood Aunt Nadine. "Well, you're home early. What happened, honey?" Nadine Mills asked her adored nephew, noting his distressed look.

Dear Aunt Nadine, always there to talk to, always supportive and especially when Nadine's brother, Cody's father, had been at his homophobic worst. "I … it didn't work out," Cody said, feeling a bit crestfallen.

Nadine was very observant and looked puzzled. "What happened to your book, Cody?"

Cody blushed a bit. "I lost it, now I'm going to have to go back to find it."

Yes, Nadine knew all about his fetish interests; he kept nothing from her.

"Oh, I'm so sorry, honey. Are you going back this evening?" she asked with true concern.

"No, I'll stay home and go back in the morning," said Cody and slumped to his bedroom.

It was a long shot, but Cody obligated himself to return to The Caldron during the next daylight hours. It would feel much less intimidating that way, so Cody slept the night and then did just that.

Cody walked inside The Caldron's front door just after owner Tom McNeil had opened it for the early crowd the next late morning. It was Saturday and sunny out, so not many would show up for quite a few hours. Cody spied Tom as the man with the mic from the night before.

"What can I do for ya?" Tom grinned affably as he stood behind the bar's long shiny black counter-top.

"Um, I might have lost something here last night, at least I hope it's here," Cody said, standing back from the bar. Tom recognized the young newcomer right away.

"You don't have to stand back there, kiddo, I won't bite. You want a drink? It's on the house."

"I … um, I don't drink, but a Coke would be great," Cody said softly, some of the unpleasant memories of his father's drinking habits suddenly coming to roost.

"Well, you're better off. I'm Tom and you are?" Tom said, setting the dark bubbly refreshment in front of Cody.

"Um, Cody Mills. I was here for the first time last night for the book signing," Cody said shyly and picked up the dark caramel-colored beverage. "Thanks!"

Tom smiled warmly. "Hey, you're always welcome here, partner. Bet you get a lot of action, huh?" already knowing that Cody was the lost paperback's owner as Buck had given Tom the book "just in case Cody shows up for it."

"No, no action," Cody smiled shyly and sipped the cold soft drink.

Tom pulled out the lost paperback from in back of the bar. "Is this what you lost?"

Cody looked so relieved. "Yes! It is!" and Tom started to hand it to him, but snatched it back. Cody was a little taken aback.

"Wait a second there, son. Before I give it to you, Buck said to tell you that you should be spanked for being careless," and then Tom grinned and gave the book to the anxious boy. Tom had made up the part about Buck just to tease Cody.

Cody blushed and opened it. "He said that?" a bit excitedly and then saw what Buck had already done. "He autographed it!" Cody gawked.

Tom looked at the kid. Cody's honest and innocent expression of pleasure at not only reclaiming his treasured volume but also at the autograph was refreshing in an era of widespread cynicism in the local gay community, something that Tom hated.

"I just wish he would have signed it in person. He's right. I should be spanked," Cody said wistfully.

Tom sighed. "Look Cody, I know where Buck is staying while he's in town. He's going to be at the bar tonight, but maybe you want to meet him before that?"

"Me? Meet Buck … well, I guess … um … no, I shouldn't," Cody said allowing doubt to creep in as usual.

"Why not? What's the worst that could happen, huh? A spanking over the spank-master's knee?"

"Me? I've never been spanked, hell, I never … "and Cody's voice caught and he turned and started for the front door with mounting embarrassment.

"Cody! Don't leave, man, I was just kidding!" but by now Cody was out the door again. Tom just sighed and shook his head.

Once again holed out in his bedroom at Aunt Nadine's, Cody Mills was quite put out with himself for having been such a jerk. Tom had been decent, even kind and Cody had acted in a very uncharacteristic but still disappointing and unseemly manner.

Not one to squander a rare opportunity to fill the shoes of a "bad boy" for what he had done,

Cody quickly locked his bedroom door and stripped naked. His cock started to harden as he reached under his bed to get out a shoebox. He found and opened it.

His eye caught the target in the box, a cherished old wood-backed hairbrush; but then also saw the carefully folded-up white lined paper, twenty or so pages, a story he had hand-written inspired by his favorite author. He swallowed hard, ignored the story, fisted his hairbrush and then stood up and looked at the brush.

"Cody Gregory Mills, you've been a bad boy, a really bad boy. You need a spanking!" and then Cody pushed the shoebox aside and lay himself supine onto the length of his bed, and pulling back his legs high and back over his head, started to paddle his own bare butt with the brush.

This time he meant business. Wielding the hard flat business side of the brush, Cody rapidly paddled all up and down his fairly tender bare buttocks until he could just barely stand the sting and burn. Unfortunately, Cody misinterpreted the effects of feeling genuinely "bad" and instead of hardening, Cody's cock started instead to soften.

Cody sighed with frustration and gave up on the effort. He tried to rekindle some lust using aggressive play-talk, albeit using words that he had heard from his father's sour attitude about gay people.

"You're a filthy masturbator, Cody Mills! You're a … a … sinful fudge packer! You need to be punished on your bare ass!"

To purchase the book, look for **Over His Knee by P.J. Franklin**.

* * *

Andrew Todd

Riding High

Hot Gay Romance Erotica

The sharp rap on the door, followed by an urgent, "Zak, are you up!?" made Zak bolt upright in bed.

"'M up, Mom, I'm up," he mumbled.

"We have to leave in a half hour; you need to be downstairs in 15 minutes if you want to have breakfast before I drop you off at work."

"Ok, I'll be right down."

He heard her walk away from the door and head back downstairs. He lied back down on his bed, pulled his pillow over his face and screamed as loud as he could. Being awakened at 6:30 on a Saturday morning was not his idea of a great start to a weekend. When his mom had suggested he get a summer job, he had at first been excited. He was turning 19 and his mom had promised him he would inherit her old Toyota, but he would have to be able to pay for the insurance and gas.

He had gone right to the library and Mrs. Clinton the librarian was thrilled to offer him a job as an assistant librarian. He would mainly work in the kid's section helping younger kids with their summer reading and helping out in general in the library. He thought he was set for a nice, easy, air-conditioned summer. But, his mother had other plans. She had secured him a job at a local ranch. She insisted that he be outdoors during the summer, and that he be more active. His only physical activity during the school year was swimming at the YMCA two or three days a week. He was a great swimmer, but he was not interested in joining the team. Her insistence that he take this job had resulted in Zak basically giving his mom the silent treatment for the past week.

And what was worse, in order to get him 'ready' for his new job, he had to spend every Saturday and Sunday there for the last month of the school year. After school ended he would work there five or six days a week. He wasn't exactly sure what would be expected of him. He figured he'd be shoveling shit most of the summer. However, he figured if he screwed up enough this weekend, maybe they would fire him and he could get his library job back.

Looking at the clock he realized time was getting away from him. He jumped out of bed and ran to his bathroom. He turned on the shower and, after dropping his briefs on the floor jumped in. He quickly showered and then stepped out and started to towel himself off. He caught a glimpse of himself in the mirror. His blond hair was starting to get shaggy, but he had decided to let it grow out this summer. He didn't think he was the worst looking person in the world. In fact, he considered himself plain, but had heard some girls at school whispering about him. Apparently they thought more of his looks than he did. He had a slight swimmer's build, lean and taut. He was slender and short for his age, barely measuring 5' 4". He was hoping for a growth spurt this summer, but since his mom topped out at 5' 3" and his dad had been only about 5" 7' (at least according to his mom), he figured that ship had pretty much sailed.

He did not remember his dad, who had died in a car accident when he was only a toddler. His blond hair and blue eyes he got from his mom and according to her, he got his love of books and imagination from his dad. He would often look at the pictures of his dad and wonder what the last 15 years would have been like if it hadn't been just him and his mom.

After his dad passed, his mom had taken the BA in Accounting that she earned just prior to marrying his dad and parlayed it into a Vice Presidency at a local bank. She was a bit of a workaholic, but had been able to provide a nice home for Zak and her job offered them financial security and stability.

He stepped out of the bathroom and went to his dresser. He had no idea what he should wear, since he had little to no idea what his job would entail. He didn't want to wear anything that might be irrevocably ruined since he had the feeling there would be a lot of muck and dirt in his future. He figured he would go with some ratty old jeans and an old t-shirt. He also decided to wear his old sneakers since he wasn't about to run around a ranch in his new Chucks. It was only about 60 degrees out so he grabbed his old black hoodie and ran downstairs.

His mom was leaning against the counter drinking what was probably her third or fourth cup of coffee.

"Well, it's about time. I was about to go knock down your door."

"I'm ready." He looked out the kitchen window. "Mom, it's barely even light out. Are you sure I'm supposed to be there this early?"

"Yes, Jim said Mr. Jones was expecting you there at 7:30 this morning and that he would expect you to be there until 6 tonight and 4 tomorrow. He's not keeping you as long on Sundays right now because of school." Jim was a co-worker of his mom's; Mr. Jones, the owner of the ranch, was a friend of his and when Jim heard he was looking for summer help he told Zak's mom and the rest was settled before Zak knew what hit him.

"Did Jim know exactly what I would be doing?"

"Well, it's a horse ranch so I would imagine there will be a shovel in your future."

He shot his mom a dirty look as she grinned at him. "Ha, Ha," he rolled his eyes. "What makes you think this is the job for me? I've never even been to a ranch and the last time I was near a horse was the pony ride at the fair when I was five."

"Zak, Jim told Mr. Jones all about you, the work you do with younger kids at the library and the Y and about how good you are with computers; he also told him that you needed to get outdoors more."

"Mom…"

"Let me finish. I know you had your heart set on the library job, but you know as well as I do that this job will pay you a lot more than working at the town library. You'll be able to earn more, you'll be out in the fresh air, and maybe you'll make some new friends."

'Ah-ha', he thought, 'the other shoe has dropped.' His mom was always dancing around the fact that he was essentially a loner. He had a few friends at school, but they were just that: school friends. He spent most of his time alone or at the library or the Y where he mainly worked with kids that were younger than him. He was often uncomfortable and tongue-tied around people his own age. Most people at school saw him as a small, smart, shy nerd and he didn't disagree with their opinion of him.

He had known he was 'different' since he was much younger and it wasn't until puberty hit that he was able to put his finger on what made him different than the other boys at school. While they were chasing the girls, all Zak could think about was chasing them. He had never seen what his male classmates saw in their female counterparts. But just being in the boys' locker room made his heart race. He knew that if anyone of his classmates knew his secret, his life would be unlivable. They might spend a lot of time in the media telling you 'It Gets Better', but you had to survive 'It' first.

From the moment the realization of his sexuality hit him, he had found himself more comfortable with younger kids. They were honest and he had fun teaching little kids to swim and read and helping them with schoolwork. When he was working with the little kids, he didn't have to worry about being turned on or aroused. He could relax, and in those moments he could be himself, not the guarded automaton he was in school.

His mom's voice woke him from his daydream. "Well, we need to get going."

"Ok, I'm ready." He grabbed a banana off the counter and ran to the fridge to grab a bottle of juice.

They didn't talk much on the way to ranch. Zak's mom knew he was nervous about this job and she felt a little guilty about forcing him to take it, but she was concerned about him. He spent too much time indoors and with kids much younger than he was. She knew he had a brilliant future as a teacher or in some other career working with kids, but she felt he needed to get outside and make some friends his own age. She didn't know if the friends part would be accomplished with this job, but she was glad he wouldn't be spending the summer all cooped up inside. Making the deal to give him her old car was worth it to make him accept this job.

The ranch was about 15 miles outside of town. Zak was again daydreaming as they drove. He was nervous, but he knew his mom was right about the money thing. His library job would have been one step above a volunteer role. They might have been able to pay him a few dollars a day and some of the parents would pay him to tutor, but the ranch job was paying him $10 an hour. The kids working at the local fast food joints weren't going to make that much. He'd promised his mom that he would try his best and he would, knowing that if he screwed up he could still get the library job back. Mrs. Clinton had made it clear that she was creating the job for him and she would not be filling just for the sake of filling it.

He looked up to see that his mom was turning down a dirt road. Ahead of them was a large locked gate. Over the gate was a sign reading 'Triple J Ranch'. The car came to a stop.

"OK, Sweetie, I'm going to drop you here so I can get to work. Mr. Jones said to just go through the gate and go straight up the road and he would meet you at the barn. Do you have your phone, so you can call if you need anything?"

"I've got it, but I should be ok."

She leaned over to give him a quick kiss on the cheek. "I know you will. Just do your best and try to have fun, maybe you'll end up liking it."

He looked at her as if she had just taken complete leave of her senses. "I'll try, Mom."

"I'll be back to pick you up at 6."

He started to get out of the car.

"I love you, Zak."

"Love you, too, Mom."

He watched as his mom turned the car around and went back down the dirt road.

He walked over and unlatched the fence. He walked through the gate and locked it behind him. He might not know anything about a ranch, but he didn't want to get blamed for any animals getting out of the gate.

He looked up and saw nothing but woods and a long dirt road. He started walking down the road. He had walked for about 10 minutes when he finally saw a large building he assumed was the barn. He walked towards the building. When he was about 500 feet from the entrance of the building, he saw a huge dog come running out of the building and straight towards him. The dog was barking loudly and coming right at him. Zak stopped in his tracks thinking that he was going to be this dog's breakfast before he even started his job.

The dog came at him full speed and jumped up on him hitting him square in the chest with its front paws. The dog caught him off guard and Zak fell backwards and landed on his butt. He closed his eyes and waited for the jaws of this beast to go for his throat. When nothing happened he slowly opened one eye; the dog was standing over him and Zak could swear it was grinning at him. It took a step forward and licked him straight up his face from chin to forehead. Zak couldn't help himself, he sat there and started laughing while the dog continued to bathe his face.

"Ember!!" He looked up and saw a man marching out of the barn towards them. "Get off that poor boy!!"

The man stopped in front of them and the dog stopped licking Zak's face and walked over to the man. He reached down to offer Zak a hand up. "You must be Zachary."

Zak jumped to his feet and brushed himself off. 'Yes, sir, Zachary Myers, but most people just call me Zak."

"Nice to meet you, Zak, I'm Martin Jones and you've met Ember. Sorry about her greeting you that way. She's too damn friendly to be much of a watchdog. She's more likely to lick a trespasser to death."

"Oh, that's ok. She just startled me. I haven't been around animals too much. What kind of dog is she?"

"She's a Golden Retriever. They're known for being a big friendly ball of fluff and this one is that in spades. As much as I wish she was a little more of a protector, given the number of people we have come and go at the ranch, I guess I'm lucky she's as friendly as she is."

Sensing she was no longer in trouble, Ember walked over to Zak and moved her head under his hand. Zak smiled down at the dog and scratched her head.

"Well, I see she's made another friend," Mr. Jones laughed. "Why don't you come with me into the barn so we can talk some?"

Zak slowly followed Mr. Jones into the barn. Ember stayed right with him; given his small stature he was able to keep petting her while they walked.

Mr. Jones led him into a small office area. He sat in a chair behind the desk and motioned for Zak to have a seat across from him. Zak sat down and Ember sat in attention right next to him.

"Son, are you sure you don't have a dog at home?"

"No, sir, I asked my mom for one when I was little, but she thought it would be too much for me at the time and I never thought about it since, why?"

"Well, she's usually friendly and rambunctious, but I've never seen her take to someone as quickly as she's taken to you. The only other person she follows around like that is one of my other hands, but that guy has a way with animals that I've never seen in another person. Maybe we'll find out you have that same gift."

Before Zak could stop himself, he laughed out loud. Mr. Jones looked at him curiously.

"I'm sorry, Mr. Jones, I don't mean to be rude, but I have never been around animals at all. My mom sprang this job on me as a surprise. I promised her that I would do my best and give it a try, but I've never been an outdoor person or an animal person. I like animals, but I've never had any experience with them."

"Zak, I appreciate your candor. I'll be just as honest with you. When my friend Jim asked me about taking you on, I was a little apprehensive, but he spoke of you glowingly. He told me you were a smart, courteous young man who spent a great deal of his time teaching and helping others. That's what I'm looking for this summer. Yes, there will be lots of hard work and manual labor, but we have a lot of fun here as well. We're not a huge operation. It's basically me and two hands and now you. We have about 20 horses, give or take. Most are owned by me, but we do have a few boarders. We give lessons and offer trail rides. I know horses can be intimidating for some people, and you might feel a little nervous around them at first, especially given your smaller stature, but my first advice for you is to remember to let them know who is boss. I've seen a 17-hand horse follow a small child around the ring, cuz the kid let that horse know he was in charge."

"You have a horse with 17 hands?"

Mr. Jones let out a loud belly laugh. "Sorry, you're going to have a lot of horse lingo thrown at you over the next couple days. Hands are the way you measure a horse. One hand is roughly 4 inches and you measure them to the top of their withers--that's their shoulder."

"So that's a big horse?"

"Yes, very big. Most of ours are between 14 ½ and 16 hands. And most of them are extremely gentle and friendly. They have to be; if I can't trust them with inexperienced riders, I'd lose my business."

"So, what exactly will I be doing?"

"Well, for the next few weekends, I'm going to turn you over to one of my hands, Dusty. He'll go over what we expect from you and walk you through everything. The only thing I ask is that you listen carefully to everything he tells you and if anything doesn't make sense or you're not quite sure, always ask."

"Yes, sir, I will," Zak replied, thinking to himself, 'Oh, great I'm gonna spend the weekend with some old cowboy with a cliché for a name.'

As he rose from his chair, Mr. Jones said, "Dusty should be here any minute and then I'll turn you over to him. I think you'll like it here, Zak."

He offered his hand to Zak and Zak shook it.

"Thank you, Mr. Jones, I'll try my best."

"I believe you will, son. Now, I need to check on some things in the other barn. Why don't you wait here; like I said, Dusty should be here any minute. I'm sure your new girlfriend will be more than happy to keep you company."

Zak laughed as Mr. Jones left the office. He leaned over in his chair and rubbed the big dog's ears and petted her sides. He had been honest with Mr. Jones; after the one time he asked his mom for a dog, he had never thought about it again. His mom had given him a lot to try to make up for his dad not being there, but she never tried to spoil him. Even at five, he had known she was right; neither of them was in a place to take care of a dog and since he did not have many friends, he had no experience with animals at their houses either. Looking down at Ember, he suddenly thought that maybe if things went well he might ask his mom if he could get a dog now. She knew he was responsible and she always wanted him outside and a dog would get him out for walks. That was something to think about.

He sat in the office for about 10 minutes just petting and talking to the dog; he was starting to feel more relaxed and thinking that maybe this wouldn't be the train wreck he was anticipating.

He heard someone come into the barn and assumed it was Mr. Jones. Ember's ears pricked up and she took off like a shot out of the office.

"Hey, Emmy, how are you?" he heard a voice saying. It wasn't Mr. Jones.

As he was getting out of his chair to investigate, Ember came charging back into the office followed by the most beautiful boy he had ever seen. He was about 18, deeply tanned, with black eyes and long black hair pulled back in a ponytail. He was wearing faded jeans, scuffed-up leather boots, a wife beater and a denim jacket. He had to be almost 6 feet tall and was slim and muscular.

Zak just stared as the other boy offered his hand.

"Hey, you must be Zak," he said with a radiant smile. "I'm Dusty."

Zak stood up and took the offered hand and shook it.

"Oh, man," he thought. "It's going to be a long summer."

If you enjoyed this sample then look for **Riding High by Andrew Todd**.